Young lovers Greg and Tyler secretly meet to spend time together, until a moment of passion by the moonlight throws their lives into chaos. When their parents learn about their little escapade, it opens a Pandora's box that spreads family discord, resentment, and heartaches. When someone adds fuel to an already fragile situation, things get out of hands quickly. Will these two young lovers stay safe? How much can they endure before they break?

Sins of Our Sons
Copyright © 2022 Kristian Daniels
ISBN: 978-1-4874-3564-6
Cover art by Martine Jardin

Published by eXtasy Books Inc

Look for us online at:
www.eXtasybooks.com

Sins of Our Sons

By

Kristian Daniels

CHAPTER ONE: DISAPPOINTMENT

Nestled in southwest Alberta's rolling foothills lies the quaint little town of Cardston — the Miller and Bradshaw families' hometown. Cardston straddled the Lee Creek valley and served as a shopping and tourist hub for southwest Alberta, and was the unrivalled centre of Mormon life in Canada. Three-quarters of the town's residents belonged to the Church of Jesus Christ of Latter-day Saints, while the other quarter was Catholic and Baptist. The town's social life revolved around family life, team sports and religion.

Greg Miller was the captain of the town football team, the Cardston Cougars, and the proud son of John and Teresa Miller. Greg's parents owned the only shoe store in town, where Greg helped on weekends and summer holidays.

Greg and his teammates had been busy preparing for their next big game against the Calgary Golden Bears; it was the Cougars' opportunity to bring back home the trophy they lost to the Bears three years ago. Unfortunately, John and Teresa couldn't be there to cheer on their son — John had his business to run, and since Greg would be in Calgary, his mother would have to be at the store instead. Sales had been down, and closing for even one day could cause the family hardship in the coming months. Tyler had attended Greg's practices ever since they met. You could tell in Tyler's eyes how proud he was of his boyfriend—his secret boyfriend. Unfortunately, Greg and Tyler needed to be discreet and hide when they wanted to meet, a drawback of living in a small religious town.

1

It was Greg's last year of high school, and if his team won the game, it could mean a scholarship for him at the University of Alberta and a golden chance to play for the Golden Bears. Over dinner, Greg asked his parents once more if they were sure they couldn't make the game.

His father looked at him and said, "Sorry, Greg. I wish we could go, but we can't close the business. You know how important November is to us."

"Can't you ask Steve to cover for you?"

"No. Steve has decided to move on, and even if he was still with us, I don't have the money to pay for him to replace me. I'm sorry, son, you'll have to do this one on your own."

"You don't need us there," his mother said. "You'll do just fine."

"I know. It would have been nice to have you guys there, that's all. But I understand," Greg said.

"Besides," his mother said, "if we went, we'd need a hotel room and Calgary's expensive."

Greg nodded and lowered his head. He quietly finished his meal, took his empty plate to the dishwasher, and went to his room. He turned on his computer and browsed the internet for anything and nothing, then went and laid in his bed, staring at the ceiling. *Bummer. I'll probably be the only guy whose parents won't be there.*

He texted Tyler about meeting up. Thirty minutes later, Greg stopped by the living room and told his parents he was going out. He hopped on his bike and met his boyfriend, Tyler, at Lee Creek Park.

Unlike Greg, who was a Catholic, Tyler was Baptist. Tyler thought being Baptist was very similar to other denominations, but their parents thought differently. A typical week for Tyler was packed with religion, beginning with a seminar at six in the morning, youth group on Wednesdays, and bible school on Sunday. In high school, Tyler was referred to as the boy who didn't drink, smoke, or hook up with girls. There was nothing he'd like more than to be like the other guys his age, but his religion forbade it, as did his parents.

Tyler was already at the park when Greg arrived, sitting near the creek, leaning against a tree and lost in his thoughts. Greg quietly approached him from behind the tree and grabbed one of his arms.

"What the . . ." Tyler jerked his arm away, and Greg burst out laughing.

"You scared me," Tyler said.

"How's it going, dude?"

"Okay. And you? Ready for the big game?"

"I think so, but it's a bummer my folks can't come."

"Oh, that's too bad."

"Yeah, but what can you do?" Greg said with a shrug.

"Would you like me to be there? I can be your cheering section in the audience," Tyler said with a smile.

"You would do that?"

"Of course."

"That would be so cool. We could rent a room for after the game."

"Won't you have one already?"

"Yeah, but we're four of us in there, and I don't think the coach would let you crash. Besides," Greg said, leaning forward towards Tyler, "we wouldn't be able to do this." The two of them kissed.

"You have a point there," Tyler said. "I'll ask my parents to reserve a room for me. You need to keep your cash for university."

"Will they let you go?" Greg asked, excited at the prospect of being with his boyfriend alone where no one knew them.

"Don't worry about that. I'll be there to support you," Tyler said with confidence.

"I can't wait for us to be at university so we can be together. I'm tired of hiding," Greg said, looking at Tyler.

"Me too. You'll have to wait, though, because you're a school year ahead of me." Tyler grinned.

"Right." Greg made a sad face. "But you can join me the year after," he said with a smile.

"Think of what would happen if our parents found out about us," Tyler said, lost in his thoughts.

"That's a scary thought. Come here." Greg placed his hands on Tyler's shoulder and lowered him on his lap.

Tyler rested his head on Greg's lap, and Greg bent over and placed his lips on Tyler's.

CHAPTER TWO: QUESTIONING HIS FAITH

Tyler was twelve years old when he realized he was different. Growing up in a Southern Baptist circle, Tyler's parents, Layton and Adabelle, were active churchgoers. Tyler's father—a tall, black-bearded, broad-shouldered man—was an integral part of the ministry, and if his father suspected that his son was more attracted to guys than girls, he would send him to therapy.

Tyler remembered the Sunday he and his family drove to Calgary for a dedication service for their fellow church. The service went all day with hours of choral performances, fire-and-brimstone sermons, spontaneous bursts of prophecies, worship songs, and altar calls. The Spirit was running thick.

Tyler felt less like he was in a temple and more like a cage. He looked around and saw beaten-down mechanics and plumbers, their wives shushing their babies who didn't seem incredibly blessed by God, donating when the deacons passed the offering plate. Everyone came to the service to gather and pray, and they felt obliged to empty their pockets. Tyler asked himself, "How can this be?"

On the way back home, Tyler asked his father why church-goers had to pay to attend a church service.

"No one has to pay to pray," his father replied.

Tyler was confused and then asked, "But I saw people giving money when the deacon went around. Isn't this paying to go to church?"

"No, sweetie," his mother said. "People offer this as a gift to God; for the love, the work, and the food God sends us."

Now, at seventeen, Tyler was even less sure about the church's teachings. At a Sunday service when he was thirteen, the preacher had read bible verses that said homosexuality was a sin, and on Judgment Day, God would judge the sinner. For a closeted queer boy just starting puberty, this was quite the time to learn that the things that came so naturally to his mind were sinful. Tyler, who had begun discovering himself mentally and physically at that age, started to understand shame. Every time he masturbated, he felt an unwavering sense of self-loathing.

With nothing interesting to do, one Friday night, Tyler decided to meet his friends at the arena to watch the Junior Hockey game. The Cardston Eagles were playing against the Calgary Knights tonight, and all his friends would be there. Tyler wasn't a big hockey fan, but hoped they'd go out dancing afterward.

During the game, two benches up to his right, a guy kept looking over at him. Tyler didn't pay much attention and kept chatting with his friends. At halftime, Tyler went out to get a soft drink, and as he was checking his cellphone, he felt a tap on his shoulder. Turning around, he saw the guy from earlier.

"Hey," the guy said, "which team are you rooting for?"

"The Eagles, of course," Tyler replied, smiling with a bit of a blush. "You?" Tyler asked.

"Same. I haven't seen you here before. Are you from around here?" the guy asked, eager to find out more about the other boy.

"Yeah. Born and raised," Tyler proudly said.

"Your first time at a hockey game?"

Tyler nodded yes.

"Really?" he said, a little surprised.

"I'm not a big hockey fan," Tyler replied with a pouty

mouth. "I came to meet my friends." He shrugged.

"That's cool. I'm Greg," he said with a hand on his chest.

"Tyler. Nice to meet you," Tyler said, his eyes sparkling.

"So, what do you think of the game so far?" Greg asked.

"Interesting," Tyler said, smiling.

"I think you're up," Greg said, pointing to the kiosk.

Tyler walked up to the counter and said, "I want a medium Coke." He turned to Greg and asked, "What do you want? My treat."

"Hey, thanks, man. I'll take a Coke too," Greg said.

"No problem. Please make that two medium Cokes," Tyler said to the server.

"Which school do you go to?" Greg asked.

"Cardston High School," Tyler replied, taking a sip of his Coke.

"I don't remember seeing you there," Greg said.

"I usually keep to myself, but I've seen you around. You're the captain of the football team, right?" Tyler said. "You're here by yourself?" he asked curiously.

"I'm here with friends," Greg replied.

"Is that your girlfriend sitting next to you?"

"Ally? No, she's just a friend," Tyler hastened to say.

Greg smiled and nodded.

"I should get back to her. Maybe we can catch up sometime, go for a drink," Tyler said, hoping to get a yes.

"I'd like that. I owe you one. Catch you later, bud," Greg said.

"See you," Tyler said before joining his friends in the arena. As he sat down, he glanced in the direction of Greg, and Greg smiled at him. He returned it and went back to his evening.

CHAPTER THREE: LATE NIGHT

It had been a year already since Neil and Amanda became more than friends and moved in together. Lately, though, their relationship had become almost platonic. Neil seemed to be working late more and more, and Amanda spent her evenings wondering about Neil.

Neil's parents had played matchmaker and introduced their son to Amanda Freeman, their best friends' daughter. Neil and Amanda went to the same high school and spent a lot of time together as friends, and when graduation came, they decided to attend together. At this point, their friends thought for sure they were dating.

Out of university, both Neil and Amanda got jobs in Calgary. They both still lived at home in Cochrane, so they travelled together back and forth to work every day. Being on the road all the time took a toll on Amanda, which prompted her to move closer to work. She had been working for the same firm for two years, and at twenty-five years old, she figured it was time to leave home and found an apartment. But Neil wasn't quite there yet. Moving in with Amanda was a big step for him, and even though they had been dating for three years now, his feelings for Amanda were still uncertain. Neil's parents heard about the condo in Calgary and began asking Neil when he would be moving out.

Neil told his parents the apartment belonged to Amanda and didn't know if he was ready to take that leap yet. "But Amanda's such a lovely girl," his mother said. "There aren't too many like her around. If I were you, I wouldn't miss this opportunity."

For several days, every opportunity they got, Neil's parents kept asking why he was worried about moving with Amanda and if everything was okay between them. After a while, Neil threw in the towel and told them he was moving in with Amanda. They were both ecstatic. *I guess they really wanted me out.*

After a few months of living with Amanda, Neil felt some sparks growing in his heart for her, but still, he sensed something was missing. One night, coming home late from work, Neil quietly unlocked the apartment door, trying not to wake up Amanda. As he entered, he remembered he had forgotten to tell her he was working late. *Oh, shit. I hope she's asleep; otherwise, I'm in for a lecture.* Neil softly placed his keys on top of the small desk at the entrance, then gently made his way to the kitchen. Crossing in front of the living room, Amanda asked where he'd been.

"Whoa! You scared me. I thought you would be in bed. Sorry for coming in this late, we had a last-minute shipment and had to unload the truck before morning."

Amanda shook her head, looked at him, and said, "It's the third time this week you worked late."

"I'm sorry, honey. There's nothing I can do."

"Have you had time for dinner?" she asked.

"No, we were too busy," Neil said.

"Let me warm something up for you," she said.

"Thanks, honey. I'll hit the shower then and get changed."

Amanda opened the fridge, took out the leftover meatloaf her mother had made over the weekend, and warmed it in the microwave.

Neil jumped in the shower and, while towelling himself off noticed a red mark on the right side of his neck. He took a closer look, turned sideways, tilted his head, and panicked. *Oh, shit. It's a hickey.* Neil looked in the vanity and found

Amanda's foundation, applying a little bit of makeup to cover the mark.

On his way to the kitchen, Neil stopped and checked himself in the hallway mirror. His gym-going was starting to pay off; he had gone from an average body to a muscular one in the space of six months. When he arrived in the kitchen, Amanda had his plate already for him.

"You know what's funny?" Amanda said as she sat beside him. "When I called the office earlier tonight, no one answered."

"Oh, you called. Stephanie was probably out to get coffee," Neil said nonchalantly.

"Hum," Amanda replied suspiciously.

"This is delicious, honey. Is it a new recipe?" Neil said, trying to change the subject.

"She must drink a lot of coffee. I called the office every fifteen minutes, and no one answered," Amanda said.

Neil gulped down his last bite and raised his head with an innocent face, and said, "Oh, you know she runs around from her desk to the printer. She's a busy gal."

"Neil, just stop. I called your office every night you said you worked late, and you weren't there. Also, Stephanie told me no one ever does overtime there."

"What are you saying? That I'm lying? I'm hiding something? What?"

Amanda got up, and Neil tried to say something, but she'd heard enough lies for one night. She looked at Neil and said, "If you're not late tomorrow night, we'll talk about it then. Tonight, I'm going to bed, and you can sleep in the spare room."

"Amanda, please, can we talk about this?"

Amanda locked the door behind her.

"Fuck," Neil said.

CHAPTER FOUR: CLOSE CALL

Neil woke up to a cold coffee and a note: *If you're going to be late again, don't bother coming home. What a way to start the day. Well, I guess I'll grab a coffee on my way to work then.* Neil went and got ready for work, walked to the bus stop and stopped at the coffee shop just on the corner of his office.

Sitting at his desk, Trevor dropped by with his office mail.

"Hey, Trevor," Neil said. "Can you meet me during our morning break? I need to talk to you."

"Is everything okay?"

"Yeah."

Trevor was a handsome young man, slimly built and fashionable, unlike Neil, who was more of a jeans-and-hoodie type of guy. They both started working for the company on the same day and had become good friends since.

"How was it when you got home last night?" Trevor asked.

"That's what I need to talk to you about."

"Sure. See you at ten." Trevor went about his mail run.

Neil sat there, wondering how he could get himself out of this situation. He never thought that Amanda would check upon him. *Granted, I'm the one at fault here. I should have called her or sent her an email. Maybe it's time I come clean.*

Later that morning, Neil grabbed a table near the window at the coffee shop and ordered two lattes, Trevor's favourite. Trevor walked in seconds later and asked, "Hey, I thought about you all morning. What happened?"

"Amanda was waiting for me when I got home."

"So? You did tell her you were working late, did you?" Trevor asked.

"I forgot to send her an email. She called the office several times, and whoever she talked to told her that, apart from her, no one ever works late."

Trevor's eyes widened. "What did you say?"

"I tried to explain, but she didn't want to listen to anything last night. She wants to talk about it tonight, though," Neil said.

"What are you going to say?" Trevor asked.

"I don't know. I have to come up with something, or I'm toast."

"How about telling the truth?"

"I don't know about that."

"What's at stake for you if you come clean?"

"Everything. My inheritance, being disowned by my family and cursed by Amanda's family. I'd never hear the end of it."

"Well, you need to come up with a story and quick, or tell the truth." Trevor looked at his watch, "Time to get back to work. I'll call you if I come up with something."

"Okay. I need a believable story," Neil said jokingly. "Catch you later, and don't forget lunch—you're buying."

Neil went back to the office, tried to concentrate on his work, as well as coming up with a brilliant idea before five. Meanwhile, his boss came by and asked if he could deliver something for him.

"Of course, when did you want this delivered?" Neil asked.

"It doesn't have to be right now; you can deliver it later tonight. I'll pay you overtime," his boss said.

"Sure, no problem," Neil said.

"Excellent," Neil's boss said. "Please see Stephanie before you leave tonight, she'll give you an envelope. The person lives fifty kilometres south of Calgary. Is that okay with you? I may have more deliveries to the same address if you don't mind doing them for me?"

"No, I wouldn't mind," Neil said.

"Thank you, Neil."

When his boss left his office, Neil's face lit up. He picked up the phone and called Trevor. "I have the perfect story. Jim just asked me if I could deliver something for him tonight. He also asked me if I could do this from time to time."

"That's awesome," Trevor said. "Will I see you after work?"

"No, I can't. I have to deliver this package, and I need to keep a low profile for a few days."

"You're right. See you tomorrow then."

Neil arrived at home at six sharp, Amanda was sitting in the living room with a glass of wine.

"Hi," she said. "How was your day?"

"I had an amazing day. How about you?" Neil asked.

"It was okay."

"A glass of wine in the middle of the week. Are we celebrating something?"

"No," Amanda said, "just trying to relax. Tell me, honey, if you weren't at the office those nights you said you were working overtime, where were you?"

"Well, I talked to my boss today, and I told him that you called the office last night and discovered that I wasn't working."

Amanda interjected, "You told him that?"

"I did," Neil said. "Let me explain. I was delivering something for my boss."

"What?" Amanda asked.

"An envelope."

"You expect me to believe this . . ."

Neil got the envelope from his messenger bag, placed it on

the coffee table, and said, "Packages like this."

Amanda took the envelope and read the addressee and asked, "Who is Rachel Woodward?"

"I don't know. I told you I was working late on a shipment because I wasn't supposed to discuss this with anyone, not even with you. Sorry about all this, babe. It would have been much simpler to tell you the truth."

"I'm sorry I doubted you," Amanda said.

"I would have had questions too if I were in your shoes. How about dinner?" Neil asked.

"How about if we go out for dinner?" Amanda asked. "I was too upset to make anything when I got home. What do you say?"

"We have to make it quick, though, I have a delivery to-night," Neil said.

CHAPTER FIVE: GOT YOU

Trevor was an attractive twenty-two-year-old from Medicine Hat. Tired of the infighting and arguing with his parents all the time, Trevor chose to leave his dysfunctional family and moved to Calgary four years ago. Despite his misfortune, Trevor was fortunate to have found employment shortly after he arrived.

Growing up, Trevor had always been a loner. Whether it was at home or school, being laughed at was a daily thing for him. Trevor's brothers, Jake and Shawn, were the ones who outed him. Trevor came home from school one day, and one of his brothers waved the sketches of male nudes that Trevor had drawn at him. "Hey, little brother, what are these?"

"Give me that," Trevor said. But his father snatched them out of his son's hand.

"Jesus Christ," his father said. "Did you draw this?"

"I did," Trevor said.

"Where do you get off drawing that shit?"

"Let me see," his mother said, studying the drawing. "Are you a fucking fag?"

"Why would you ask this? Drawing naked bodies doesn't necessarily mean you are gay."

"Hey, bro," Jake said, laughing. "If you were like us, you'd be drawing titties instead of penises."

"Funny. You guys should be comedians."

"I'm asking again," his mother said, walking up to him. "Are you a homo?"

"No."

"Then explain to me why you only draw naked men?"

"I don't know; that's what I like to draw. Maybe I'll draw something else later; I don't know."

"I've never seen you with a girl," his father said. "I only see you around guys, effeminate ones."

"Yeah! The same ones he hangs around with at school," his older brother said.

Discerning that his brothers and his parents won't let up, Trevor swallowed his pride and decided to tell them straight up. His mother slapped him across the face and told him he was a disgrace to the family, tore his drawings up, and threw them away. His father walked away but showed him his fist on the way out, and his brothers were bent over laughing and calling him a faggot. Trevor ran to his room, locked the door behind him, and threw himself on his bed, sobbing.

After months of distant behaviour from his family, he ran and didn't look back. Finally, Calgary had allowed him to be himself and enjoy the privacy he so longed for.

Trevor hadn't been at work in more than three days, and Neil was worried. The first thing Neil did when he got to work on Thursday was to call the mailroom to see if Trevor was in.

"Hey, Trevor, how are you? I haven't seen you lately," Neil said.

"I've been sick. Nothing serious, just a cold," Trevor said.

"Hope you're feeling better, man."

"I am, thanks. What are you doing later?" Trevor asked.

"Why?" Neil asked.

"I thought we could get together," Trevor said.

"Yeah, that would be great."

"By the way, how did things work out with Amanda?"

"Fine. We talked, and everything's cool," Neil said.

"Cool, I'm glad to hear. Well, I have to get back to work."

"Yeah, me too. I'll see you after work."

Neil hung up and sent Amanda a message letting her know that his boss asked him to deliver a parcel after work and he would be home late.

Amanda replied, *Again? How late will you be?*

Neil wrote her back and said, *What do you mean, again? I told you my boss asked me if I could help him out from time to time. I'm sorry.*

It's alright. I understand, Amanda said.

I don't know what time I'll be home, honey. Isn't your mother coming over tonight?

Yeah, she is. Don't be too late then, she wrote back.

At five, Trevor walked out of the building, anxious to have that drink with Neil. Neil was equally eager and was already in front of the office, his car running.

They drove to a friendly little bar approximately fifteen kilometres outside the city. They wanted to go somewhere away from coworkers and whoever knew them so as not to start any unnecessary rumours. Inside, they spotted an empty table on the right side of the bar. The scruffy-looking table they sat at looked like it had been painted several times to cover cigarette burns and carvings. Neil waved at the waiter.

"So, your talk with Amanda went okay, you said?" Trevor asked.

"Yes, it went well. I was prepared to argue my point, but I didn't have to. I told Amanda about delivering stuff for Jim. I had the envelope he gave me, so that made it more believable."

"That was a close call. What about tonight? Did you let her know you might be late?" Trevor asked.

"I did. I sent her a message soon after I hung up with you," Neil said as the waiter arrived at their table.

"Hey, guys, what can I get you?

"We'll have two beers . . . Do you serve food here? Neil asked.

"Yes, we do. Let me get you a menu," the waiter said.

"Do you have any burgers?" Neil asked.

"Yes we do."

"I'll have a burger, all dressed, and fries."

"I'll have the same," Trevor said.

"I'll get your drinks and be right back. My name is Rick."

"Thank you, Rick," Neil said, smiling.

"Aren't you worried about her getting suspicious?" Trevor asked once Rick was gone.

"Not as long as I keep delivering these letters for the boss. I just have to be careful not to be away too many nights in the same week."

"Have you ever thought of coming clean?" Trevor asked.

Neil shook his head. "You know I have too much to lose."

"What about your happiness, isn't it important?"

"Of course it is," Neil said.

"So what if you lost your inheritance? Would that be such a bad thing if you find happiness in return?"

"I guess not."

"You might not lose anything either, depending on your family's reaction," Trevor said.

"You don't know my family."

"You might be surprised," Trevor said.

"I might; I'm not prepared to go there yet," Neil said.

"It's just a thought. If Amanda ever gets too suspicious about your after-hours activities, that would be an option," Trevor said, smiling. "You know you always have a place to stay. Speaking of which, let's finish up here and head over to my place."

"I like the sound of that."

On the way to Trevor's apartment in the southeast end of the city, Neil asked Trevor how his coming out was. Trevor said it wasn't easy. "For starters," he said, "I have a very dys-functional family. My parents are controlling; they have no empathy for anyone and fight most of the time. I didn't come out, my brothers outed me to my parents. I almost got punched by my father, and my mother called me faggot. So you see," he continued, "I didn't have it easy back home. Before I left, I looked my father in the face and told him it was the last time he'd ever lay a hand on me. What about your situation?"

Neil sighed. "Let's say I was pushed to move in with Amanda. Mr. and Mrs. Tamblyn, Amanda's parents, bought her the condo, then spoke to my folks to persuade them to convince me to move in with their daughter. The thought of not living at home anymore was appealing to me, but my gut told me otherwise. I should have listened to my instincts, telling me it wasn't a good idea."

"Any regrets?"

"Lots. Here we are," Neil said, nearing Trevor's place.

Neil was coming home late yet again. Amanda, not impressed, decided to shower and relax after a hectic day. While in the shower, she kept thinking about Neil's message, and wondered why wouldn't he come home first before delivering whatever it was. It didn't make sense to her.

After her shower, she called her mother and asked her if she would come by tomorrow instead. She told her she was tired and wanted to rest. Then she called Neil's office, hoping someone would still be there at this time, even though it was seven o'clock.

"Hello, who am I speaking to?" Amanda asked.

"Stephanie."

"Hi, Stephanie, I'm Amanda, Neil's girlfriend. He told me he had to deliver something tonight, but I can't remember where he was going? Has he left already?"

"Neil left earlier with Trevor. I don't know anything about

a delivery, though," Stephanie said.

"Maybe that was it. Do you know Trevor's last name? I forget," Amanda asked.

"Porter," Stephanie said.

"Thank you. Sorry to have bothered you. Have a good night."

Amanda searched for a Trevor Porter in Calgary and found his address: 13531 Deer Run Blvd SE, Apartment #2. *What business does he have with this Trevor Porter?* She hopped on a bus to Deer Run Boulevard, hoping to find some answers. *Neil never mentioned him before. Could it be that . . . No, he couldn't be having an affair with another man.* The ride there seemed to take an eternity.

En route, she tried reaching him on his cell, but Neil didn't answer. She tried several times again with no answer, then she became even more suspicious. *Neil practically lives on his cellphone.* She got off at the corner of Deer Run and Deermoss Crescent and walked towards the apartment building.

Stephanie saw Neil's car parked in front. She decided to wait around at the nearby park. She walked to the park and sat near a bush where the branches would make it challenging to see her, but still gave her a good vantage point of the apartment building's entrance.

An hour later, Neil strolled out of the building with Trevor. Neil leaned in and kissed Trevor passionately. Amanda's jaw dropped.

Oh my God, Oh my God. This is not happening. "That bastard," she said, fighting back her tears. She waited until Neil left before leaving herself, calling a taxi to take her back home.

CHAPTER SIX: WHAT A MESS

Amanda carefully unlocked the door of the apartment, thinking Neil must be home before her. She called out his name, then looked in the living room and the bedroom. He wasn't home yet. Calmly, she poured herself a glass of wine and went to wait for him in the living room.

Is this what he was doing all this time, spending his evenings with Trevor? Replaying the scene where Neil kissed Trevor, rage flooded through her veins. "I need to calm down," she said, gripping the cushion beside her, ready to throw it across the room. She took a deep breath, dropped the cushion back on the sofa, took a sip of wine, and inhaled again. When she heard Neil's key turning in the lock, she sat back and pretended to read a magazine.

"Amanda, I'm home."

"Hi, honey," she said nonchalantly. "I'm in the living room."

"Hey," he said, going to kiss her.

Amanda kissed him back, even though her hand was itching to slap him across the face.

"How was your day?" Amanda asked.

"Busy. I hope you got my message."

"Yes, I did. Thank you. How did it go?" she asked.

"Good. I had to wait around for the recipient to come home, but other than that, it was fine," Neil said.

"So it's a woman. Must be his lover then," Amanda said.

"Why would you think that?"

"Why would he keep sending her letters via courier?"

Amanda said.

"I don't only deliver letters. Sometimes they're packages. Anyway, I'm not one to pass judgement."

"Why doesn't your boss deliver them himself?" Amanda asked.

"I don't know. I never asked. Besides, he's paying me for this, so I don't care."

"I'm sure you don't."

"Hum. What's that supposed to mean?"

"Oh, nothing. Just saying, why would you mind when you're getting paid?" she said, smiling.

Amanda shrugged and got up to pour more wine into her glass. She asked Neil if he wanted some, but he declined and said he was going to shower. "Calm down, Amanda," she said while gulping down her freshly poured glass of wine. Then she poured herself another and went back to the living room.

Neil returned after his shower and sat beside Amanda. "How was your day, I forgot to ask."

"Well," Amanda said, "it started well but ended with a bombshell."

"Oh, that doesn't sound good. Sorry, you had a bad day," Neil said.

"Oh, I didn't have a bad day. I had an eye-opening day."

"Really, what do you mean?" Neil asked.

"You know my friend Isabelle from work? She was telling me that she had a feeling her boyfriend was having an affair."

"Wow," Neil said, sensing a shiver all over his body. "How can she tell?"

"Well," she said, "lately her boyfriend has been working late, something he rarely does. So one day she said she called his work and asked to talk to him and he wasn't there. She was devastated," Amanda said as she took a sip of wine.

Neil felt a rising panic take over his body. *Breathe, breathe.*

"Are you alright?" Amanda asked.

"Yeah. Why wouldn't I be? He probably went out with the boys and forgot to tell her," Neil said.

"You know, that's what he told her," Amanda said. "But the next day, she decided to follow him and saw him with someone else."

"It could have been just a friend," Neil said.

"That's what I said to her, but she saw them kissing. Can you imagine what went through her head when she saw this?" Amanda took a sip of wine and glanced at Neil, who suddenly started to feel sick.

"Did Isabelle confront him? Maybe she overreacted?" Neil asked.

"I don't know if she did. What I know is, how can you over-react when you witness something like that?"

"You have a point," Neil said.

"So tell me. How is Trevor?" Amanda asked.

"Who?" Neil asked.

"Trevor. You know, the guy you kissed tonight and prob-ably have kissed last week, and God knows how many times before that," Amanda shouted at the top of her lungs.

"Can you lower your voice, please? What are you talking about?" Neil asked.

Amanda picked up her cell and gave it to Neil. He turned several shades of red when he saw the picture. He didn't dare look at Amanda.

"How long has this been going on?" she asked.

Hesitantly, Neil blurted out, "Nothing is going on. He's just a friend." Then he realized how dumb that sounded.

"Do you kiss all your friends like this?" Amanda said. Neil sat there expressionless. "Say something."

"I don't know what to say. I know if I tell you I'm sorry,

you won't believe me, but I am."

"You're right. I won't believe you. You haven't answered my question. How long has this been going on?"

"A few months."

"Is this where you were all those late nights you told me you were working?"

Neil nodded yes, scratching the back of his head and gazing downward.

"Have you slept together?" Amanda asked.

"We did," Neil said, his eyes tearing up.

"You bastard," she yelled.

Amanda's harsh tone struck a nerve in Neil. He gently placed his hand on her arm to calm her, but she yanked her arm under his hand and said, "Don't touch me. You disgust me."

Neil got up to leave but turned to Amanda. "I'm sorry. I know I should have been honest with you. You have to believe me when I say I never wanted to hurt you."

"Go to hell," Amanda said. "I want you out of here by the weekend." With that, she picked up her glass of wine and threw it against the wall.

"Give me time to find a place to stay, for fuck's sake," Neil said.

"Go stay with your boyfriend. I don't care as long as you're out of my face," Amanda said.

She marched to the bedroom and slammed the door shut.

"Fuck, what a mess." He went to the kitchen, came back with the broom and dustpan, and picked up the broken glass.

CHAPTER SEVEN: IT'S MY LIFE

Six o'clock already, and Neil had barely slept. *Where did the night go? I might as well get dressed and leave before Amanda wakes up. I'm not in the mood for another argument.*

Sitting in his car before taking off, he dialled work and left a message with Stephanie to let everyone know he wouldn't be in today.

Neil picked up a newspaper in the stand outside the coffee shop and went in to order breakfast. Perusing the rental section, he muttered, "There is hardly anything for rent in this city. Where am I supposed to stay?" Reading through the paper, Neil came upon an article about Calgary's vacancy rate. "The vacancy rate in Calgary is at an all-time low. Rentals are rare in Calgary, and renters must look outside the city and be ready to commute."

His choices were limited: ask Trevor if he could move in with him, or move back to his parents' place until he found an apartment. While his preferred route would be to go live with Trevor, he remembered his parents' questioning temperament and what a headache it would be to explain to them, so he decided to drive to his parents in Canmore to see if he could crash there. *Mom will be full of questions regardless. "What happened, and why did she throw you out?"*

Neil steeled himself for a painful visit.

Amanda looked in the spare room to see if Neil was still asleep on her way to the kitchen, but he was already gone.

She grabbed a coffee and sat at the table, her eyes puffy, having wept most of the night. *How could he do this to me? Is it me?* With fresh tears falling, she picked up her cellphone and called her mother.

"Are you okay?" her mother asked.

"No." Amanda began sobbing.

"What is it? Why are you crying?"

"Neil . . . Neil is seeing somebody else."

"Who?"

"He's having an affair with another man," Amanda said. "I caught the two of them kissing."

"Another man?"

"Yes. I could hardly believe it when I saw them? I think I would be less upset if he were having an affair with a woman," Amanda said through her tears.

"What did he say? Is he sorry?"

"He tried to tell me he's sorry, but I didn't let him. If he were sorry, he wouldn't have been unfaithful in the first place."

Her mother sighed. "Well, sweetie, you could have let him explain why he strayed?"

"Not after he told me they slept together. It's disgusting."

"Will you be alright?"

"Yes, I will. I asked him to move out by the weekend. I don't want to see him. I have to get ready for work, Mom. I'll call you tonight. Thanks for listening." With that, Amanda hung up and went to her room to get ready for work.

No sooner had she hung up with Amanda than Suzanne called Beatrice, Neil's mother.

"Hi, Bea, how are you?" Suzanne asked.

"Suzanne, I'm fine. How's life in Cardston?" Beatrice asked.

"Peaceful. I love it here," Suzanne said.

"And to what do I owe the pleasure of your call this morning?" Beatrice said.

"Just wanted to get some news. I haven't spoken to you in a while. Have you heard from Neil?" Suzanne asked.

"No, not this week. Why?" Beatrice said.

"Nothing special, just curious," Suzanne said.

"What's going on, Suzanne? I know you. You don't ask something just because you're curious," Beatrice said.

"Well, Amanda called this morning. She was upset, and she told me that she asked Neil to move out by the weekend."

"Why? What happened?" Suzanne asked.

"I'm not sure how to tell you this, Bea . . . Amanda told me that she caught Neil having an affair."

"What? How did she find out?"

"Neil had been working late recently, and Amanda became suspicious. Anyway, she found out he'd left work early with someone."

"I'm sorry to hear that, Suzanne. Why would he do such a thing? Who is she?" Beatrice asked.

"*His* name is Trevor."

"What do you mean, *his* name?" Beatrice said sharply.

"Neil is having an affair with a man."

"Neil isn't like that," Beatrice said. "It must be a mistake."

"Amanda confronted him last night, and he didn't deny it, unfortunately."

"Well, that son of a bitch. I don't care if he's twenty-five, I can still whip his ass. Thanks for letting me know, Suzanne, and tell Amanda that I will make sure he doesn't do it again."

"Alright, Bea, I'll let her know. What will you do?"

"His dad and I will have a serious talk with him. I will send him to see a therapist if I have to. Something is wrong with his head, that's for sure."

Moments later, Beatrice heard the door.

"Hi, Mom," Neil said.

"Neil? What are you doing here?" She was surprised to see him. "I'm making coffee, do you want some?" she asked.

"Yeah, sure, coffee would be excellent," Neil said.

"How come you're not at work today?" she asked.

"I took the day off and decided to come to visit," Neil said.

"Everything alright?" she asked.

"Yes, things are good."

"How is Amanda?"

"Amanda is fine," Neil said. "Actually, we've decided to take a little break."

"Oh? Why is that? Everything okay between you two?" Beatrice asked.

"We had an argument last night, and she asked me to leave by the weekend."

"She asked you to leave just because you guys had an argument? There must be more to it."

"I worked late a couple of times in the last few weeks, and somehow she got it in her head that I was having an affair, which I'm not. She said she needs time to think."

"Are you having an affair?"

"No, I'm not. Come on, Mom. You know me better than that," Neil said.

"That's why I'm asking?"

"What's that supposed to mean?"

"Are you telling me the truth?"

Neil felt his face flush. "You don't seem to believe me. Anyway, I was wondering if I can stay with you guys for a while until I find an apartment."

"Your room is still in the basement. Won't you find it far to commute to work every day?" she asked.

"It's only for a short while, it'll be fine."

"Are you sure everything is alright?"

"Yes. Why do you keep asking?"

"You know you can tell me anything."

"Yes, I know." *Not this, I can't.* "Thanks, Mom. Where's Dad?"

"He's gone to visit a friend in Banff. Are you staying for dinner?"

"I can," Neil said

"Good, your father will be glad to see you."

"I'm going to see if Sean is at home. I haven't seen him since I moved to Calgary." Sean Freemont was Neil's best friend from university.

"Supper is at five, don't be late," Neil's mother said.

Roger, Neil's father, came back early from Calgary. When he walked in, he noticed his wife sobbing in the living room.

"What's wrong, Beatrice?" he asked.

"I found out that our son is gay," she said.

"Who told you that?"

"Amanda caught him kissing another man yesterday."

"Impossible, Neil isn't like that. Have you asked him if that was true?" Roger asked.

She shook her head. "No, I was waiting for you to get home."

"Why? You didn't have to wait for me to be home to call him."

"Neil came down this morning. He's at Sean's and will be back for dinner."

"Alright, we'll talk to him tonight. I want to hear what he has to say. I'm sure it's a mistake," Roger said.

After dinner, Neil and his parents went into the living room.

"Neil, your mother and I would like to know something," Roger said.

"What?" Neil said.

"Amanda's mother called your mom this morning." As soon as Neil heard Amanda's name, his heart started to beat faster. "She told your mother that Amanda caught you with another man. Is this true?"

Neil's blood froze in his veins, and he hesitated an instant before he said, "I was with a friend, yes. What exactly did she tell you?"

"She told me that Amanda saw you kissing another man and confronted you last night when you got home," Beatrice said.

"Are you a homosexual?" his father asked.

"Nobody says *homosexual* today. *Gay* is more appropriate, and she had no business telling you this. How dare she," Neil said.

"Is it true?" his father asked.

"This is between Amanda and me," Neil said.

"It's more than that," his father said. "It's our family honour."

"It's my life," Neil said.

"It may be your life, but this behaviour will stop immediately. Otherwise, you will never get a penny from me. Do you understand?" his father said bluntly.

"I do," Neil said.

"We're serious, Neil," his mother said. "This is not how we raised you. You need to ask God's forgiveness." Neil bowed his head and stared at the floor. *Whatever. It's pointless trying to explain how I feel; they won't listen.*

"When do you think you'll come to stay with us?" his mother asked.

"Is tomorrow okay? I'll go back to the apartment tonight and pack my things," Neil said.

"That's fine," his mother said.

"Then I should go and get packed. Thank you for letting me stay. I'm sure I'll be able to find an apartment soon."

"Don't worry about it, stay as long as you like. Drive carefully. We love you."

"I love you too."

Neil got in the car and pounded his hands on the steering wheel. *Fuck. Why did Amanda have to open her big mouth to her mother? This was between us, and now the whole world will hear about it. What am I supposed to do now? If I don't do as they say, I will lose everything. But how can I see Trevor without getting caught?*

CHAPTER EIGHT: ONE LAST NIGHT

Neil thought it was strange his cellphone didn't buzz all day. He was accustomed to checking his messages and emails several times a day. He reached in his pants pocket, pulled out his phone, and noticed that it was turned off. He turned it on, and his phone instantly started pinging. He stopped at a gas station to get a coffee for the road and scrolled through his messages, noticing Trevor had called several times.

The poor guy must be worried sick. He decided to call him.

"Sorry I missed your calls. I'm fine. I didn't feel like working today, especially after the night I had."

"What happened after you got home?" Trevor asked.

"She found out about you and me," Neil said.

"How?"

"Do you mind if I stop by? I'll tell you all about it," Neil said.

"Come on over."

"I should be there in about one hour."

"Cool. I'll be waiting for you."

Neil thought about what his father told him. *Of course, he would threaten me with the inheritance. What else do they have to get me to conform? Do I really want to live my teenage years all over again? What are you doing, dickhead – this is your chance to be who you are.*

Neil stopped by the apartment before heading out to Trevor's to pick up his belongings. Amanda was sitting in the living room when he walked in, and her eyes never left her book, not even for a second.

Suitcase in hand, Neil walked towards the hallway closet, checked inside and, as he closed the door, he jumped when he saw Amanda standing there.

"Woah, you scared me."

"Can I have your keys?"

"I know you're upset, I understand. I want you to know I'm truly sorry for what I've done. I hope you can forgive me someday."

"Give me your fucking keys,"

Neil took the keys from his keyholder and held them in front of Amanda. She reached for them, and he let them drop to the floor as he walked out, slamming the door.

Neil's mother called as he parked the car near Trevor's building.

"Hi, Mom," Neil said.

"What did you do to Amanda?" she asked.

"What? What are you talking about?"

"Suzanne called me."

"About?"

"She told us you were rude to Amanda? What did you do?" she asked.

"How could I have been rude? I didn't say a word to her. I got my clothes and left, that's all," Neil said.

"Couldn't you have stayed and tried to apologize for what you did?" his mother asked.

"I did apologize and she screamed at me, so tell me, why should I have stayed one more minute?"

"Where are you going to sleep tonight?" she asked.

"At a friend's place," Neil said.

"Your sissy friend?" his mother said rudely.

"His name is Trevor, and he's not a sissy. Where did you hear that word anyway? Isn't it a sin belittling someone else?"

"How dare you speak to me this way. I'm still your mother.

When are you coming over?"

"I told you, I'll be there tomorrow, and don't worry—it'll only be until I find an apartment," Neil said.

"You know our conditions," she said. "Your father and I will set up an appointment with the Hope and Faith Wellness Centre. They've helped lots of young men that strayed like you, and they are all happily married now."

"What are you talking about?"

"It's a therapy centre near Banff."

Neil frowned. "You guys never mentioned conversion therapy. Do you know what goes on in those places?"

"Yes. You pray and ask God to help you see the light. They have psychiatrists to help in your conversion."

"No, Mom. They resort to torture, shame, and isolation. They treat people like prisoners."

"That's not true. The bishop at my church told me what they do. The bishop said that homosexuality is caused by nurture, not nature, and with therapy, it can be reversed. There are classes on how to act less *gay*."

"Well, that's bullshit. If I were you, I'd ask somebody other than the bishop."

"Neil, you are going to therapy," his mother said firmly. "Homosexuality is a sin. It's a transgression against God's heart and mind. Your soul needs saving."

Neil swallowed down his frustration. "Got to go, Mom, see you tomorrow." He hung up. *Aargh, how stupid can someone be?*

Neil called the elevator. In the elevator up to the fifteen floor, fists clenched, he was quivering with anger. He took a deep breath and knocked.

"Hey," Trevor said when he opened the door. "How are you feeling?"

"Horrible," Neil said.

"That bad, hey. Come here," Trevor said, taking him into his arms. How about if I give you a massage. Let me move the

34

coffee table . . . There, lie on the carpet. Comfortable?" Trevor kneeled between Neil's hips, placed his hands on his shoulders, and started kneading. "Feels good?"

"Yeah, hmm, it feels great," Neil said.

"Here, let me take off your sweater." Trevor took Neil's arms and moved them up over his head, then pushed the bottom of his sweater up past his chest and pulled it off.

"So, tell me, how did Amanda find out?" Trevor asked while working on Neil's shoulder.

"She called the office, and Stephanie must have told her we left together. She also told her your name, and she searched for your address. She took the bus over, saw us kissing, and even took a snapshot of us."

"What? Why would Stephanie do this?" Trevor said, getting up and sitting beside Neil on the floor. Neil rolled on his back, his hands behind his head, and shrugged.

"What happened when you got home?" Trevor asked.

"I tried to tell her I was sorry, but she wouldn't hear it and gave me until the weekend to move out. To top it all, she called her folks, and her folks called mine, and now my parents are on my back, and I got a lecture to boot."

"Ouch. No wonder you're stressed."

"Maybe it's better this way. Like you said, I should have come clean. But I've been outed instead," Neil said.

"I'm sorry. Unfortunately, it happens to the best of us. Where will you go?" Trevor said.

"I was wondering if I could crash here tonight?" Neil asked.

"Sure, you don't need to ask," Trevor said.

"I'll be staying with my parents until I find an apartment."

"You're welcome to move in here if you want," Trevor said.

"Thanks. I thought of it, but I don't want to subject you to the backlash that will be coming my way from my folks and

Amanda's folks," Neil said.

"I've got thick skin," Trevor said.

"I know you do, but I care about you too much to let you go through this," Neil said.

"Go and get comfortable. I'll pour us some wine."

Neil showered and came back in boxers and a T-shirt. A glass of wine was waiting for Neil on the coffee table.

"What do you feel like doing? We can watch television or just sit here?" Trevor asked.

"Let's just be together. I don't know when I'll next be able to do this with you," Neil said sadly.

"I don't understand," Trevor said.

"I'll see you at work. We can have lunch every day if you want to. But to come over and spend this wonderful time together will be challenging," Neil said.

"Don't say that. You're no longer with Amanda. You're a free man," Trevor said.

"Not quite, I'm afraid. You see, the lecture I got from my parents was because they are absolutely against this *lifestyle*, as they call it. They want to send me to conversion therapy," Neil said.

"Conversion therapy? You're kidding, right?" Trevor said.

"I wish I were. Just before I got here, my mom called me, and when I told her I would be spending the night here, she lost it. She said they would be sending me to therapy," Neil said.

"They can't do this to you. They can't force this on you."

"No, they threatened me with it."

"Otherwise, no inheritance?" Trevor asked.

"Yep."

"This is blackmail. How can you go through with it?" Trevor asked.

"I don't know," Neil said.

"Be careful. The people that run these places have no

scruples. They could break you."

"I know. Can we go to bed?" Neil asked.

Trevor leaned over Neil and kissed him. Neil pulled Trevor's T-shirt off and took his off too. Trevor stood, took Neil's hand, and led him into the bedroom.

CHAPTER NINE: HOPE AND FAITH

Beatrice and Roger Fallon had devoted their lives to serving the church. Before moving to Canmore, Beatrice cleaned the rectory and cooked for the parish priest, while Roger helped with minor repairs and replenished the candles and lanterns in the church.

Beatrice spent two years at a convent when she was sixteen. After returning from the market, her mother heard her daughter crying and screaming in her room. She dropped her shopping bags on the floor in a state of panic and ran to see what was going on. When she saw her husband on top of her daughter with his pants down, she pounced on him like a panther and threw him on the floor. She asked Beatrice how long had this been going on. Beatrice didn't answer, but curled up in bed and cried. To protect the family's reputation, Beatrice's mother remained married to her husband and sent Beatrice away to a convent.

When Beatrice turned eighteen, she left the convent ready to serve God in her own way. Beatrice went to live with her unmarried aunt and found work as a housekeeper for an upper-class family. Roger Fallon, hired to build a gazebo for the residence where Beatrice worked, spotted Beatrice one day. He called her over and ask for a glass of water, and then later asked for coffee. She brought him lunch every day, as instructed by the head housekeeper, and got him when the head of the family wanted to see him.

Soon, Roger began making conversation and eventually asked her out. A few months later they started dating, and finally, Roger asked her to marry him. Neil was the only child Beatrice had because she had no sexual appetite, due to the emotional scar of having been raped at a young age. When they moved to Canmore after Roger's retirement, Beatrice dedicated her time to church events and helping the community.

Beatrice was determined to set her son on the right path. She called upon Grant Manley, the founder of Hope and Faith Wellness Centre.

The Hope and Faith Wellness Centre was located in Southern Alberta, at the far end of the only avenue in downtown Chelsea. White peaks surrounded the complex, snow-covered slopes and charcoal stone interspersed by the Cascade Mountains' evergreens. The main building appeared minuscule, and the guests' quarters stood behind the main building at the edge of the mountain. If you listened closely, you could hear the water stream splashes flowing down from the hill into a pond.

In a recent interview, Grant boasted that the centre had helped hundreds of young people on the road to sexual liberation under his command. He and his staff utilized prayer and reparative therapy, sometimes called conversion therapy. Everything was rooted in their guests confessing that same-sex desires were a sin and a disease.

Beatrice heard about Hope and Faith Wellness at a church function. Grant Manley created the centre with the support of several small church ministries across the United States and Canada, and Beatrice's parish was a supporter of the centre.

For Beatrice and Roger, having a straight son was non-negotiable. They called the centre and made an appointment to find out how they could help. And now here they were, driving down Hope Avenue, their hearts palpitating when they saw the blue archway with the centre's name etched in silver.

Following the U-shape driveway, they approached this

cobalt-blue building with a red metal roof. Stepping onto the veranda, mesmerized by the surrounding beauty and tranquillity, they took deep breaths, looked at one another, and went inside.

"Good day," Beatrice said to the receptionist. "We have an appointment with Mr. Manley."

Grant Manley was a zealous and devout Christian. He believed that homosexuality can be reversed and homosexuality is caused by childhood sexual abuse or alienation from one's parents. He built a faith-based wellness centre to help men who experience unwanted same-sex desire turn towards the "truth" and change their sexual orientations.

"Mr. Manley will be with you in just a moment. Please have a seat," the receptionist said.

A young man dressed in a white shirt and black pants stopped and asked Beatrice and Roger if they would care for a coffee while they waited.

"No, thank you," Beatrice said, clutching her purse.

"Mr. and Mrs. Fallon," Grant Manley said, walking towards them. "How nice to meet you both. Please follow me."

They all took a seat in Grant's well-appointed office.

"So, how can I help you?" said Grant.

"We're here for our son, Neil Fallon," Roger replied.

"Our son Neil told us that he is gay. We are a good Christian family, and when he told us this, it was as if the world ended around us. You are Christian, Mr. Manley, you must know this is not an acceptable lifestyle," Beatrice said, tearing up. "We don't want our son going to Hell. Can you help him?"

"Here at Hope and Faith Wellness, we have successfully cured many young men such as your son from their homosexual tendencies," Grant said.

"I'm so happy to hear you say this. I knew we made the right decision calling here," Beatrice said.

"How does it work?" Roger asked.

"First, our therapy never involves coercion. Our therapists, with the clients' assistance, will work to rid him of his unwanted same-sex desire. The counsellor, with his professional experience, helps our clients meet their own goals. We call this a collaborative relationship," Grant said.

"How long is the therapy?" Roger asked.

"It all depends on the client and his commitment to the therapy. Is your son ready to commit to this therapy?" Grant asked.

"He is," Beatrice said.

"When would he like to start? I'm curious, why isn't your son with you today?" Grant asked.

"Neil had to work today, but he is aware of our thoughts on homosexuality and our intent to send him to get rid of this disease," Beatrice said.

"Very well. Our therapy can change that for Neil," Grant said.

"Thank you, Mr. Manley. What does he need to do to get started?" Beatrice asked.

"There is a consent form that Neil needs to fill out, as well as a registration form. I will give you some reading material for Neil as well. Eva will call you with a start date once we receive Neil's paperwork," Grant said.

"Thank you again, Mr. Manley," Beatrice said.

"Here is a brochure, the form I was mentioning, and a few pamphlets." Beatrice took the envelope that Grant just prepared and carefully placed in in her oversized purse. She smiled, almost teary-eyed as she was walking out of Grant's office, at the thought that her son would be cured after his passage at the centre. Beatrice and Roger sat in the car for a moment, smiling and reassured. Beatrice looked at the brochures — one was entitled *Jesus and Sexuality* and the other *The Healing Touch*.

"I hope that Neil doesn't change his mind," Roger whispered to his wife.

"I will drive him here myself. We are his parents, and we know what's best for him," Beatrice said

"Bea, our son is an adult. You can't force him to do anything."

"Maybe being disinherited will bring some sense into him."

"What if he doesn't care about the inheritance?"

"He's our son, isn't he? He will care. Just like we cared when your parents left you nothing, and we sued the estate to get your share."

CHAPTER TEN: EIGHTEEN

Tyler woke up to a brand-new day. Today he was becoming a young adult. He stood in front of the mirror and surveyed his body to find any changes. Besides a few more pubic hairs, nothing else seemed different. He was still a handsome, blond-haired, lean, and muscular young lad. He got dressed and brought his empty water glass to the kitchen.

"Good morning, today's your big day!" Tyler's mother said. "Happy birthday, sweetheart."

Tyler looked at his mother, smirked, grabbed his backpack and headed for the door.

"Oh, someone is cranky on his eighteenth birthday?" his mother said. "Is there something the matter?"

"No. I'm fine. Have a nice day, Mom," Tyler said, leaving for school.

What's there be cheerful about? My birthday fell on a weeknight two weeks after school started, there won't be much going on.

He was right; not much would be happening that evening. As Layton and Adabelle Bradshaw had raised Tyler in a Baptist household, their parenting style was entirely connected to lessons that could be learned from the bible. When it came to teaching Tyler how to be self-sufficient, speak about his emotions, or what constitutes a healthy relationship between two people, there was never an answer that didn't involve God. Prayer sessions ruled over anything else in their home. Tonight was no exception. There would be a family dinner and a birthday cake, followed by a prayer and then homework.

Tyler strolled in at school, his hands in his pockets, looking sad. Greg noticed and came over.

"Hey," Greg said.

"Hi," Tyler replied, expressionless.

"You look down. Is everything okay?" Greg gently grabbed Tyler by the shoulders.

"Yeah." Tyler flashed a forced smile.

"So, are you excited about turning eighteen today? I would be. I mean, I was when it happened last year."

"I am. I'm just bummed out about not having a party. It's a weeknight, and my parents won't let me have anybody over," Tyler said.

"That's a bummer," Greg said. "Then we'll have to celebrate this big event on Saturday. What would you like to do?"

"How about if we go out to eat and hang out?"

"Cool. It's a deal. Cheer up, now you've got something to look forward to. Let's see that smile of yours."

Tyler smiled at his new friend.

"There you go. I've got to get back to class. Happy birthday, Tyler."

"Thanks, man."

Greg had made his day. That is how Tyler wanted to celebrate his eighteenth birthday — with friends, somewhere other than home. Tyler went on about his day cheerfully, looking forward to the weekend but also his birthday cake at home.

When he walked in the door that evening, Tyler hoped his parents had prepared a little celebration for him after all — it's not every day your son turns eighteen. He didn't expect anything big, maybe a Happy Birthday sign or a balloon tied to his chair. Tyler peeked about, but didn't see anything. *Maybe they'll bring out the cheers at dinner.*

Dinner was called, and all he got was a simple *Happy Birthday, Tyler* from his parents. He forced a smile, sat, and listened to the endless conversation about school and work. There was no birthday cake or birthday card, or any signs of a gift. Upset,

Tyler got up, brought his empty dishes to the kitchen counter.

"Oh, by the way, we've planned a party this Saturday with family friends. That's why we didn't prepare a celebration for you tonight," his mother said brightly.

"I have other plans for Saturday," Tyler said. "My birthday is today, not Saturday. My friends are taking me out then."

Adabelle turned towards her son, placed her hand on Tyler's arm resting on the table and said, "We know your birthday is today, but this is a weekday and schoolwork is more important than a party. You should know this by now."

"Well, this year is the only year I'll be turning eighteen. A little exception wouldn't have hurt anyone," Tyler retorted.

"I've already invited our friends, and everybody is looking forward to getting together on Saturday. Your father and I haven't had them over for dinner in a while, so tell your friends thanks but no thanks."

"You guys can have your friends over and celebrate without me."

"No," his mother insisted. "Saturday night is family night, the McNichols are coming over for your birthday, you are spending it with us, and that's final."

"That's not fair. You guys get to spend time with your friends, and you're preventing me from seeing mine, just so you have someone looking after their kids while you guys sit and drink all frigging night."

"Watch your mouth, young man," his father said.

"That is not a birthday party," Tyler said, stomping off to his room and slamming the door shut.

Tyler texted Greg. *Hi Greg, hope you're having a better evening than me. My folks just told me they've invited their friends for dinner Saturday to celebrate my birthday. I told them I was going out with friends, but they wouldn't hear of it. There is no way I'm spending my Saturday night at home with my parents' friends and their kids.*

Greg replied, *Hey bud. I hear you. What if I send you a message*

*to let you know where I'll be? Can you escape without being no-
ticed?*

I can for sure. What time were you planning to have dinner?

Around seven on Saturday. Does this work?

*It's perfect. My parents will be busy greeting their guests around
six-thirty,* Tyler wrote back.

*Great, I'll be able to have my chill night with Greg and spend a
wonderful birthday my way.*

Saturday night came around. Tyler felt terrible doing this
to his parents, but it was his eighteenth birthday, and he
didn't want to spend it babysitting the McNichols kids while
the adults had their grown-up dinner party. When the front
doorbell rang, Tyler exited through the back door and was on
his way to meet Greg.

"How was the getaway?" Greg asked when Tyler arrived
outside Cardston Pizza.

"Smooth. Thanks for the great plan. My parents do this to
me all the time."

"Ouch. What a way to spend your birthday."

"It's not only birthdays. It's Christmas and New Year too.
I always end up having to keep the kids busy while they have
their fun," Tyler said.

"I'm glad I rescued you, then. Here's what I have in mind.
We'll have a bite to eat, then we'll see a movie, and after we
can go to the park and shoot the shit. How does that sound?"

"It sounds like my kind of way to spend a birthday," Tyler
said.

They went into the restaurant, and the hostess brought
them to their table and gave them each a menu.

"What did your parents do for your birthday on Wednesday? I bet you had a cake."

"I wish. No. Since they decided to celebrate my birthday
tonight, I didn't have anything that day."

"That sucks. Well, I'll try and make up for it."

"You already did." Tyler smiled. "Are you guys getting ready for your big game in Calgary?"

"We are. It's coming up fast.

They looked at the menu, and Tyler said, "There sure are a lot of pizza toppings, aren't there?" It took them quite a long time to decide; finally, after the third time the waitress came to check up on them, they ordered.

After their pizza, Greg had made arrangements to have a birthday cake brought out for Tyler. Greg watched Tyler blow out the candles and noticed some tears in Tyler's eyes.

"It's the most thoughtful thing someone has ever done for me," Tyler said, drying his eyes.

"You deserve it."

Dinner and movie over, Greg and Tyler walked to Lee Creek Park to finish this beautiful birthday evening. On the way, Greg took Tyler's hand, and they strode along the dimly lit path to the park. At the park, sitting under a tree with Tyler's head resting on Greg's lap, they gazed at the starlit sky. Greg looked at Tyler and said, "Now that you're eighteen, can I give you a happy birthday kiss?"

"Sealing this beautiful birthday celebration with your kiss . . . I couldn't ask for anything better," Tyler said.

After their kiss, they stared at the evening sky, and the stars shone in their eyes. Greg and Tyler left the park around ten o'clock, and Greg sensed Tyler was getting anxious as they approached his house.

"Everything will be alright. Just keep remembering our beautiful evening. I'll see you Monday," Greg said, squeezing Tyler's hand.

Tyler, reluctant to go in and knowing his parents would be furious, took a deep breath and opened the door.

"Where were you?" were the first words Tyler heard walking in the door. "How could you embarrass us like this? Everyone came over for you. I worked hard preparing a nice dinner, and what do you do? Leave without a word," his mother said.

"I told you I had plans tonight. I wanted to spend my birthday with my friends, not your friends. Their kids are not my friends, they're much younger than me. Besides, while you and your Baptist friends would be having fun, I would have been stuck watching their kids. Not my idea of a birthday bash."

His mother got up and stomped upstairs.

Tyler's father, through clenched teeth, said, "You and I will have a serious discussion tomorrow. Now go to bed."

CHAPTER ELEVEN: SCHOOL TRIP

When he returned from the church service with his parents, Tyler went to his room to put on his jeans and hoodie. Thinking he was in the clear about his escapade, his father knocked on his bedroom door and said, "You and I need to talk, remember."

Shit, I thought he forgot about it. "Come in, Dad," Tyler said.

"The stunt you pulled last night almost destroyed your mother. Why on earth would you do something like this? Your mother worked all day to prepare a meal and a birthday cake for you."

"I told . . ."

"I'm not done," his father said. "Do you know how embarrassing it was for your mother and me when asked where you were, and we didn't know?"

"I sent you a message telling you where I was," Tyler said. "When Mom told me what she wanted to do, I told her I had been invited to dinner by friends. I couldn't let them down. I'm sorry for embarrassing you and Mom, it wasn't my intention. I just wanted a quiet get-together with my friends and to chill with them."

"You could have joined your friends after dinner, Tyler," his father said, looking at his son with his arms crossed.

"But you would have made me babysit the kids. Besides, my birthday was last Wednesday — a cake and a birthday card would have been nice then, not four days later. I wasn't asking for a big party. I never asked for a party," Tyler said, sitting down on his bed, his hands clutching the edge of the mattress.

"That is not an excuse for your behaviour," his father replied pointing his finger.

"My behaviour? How do you think I felt?" Tyler answered, irritated.

"I am very disappointed in you, and I don't want it to happen again. This afternoon, you will go and apologize to the McNichols' for your disrespect, otherwise, you can forget the school trip next weekend," his father said as he turned to leave.

"It won't happen again, I can only be eighteen once," Tyler mumbled as his father was leaving.

"Did you say something?" his father asked.

"I said it won't happen again."

There was no way Tyler was going to miss Camp Pioneer. The high school seniors were part of this trip, which meant Greg would be there; it would be their first time away together.

Camp Pioneer was three hours away from Cardston. Everyone had to be at school, ready to leave at five in the morning. Having not slept much, partly due to excitement and fear of not waking up on time, Tyler was up at four o'clock, already dressed and ready to go. Leaving his room quietly, Tyler was surprised to see his mother getting breakfast ready for him.

"Mom, what are you doing up at this time?"

"Getting you breakfast before you go. Are you excited about this trip, Tyler?"

"Yes, I am. Did you know we were going to a Christian camp?" Tyler asked.

"Yes, I knew. It was in the school letter. Don't tell me you didn't read it?"

Tyler shook his head, wolfed down his breakfast, and ran

to the door, backpack on his back. Then he rushed back to the kitchen and kissed his mother goodbye, as he ran out the door whooping with joy. Within fifteen minutes, he was at the school with all the others.

"Hi, Tyler," Greg said

"Greg, are you excited about the trip?"

"More than ever. A weekend away from this place and our parents, what else could you want?" Greg said.

"I agree."

"I wonder what a weekend at a Christian camp will be like," Greg said.

"Probably lots of sermons and prayers," Tyler said.

"You're kidding, right?" Greg said.

"Well, not entirely. If I think about how Baptist camp was, we had some of those, but it was mainly activities."

"Phew. You scared me for a minute. I thought you were going to say it would be prayers and lectures all weekend. Time to board the bus," Greg said.

"See you there," Tyler said.

"Maybe I can pretend to be in your class and get on your bus," Greg said, chuckling.

"That would be cool, but I doubt you can get past Mrs. Lawson," Tyler said.

Driving down a winding road, the driver asked his passengers right or left as the bus came to a crossroads. Mrs. Lawson said the camp is on the left. "I guess she's been there before," Tyler said to Amy, sitting next to him.

Looking out the window, Tyler thought he saw a deer running through the forest. Amy looked but was too late. The sight was breathtaking—the foliage in the forest was dense, and the evergreens stood proudly with their branches reaching out as far as possible. Tyler smiled at the thought of the animals roaming freely in this beautiful setting.

Tyler looked out front, and peeking out through the dense

foliage was the lodge. It was constructed from lumber taken from the forest, and it stood in front of a barn and arena where students could learn how to ride a horse.

The lodge coordinator met them outside. "Welcome to Camp Pioneer," the counsellor said. "You have an invigorating and spiritual weekend ahead of you."

Greg's face went blank, and he shot a look at Tyler, who couldn't help but giggle. He shuffled his way towards Tyler and said, "Dude, this is not what you promised. This sounds like praying until our knees bleeds."

"Don't believe everything he said. They all say this when you arrive," Tyler shot back.

"I will show you to your dorms," the counsellor said. "Girls, please follow Kate, and you guys follow me." Booing was heard from the guys. "Yeah, I know," the counsellor said. "It sucks, but this is a Christian camp, not Woodstock." The puzzled look on the guys' faces made the older counsellor laugh.

Unfortunately, Greg and Tyler ended up in separate dorms. After they unpacked, they were told to go to the lobby and await further instructions. Tyler waited for Greg outside their building, which was the third cabin from the main building. On their way to the main hall, Greg and Tyler saw a sports centre that included four basketball courts, a skate park, a go-cart track, and zip lines, plus an enormous pool.

"Wow," Greg said. "I wouldn't mind staying here for a couple of weeks if it wasn't a Christian camp. Look at all the fun stuff we can do around here."

At the main lodge, the school supervisors gave them their weekend schedules. There were icebreaker activities, a bible trivia game, a campfire lecture plus some free time. Tyler looked at Greg and winked; he knew he'd be freaking out at the Christian campfire events happening tomorrow night.

The cafeteria's huge dining hall was set up like a Western

town with faux-storefronts. With dinner over, and free time for all, Greg and Tyler opted to take a walk in the forest. They ventured behind the barn and noticed a trail, so they decided to follow it and check out where it led.

"What do you think of the start of the weekend so far?" Tyler asked as they followed the trail.

"Aside from the Christian campfire and bible trivia, it looks like we'll have fun after all," Greg said, laughing.

"I knew you would bring that up. It shouldn't be too bad. The camp team leader will talk about the bible and Jesus and our relationship with God. Then we'll probably sing a few songs, and then they'll leave us to have fun," Tyler said.

"If you say so," Greg said, smiling. "It sounds like you've been to a few of them before."

"Mostly Christian summer camps my parents sent me to. Have you never been to a summer camp?"

"Yes, but not a Christian one. Do you see what I see?" Greg asked.

"Is this a lake?"

"Come, let's take a look," Greg said.

Greg and Tyler made a run for the lake. They jumped on the pier and made their way to the end of it. They sat, letting their legs hang over the water, both mesmerized by the ethereal glow on the lake.

"Isn't this amazing? Look at this star-filled sky," Tyler said.

Greg turned to Tyler, looked around to make sure no peering eyes were nearby, leaned in, and kissed him in the moonlight.

"I'm happy I came on this trip," Tyler said.

"I was so happy when they included your class in this trip. The school board never brings two classes. I guess with the local church footing the bill, the school took advantage of it," Greg said.

"I almost didn't make the trip. My father came close to

grounding me for what I did the night of my birthday," Tyler said.

"Oh, I remember. I forgot to tell you something. Come closer," Greg said

"What?" Tyler asked.

Greg took Tyler's face between his hands and passionately kissed him. After the kiss, they walked back to the camp.

Chapter Twelve: Campfire

Huddled around, hypnotized by the flames spitting sparks at the sky, Greg and Tyler watched the fire and noted how the flames' warmth brought people closer together. It took a lot of air to ignite the campfire this evening, but its spell was broken by their counsellor.

"Don't let anyone look down on you because you are young, but set an example for the believers in speech, in conduct, in love, faith, and purity," the group counsellor said.

Greg, startled, looked up and noticed the leader's voice capturing the attention of all of them.

"Just because you're in school doesn't mean you don't know anything. Grown-ups sometimes think because you are young, you don't know much about God. Do you know much about God?" the counsellor asked.

Everyone looked at each other with faint smiles and then gave a barely audible mumble.

"I didn't hear you," the counsellor said.

A penetrating *Yes* echoed throughout the forest.

"Speak out. Listen to what your parents and churches teach you. We make mistakes. No one is perfect. It is your personal decision to act the way you want, but we should act in a way that pleases God. Now enough of my preaching. Enjoy yourself and this opportunity to make new friends," the counsellor said.

A roar of excitement shook the crowd as everyone got up to stretch and mingle. Tyler walked over to Greg.

"Did you want to take a walk?" Tyler asked.

"Yeah, I'm tired of sitting around. Let's walk to the lake," Greg said.

While everyone was busy chatting amongst each other, Greg and Tyler tiptoed out of sight. Cellphones tucked under their belts, flashlight modes on, they strolled along the guided path to the lake.

"You survived your first campfire spiritual speech," Tyler said.

"I felt like I was at home. My parents come out with stuff like that occasionally," Greg said.

"That makes me feel less alone," Tyler said.

"You're eighteen now. You should be able to decide whether you want to go through this or not," Greg said.

"What about you, can't you decide?" Tyler asked.

"I tried. As long as I'm at home, eighteen or not, what my parents say, I do," Greg gently said. "When did you know you like guys?" he asked.

"Around my twelfth birthday. I've always had this peculiar feeling whenever I was around guys, especially when I was with Eric, my best friend. I couldn't pinpoint or put a name to it at the time. One day, Eric announced that he was moving to Toronto. I suddenly felt this void in the pit of my stomach, and cried myself to sleep that night, heartbroken. Then I realized a few days later, that my feelings for Eric were more than friendship. I loved him," Tyler said in a halting voice.

"I've known as far as I can remember. I thought by going out with girls, it would make those feelings go away. It just made things more complicated. I couldn't get sexually excited with any of them," Greg said.

"Have you ever had sex with a guy?" Tyler asked.

"No. I dream about it and want to. Can you imagine what would happen if two guys were discovered making love in our small town? It'd be on a billboard," Greg said with a chuckle.

"Come, let's go and sit on the beach," Tyler said.

With only their cell flashlights to light the way, they ran to the beach, almost tripping over tree roots rising through the ground.

They came upon the moonlit beach. Tyler said, "Look, a shooting star. Make a wish, quick."

"Where, I don't see it?"

Tyler rose and pressed his lips against Greg's and said, "Here is your shooting star."

"Now I see it," Greg said, looking in Tyler's eyes as he kissed him back. "This was my wish."

Greg swiftly tossed Tyler under his body and began exploring his body with his hands. He unbuttoned Tyler's shirt, and his lips found his chest. Tyler moaned when he felt Greg's lips around his nipples. They both undid their pants and removed their underwear, and in the glow of the moonlight, they kissed and pleasured themselves.

In the darkness of night, hiding behind a tree, Amy and her friend Jason stood there, shocked by what they saw. Amy covered her eyes with her hands, and dried the tears rolling down her cheeks. *I thought he liked me. He talked to me on the bus.*

"What the fuck?" Jason said. "Fucking queers. Let's go back to the camp. I've seen enough. It's disgusting."

But Amy couldn't move.

"Amy," Jason said. "Come, let's go."

They left the two lovers making out on the beach and carefully made their way back to camp.

Chapter Thirteen: Stool Pigeons

Amy was a dark-haired Spanish girl who fell in love with any guy who passed the time of day with her. The next morning she entered the cafeteria with a bloated face, thick under-eye bags, and an overall drawn look. Grabbing a coffee, she joined Jason and his friends, dropping on to the seat beside him.

"You look like you had a rough night," Jason said.

"What night?" she said.

"What happened?" Jason asked, clearly wondering what she'd been up to all night.

"My head was spinning, all night," Amy said, looking around to see if Tyler and Greg were there.

"About what we saw?" Jason said, sneering.

"And more."

"Like . . ."

"I thought he was into me," Amy said, feeling betrayed.

"Guess not," Jason said. "It looks like he's more into Greg."

Amy turned to Jason and looked at him severely. At that moment, Greg and Tyler walked in.

"Look at all this food," Tyler said.

"I'm starving. I think I'll have a bit of everything," Greg said with a laugh as they made their way to the breakfast buffet.

They walked by Jason and his friends, who were grinning and winking at them. Tyler looked at Greg. "What's their problem this morning?" Greg asked.

"Good morning, Amy," Tyler said. But she turned away

without saying anything.

"What's up with those guys today?" Tyler said.

Amy leaned over to Jason and said, "You told your friends? I thought we said we would keep this to ourselves and only speak to Mrs. Lawson."

"Sorry, it just came out. Don't worry. I had them swear not to tell anybody else. You can trust them," Jason said.

"Like I trusted you?" Amy said.

Jason smirked and looked away. Amy got up, grabbed an apple and walked out, giving Jason the finger.

Mrs. Lawson stood up and shouted, "Listen up." At that moment, you could have heard a pin drop. "Today we are going mountain climbing." The whole cafeteria erupted in cheers. "Go back to your dorm, get your things and be out front in thirty minutes. We won't wait for stragglers."

Everyone jumped up, yelling, and like a stampede, they plowed through the cafeteria doors and ran to their rooms. The only ones left were Greg and Tyler, still eating their breakfast.

"Didn't you guys hear me? We are leaving in thirty minutes," Mrs. Lawson said.

"We're ready to go, Mrs. Lawson. We have our backpacks," Greg said.

Mrs. Lawson walked out of the cafeteria to pick up her gear and, coming out of the team leader's office was Amy. Intrigued, she asked Amy to wait a minute because she wanted to talk to her. Shawn, the team leader, came out of his office and noticed Mrs. Lawson.

"Ah, just the person I want to see. Do you have a minute?" Shawn asked.

"What can I do for you, Mr. Jackson?" she said.

"Can I speak to you in my office, please?"

Mrs. Lawson walked in.

"Please sit down. I have a delicate situation and would like your opinion on it," Shawn said.

"What is it?" she asked.

"It came to my attention two students from your school were seen having sex at the lake last night. It's disconcerting because this is a Christian camp, and I do understand that hormones are out of control at their age, but unfortunately, that kind of behaviour is not acceptable here," Shawn said.

"I'm sorry this happened. I agree this isn't acceptable. Do you know who those students were?" Mrs. Lawson asked.

Fidgeting, thinking how to approach this subject, Shawn sat up straight and said, "It was Greg Miller and Tyler Fallon."

Mrs. Lawson shook her head. "Who were the girls with them?"

Shawn sighed and said, "The guys were alone."

Mrs. Lawson didn't move, looked at Shawn, waiting for him to burst into laughter. "You're kidding, right?" she asked.

"I'm afraid I'm not. Amy was taking a walk in the woods after the campfire and saw them on the beach. She watched for a minute and left."

"It must have been dark, how can she be sure that's what happened?"

"She took this." Shawn turned his monitor around and showed her a picture of the guys having sex. "I had her delete it from her phone."

Mrs. Lawson got up, thanked Shawn, and drifted towards the exit.

The bus arrived, and Mrs. Lawson asked the driver to board the students while she tended to a business matter. She returned ten minutes later, boarding the bus. "Listen up, students." Everyone kept on chatting away. Then she took out her whistle and blew. "Now that I have your attention, this weekend is meant for you to think of your future, what you want to do in life. This is the beginning of your school year;

this is the time to apply yourself and get the best grades you can. This weekend is not to let your hormones run wild — remember you are in a Christian camp. So please, refrain from doing anything you might regret. That's all, enjoy your excursion."

Two hours west of the campsite was where the crew would be hiking, walking and exploring some of the wilderness. The mountain itself was a strenuous hike, interspersed higher up with a few sections of moderate and difficult scrambling, all of which could be avoided by staying on the trail that has been built for those who wish to enjoy walking instead of hiking. From the top, you could see the green meadows of the ranch below, the field of lavender flowers on the adjacent farm, and the petting zoo nestled in between.

Halfway down Scalp Creek Trail, Jason rushed in front of Greg and Tyler and displayed a disdainful look. Greg called out to Jason, "Hey, what was that all about?" But he kept on walking. Amy ran to Jason and punched him in the arm. Her look when she hit Jason was stern.

"What's his effing problem?" Greg said to Tyler.

"Who knows. I said good morning to Amy this morning, and she looked away," Tyler said.

A few miles up the trail, Greg pulled Tyler off to the side and dragged him off the beaten path. Greg took Tyler, pinned him against a gigantic pine tree, and kissed him. "Too bad we're not alone," Tyler said. I would make love to you right at this moment."

"Me too," Greg said. "We should get back, or Mrs. Lawson will have a fit."

They came back on the trail, and Mrs. Lawson asked, "What were you guys doing out there?"

"Hum, sorry, Mrs. Lawson, we both had to go relieve ourselves. Too much coffee this morning."

On top of Eagle Mountain, lunch was waiting, ready to

satisfy the hungriest of stomachs. While the gang was hiking, the camp staff brought up sandwiches, snacks, and drinks. The first ones to arrive were Jason and Amy, followed by Jason's friends. The others trailed behind, and when they saw the buffet in front of them, they rushed to get a plateful.

Greg went to sit with his longtime friends James and Carl. "Hey guys, how's it going?" Greg asked. "Enjoying yourselves?"

Both of them nodded yes. "Too bad we can't act on our raging hormones," James said, laughing. "There are some good-looking girls here."

"Down, boy," Greg said. "Glad you're having a good time. What about you, Carl?"

"It's my first time at a camp, so it's terrific. My idea of a camp wasn't like this at all. I thought we would spend days in an auditorium listening to lectures."

"For me," Greg said, "it was *Christian camp* that spooked me. I imagined being preached on all day and going to church every morning. Apart from the counsellor's speech at the campfire, everything's been perfect."

Tyler joined them and asked, "Do you guys know what's wrong with Amy? She seems kind of moody today."

"Maybe it's Jason's personality rubbing off on her," Lucas said, chuckling.

"Maybe she likes you, and she's shy. I saw you guys talking when we drove up yesterday," Carl said.

"I was only making conversation."

"Well, maybe your charming voice dazzled her, and she was rendered speechless," Lucas said.

Lunch over, Mrs. Lawson gathered everyone to help put leftovers away in the coolers. "Now, let's get back down, the buses will be arriving soon."

The buses arrived a few minutes after the gang made their way back. Tyler sat with Lucas and Carl, and Greg got on the other bus. Bodies slumped in seats and heads rested on seatbacks. Not a word was heard from anyone, and the buzzing of this morning was replaced with tired silence.

The buses pulled into camp a little after three. Groggy from their naps, everyone slowly got up from their seats. Then Mrs. Lawson said, "Dinner is at six o'clock sharp in the cafeteria. Get some rest." When Greg stepped out, she told him to wait by the bus, and she marched to the other bus and asked Tyler to follow her. "Can you guys come with me? The counsellor wants to see us."

They followed Mrs. Lawson, wondering what was going on. As they approached the counsellor's office, Tyler's hands began to shake, and they felt cold. Tyler looked at Greg, and he looked back at Tyler, his eyebrows raised. Upon entering Mr. Jackson's office, the boys saw their parents standing there, arms folded.

"Mom, Dad. What are you doing here?" Greg asked.

"I asked your parents to come up," Mrs. Lawson said.

"What for?" Tyler said.

"I think we all better sit down," Shawn said. "Boys, your parents are here because we need to discuss a delicate matter with you."

"What matter?" Greg said.

Shawn looked at Greg and Tyler's parents, then at Mrs. Lawson.

"Oh for God's sake," Greg's father said. "Someone said they saw you having sex at the lake. Is this true?"

"That's bullshit. Who told you that?" Greg asked.

"It doesn't matter who. Is it true?" Shawn asked.

"No," Greg and Tyler said in unison.

"You're saying that this person lied," Shawn said.

"Of course. Why would they say something like that?" Tyler asked.

"It was more than one person. They saw you leave the

campfire together last night. They followed you and saw you guys having sex on the beach," Shawn said.

Suddenly the door opened, and Jason barged in. "You fucking queers. You cocksuckers," he yelled.

"Get out," Mrs. Lawson said. Jason ran out the door, slamming it behind him. Greg's father stood, grabbed his son by the scruff of his neck, and moved to slap him.

"Mr. Miller, there is no need for violence," Shawn interjected.

John lowered his hand. "It's none of your business how I raise my son," John said, dragging Greg out. Teresa followed swiftly behind.

"Did he force you into this?" Tyler's father asked.

"No, I wasn't forced into anything," Tyler said.

"What are you saying?" his father asked abruptly.

"Just that. I wasn't forced," Tyler said.

"Do you realize you've committed a sin?" his father said. "A sin in the eyes of God? Thank you, Mrs. Lawson and Mr. Jackson. We're so sorry about this," Tyler's father said as they exited.

Tyler followed his parents to the car, his head down and his hands in his pockets.

Chapter Fourteen: Long Ride Home

Greg kept his eyes glued to his cellphone on the ride home. *I'd like to find out who spied on us. Do they realize how embarrassing this was? I'm fucking eighteen years old, and they treat me like a ten-year-old.*

Greg's mother, sobbing in the front, turned to Greg and asked, "Are you . . . I can't even say the word."

What if I was? I wonder how Tyler is faring out on his side.

His father gripped the steering wheel. "Do you have any idea what the neighbours will think of your mother and me if they find out what you've done?"

"Is that all you care about? What will the neighbours think?" Greg said, anger rising in him like a tide.

"Don't you take that tone with me," his father said.

"Do you know what it feels like to be confused about who you are? Do you know the battle going on inside me? Do you even care?"

"It's simple, boy. Guys go out with girls, full stop," his father said.

"You don't understand," Greg said.

"No, *you* don't understand. If you want to be like that, then go somewhere else," his father said.

"Honey," Teresa said, "don't say that."

"You can't tell me what to do. I'm old enough to make my own decisions," Greg said.

"Greg," his mother said, "stop it."

His father suddenly turned on a side road, stopped the car, turned towards Greg, and looked at him straight in the eyes.

"Now listen to me. You may be eighteen, but as long as you live under my roof, you will live by my rules. Is that clear? You are forbidden to see this guy ever again, and you better get your sexuality straightened out, or I will. Do I make myself clear?"

Greg just kept on staring at his father.

"Do you understand me?" John shouted.

Greg lowered his eyes and said, "Yes, I understand you."

He grabbed his cellphone and texted Tyler: *How is it going with your parents? I've just been blasted by mine.*

John backed out onto the main road and slammed on the gas; the tires squealed as he sped forward, causing the rear of the car to swerve slightly right.

"John," Teresa yelled, "calm down. You're going to kill us all."

Same here, Tyler replied.

I'll text you later when I get home and alone. Sorry about all this, Greg texted.

"Who are you texting?" Greg's mother asked.

"Rebecca, a girl from school who was at the camp with us," Greg said.

"Why don't you ask her out?" his mother said.

"Why would I? I'm not interested in her," Greg said.

"One more thing," his father said. "You're grounded for a month."

"What? I've got football practice. We have a big game in Calgary at the end of the month. You can't do this. What about my scholarship?" Greg said.

"You should have thought about that before," his father said.

"Then you'll have to pay for my tuition," Greg said.

"No, I don't. You can work to pay for it. My father never paid for my education. Your generation thinks everything is owed to you. Well, I've got news for you," his father said.

"I'm already working for no pay at the shoe store. How do

you think I'll pay for university? This is my one chance, and now you want to fuck that up as well?" Greg said, irritated.

Greg's father opened his mouth, and his wife put her hand on his shoulder, looked at her husband to calm him down, and said, "We'll continue this conversation when we get home. You, young man, will not speak to your father this way. Am I making myself clear?"

Greg set his cellphone on the seat and stared outside, simmering with anger. *I'll sneak out. I'm sure they won't notice I've gone to practice. They get so engrossed in their TV shows. Nobody is going to blow my chances at a scholarship and playing for the best team in Alberta.*

Greg stewed all the way home. As they made their way up the driveway, Greg grabbed his cell and stuffed it in his front jeans pocket. As soon as the car stopped, Greg practically jumped out, holding his backpack. His mother unlocked the door, and Greg ran to his room and slammed the door.

His father yelled, "You better watch out, young man."

Teresa said to her husband, "Leave him be. We should let him go to practice. There are other ways to punish him if you want to punish him. Boys having sex together doesn't mean they are gay. It could have been just a spur of the moment thing. We should count our blessings that he didn't get a girl pregnant."

"I would have preferred that to him fornicating with another boy," John said.

"You don't mean that," Teresa said.

"At least he would be normal," John said.

"Greg is a normal young man, John. He is going through a self-discovery phase, and instead of yelling and screaming at him, maybe we should sit with him and help him through this."

John got up, looked at Teresa and shook his head. "If you like having a queer son, that's your choice, but I don't." Then he walked towards the front door.

"Where are you going?" Teresa asked.

"I'm going to the bar," John said.

"Oh! That man . . ." Teresa said. She went up the stairs and walked down the corridor to Greg's room.

"Greg?" his mother said, gently opening his bedroom door. "I want to talk to you."

Greg lay in his bed, staring at the ceiling. "What?"

"I talked to your father, and we'll let you go to football practice. But that's the only outing you'll be allowed. After practice, you come straight home," his mother said.

"Thanks, Mom," Greg said, lowering his eyes to look at her.

"Greg," Teresa said. "I know you're going through a difficult phase, but I'm here if you need to talk."

"Alright," Greg said turning onto his side away from her.

CHAPTER FIFTEEN: GETTING ME FIXED

Tyler's father's eyes never left the road. His mother was praying all the way home, asking for God's forgiveness for the sin her son committed. Now and again, his mother would say to her husband, "We need to get him fixed," as if their son was a broken piece of machinery or something.

When they got home, the first thing his mother asked him was if he saw a girl in his future. Tyler didn't respond because he didn't want to lie.

"Maybe you're confused," she said. "It's just a phase; you'll grow out of it. Ask the Lord to guide you."

He smiled. Tyler was pretty sure he wasn't confused. He had always tried to please his parents, and disappointing them was not an option—even if it meant forgetting himself in the process. But a powerful sentiment he could not shake was his sexual attraction towards men. His father believed the devil was inside him and had tempted him.

"Sit down," Tyler's mother said. "How do you know you don't like girls if you've never been with one?"

"I like girls. I'm just not attracted to them. It's not a choice. It's how I feel," Tyler said.

"It is a choice to act upon your feelings," she said.

His parents were stubborn.

Unbelievably, his dad thought that it would be easier for him to hook up with men than women, and he was just taking the easy route. *Have I heard this right? How can it be easier to date men than women?*

"Tyler," his mother said. "Your father and I will always love you, but we can't accept this."

Tyler went to his room and threw himself on his bed. *How do I make them understand that I won't change? Girls don't excite me, but having a dick in my mouth does.*

"Pray, Tyler. It will cleanse your soul and guide you towards the righteous path," his mother called to him.

Tyler took his earbuds and stuffed them in his ears to tune his parents out. "Their answer to everything — prayer," Tyler said.

Hey, Tyler, how are you doing? Greg texted.

Hey man, not too bad. You?

Angry. My folks have grounded me for a month. I managed to get them to let me go to football practice, as I have the game in Calgary coming up in a few weeks, Greg said.

I hope they won't forbid you from going. You're the captain, after all, Tyler wrote back.

My dad is a football fanatic on top of being a religious freak, so I'm banking that he will soften his stance and let me go. Will you still be able to go to Calgary with me? Greg asked.

I think so. I'm not grounded. I have to think about what I'm going to tell them, though, Tyler texted.

I can't believe we were spied on. They must have followed us when we left the campfire, Greg wrote.

I wonder who it was? Tyler replied.

Do you think it was Jason? He did call us cocksuckers. What about Amy? She was in a strange mood. After all, she's all lovey-dovey when you're around, Greg texted back.

She did look upset when we met her and Jason on the trail. What I'm having a hard time with is not the fact we got caught, but the fact they called our parents, Tyler wrote.

To embarrass us. I bet you if it had been Jason and Amy, they wouldn't have called their parents on them. This is discrimination, pure and simple, Greg texted back.

"Tyler, dinner will be ready soon," his mother shouted.

I've got to go, my mother just called me down to dinner. Call me tonight, Tyler said.

"Are you gay?" his father asked at dinner.

"I think I am. No. I know I am," Tyler said.

"How do you know?" he asked.

"I don't look at girls the same way I look at guys."

"What do you mean?" his mother asked.

"When I look at a guy, I get weak at the knees, and my heart starts beating faster."

"I spoke to our priest just a minute ago, and he said gay people could go to Heaven if they repent their sins and accept Christ. He also said that you could not stay gay and continue to call yourself a Christian."

"Why did you call the priest? What does he know?" Tyler said.

"He knows that two people of the same sex cannot sleep together. He knows that the Lord condemns this type of behaviour," his mother said.

"We called the priest because we want you to get better," Tyler's father said.

"You guys keep talking about me getting better. I'm not sick," Tyler said, raising his voice.

"Yes, you are," his mother said. "Homosexuality is a sickness and can be cured. The priest said so."

"The priest isn't a doctor, and if you ask any doctors, they will tell you it's not a sickness."

"It's not a sickness like that, it's a sickness of the soul. Your father and I were just talking about sending you to see someone, some sort of therapist."

"What? I'm not going to go to a therapist. I'm not troubled," Tyler said.

"Well, we think it's a good idea. It will be good for you," his father said.

"How will this be good for me?"

"They will help you see the harm you are doing to yourself. We think it's the best thing for you at your age. You're still young and can be guided back to the righteous path."

"How do you guys know what's best for me? You're not me," Tyler said.

"Tyler, we are your parents and we know what is best for you—besides we've made up our minds," his mother said. "You're going whether you like it or not."

"Where are you sending me?" Tyler asked.

"We don't know yet," his father said.

"That's just wonderful," Tyler said as he got up and left the table, slamming the door to his room.

CHAPTER SIXTEEN: PRE-GAME PRACTICE

It was the weekend of Greg's big game in Calgary, and Tyler needed to find a way to go to the game without raising suspicion. After a bit of research, Tyler found out that there was a Baptist event happening that weekend. *I can drive down Saturday morning, attend the Youth Ministry and come back Sunday after Greg's game.* This way, he wasn't lying to his parents, and they didn't have to know that Greg would be there.

"Mom, Dad, there's a Youth Ministry in Calgary on Saturday, and I'd like to go," Tyler said.

"Where?" his father asked.

"It's at the Trinity Baptist Church. It starts at two in the afternoon," Tyler said.

"Where will you stay?" his mother asked.

"Well, I'll need to stay overnight since the event will finish late. I thought you could get me a hotel room," Tyler hesitantly said. "And I will need to borrow the car too."

"I'll talk it over with your mother and let you know," his father said.

"Thanks, Dad," Tyler said. "I'm going for a run."

"What do you think, Teresa? Should we let him go to this Youth Ministry thing?" John asked.

"We used to go to something similar when we were young. The day was full of prayers and sessions which brought us closer to God. When we left, our hearts and souls had been renewed and engaged with Jesus. With what has been going on with Tyler, maybe this will enlighten him, and you know, help him get on the righteous path," Teresa said.

"You have a point there. I'll book him a hotel room not far from the Ministry," John said.

The Cardston Cougars were almost through with their football practice. Tyler had run a couple of laps around the track and field at Lions Park and elected to wait around, hoping to have a few moments with Greg before heading back home.

"Good practice, guys," Greg said. "I think we're ready for the game this weekend. Listen, before we go, most of you have heard what happened to me on the school trip. I just wanted to say that I didn't say anything to you guys about me because I wasn't sure where I stood. I don't know if you're cool with it or not, or if some of you have a problem with LGBTQ people. If you do, I can't do anything about it, and I understand. All I'm asking is, let's focus on the game and make Cardston High School proud. Now let's get some well-deserved rest."

"Greg," James said. "To us, it doesn't matter whether you're gay or not. You're our captain, our friend, and we're behind you."

"I second that," Carl said.

"Thanks, guys. That means a lot to me," Greg said.

"Did you want to come hang with James and me?" Carl asked Greg.

"I'd like to, guys, but my folks have me on a short leash since camp," Greg said, laughing.

"Whoa," Carl said. "We have a curfew, do we?"

"As ridiculous as it sounds, I do," Greg said.

"Maybe next time," James said.

"For sure. See you guys tomorrow." Greg took off his gear and stuffed it in his sports bag, and decided to cut through

Lions Park to get home. As he was walking across the field, he saw Tyler sitting on a bench. His face brightened up, and as he was about to shout Tyler's name, he heard a horn honking. *Fuck. It's my old man. What is he doing here? So much for trusting his son.* He turned and marched towards the car.

Tyler got up and saw Greg's dad waiting for him. Disappointed, Tyler decided to run one more lap before going back home.

"Tyler," his mother said. "Can you come here for a minute?"

"Hey, what's up?"

"Your father and I agreed that the Youth Ministry event would be beneficial for you. Your father will rent a room for you at the Delta. As for a car, you can borrow mine. When is it exactly?"

"It's this Saturday," Tyler said. "Thanks, guys. I can't wait to attend my first Youth Ministry."

"Your father and I had lots of fun at ours when we were your age. We met some terrific friends. That's where we met the McNichols," his mother said.

Lying in bed, listening to music, Tyler fantasized about the weekend with Greg after his shower. He could still feel Greg's body against his from their moment on the beach. The softness of his skin, the hardness of his penis caressing his own. At that moment, Tyler knew what he felt was right.

Hey, Greg, Tyler texted. *I have good news. I'm going to Calgary this weekend. I told my parents that I was going to the Youth Ministry on Saturday. It's an afternoon thing, so we can spend the evening together. My father rented me a hotel room for the weekend. Have a great evening. Can't wait to see you.*

Chapter Seventeen: Youth Ministry

Even though the drive to Calgary was about two to three hours, the anticipation of spending a weekend with Greg made Tyler want to get there sooner than later. As he was getting ready to leave, his father said, "Enjoy yourself and try to stay out of trouble." He gave him his credit card to pay for the hotel, meals, and gas, plus a little cash as well.

"Thanks, Dad," Tyler said. "You didn't need to do this."

"Well, your mother and I are proud of you for making an effort to steer your life towards a normal one, so we wanted you to have a worry-free weekend. But don't go crazy with the credit card," his father said with a laugh. "Enjoy your time this weekend with your fellow God-loving youth."

Tyler just smiled. "I'll be on my way then. I'll call you before the ministry starts. Bye Mom, bye Dad."

If they only knew who I was meeting this weekend, they'd probably disown me. He made a pit stop at the drugstore out of town to get condoms. There was no way he was going to buy those in Cardston. News travelled fast there. Tyler couldn't help thinking, though, that what he was doing was not totally above board. He couldn't tell his folks about Greg being in Calgary as well; he never would have gotten his parents' blessing to go. But he couldn't let this chance of spending a weekend with Greg slip through his fingers either. After all, when would they have been able to be with one another for a few days? Certainly not in Cardston. *What they don't know won't hurt them.*

Tyler went directly to the hotel to check in, pay for the

room, and drop off his bags. Since the event was in the early afternoon, Tyler texted Greg to let him know he had arrived. Greg replied, saying he couldn't wait to see him.

Meet me at Denny's around six. I have to practice all afternoon, and Denny's is close to my hotel and MacMahon Stadium, where we're playing tomorrow.

Sounds great. See you then, Tyler texted.

Uplifted and eager for the afternoon to be over with, Tyler got in his car and drove to the Trinity Baptist Church. Tyler checked in with staff at the door, got his welcome package, and entered a huge hall decorated in black and white. The tables were square and had black chairs strategically placed around them, so everyone could see the centre stage. The walls were adorned with paintings of Jesus, Mary, and the crucifixion.

The buzz around the room was suddenly broken. "Good afternoon, everyone. It's terrific to see such a turnout for this event. My name is Garth Beddington, and to my right is Meredith Goldstein. We are your leaders for this afternoon. Meredith, can you present today's topic?"

"Hi, everyone, please take a seat at a table, any table. The people sitting with you will be your partners for the activities that we have for you. Today we'll be discussing *Hatred in the eyes of God.* The meaning in today's discussion is this: Loving God means you love people. Hatred is the opposite of love, and only love rooted in God can conquer hate."

"Thank you, Meredith," said Garth. "Hate is a powerful word. You may have been forbidden when you were young to say you hated someone. Why? Because the word *hate* carries substantial implications. The dictionary defines it as *an extreme dislike or disgust.* The opposite of kindness, love, compassion, or grace. Nothing about *hate* reflects the character of God. Can you think of anything that triggers hatred in people?" Garth asked.

Tyler stood up. "Two people of the same sex walking

holding hands."

"This triggers hatred because?" Garth asked.

"When society sees this, it causes extreme dislike or disgust and aversion towards those individuals holding hands," Tyler said.

"Perhaps. Why do you think that is?" Garth asked.

"Because it is contrary to what society has determined to be normal," Tyler said.

"What the church sees is two people struggling to find God's path," Garth said.

"Why do you, or the church, see this?" Tyler said.

"Because being intimate with someone of the same sex goes against church teachings, and is a sign of struggling with their faith. Society has an aversion towards same-sex people because it is abnormal behaviour in their eyes and those of the church."

"The struggle they face is because of hatred, not because of sin or their faith," Tyler said. "Is walking hand in hand a sin?"

"No," Garth said. "But homosexuality is."

"But two people of the same gender walking hand in hand does not necessarily mean they are homosexuals," Tyler said. "People make that assumption. They could be friends, brothers, or family. Women are allowed to be open and intimate amongst their friends, but the moment a guy decides to do the same thing amongst his guy friends, it's immediately labelled as *gay*."

"What is your point?" Garth asked.

"My point is, you asked for an example of something that triggers hatred. I gave you one, but you don't seem to agree that with that. Hey, I'm okay with that. I'm just debating my point, that's all," Tyler said.

"Thank you for your point of view," Garth said. "Your example . . . What's your name?"

"Tyler."

"Tyler, two men or guys would not normally hold hands," Garth said. "They would pat each other on the back or make another manly gesture. Two guys holding hands is a simple, defiant act homosexuals choose to spark hate onto themselves."

"Why would they seek hate? I'm sure they have gone through a lifetime of hurt and failure and probably been teased, bullied, and threatened with violence. Why would they add hate? Didn't Meredith say that *Loving God means you love people*? Does God preach you shall love all except those who are different? In my example, people don't even know who the two guys are, but they think they do based on their once-over assessment. Is there anybody else here that thinks judging and hating someone based on what they see or hear is fair?"

"Tyler, thank you. Let someone else speak. I recommend you speak to your minister at your church. He may help you in your struggle. Does anybody else have an example of what would cause hatred, besides people struggling with their sexuality?"

Tyler got up and left.

"I can't believe what I just heard in there. How can they speak of hatred when they can't accept that the LGBTQ community is subject to hostility and disgust? Gay people don't struggle with sin, they struggle with being accepted. It is the church that struggles with them and who defines them as sinners," Tyler muttered to himself, burning up in anger.

Chapter Eighteen: Alone at Last

Tyler got back to his hotel room, threw his backpack on the bed, and thought about the narrow-mindedness of today's church and people. *They forget we are all on the same journey. It's sad to diminish the workings of God in the world because of narrow-minded bigotry. With their groundless and malicious words, they play with people's lives in more ways than they know.*

Someday, I'd like to dedicate my time to help those who struggle, as the church put it, to accept themselves and love themselves. God made us this way for a purpose.

Oh my God. Tyler looked at his watch. *It's almost six.* He rushed downstairs, hopped in his car, and met Greg at Denny's.

"Sorry I'm late," Tyler said, going over to sit with Greg.

"Just got here myself. So how was your meeting?" Greg asked.

"If you don't mind, let's not talk about it right now." Greg nodded. "I want to hear how your practice went. Ready for the big game tomorrow?" Tyler said.

"I think we are. Now, all we have to do is win," Greg said.

"I'm sure Cardston will give Calgary something to remember. I'll be there cheering for you," Tyler said.

"So, why don't you want to talk about your meeting? What happened?" Greg asked.

"It reaffirmed what I thought of our religious leaders. I went to it because I wanted to find out if everyone in the Baptist world thinks alike," Tyler said.

"What do you mean?"

"We started talking about hate. God's view of us is being kind, compassionate, accepting, and loving. Hate is contrary to this. Then the leader asked us to give an example of something that would spark hate in people, and I said two persons of the same sex walking, holding hands," Tyler said.

"No, you didn't say that?" Greg asked, chuckling.

"I did. It took nerve, but I did. But what got me angry was the position of the church. They associated the struggle of gay people being accepted as their struggle with the sin they commit. Then this guy had the guts to say that two guys holding hands do it to defy society and bring hatred onto them. They wouldn't acknowledge the hate we are subjected to," Tyler said.

"It's the same with the Catholic Church and with my parents. If they knew I was sitting here with you, I would be on the next bus to conversion therapy," Greg said.

"Oh, you've been threatened with therapy too."

"And grounded for a month," Greg said.

"I'm not going to therapy to get fixed as my parents put it. I am who I am. Now I have to let them know this," Tyler said.

"It looks like a rough road ahead of us. Let's order and go back to your place," Greg said.

"What time do you have to be at the stadium tomorrow?" Tyler asked.

"Why?"

"So that I have an idea of how long I can have you to myself tonight," Tyler said with a grin on his face.

"Sounds promising," Greg said.

"When will you hear about your scholarship?" Tyler asked.

"It depends. If I get recruited for the football team, I should get offered a scholarship. I asked the coach for the Golden Bears to attend the game tomorrow to see me play. I hope he'll be impressed and recruit me. If not, well, I don't know what I will do. My family can't afford to send me to university," Greg said.

"You can always work for a year and do some correspondence courses," Tyler said.

"That would mean living at home for one more year and working at my dad's store," Greg said, sighing.

"Have you thought of finding a job outside of Cardston?" Tyler asked.

"That would mean paying rent, though," Greg said. "Shall we go? I have to be back at my hotel by eleven."

"I'm ready," Tyler said.

Greg took out his wallet, and Tyler waved him away. "My treat. Well, my dad's," he said, flashing the credit card.

Driving to the hotel, Greg asked how things were at school for him.

"Things are pretty cool, you know. I think the ones that were grossed out by our little escapade are the teachers and the teacher's pets. For me, it hasn't changed. What about you?" Tyler asked.

"My football team told me just before we came to Calgary that they didn't care who I dated. At school, nothing changed either. The only ones that freaked out were my folks, but that's to be expected I guess," Greg said.

"Here we are. I told you my hotel wasn't far from yours," Tyler said.

"Cool. I must warn you that, as an athlete, I'm not allowed to exert myself before a game," Greg said, smirking.

"I'll make sure of that," Tyler said as they climbed the stairs to Tyler's hotel room.

Tyler opened the door, and as soon as they were in, Greg picked Tyler up, brought him to the bed, laid on top of him, and kissed him.

"I thought you weren't supposed to exert yourself," Tyler said with a grin.

"Kissing you isn't exhausting. It's energizing," Greg said.

"Do you think we can take off our jackets? It's getting hot in here," Tyler said.

"We can take off more than our jackets," Greg teased.

Tyler pulled Greg's hoodie off. He stood there admiring Greg's well-defined upper body when Greg grabbed Tyler by his hoodie, pulled him closer, and kissed him. Reaching under Tyler's hoodie, Greg's hands felt every hard inch of Tyler's abs and chest. Tyler undid Greg's belt, unbuttoned the waistband, slid his hand inside Greg's jeans and underwear, and grabbing the flesh of his hard bubble butt. Then he pushed his hands down and thrust Greg's jeans and underwear to his ankles. Greg stepped out of his jeans and stood entirely naked in front of Tyler. Tyler unbuckled his jeans and stepped out of them and his underwear in one motion. Now he too stood entirely naked, fully aroused.

Tyler picked his jeans up, reached into the back pocket, pulled out a condom, and set it on the night table. Softly pulling Greg towards the bed, Tyler climbed on top of Greg's body and started kissing him all over. The lower his lips went, the louder Greg moaned.

"Oh my God. Ahh, don't stop. Fuck, it's oh fuck, it feels good." The passion of Tyler's love sent an electrifying spasm all over Greg's body.

The warmth of Greg's thighs under Tyler sent shivers up Tyler's back. Then their bodies moved in unison, and the excitement took over their bodies. They abandoned themselves to the pleasure, one they'd been longing for. As Tyler got closer to climax, Greg's body tightened, and his breathing became heavier and faster. Then the warm flow from their lustful desire erupted, and Tyler collapsed on Greg with their lips locked into a passionate kiss.

Still panting, they both lay there side by side, recuperating.

"Now I know I like dick better," Greg said, laughing.

"Man, that was insane. I've never had an orgasm that power-ful."

"How will we be able to keep our hands off each other back home? Tyler said. "We'll have to find a secluded place so we can be with each other."

"I agree," Greg said.

CHAPTER NINETEEN: KICK-OFF DAY

It was two hours before kick-off. Greg walked into the locker room and spotted his jersey hanging in front of his locker. The new jerseys were ordered especially for this game. Printed on the front of the jersey was a white cougar with Cardston Cougars written around it in orange letters. Seeing his name and number on the back, Greg felt butterflies starting to flutter in his stomach. *It must be what pop stars feel before walking on stage.*

The programme was neatly placed on the bench in front of the locker, waiting to be read. This was one thing that helped most of his teammates relax before a game. A few minutes later, the guys started to arrive one by one, some looking as if they hadn't slept in days and others slightly hungover.

"Hey, Captain, you look energized today," Chucky said. "Where did you go last night? We searched all over for you."

"I had dinner with a friend, and we went out after," Greg said.

"Must have been a hot night then," his teammate said, which had the other guys in stitches.

"Hilarious. It looks like you guys had a wild night too. Some of you look like zombies, and the smell of booze from your breath . . . wow," Greg said, chuckling. "Come on, let's hit the showers, it'll wake us up."

An hour left before the game, the energy in the room was pretty much quiet. Most of the team were trying to visualize making a big play. Greg was lying on the ground, a towel over his eyes, looking in a meditative state, but thinking of his night with Tyler.

Thirty minutes before the game, Greg asked the guys to get ready. Proudly wearing their jerseys, they gathered for the team prayer. The head coach had the entire team, including himself, take a knee, hold hands and bow their heads for the Lord's Prayer. Religious or not, saying a prayer was very effective at unifying a team.

Pumped and ready for action, Greg couldn't wait to get the game started. *I hope the coach from the University of Alberta is here today.*

"Alright, guys, this is your moment to shine and show those Calgarians that we Cardstoners are here to win. What do you say?" the head coach yelled.

All the guys yelled out, "Let's win this game. *For Cardston!*"

"It's time, guys," Greg said. Everyone stood in line, and soon they announced, "Ladies and gentlemen, the Cardston Cougars." Greg and his teammates ran out and positioned themselves on the field.

In the tenth row behind the Cougars goalpost, Tyler was cheering and yelling, "Go Cougars." He wanted to sit lower and closer to the school team, but he thought if someone else from the school was there, he didn't want to have the news travel back to his or Greg's parents.

The scouting agent from the University of Alberta was seated behind the university's team. He wanted to have the best view to watch the game and to see how Greg Miller performed. As a potential recruit, Greg needed to meet their specific physical and performance requirements.

In the third quarter, the game was not going well for the Cougars. The team was ten points behind, but Greg refocused his team on the game, and before long, the coach and everyone in the stands could not believe their eyes. The Cougars were doing everything right. The opposing team could not stop them. They ran, passed, blocked, and tackled like stars.

The score was tied and it was their chance to win the game.

Their opponent had the ball, and a player was gearing up for the kick. They had their best player kicking the football, then the kick came, the ball was rolling in the air, then in the closing seconds of the game, the ball started coming down—the kick didn't send it far enough to reach the goal. The player caught the ball and threw a pass to one of his teammates. Greg leapt towards the ball and intercepted the pass and ran for the winning touchdown.

The fans went wild. Greg's teammates hoisted him onto their shoulders, and cheers and screams from their fans drowned the boos of the losing team fans.

In the locker, the coach popped a bottle of champagne and passed it around. "Outstanding play, you guys," the coach said. "You scared me for a minute in the third quarter, but what a comeback. Well done."

Finally, after the stands had emptied and the team had showered, Greg went to see if Tyler was still around. He was waiting for Greg out on the field. They sat on a bench nearby, and Tyler was speechless at what he'd seen. "I'm so proud of you," Tyler said. "That was one heck of a play you did. Man, you're good."

Greg leaned over and kissed Tyler. "Thank you for being here," Greg said.

"If the scout saw that touchdown, you're sure going to get a scholarship. You're awesome and beautiful. I think . . . No, I know, I'm falling in love with you."

"I love you too," Greg said. "When are you heading back?"

"As soon as I get another kiss," Tyler said.

"I have to get back to the team. I'll see you back in Cardston." They embraced once more, and Greg went back to the locker room.

Tyler got up and walked towards the exit but sensed eyes peering at him from the seating area. He looked up and saw a shadow disappearing out the last row exit.

Chapter Twenty: Sunday Worship

"Welcome, everyone, to today's worship service," Father William said. "Seek wisdom from above. Repent of our love for the things of this world. Receive the grace of God. Today's service is about repentance.

"Repentance allows us to have single-minded devotion to the Lord. It keeps us from trying to maintain a friendship with the world while seeking to obey God at the same time. It keeps us from behaviour contrary to what the good Lord expects from us, and what is written in the scripture.

"Genuine repentance involves sorrow and prayer. Turning away from sin is painful. It is heartbreaking when we transfer our love for the world to affection for God. But once repentance is complete, God lifts our spirits from sadness to gladness, from sorrow to joy.

"My friends, let's pray and ask forgiveness from God for our sins. May the Lord forgive us."

"Please join me in our reception area for coffee and dessert to welcome the new members of our community and our church," Father William said at the end of the service.

"Where are you going, Mom?" Tyler asked.

"To the reception," she said.

"Really? Well, I'm going home then," Tyler said.

"Alright. See you at home."

Adabelle and Layton walked down the stairs to the church basement hall. Pouring herself a coffee, Adabelle felt a tap on her shoulder. She turned her head. "Suzanne, my goodness, where have you been? I haven't seen you in ages," Adabelle said.

"Hi, Adabelle," Suzanne said. "I've been busy going back and forth from Cardston to Calgary. How are you?"

"I'm okay. I'm busy with church and raising an eighteen-year-old," Adabelle said, smiling.

"Oh, I know what you mean. When Amanda was that age, she thought she could do anything because she was eighteen," Suzanne said.

"Well, it's the same with Tyler. How is Amanda?" Adabelle asked.

"Not too good these days. A few weeks ago, she found out her boyfriend, Neil, had been unfaithful," Suzanne said. "That's why I've been going from Cardston to Calgary almost every second day."

"That's too bad. Neil has family in Cardston, doesn't he?" Adabelle asked.

"Yes. Do you know the Springfields?" Adabelle nodded yes. "Shirley Springfield is related to Neil's mother," Suzanne said.

"How did Amanda find out?"

"Amanda started getting suspicious when Neil began working late a few nights a week. So, after calling the office one night, she discovered Neil wasn't at work and had left with a co-worker. She got the address of the co-worker he left with and went there and caught Neil kissing another guy," Suzanne said.

"What?" Adabelle said. "Neil was sleeping around with another man? Is he, you know, that way?"

"Looks like it," Suzanne said. "I still cannot believe it. I would have never guessed."

"He seemed like a nice young man. Well, between us, my Tyler got caught having sex with another boy on a school trip recently," Adabelle said.

"Oh no," Suzanne said, shaking her head. "What's this world coming to? Neil's mother Beatrice, she's a good friend of mine, told me she would be sending him to conversion therapy. They drove down to Hope and Faith Wellness to meet with the director. They told her that ninety-nine percent of the boys that are sent there are cured," Suzanne said.

"Is that so? I told Tyler the same thing. We don't accept this behaviour, and we were thinking of sending him to therapy also. Thank you for mentioning this place. I will look into it," Adabelle said.

"One of these days, we should get together and catch up properly. Oops, there's Robert waiting for me over by the stairs. I have to go. It was nice talking to you."

CHAPTER TWENTY-ONE: MEETING PLACE

Tyler couldn't get out of his shirt and tie fast enough when he got home. *Why do I have to dress like this for church? Why do I go to church in the first place?*

His cell buzzed while he was slipping his jeans on. Grabbing his phone, his jeans halfway up, he almost fell over, then saw Greg sent him a message. *Hey, Tyler, do you want to get together this afternoon? I found a quiet place under the Carriage Trail bridge. Meet me there at one.*

He looked at the time. *Shit, Mom and Dad will be home soon.* He ran back to his room, grabbed his runners and his hoodie and left for the bridge. Tyler took Cardston's nature trail, which was the quickest path there. The footway was interspersed with stones once washed up by the Lee Creek river in the early seventies. Tyler had sprained an ankle last year, running along this path when his foot stepped on one of these stones.

Eager to see Greg, he felt butterflies in his stomach at the sight of the bridge. *Almost there.* Picking up the pace, Tyler spotted Josh and Elaine coming towards him. *Not Elaine. Miss Blabbermouth herself.* Tyler slowed his pace.

"Tyler, where are you headed, man? All by yourself?" Josh asked.

"Just going for a walk. Hi, Elaine." Tyler smiled at her. "What about you, guys? Going somewhere special?"

"No, we were just walking. Our Sunday get-together. Right, Josh?" Elaine said.

"Yes, babe," Josh said. "Meeting someone?"

"No. My folks are at a church function, and I didn't feel like going with them, so I thought I would take a walk to the Carriage Museum and back."

"I know what you mean," Josh said. "My folks try every Sunday to bring me along with them."

"Well, I'll be on my way. Enjoy your walk. I'll see you both at school," Tyler said.

"For sure, man. Ciao," Josh said.

Tyler went on his way, checking behind him now and again, making sure Josh and Elaine didn't decide to turn around and follow him. At the bridge, Tyler stopped and looked around. Then he heard, "Psst, over here." Greg was waving to him.

"Oh, that's where you're hiding," Tyler said, following the trail leading down to the river.

"Hey," Greg said, pulling Tyler by the hand. "Come here, you," he said, wrapping his arms around Tyler and kissing him. "I missed you."

"I missed you too. How did it go after I left the stadium?" Tyler asked.

"We were so pumped winning the game. The coach was still in awe. We went out for a drink, and then got the bus home," Greg said.

"Was your dad impressed when you told him you won?" Tyler asked.

"He was very proud. Thanks for being there. It meant a lot to me," Greg said.

"Even though I'm not a football fan, I wouldn't have missed my favourite player for the world. I'm glad we had the chance to spend time together. It's not going to be easy getting together here with both our parents watching our every move. And, guess who I ran into on my way here? Josh and Elaine," Tyler said.

"Not Elaine?" Greg said.

"Yes. Oh, I forgot to tell you. After the game, when you left, I saw someone leaving from the last row. I don't know who it was, but I think they saw us," Tyler said.

"It could have been anybody. No one from my team came down with their girlfriend, and I don't remember anyone from school who said they would be there," Greg said.

"Is this going to be our meeting place from now on?" Tyler said, smiling. "Not that I mind, but it's kind of hard on the ass, wouldn't you say? How do you expect us to make love?" Tyler straddled Greg's legs.

"Aren't you a tease? I love it," Greg said. "I agree, we should find a place no one would think of looking. Any ideas?"

"Wait a minute," Tyler said. "Our neighbour has a tree-house they made for their kids. We could meet there after sundown. They built it a few yards away from their house, they won't see us getting in, and it's out of sight from my house."

"That's a possibility, as long as your neighbour's kids don't come up while we are there," Greg said.

"No worries, they moved in with their mother, who lives out of town. The treehouse isn't used except when they visit," Tyler said.

"Cool. However, we should find somewhere warmer. I don't see us making out in the treehouse in the winter. We'll freeze our balls off." Greg said with a grin.

"Do you want to meet there tonight?" Tyler asked.

"Sure. What time?" Greg said.

"When it starts to get dark, maybe around eight."

"Eight it is." Greg looks around. "The coast is clear, but I'll let you leave first. See you tonight."

Tyler leaned in and kissed Greg. He then got up and left.

Dinner over, Tyler got up and went to the kitchen to help

his mother with the dishes. "Mom," Tyler said. "Why do the dishes by hand on Sundays? Why don't you use the dishwasher?"

"It's a habit of mine. My mother always did the dishes on Sundays, while my brothers and I did them during the week. You don't have to help, honey. I can do them myself. It relaxes me. Don't you have homework to finish?" she said.

"I do. I'm almost done." Tyler kissed his mother and went to his room. Shortly after, he walked past the living room carrying a jacket, and his father asked where he was going.

"I'm going to meet a friend," Tyler said.

"Don't get home too late, you've got school tomorrow," his mother said.

"No. Promise," Tyler said, closing the door behind him.

Walking down the street to Tyler's home, Greg ran into Elaine. "Hi, Greg," she said. "What are you up to?"

"I'm just heading over to James's place to talk about the game," Greg said.

"Yeah, congratulations, I heard you guys beat the shit out of them," Elaine said.

"Not quite. They played an excellent game. We got lucky at the end with the winning touchdown. I've got to get on my way, I'm running late. It was nice seeing you," Greg said.

"Yeah, see you in school tomorrow," Elaine said.

Just as he was approaching Tyler's house, his father drove by. "I thought you were going over to James's place," he said, slowing down.

"I am. Are you checking up on me, Dad?" Greg asked.

"I'm going to the store for your mother. Of course I'm not checking up on you," his father said.

"The store is the other way, Dad." Greg pointed his finger in the opposite direction of where his dad was driving.

"I'm sorry, son. Your mother asked me to check where you were going."

Greg stopped in front of James's house, turned and looked at his father. "I'm here, you can go home now."

Greg knocked, and James answered the door. "Greg, what are you doing here?" he asked.

"Can I come in? I'll explain," Greg said

"Yeah, sure. Come on in."

Greg looked outside before closing the door and saw his father leaving. *They better not start following me around like this.*

"So, what is it?" James asked.

"I was on my way to see Tyler. Then I saw my father following me in his car. Before I left, I told them I was coming to see you. I guess they didn't believe me, and they don't trust me. He followed me here, and here I am."

"Wow. I don't know how I would react if my father did this to me. It sucks. Let's go down to the basement, we can sit and chat," James said.

"Let me call Tyler to let him know that I won't be meeting him," Greg said.

"I'll get us something to drink," James said, going back upstairs.

Greg got up, still shaken from having been followed by his father, pulled out his cell to call Tyler.

"Hi, Tyler, I'm sorry but I won't be able to see you tonight. My mother had my father trailing me. He followed me until I went into James's house."

"What?" Tyler said. "How could they do this?"

"They did. So much for trust. But to go as far as following me, it's shit, man. I'm really sorry about this. I wanted to see you tonight more than anything. Let's try again tomorrow night."

Greg slid his cell in his front pocket.

"Here, is cola okay?" James asked.

"It's fine, thanks. I won't stay long. Thanks for understanding," Greg said.

"That's cool. Sorry about what's happening, though," James said.

"Me too. I didn't think my folks would be like this. Ever since what happened at camp, they've become impossible. Watching my every move and wanting to know where I go and who I'm hanging out with. I've come to lie because whatever I say, they don't believe. Tonight was proof."

"Are you and Tyler an item?" James asked.

"I think so. He came down to the game. We saw each other the night before. But back here, we have no place to meet. I can't bring him home, and I can't go to his house. Tonight we were meeting in a treehouse behind his neighbour's place. Can you believe that?" Greg said, laughing.

"We have a camper at Lee Creek campground. We use it when we have a lot of people over. You and Tyler can use it whenever you want to see each other. I use it sometimes with my girlfriend. I'll give you a key," James said.

"Are you sure? That's really cool of you," Greg said. "But you don't have to do this."

"It's not right what this town is doing. Discriminating against people, young and old, because of their sexual orientation, race and ethnicity. My parents always taught me to treat everyone the same. I'm offering the camper because you're my friend, my teammate, and you and Tyler need somewhere to be together," James said.

"Thanks, man. I really appreciate it," Greg said.

"No sweat," James said.

"I'm going to head back. Thanks for being there."

They walked up from the basement and James told Greg to wait a minute while he went and got the key for the camper. James came back holding a caravan key ring with the key attached to it.

"Here's the key to the camper. It's behind the building when you drive in. I told my father that you would be using it. He's cool with it. The campground owner won't bother you. We told them that we would be using it in and out of season."

"See you tomorrow at school then," Greg said, giving James a hug.

When Greg got home, his parents were still up. Greg went in and went straight to his room. His father kept knocking and asking Greg to open the door. Greg yelled, "Go away. I have nothing to say to you."

"Greg, your mother and I are sorry for not trusting you," his father said.

Greg plugged in his earbuds and turned the music loud to drown out his father's constant knocking. The knocking stopped a few minutes later, and Greg fell asleep listening to music.

CHAPTER TWENTY-TWO: NO MORE DOUBT

Neil woke up groggy, dragging himself to the bathroom. He stopped and stared in the mirror before showering and thought, living at home at twenty-six sucks. I have to find another solution. Getting ready for work, Neil told his mother not to wait for him for dinner.

"Why? I was making your favourite beef stew."

"Thanks, Mom, but I'm meeting a friend for dinner and drinks."

"Who? That guy? You know how we feel about this," his mother said.

Neil stopped at the door, turned to look at his mother and said, "Mom, I'm an adult capable of making my own decisions. I didn't come here to be lectured, or scolded like a teenage boy. Don't worry about me." Neil said to his mother before walking out the door.

"I can't go on living like this. I lied to myself for too long, and now Trevor is on my mind all the time."

Around lunchtime, Neil called Trevor and asked to meet him for a drink after work.

The workday couldn't end fast enough for Trevor. He left work at five o'clock sharp and made his way to the bar Neil had suggested. He stared out of the windshield. *Is this the place? It doesn't look like a bar.* He checked his cell, thinking for sure he'd taken a wrong turn. The front window of the building looked like a garage door with six glass panes. The signage on the building read *After Hours Blue Bar,* but the building looked far from a bar. Trevor decided to go in anyway, and when he entered, he stood there in awe. He then saw Neil wave at him.

"Wow. This is really a bar. I was sure this was a garage," Trevor said.

"Cool, isn't it. Thanks for coming over. I know we see each other at work, but we can't speak freely with everyone around. What I mean is, while I've been staying with my parents, I've come to realize how much I missed you. I'm not sure if you feel the same when you said I could move in with you," Neil said.

"Of course I do. I meant it. You know I have feelings for you. Can you move in this weekend?" Trevor asked.

"I don't have much to move, just my clothes and me," Neil said.

"What about your parents' threat to disinherit you?"

"My inheritance is you. The other doesn't bring happiness."

"You know they will use it to try to convince you to change?" Trevor asked.

"I know they will, but I can't live my life pretending to be someone else to please them. I hid behind Amanda to please my parents," Neil said.

"I think we all tried to please someone at some time or other. It's easy to put someone else's desires before our own," Trevor said.

"Do you want to go eat somewhere?" Neil asked.

"I have a better idea. Let's go back home and order in," Trevor said.

"That's an even better idea."

Neil left Trevor's apartment a little after eight. *I am making the right decision. My life makes sense when I'm with him.*

Neil noticed the lights were still on in the house when he pulled into his parents' driveway.

"Neil, we're in the living room. Come join us," his mother said.

"Sit," his father said. We wanted to talk to you before we went to bed."

"About what?" Neil asked.

"Your mother and I went to the Hope and Faith Centre to speak with their director," his father said.

"What's this centre? A retirement village?" Neil asked.

"No, no," his mother said. "It's a centre where they help young men like you get rid of their same-sex attraction. It's a nice place, you'll like it there."

"Why would I want to go there?" Neil said.

"To get better, son," his father said.

"But I'm not sick. Same-sex attraction is not a sickness. I have no issues with who I am."

"What do you mean you don't have issues? Of course you do. You cheated on Amanda with another man. Don't tell us you don't have problems," his mother said.

"I cheated on Amanda, yes, and I regret hurting her. But I've been attracted to men since high school, and Amanda was my hideaway. I went out with Amanda, moved in with her, to please you. I've had time to think about my life and who I am, and I don't want to live a lie anymore. I love Trevor, so I've decided to move in with him," Neil said.

"You are *what*?" his father said, raising his voice. "You will not live with a man. It's a sin."

"Dad, I'm an adult, and I don't need your permission, nor is it any of your business who I go to bed with," Neil said.

"Maybe Amanda wasn't the right girl for you," his mother

said. "You'll find another, and maybe she'll make you happy."

"No, Mom. What don't you understand? I love Trevor, this is who I am. I am attracted to men. I'm tired of pretending to be someone else. I'm moving in with Trevor tomorrow. I love you both with all my heart, but I need to live for me, not you," Neil said.

"Your happiness is not worth the price of giving up being normal," his mother said.

"I'm sorry for being abnormal in your eyes and those of your church," Neil said. "I consider myself to be quite normal." He got up and went to pack his bags.

"Get back here," his father said. "We're not done talking."

"I am," Neil said.

Neil opened his suitcase and threw his clothes in it. He grabbed his backpack and stuffed his shoes and toiletries in it. Returning from his bedroom with his bags, he stopped by the living room and said, "Thanks for putting up with me in the last two weeks. I love you. I'll call you."

"Where are you going at this time?" his father asked.

"Back to Calgary."

Neil sent a message to Trevor, letting him know he was on his way to his place tonight.

Chapter Twenty-three: Elaine

Elaine Thompson grew up in a wealthy family. Her father was a real estate mogul whose business, Thompson Realty, had offices all across Western Canada. Elaine, from the day she was born, got everything she wanted from her parents. When Elaine's parents bought their five-bedroom mansion on Hillstreet two years ago, Elaine wanted the master suite for her bedroom.

"Dad," Elaine whined. "I want this room."

"Absolutely not," her mother said. "This is our room. There are four other bedrooms in this house, I'm sure one of them will suit you."

"I want this room," Elaine said. "I want a walk-in closet and an en-suite bathroom. Dad, please say yes."

"I tell you what, pick a room, and I'll have it remodelled to your liking," her father said. Elaine looked down her nose at her mother and, with a fake smile, turned around and walked away.

"Jack, stop giving her everything. She's becoming a spoiled brat," Sarah said to her husband.

"Honey, she's our only child. A little spoiling never hurt anyone."

Three weeks after they moved in, Elaine had her addition built: a private room furnished with a flat-screen television, a desk, and a leather sofa. The couch had to be white to match her pink and white drapes and beddings. Her room was off-limits to everyone unless you were invited. God forbid if her mother entered her room without asking, even just to bring her laundry. Elaine would scream at her to get out of her room.

Elaine was now a senior at Cardston High, and needed to improve her grades if she was to attend university.

Mark, Elaine's neighbour, had invited a girl over for dinner while his parents were out. Mark was notorious. Whenever he wanted to have sex, he wined and dined a girl, got her into bed and then dumped her the next day. Elaine noticed a glow outside her bedroom window, and she peered out to see Mark and this girl having dinner on the terrace. *I see Mark is up to his tricks again. That looks like Cindy Roberts. I know her. She's the smart-ass who aces every exam. I wonder if she would help me with mine.*

Cindy was the middle child of Mr. and Mrs. Roberts, and belonged to a good Mormon family. Being the new girl in town, Elaine spotted her right away when she began at Cardston. Cindy was somewhat reserved, so Elaine pondered how Mark got her back to his place. *Ah, there goes Mark and this girl inside the house. Way to go, Mark.*

Tired of being cooped up in her room, Elaine decided to go out for some fresh air. She grabbed her cell, and walked up the street towards Mark's house. *I wonder if Mark got his way with Cindy.* Elaine, curious, couldn't resist and went and snooped.

She snuck to the back of Mark's house, she remembered from her visit, his bedroom was at the back. The house was a bungalow, so peeking into a room was no issue. Elaine ducked as she approached Mark's bedroom window, then she carefully lifted herself to look inside and there was Mark and Cindy going at it. She grabbed her cell and began snapping pictures of the two making out. She sat on the ground looking at her snapshot and she heard Mark moaning. She put her hand in front of her mouth trying to keep herself from bursting out in laughter. She silently made her way back to the street.

Grinning, on her way home, she, saw Cindy leaving Mark's house, she hurried up her driveway and went inside, not wanting Cindy to become embarrassed seeing her and perhaps lessening her chances of getting her help. Elaine was barely back in her room before Mark came over to brag about his conquest.

"I see you had your girlfriend over for dinner," Elaine said.

"Cindy? Yes, she came over for dinner, but she's not my girlfriend," Mark said.

"Oh, no?"

"Well, she thinks she is."

"Maybe you got her to believe it to get your rocks off tonight," Elaine said.

"I almost didn't. She didn't want to at first. I had to use my favourite line: *I love you, and making love would prove to me that you love me too.* It works every time," Mark said with a smirk on his face.

"Oh, you're pathetic," Elaine said.

"Elaine Thompson, don't be such a prude. You do exactly the same with guys, so don't give me that bullshit."

"What was her name again?" Elaine asked.

"Cindy Roberts," Mark said.

After Mark left, Elaine went and asked her father if she could have a car. "A car would be useful, Dad. I'm eighteen, and you told me you'd get me one."

"Let me talk it over with your mother first," he said.

"Why? You know Mom, she'll find all kinds of reasons for me not to have a car," Elaine said.

"I'll talk to her. I don't think she'll object."

The following evening, Jack and Sarah asked Elaine to come to the living room. "Your mother and I have decided to get you a car only if we see improvement in your marks."

"What? It's not fair," Elaine said.

"Elaine," her mother said. "Your marks have been

suffering for the last two to three years. I don't know how you have managed to go from one grade to the next. This is your last year of high school, and you need the marks to get into university."

"What makes you believe I want to go to university?"

"You will go to university, Elaine," her father said. "No university, no car and no more money. These are the terms. You will need to show us some improvement and an acceptance letter from a university."

"This is bullshit," Elaine said, storming to her room.

In her room, Elaine browsed her cellphone and pulled up photographs of Cindy and Mark having sex that she took through the Mark's bedroom window, on her walk the previous evening. *If Cindy refuses to help me, then I could use these. I need that car and my father's financial support, and nothing will stop me.*

Elaine approached Cindy the following day in the schoolyard and said, "Hi, Cindy? How was your weekend?"

"Elaine, hi. My weekend was quiet. What can I do for you?" Cindy asked, knowing that Elaine Thompson didn't talk to people like her for no good reason.

"I need help with my marks. I was wondering if you could help me with them."

"What kind of help?"

"Oh, nothing much. I need to achieve high enough marks to get into university next year; otherwise, my father will cut me off financially. That's not going to happen, so, I was thinking that I'd like you to help me with homework, assignments and other school stuff."

"Are you insane? I can hardly keep up with my own, I'm certainly not going to help you with yours. No, sorry."

"I knew you were going to say that. Do you recognize this photo?" Elaine asked, bringing out her cellphone.

"What's this?"

"Look closer."

Cindy's eyes opened wide. "Who gave you this?"

"I have more, do you want to see? It would be a shame if these made their way onto social media."

"No, no, I'll help you. Please don't share these with anyone."

"Oh. Thank you, Cindy, for offering me your help. As long as you help me, the photos are safe with me. Have a nice day," Elaine said, walking away.

Elaine started dating Peter Harmon, and told everyone he was the wealthiest guy in her senior class. Peter was pretty nerdy and had never gone out with a girl before, so he was grateful that Elaine wanted to date him. Elaine's motive in dating Peter was to make all the other guys jealous. Elaine loved variety in bed, so dating someone she didn't want to have sex with was her way to entice the other boys for a night of fun.

Peter wasn't so nerdy after all. One night he asked Elaine out for dinner, and she told him she had other plans. It wasn't the first time that Elaine turned down Peter's invitations, whether it was dinner or a romantic night together. Peter decided to find out why she never has time for him, so he followed her.

Where is she going? Why is she going to the park? Peter followed the Carriage pathway. As he spied on Elaine, he stepped on a branch, and came to a complete stop. Elaine looked back, and Peter dove behind a tree. Tiptoeing back onto the trail, Peter hid behind a nearby tree and saw Elaine getting into a car with another guy. The guy looked older than her, and drove a Jeep Cherokee. Then Peter saw her kissing this other guy, and that was enough for him.

The following day at school, Peter, in front of everybody said, "You're a rotten spoiled brat who only thinks of yourself and cries to get what you want. Why did you want to date me again? Oh yeah, so that you can fuck someone else behind my back? Grow up, little girl, you're not in Kansas anymore."

"I never liked you anyway," Elaine said. "You're a pathetic mommy's boy."

"I wouldn't talk if I were you," Peter said. "Everyone knows about your whining to get what you want from Daddy. I'm sure all the football team had a piece of you."

Elaine gave Peter the finger. "Fuck you, Peter Harmon. How dare you say I'm a slut? If you could get a hard-on, maybe I wouldn't have slept around," Elaine shouted.

"Maybe my dick would have gotten hard if you had given it a chance, instead of blowing me off to go suck someone else's dick. Bitch."

"Shut the fuck up," Elaine said, all eyes upon her.

Chapter Twenty-four: The Letter

Still smouldering with resentment from having been fol-lowed, Greg went straight to his room after school.

"Greg, dinner is ready," his mother hollered. He came downstairs for dinner and sat at the table in silence.

"How was your day?" his father asked.

Greg kept looking at his cell, scrolling through it while eat-ing.

"Greg," his mother said. "Put your cell down. How many times do we have to say we're sorry for what we did? We made a mistake. Yes, we make mistakes, just like you."

"Do you know how much it hurts finding out your parents don't trust you?" Greg said, staring at both of them.

"We know how much we've hurt you. It was uninten-tional, believe us. Can we be a family again? Soon enough, you'll be going to university. Speaking of university," she reached back to the buffet behind her, "this letter from the University of Alberta came for you today."

Greg sprang up from his chair and grabbed the letter. His hands were shaking from the suspense; anxious to find out its contents, he managed to tear open the letter.

"What is it?" his mother asked.

Greg unfolded the letter, and suddenly he jumped up with excitement. "I've been invited to a Golden Bears game this Saturday. The coach wants me to meet the team," he said.

"That's wonderful, Greg." His father got up and patted Greg on the back. "I'm proud of you, son."

"Thanks for dinner, Mom." Greg forgot his dispute with

his parents for a minute and promptly went back to his room to text Tyler.

Hey, Ty. I've been invited to meet the Golden Bears this Saturday. Isn't it cool?

That's great, babe. You may get that scholarship after all, Tyler wrote back.

I hope so. Will you come with me Saturday? I'd like you to be there, Greg wrote.

I think it might be too risky. I'd love to go with you, but I'd be hard-pressed to explain to my parents that I'll be gone all day without telling them where and with who, Tyler replied.

You're right. It will be a long trip without you, though, Greg wrote back.

That's sweet. Just think, that part of your dream will soon be realized. Then when you get back, you can stop by the camper, I'll be there waiting for you ♥ ♥.

Alright, now I can't wait for the weekend, Greg texted.

Are you going to make me wait four days? It's cold in the trailer tonight, Tyler wrote back.

By the time you get to one, counting backward from ten, I'll be in your arms, Greg texted as he made his way out of the house.

"Going out?" his mother said.

"Not for long. I'll be back soon," he said as the door shut behind him.

Greg never ran so fast in his life. Had it been summer, all you could have seen was a cloud of dust suspended in mid-air. On his way to meet Tyler, still unsure about his parents' trust, he checked behind him now and again to make sure he wasn't being followed.

Huffing and puffing, he stepped into the camper. "You wouldn't think I play football," Greg said, standing in the trailer, almost out of breath. "Are you still cold?"

"Not so much now that you're here," Tyler replied with a grin.

"Scoot over, I'm coming to join you in that bed," Greg said.

"There's a dress code." Tyler lifted the blankets, flashing his naked body. "You can only come in wearing nothing."

"I'm ready," Greg dropping his jeans.

"No underwear, I see," Tyler said.

"They were stained with pre-cum from your teasing earlier. Look, it's coming alive again just at the sight of you," Greg replied.

Greg climbed into bed with Tyler, looked at him and kissed him fervently. Tyler kicked the blanket off the bed, then he wrapped his legs around Greg's butt and guided his hips towards his ass. Greg reached into his jeans and pulled out a condom. Greg was about to roll it over his erection when Tyler grabbed it and put it on Greg's manhood himself. Greg, reached the lube sitting on the night table, squeezed gel on his fingers, and then rubbed some on his erection. He poured more in his hand and ran his open hand between Tyler's ass cheeks, then he inserted a finger in Tyler's anus. Tyler then took Greg's erect penis and steered it to his hole.

Slowly, gazing into Tyler's beautiful green eyes, his hips began pushing against his opening, the head of his cock disappeared inside, and Tyler let out a cry. Moving his hips a little closer to Tyler's smooth ass, Greg inched his penis farther inside. The warmth inside made Greg's hard-on grow bigger, stretching Tyler's tunnel even wider. Tyler couldn't help but grab his cock and slap it against Greg's tight abs. One more thrust, and Greg was in, the tip of his head tickling the edge of Tyler's prostate. "Oh, fuck," Tyler moaned, "make me cum, babe."

Greg began moving his hips, holding on to Tyler's legs while watching Tyler stroke his hardness. Tyler's eyes were closed, Greg knew he was enjoying every thrust he gave him. Greg filled the condom inside Tyler while Tyler covered himself with his own juice.

Fulfilled, Greg and Tyler lay side by side, their chests heaving and beads of sweat all over their bodies. They sealed the moment with a kiss.

CHAPTER TWENTY-FIVE: NEIL AND TREVOR

Neil carefully rolled over onto his side to check the time on his cell. With the curtains drawn shut, he couldn't tell if it was night still or morning. Six in the morning was when Neil usually got up to get ready for work and drive from Canmore to Calgary. He turned and faced Trevor, who was sleeping on his back. *What a beautiful man. This is my first time waking up with a man at my side.* Trevor looked so peaceful and vulnerable. His smooth, bare chest lifted lightly as he breathed, and his skin looked so soft.

Neil stared at Trevor, thinking about their lovemaking the night before and how he hadn't felt that aroused in years. Smiling, he crawled out of bed and headed for the shower.

By the time he was out, Neil could smell the coffee brewing in the kitchen. He wrapped a towel around his waist and walked through.

"Good morning," Neil said.

"Good morning," Trevor replied, giving Neil his coffee. "How did you sleep?"

"I slept like I've never slept before," Neil said.

Neil looked at Trevor getting breakfast ready and saw every detail of him. How his thin eyebrows arched over his green eyes, his wavy hair messy in the morning. Trevor had long, beautiful eyelashes and his lips were full and smooth.

"You've showered already?" Trevor asked.

"Yeah. I woke up at six and watched you sleeping for a

minute, thinking of the beautiful night we shared. Also, my body's internal clock is used to waking up early.

"Do you want to drive in together? I'll only be a minute," Trevor said.

"Why use two cars? We're going to the same place," Neil said.

"What about what they'll think when they see us together?" Trevor said.

"It doesn't matter. I want them to see us together. Besides, they're already speculating about us. Now they'll have more to talk about."

"I'll be ready in a minute," Trevor said.

Neil and Trevor arrived at work, and as expected, there was a lot of whispering going on. Trevor went to his office and Neil to his. Sitting in the office next to Neil, Pamela peeped over the wall separator and asked, "Hey," she whispered. "Are you and the mail guy an item?"

"Yes, we are."

"Oh. Weren't you with a girl?"

"I was. Why?"

"Just curious."

"Okay. I have to get back to work. I'll talk to you later."

Jeff, Neil's network administrator, walked into his office. "Neil, we're having an issue with one of the main systems this morning. Do you have a minute to check it out?"

"Sure."

Neil and Jeff went to the basement where the company networking system was located. Entering the vault, Jeff showed Neil the computer that was reaching its end of life and required replacing. "How long do you think before it crashes?" Neil asked.

"I've been able to replace a part temporarily, but I think we need to replace it no later than three weeks from today.

Otherwise, we might lose some data," Jeff said.

"Can we change our data back-up to daily so if this computer crashes, we lose a minimal amount of data?"

"Already done," Jeff said.

"Good. I'll get you another computer," Neil said. "Send me an email with the details, and I'll get on it."

"Thanks," Jeff said.

Neil reached one of his suppliers and ordered the computer. After spending his day dealing with network issues and going over employees' performance reports, Neil thought a celebration was in order instead of going straight home after work—a celebration to mark his first gay relationship.

"Are you okay? You look distant?" Trevor asked over dinner.

"I'm okay. I was thinking about how our relationship started. First, casually getting together for sex, then seeing each other more frequently, and here we are. We've come a long way, don't you think?" Neil said.

"We sure have. I always hoped that we would end up living together one day," Trevor said.

They went for a stroll in the park near their apartment to walk their dinner off. Trevor wrapped his arm around Neil's waist and pulled Neil closer, then Trevor whispered, "I love you." They slowed down and stood still for a moment, then Trevor gently guided Neil towards the evergreen behind him. He looked at Neil with those big innocent eyes, leaned in, and pressed his lips to Neil's. Neil shivered.

They hurried back to the apartment, and Neil drew Trevor's body against his and softly, gently kissed him. Emotions welled up inside Neil as he felt Trevor's hand slide under his shirt, before they began kissing more aggressively.

Trevor unbuttoned his shirt, then unbuttoned Neil's. Their

bodies touched, and Trevor took Neil's face between his hands and brought it towards his lips. *I love how his smooth chest feels against mine. How our soft cocks rub against each other.* Neil's fingers slipped under the back of Trevor's pants, and he squeezed Trevor's firm butt.

Trevor took a step back and began to undo Neil's belt. Trevor unzipped Neil's pants and let them drop to his ankles, then tugged at his underwear and slowly pulled them down, allowing Neil's hard-on to spring out. Neil's hard cock pressed into Trevor's flat soft, smooth stomach. Trevor and Neil lay on the bed, side by side. Their noses nuzzled as their hard cocks brushed against each other. They explored each other's chests gently with their hands, then their backs and asses. Trevor's hand ran down Neil's stomach, then down the underside of Neil's hard cock, and he slowly began stroking him.

Their foreheads pressed together as they each stroked the other slowly. It was the most intimate moment of Neil's entire life. Neil felt connected to this wonderful man, and all he wanted was to give back to Trevor. As they cuddled and jerked off, Neil's breathing became erratic. Trevor pawed his hard-on more roughly and buried his forehead into Neil's shoulder. Neil could feel Trevor's pre-cum on his thumb, and he used it to rub that spot on the back of his cock.

Trevor's head rose off Neil's shoulder and craned backward. Trevor let out a muffled cry, and Neil felt the warm wetness of Trevor's seed shoot onto his stomach and chest. Trevor's eyes glazed over as the pleasure coursed through him. His stiffened body relaxed, and he refocused on Neil. Some of his jizz was on Neil's dick, and Trevor used it to lube Neil's cock before finishing him off. Neil had one of the strongest orgasms of his life.

Neil ran his hand down Trevor's side and into the dip of his waist. They stared at one another in silence. Trevor's chest heaved, and his cheeks were flushed. Neil felt like nothing he had felt after sex with Amanda. It was a relaxed, glowing feeling, knowing he had brought pleasure to someone he cared for.

They lingered like that for a good fifteen minutes before showering and sitting in the living room, cuddling and relaxing.

CHAPTER TWENTY-SIX: MEETING THE TEAM

Greg got up at the crack of dawn, excited at the prospect of meeting his favourite football team. He weighed two options for what to wear: his Golden Bear jersey and ball cap, or jeans and a hoodie. He took out everything and laid it out on his bed, and went to shower. *Too bad Tyler isn't coming with me, it would make this trip even more special.*

His appointment with the Golden Bears was at noon, and it was a three-hour drive to the university. An hour went by and Greg still hadn't decided what to wear, but it was nearing eight o'clock, and if he wanted to make it in time, he had to decide now. Sitting in the car, in his hoodie and jeans, Greg texted Tyler to let him know he was leaving and that he would meet him at the trailer at seven that evening. The weather couldn't have been more beautiful. The sun was shining and everything seemed possible.

With clammy hands and a racing heart, Greg entered the university. Down the hall, standing near the gym, Coach Hudson waved at him. "Good to see you, Greg. The guys are in the gym."

Walking through the locker room, Greg's hands started shaking and his breath quickened. Entering the gym, Greg saw the team playing and warming up, and he was stars truck instantly. A shout from the coach and the boys stopped shooting baskets and gathered around. "Guys, here is Greg Miller, the young lad who scored the winning touchdown a few weeks ago."

"Good to meet you, Greg," Dave Townsend said.

Oh, my God, it's him, Dave Townsend. So I'm finally meeting the star player of the team. "I've been watching you guys play since forever. It's great to meet you all."

"You're the captain of the Cougars, right?" Dave asked.

"I am," Greg replied.

"You want to shoot some hoops with us? It's not football, but the guys like the game, and it's a good way to warm up too," Dave said.

The coach sat in the bleachers and watched Greg's physical form and play tactics. Greg played like a pro—he passed the ball to his teammates, scored some baskets, and kept his teammates in stitches. His footwork, balance, and upper-body strength impressed the coach. Coach Hudson signaled Dave to foil Greg, to check out how Greg would regain control of the ball. The coach watched the two of them play off each other and was captivated. He blew his whistle, and the guys stopped playing, congratulating Greg for an impressive performance.

Coach Hudson handed Greg a questionnaire and said, "You know, Greg, I was impressed by what I saw today, so I tell you what . . . Once you send me what I gave you, I'll see what I can do about getting you up to our camp."

"Really, wow! It would be a dream come true being invited to the Bears football camp," Greg said.

"It would be a pleasure for us to have you there. Safe drive back, and we'll talk to you soon."

Greg shook the coach's hand and said goodbye. The guys from the team gathered and all wished him well.

"Thanks, guys. I enjoyed meeting you all too. I'll see you soon, I hope," Greg said as he left the gym.

Monday morning at school, Greg told his pals how he hung

out with the Golden Bears players.

"Are you being recruited?" James asked.

"I don't know. It would help me financially if they did. Coach Hudson gave me a questionnaire to fill out," Greg said.

"It sounds like he's interested in you. I hope they give that scholarship," James said.

"Thanks, man," Greg said.

Not to get their hopes up, Greg didn't tell his parents about the camp and the questionnaire.

CHAPTER TWENTY-SEVEN: NEIL'S FATHER

Neil got up, went to the bathroom and crumpled to the floor. Unable to contain the crushing pain inside of him, he started to weep, curled up in the corner of the bathroom. Chris, a co-worker, noticed Neil didn't look well after he hung up the phone. Chris called Trevor and told him he had better come up to see Neil.

Trevor came up to Neil's office, and Chris motioned that he was in the bathroom. Entering, he saw Neil on the floor, bent over and holding his head and crying. Trevor rushed to his side, sat beside him and wrapped his arms around him.

"What's wrong, sweetie? What's happening?" Trevor asked.

"It's my father."

"What about your father?" Trevor asked.

"He suffered a heart attack this morning. My mother called from the hospital, and . . ." Neil tried to stop crying long enough to speak, "and she told me that they don't know if he will make it."

"Come, I'll drive you home. I'll tell Chris what happened so if your boss comes around, he can tell him."

Trevor took Neil home. "I think you should rest before going to the hospital, honey. I'll set the alarm for an hour from now. Text me when you get there." Trevor kissed Neil and left for work.

Unable to sleep, Neil's thoughts kept returning to his father and the last discussion they had. *I wish I hadn't said what I said. I should have agreed to go to therapy. Maybe he wouldn't have suffered a heart attack.*

Neil got out of bed, went to the living room and stared out the patio door, tears running down his face. He went back to the sofa and picked up the phone to call his mother.

"Mom, how is he?" Neil asked, his voice shaking from distress.

"He's in intensive care," his mother answered.

"I'm leaving for the hospital now. I'll see you there."

His whole life was shattered the moment he entered the hospital. His father passed away minutes before he got there. Neil rushed to his mother's side and took her into his arms to console her. She suddenly pushed him away. "Don't," she said.

Neil stepped back, tears rolling down his cheeks. "Why didn't you tell me he had a heart condition?" Neil said in a quivering voice.

"He didn't," his mother said. "He was fine when he got up, and then we started talking about you during breakfast. Your life and what you've become. That's when it happened."

"No warnings?"

"No. It was sudden. He was drinking his coffee, and then he fell to the floor complaining about a pain in his chest."

"Did he complain about chest pains before?" Neil asked.

"He complained about not feeling well a few days after you refused to go to therapy."

"Why didn't he see a doctor?"

His mother sighed. "You know your father, him and doctors."

"Yeah, I know."

"How are things with your *roommate*?" his mother asked coldly.

"Mom," Neil said. "Trevor's not my roommate. He's my partner."

"You've chosen a tough lifestyle, Neil. You'll be very lonely, you'll have no friends, and you'll be ridiculed and bullied."

Shattered by what his mother said, Neil asked, "How can you say that? I have a wonderful life with Trevor."

"You call that a life? It's an abomination."

Neil didn't want to listen to this anymore. "You know what, Mom, I'm not going to debate you on this because I don't want to fight with you. Dad just died, and your concern about how I'm going to hell, well, we can have that discussion some other time. I'll see you at the funeral. Let me know if I can help with the arrangements. Goodbye."

On his way to the car, Neil texted Trevor to let him know he was on his way back home. Trevor asked how his father was, Neil wrote back that he had passed away minutes before he arrived. Sitting in his car, Neil broke down.

Dad, I'm sorry if I caused you to become ill. I'm sorry if I didn't turn out to be the son you and Mom wanted me to be. I hope you understand and forgive me. I love you and will miss you forever.

On the day of the funeral, Trevor and Neil were standing near Neil's father's urn, talking with friends and co-workers, when Amanda came in with her parents. Suzanne and Robert extended their condolences to Neil's mother; Amanda asked where Neil was, and his mother pointed over.

When Amanda saw Neil with him, she felt a knot inside her. He'd destroyed their relationship. She took a deep breath and put on her fake smile, which Neil was too familiar with and walked towards them.

"My condolences, Neil," Amanda said. "How are you doing?" Then she turned to Trevor. "You must be Trevor."

"Pleased to meet you," Trevor said.

"I'm sure," Amanda said.

Neil looked at her with scornful eyes. "I'm fine, thanks."

"He went fast," Amanda said.

"He did. How are you?" Neil asked.

"I'm fine. I got a promotion at work, and I am moving to Vancouver," Amanda said.

"Congratulations. Why Vancouver?" Neil asked.

"That's where the new office I'll be managing is," Amanda said.

Suzanne and Robert came over. "Neil, I'm so sorry for your loss," Suzanne said.

"Thank you. This is Trevor, my partner," Neil said.

"Nice to meet you," Suzanne said. "Beatrice, why don't you come to Cardston after the funeral? You need the rest."

"I don't know," Neil's mother said. "Maybe next week. I have a few things to do after this, and I'd like to be alone for a few days."

"Sure, I understand. If you want, I can come to pick you up next week," Suzanne said.

A few days later, Beatrice asked her son to meet her at Canmore Café. Neil walked into the café and saw his mother sitting sipping her coffee.

"Hi, Mom," Neil said, leaning in for a hug. Rather than a hug, a comfort Neil needed, she offered poison.

"You killed your father with your homosexuality. It's your fault he had a heart attack," she said.

"No, no, no. I can't believe you just said that."

"If you had listened to us and gone to therapy, your father would be alive today."

Stunned by what he just heard, Neil said, "Are you mad? Why are you saying this?"

"Your lifestyle is against all we ever taught you. You are an abomination in this family."

"I can't believe what I'm hearing. Mom, how can you look

me in the eyes, your *son*, and say this to me. Do you hear your-self?"

"I want you to return the key to the family home," she said harshly.

As Neil removed the key from his keyring, he slid it across the table in disbelief, and said, "One day, on your deathbed, your one regret will be you disowned your only son, who loves you. Stop waiting for the miracle that will never come. I'm gay, and I will not change."

Neil got up, feeling sick to his stomach, and ran out. He leaned on the hood of his car, looking at everything and noth-ing, and suddenly leaned over and was sick.

CHAPTER TWENTY-EIGHT: TYLER AND GREG

The school bell echoed through the school's empty hallways, then suddenly, the classroom doors swung open, and a stampede of students ran to their lockers. Reaching for his backpack, Greg heard the coach's voice, "Greg, before you go, you want to come by my office?"

"Sure, I'll be there in a minute," Greg said.

Tyler was walking by, and saw Greg reaching in his locker. "Hi."

"Hey," Greg said, looking around. "Aren't you afraid people will talk?"

"Why? We're not doing anything wrong. We're just talking," Tyler said.

"True enough. Some days I just want to tell everyone to fuck off and leave us alone, you know. This business of continually watching our backs is getting me paranoid. Why can't we be who we are?" Greg said.

"The people who cling to the Old Testament instead of the new, like your folks and mine. I know this is hard, and if it were up to me, I'd be with you every day. But we're at the mercy of the religion and our parents, neither of whom have progressed with the times," Tyler said.

"This is so true. Will I see you tonight?" Greg asked.

"Of course. A day without seeing you is a day without sunshine, as they say," Tyler said.

"I knew there was a reason why I loved you," Greg said,

smiling. "I've got to meet the coach. He asked me to stop by his office before leaving. I'd kiss you, but there are too many eyes around. See you tonight."

Greg shouldered his backpack, ran down the stairs to the lower level where the coach was, and as he approached the coach's office, he saw Elaine. She stepped back from the water fountain and purposely bumped into Greg. "Oh, I didn't see you," Elaine said.

"Really, I could have sworn your eyes were looking at me while the water was running over your lips and on the floor," Greg said with a grin.

"Maybe I was, then," Elaine said in a seductive voice. "Where are you going?"

"The coach wants to see me," Greg said.

"Oh, sounds serious," Elaine said. "Are you free later? We could hook up later tonight for an intimate moment," she suggested.

"An intimate moment, wow. Aren't you dating . . . er, what's your new boyfriend's name?" Greg asked.

"Patrick, yeah, but we have an open relationship," Elaine said.

"Does Patrick know this?" Greg said nonchalantly.

"Of course he does," Elaine said.

"Sorry, I'm busy tonight," Greg said.

"With Tyler, I suppose?" Elaine said.

"You know Elaine, it's none of your business who I hang out with," Greg said, walking away.

The coach's door was ajar. Greg poked his head inside and knocked, and the coach signalled him to come in.

"How are you, Greg?" the coach asked. "I got a call from Coach Hudson this afternoon."

"Oh yeah? Good or bad?" Greg asked.

"Let's just say he was asking about you, how you were in school and your grades. All the questions a recruiting coach would ask when they are thinking of awarding a scholarship."

"Are you serious?" Greg exclaimed. "Do you think I have a chance?"

"I'm sure you do. You'll probably be invited to their summer camp, which is usually a good sign. It means that they're interested in you."

"Thanks, Coach. It's so cool."

"If someone deserves this, it's you. Have a good night."

Greg left and was walking with a spring in his step. *I can't wait to tell Tyler tonight.* Thinking of the prospect of being with his favourite football team under the same roof for three to four weeks this summer got Greg smiling all the way home.

"Mom, I'm home," Greg said, closing the front door. "When is Dad coming home?"

"He should be here soon. Why?" his mother asked.

Greg went to his room and let himself flop on his bed. He reached on his night table for his earbuds, plugged them into his cell and lay there listening to his favourite tunes. An hour later, he was called down to dinner.

"Hey, sport," his father said. "How was school?"

"Cool," Greg said. "My coach told me that Coach Hudson from Calgary called him to ask about me."

"That is wonderful news," his father said.

"And the coach said that there is a good chance that I'll be asked to go to the Bears camp this summer. That would be so cool," Greg said.

"I hope it comes through," Greg's mother said.

"Tell me," Greg's father asked, "that boy from the camp, have you seen him since?"

"He goes to the same school as me. I see him every day. Do I talk to him? Is that what you want to know? I say hello to him now and again, that's about it. Why?" Greg asked.

"Just wondering if you and he were seeing each other after

class."

"Would it be that terrible if we did?" Greg said.

"Yes, because you would be going against what we agreed," his father said.

"We're not. I only see him at school," Greg said.

"Any girlfriend yet?" his mother asked.

"Mom, with football and school, I don't have time for a girlfriend. I'm going to my room to study," Greg said.

Around eight o'clock, Greg walked by the living room and told his parents he was going out for a run. He jogged to the school track as his warm-up and ran a few laps around the track before running to the trailer where Tyler was patiently waiting for him.

Still upset after being rejected by Greg, Elaine saw him running on the school track, so she decided to stick around and watch him for a while. Carl was out for a walk and saw Elaine sitting alone near the track and field. He ran over and tapped her on the shoulder. Elaine shrieked and punched Carl on the arm. "You scared the shit out of me."

Carl couldn't help but burst out laughing. "So," Carl said. "What are you doing here by yourself?"

"Nothing much. I came out for a walk. I like coming here, it's quiet, and I saw Greg running, so I sat down to watch. What about you?

"About the same. I was bored, so I decided to go out for a walk. How long has Greg been running?"

"I don't know, he was here when I got here. Is it true what they say?" Elaine asked.

"About?"

"Him and Tyler?"

"It is. James told me."

"Oh. I suspected it. I've never seen Greg with a girl, so I

wondered if he was."

"Well, it's not as if two guys can walk around holding hands in Cardston," Carl said.

"And there are no gay bars or meeting places here either," Elaine said. "It must be hard for them to be together. I don't think they're welcome at each other's homes, either."

"James told them to use his parents' trailer at Lee Creek. But don't tell anyone. I promised James I wouldn't," Carl said.

"Your secret is safe with me," Elaine said, smiling.

"Well, I'm going back home," Carl said, getting up. "I'll see you at school tomorrow."

"Ciao," Elaine said.

Elaine had to get to the bottom of this, so she followed Greg to Lee Creek Campground. When she saw the *Campground closed for the season* sign, she thought, ah, they won't be disturbed. Elaine looked to her right. *Where did he go?* As she was exploring the site, a glow caught her eyes, just before the tree line at the back of the lot. A dimmed light appeared to be lit in a trailer over that way. Curious, she followed the light.

As soon as the trailer door closed behind Greg, all he could do is smile when he saw Tyler sitting waiting for him. The first thing Greg did was to take Tyler in his arms and kiss him. "This is the kiss I wanted to give you this afternoon." Greg kissed him again. "And this one is for tonight."

"How did it go with the coach?" Tyler asked.

"It looks like Coach Hudson has been checking up on my grades and school. He called the school coach to ask about me," Greg said.

"That's so cool," Tyler said. "Did you tell your parents?"

"I did. They're both excited about it. Funny thing, though. At dinner, my father asked me if you and I were still seeing each other. I lied, of course. It made me wondered if he suspected something. Well. Let's not talk about it now. Come here," Greg said, opening his arms.

Undressing as they made their way to the bedroom, Greg and Tyler embraced as their hard-ons danced between them. Greg lightly kissed Tyler down his neck and chest, savouring his soft skin and sweet scent. He lingered over Tyler's nipple, sending Tyler to cloud nine. Greg continued down, lifting Tyler's hard dick, kissing his soft pubic hair, which made Greg's own cock twitch.

Greg kissed Tyler's perfect manhood, then Greg gently put his lips over its inviting mushroom head. Tyler's back arched, and he inhaled as Greg ran his tongue around it. Greg licked Tyler's flowing pre-cum and moved down his shaft. Greg worked his way up and down Tyler's cock, and he could tell Tyler was close to losing it. He took him as far as he could and felt Tyler's stomach tighten. Tyler moaned, spasmed, and released his cum into Greg's mouth.

Tyler pulled Greg up and kissed him hungrily, then he rolled Greg on his back and swallowed his dick. Greg warned him he was about to cum before spraying his juice into Tyler's mouth, until the last drops oozed from him. They snuggled and laughed, saying the cleanup was a lot easier than their first time in Calgary.

All the while Greg and Tyler were making love, Elaine was outside their trailer and heard everything. Shocked, she left quietly until she reached the park nearby.

So the rumours are true. Now I get why Greg rejected my offer.

Chapter Twenty-nine: Heartless

Elaine was up all night, thinking about Greg and Tyler. Apart from those who were on the school trip, no one else knew their little secret, and now she did. When she arrived at school, Greg was outside talking with James. Elaine coolly walked up to them and purposely dropped a book in front of James.

"Oops."

James looked at the book and then at Elaine and said, "I think you dropped something." Then James said to Greg, "Do you want to go in?"

Elaine swiftly picked up her book, mumbling, "Fucking jerks," then went to her class.

"Miss Thompson," said the teacher. "Where is your assignment? It's due this morning."

Cindy, where the fuck is my assignment. She forgot to give it to me. Now what am I supposed to do . . . Elaine suddenly said, "I'm sorry, I left it on my desk at home. Is it alright if I bring it tomorrow?"

"It's not the first time your assignments are late, Miss Thompson. I'll allow it this time, but I will deduct marks for it."

Elaine silently sat the rest of the class, contemplating what she would do to someone come break time.

In the middle of his French class, Greg sneakily pulled out his cell and texted Tyler to meet him behind the school after lunch.

"Greg," the teacher said. "Qu'est-ce que tu fais?"

"What?" Greg said. "I didn't understand?"

"I asked you what you were doing. You're supposed to be listening and not texting."

"Sorry, sir," Greg said, stuffing his cell in his backpack.

"En français, s'il vous plait," the teacher said.

"Je m'excuse," Greg said.

Greg wolfed down his lunch, anxious to see Tyler. He told his friends that were having lunch with him, he was going for a walk before his next class. He grabbed his empty lunch bag and threw it in the bin on his way out of the cafeteria. Once outside, he glanced around him, didn't see anyone, then he ran to the back of the school.

"Hey, good looking, how's your day?" Tyler said.

"Come here and kiss me," Greg said. Tyler walked over, placed his hands on the wall on each side of Greg's shoulders, leaned into Greg, and planted a gentle kiss on his lips.

"Aren't you afraid of getting caught?" Tyler said.

"No one ever comes back here. When I need to be alone, this is where I come," Greg said.

"You know, I wish we could be together like we were last night without having to watch our backs all the time. I'm happiest when I'm with you, and it's becoming harder not being able to see each other more often," Tyler said, turning to the right of Greg and leaning his back against the wall.

"This is why I asked you to meet me back here. I want to spend every moment I can with you. If I'm invited to the Bears summer camp, I'll be gone for three to four weeks, and you'll miss me," Greg said, smiling. "Seriously, I'm not sure if I can be away from you that long."

"You'll be training all day, and you'll be so tired, you'll

sleep like a baby. Time will go by in a flash, and you'll be back in my arms," Tyler said.

Greg turned to Tyler and kissed him.

Elaine, still upset from having been put on the spot in class, couldn't wait to have a chat with Cindy. "Cindy, what the fuck. Where is my assignment?"

"What assignment?" Cindy asked.

"The one that was due today. I asked you to do it two weeks ago. The teacher embarrassed me in class this morning, and it's all your fault. Is it done?" Elaine said, raising her voice.

"I gave it to you last week, I don't have it," Cindy said, leaving for lunch.

What am I supposed to do now? I need to find that assignment.

Leaning against the school wall, thinking about what would happen if she didn't find this paper, Elaine heard laughter from behind the school. Quietly, she walked and peeked around the corner and saw Tyler and Greg chatting. Silently, Elaine pulled out her cell from her designer jeans back pocket and looked around the corner again as Tyler was moving closer to Greg and took a shot of the two of them kissing passionately. *Holy shit. No guy has ever kissed me like that.* Quietly she returned to the front of the school. Tyler and Greg did the same, but they took a different route.

That night, Elaine tried to figure out what to do with the picture.

The following day Greg noticed an unusual atmosphere walking down the hallway at school. He went to talk to a classmate, but when he saw Greg, he walked away. Greg saw James standing at his locker; he approached him and asked,

"What's with everyone today?"

"Have you been on your social media this morning?" James asked.

"No. Why?" Greg reached for his phone and opened the app, and said, "What the fuck? Who posted this?"

"We don't know. It's fucked up, man. Whoever did better stay anonymous, or I'll personally break his or her face."

"Oh my God, I'm so fucked. Did Tyler see this?"

"I haven't seen him yet," James said. "Listen, don't panic. I'll help you find out who sent this."

Greg texted Tyler, *Hey, I don't know if you've gone on your social media. Someone posted a picture of us kissing. Call me, text me when you get this. I'm so sorry, Ty.*

James and Greg went to their class, and no one dared to look in Greg's direction. Greg decided to skip his next class and went behind the school to be alone and process what just happened. *I hope this doesn't get to my dad. What am I going to do or say if it does? He will snap for sure.* Greg dropped to the ground in tears.

After reading Greg's text, Tyler went to look for him. He asked James if he saw Greg, and James shook his head. Then he knew where he could find him. Drawing near the back of the school, Tyler heard Greg crying. His heart broke at the sound of his love weeping. Rushing over to his side, Tyler fell on his knees and took Greg into his arms and said, "It's alright. We'll get through this, babe."

"I'm afraid that if my father sees this, I'll be sent away. I might lose my chance to play with the university football team because of some heartless asshole who thinks it's funny to post shit like this," Greg said.

"Listen, I'm not sure about your parents, but mine are not on social media. The only way they can find out is if someone tells them. Babe, if you look around, no one really cares in school if someone is gay or not. Yes, there are a few who will mock us, but we can handle them," Tyler said, kissing Greg.

"You're right. My parents aren't on social media, either," Greg said, drying his eyes. "I think we should go back in."

CHAPTER THIRTY: CYBERBULLIED

Greg knew Patrick quite well; they grew up in the same neighbourhood, and his family was very religious, so for him to agree to an open relationship didn't make sense. Greg texted Patrick asking him that very question.

Elaine began dating Patrick a month after breaking up with Peter. Elaine went from boyfriend to boyfriend without flinching and most were sensitive types. She would tap their sensitive side and get what she wanted out of them, even deciding when they would go out or not. Patrick, had gone through several heartbreaking relationships. His last relationship he was ghosted. He tried to reinitiate contact. He was successful, but came at a high emotional cost for him, but soon after, she ghosted me again, perhaps because of him appearing clingy. So when Elaine expressed interest in him, he was elated and has been at her mercy for the last six months.

Elaine would say anything to get any guy into the sack; Greg had seen her in action too many times to believe her. Patrick replied to Greg's text, asking him where he heard such nonsense. *Should I tell him? I'd hate to see someone else being cheated on by Elaine.*

If I were you, Greg texted, *I'd be careful. Ask around, ask her exes why they dropped her.*

I will. Who told you we had an open relationship?

Elaine did. She hit on me, I turned her down, and then I asked her if you guys were still a pair. Sorry, man.

Thanks. No worries.

Shortly after their texting, Patrick called Elaine.

Elaine was filing her nails and just about to put nail polish on. "Oh," she said, "hi, honey, to what do I owe the pleasure? Did we have a date tonight?"

"No, we didn't. Actually, I'm going out with Barbara tonight. Just calling to let you know and say goodnight," Patrick said.

"What the fuck? You called me to tell me you were going to cheat on me? Why, you bastard?"

"What's the matter? Don't we have an open relationship?" Patrick asked.

"What?" Elaine said, pretending not to know what Patrick was talking about. "What's this about an open relationship?"

"Isn't it what you tell guys you want to sleep with? You know, Elaine," Patrick said, "I've texted some of your exes to find out why they broke up with you. Funny, they all said the same thing. A slut will always be a slut." Patrick hung up before Elaine could say anything.

A wave of anger overtook Elaine. She threw her phone across the room, which went flying and smashed her dresser's mirror. *I'll bet you Greg opened his fucking mouth. I will destroy his ass.* "Nobody fucks with Elaine Thompson," she yelled. With that, she flipped her laptop open and logged in to social media. She was on a mission.

The following day, Elaine stopped in Cardston Electronics to have her cellphone replaced before going to Greg and Tyler's trailer. Elaine opened the door carefully, peeked inside to make sure nobody was there and walked in, closing the door behind her. She sneaked around, opening cabinet doors and overhead bins. She sat on the sofa and scanned the place. As Elaine got up from the sofa bed, a light went on in her mind. She lifted the sofa bed seat, reached into her jacket pocket, and placed her cellphone inside. Mission accomplished, she left and went back home.

Elaine followed Greg that afternoon, stopping short of entering the campground. Across from the campground was a park, so Elaine sat on a bench closer to the wooden area to hide quickly if Greg or Tyler came her way.

Her wireless earbuds in her ears, she heard the door open and Tyler greeting Greg with what sounded like a kiss. Then Tyler asked Greg how he was doing.

"I'm okay, thanks to you. You know how to calm me down. I was so taken by my fear of my parents finding out we were still seeing each other that I forgot common sense."

"When I got your message about the pic on social media, I panicked too. Do you know who posted it?" Tyler asked.

"No," Greg said.

Elaine laughed. *Good luck finding out.*

"Who from school would be so malicious as to post something like this?" Tyler asked.

"I can see a heartless bitch like Elaine doing it," Greg said.

Elaine stood up when she heard this, and raised her middle finger and aimed it at the trailer. "Fuck you, you fucking faggot." Then she sat down again, mumbling to herself.

"I forgot to tell you what Elaine did the other day," Greg said. "I was heading to meet the coach when she purposely bumped into me and tried to get me to go to bed with her."

"No way," Tyler said. "That slut."

How dare you call me that?

"It gets better. She told me that her and Patrick had an open relationship. Can you believe her? I had to ask Patrick, knowing she must use this line on every guy, and he told me it was nonsense," Greg said.

I knew it was you who alerted Patrick.

"Knowing Patrick, he must have been delighted to hear that," Tyler said.

"I hope he broke it off with her. I can't imagine going out with someone like that. I would never cheat on my love," Greg said, looking at Tyler.

"I wouldn't either," Tyler said. "Besides, I don't want anybody else in my life but you."

"I think we should go," Greg said, looking at the time. "I'll text you when we can meet again."

Greg grabbed Tyler by the waist and pulled him closer, and kissed him passionately. They both left the camper. Elaine waited around so she could retrieve her cellphone without being seen.

Back in her room, Elaine posted on social media anonymous rumours about Greg having a lover in Calgary and cheating on Tyler. Then she wrote another post saying that Tyler was thrown out of a recent Youth Ministry for promoting same-sex attraction. Elaine hoped to harm their reputation with her posts, break them up or else make them fight. But her hateful posts only elicited sympathy for the guys.

The next day, Elaine's friends couldn't believe the nasty things that had been posted and felt terrible for Greg and Tyler.

"I'm sure," Joan said, "what is being posted is all made up. Probably by some heartless bitch."

"You don't know this," Elaine said.

"Of course I do. These are some of the nicest guys at this school," Joan said. "Only a mean bitch would write something like this."

Elaine shook her head and walked away, anger flooding her veins. *Time to step up my game.*

Leaving school, Elaine decided to stop by the coffee shop on her way home. Sipping her coffee, she browsed the few stores on main street. A few blocks up from the coffee shop was Greg's father's shoe store. Walking by the store, Elaine had an idea. She stopped and walked back and stood in front of the store for an instant before entering.

"Good day, young lady," Greg's father said. "How can I help you today?"

"I'm looking for a pair of heels to go with my prom dress. I'm looking for a white shoe?" Elaine asked.

"White? What colour is your dress?"

"White. I only wear white for my evening and holiday wear," Elaine said snobbishly.

"I see. Well, I have these," he said, showing her a pair of white leather heels.

"Do you have anything with either a bow, sparkles or any special design? These are too common," Elaine asked.

"I'm afraid I don't. The only shoes I have in white are the ones I showed you," he said.

"Alright. Can I try them on?" Elaine asked.

"Of course, what size do you wear?"

"Size six, please," she said.

"I'll be right back."

Elaine snooped around the store, her nose wrinkling. *Who buys this crap?* Then Greg's father returned with her shoes.

"Please have a seat. Can I have your right foot, please? Thank you."

"How is Greg?" Elaine asked.

"You know Greg," he said.

"I go to school with him," she said. "You must be so proud of Greg, being out."

"What do you mean, being out?" he asked.

"You know, not hiding his homosexuality. He and Tyler make such a great couple. They have this little trailer at Lee Creek campground where they meet. Is it yours?" Elaine asked. "Ouch, you're hurting me. The shoe is too small, and I don't like them after all."

Sudden rage seemed to grip Greg's father. He picked up

the shoe and threw it against a wall, then he grabbed the phone and called his wife. "You are not to let Greg leave the house, football practice or not."

Elaine just smiled and left the store.

CHAPTER THIRTY-ONE: STUBBORN

Neil entered the apartment with red eyes, sniffling, and Trevor was about to ask how his mother was holding up, but instead he opened his arms. That was enough to make Neil collapse in tears.

"What's the matter," Trevor asked. "What happened?"

"My mother told me, without flinching, that my father died because I am gay," Neil said, his head buried on Trevor's shoulder.

"What? That's ridiculous. She probably didn't mean what she said. She's still grieving," Trevor said.

"She meant it. I know my mother. I know she's grieving, but she was serious. She might as well have knifed me in the heart, that's how it felt," Neil said, walking to the couch.

"Why would she believe your father had a heart attack because you are gay?"

"She told me my refusal to go to therapy caused it. Her parish priest told them I needed to cleanse myself of this sin. She said when I moved in with you is when my father started not feeling well," Neil said, sniffling.

"I'm sorry, but your father's condition and death have nothing to do with you or your sexual orientation," Trevor said. "Maybe with time, she'll come around."

"Don't count on it. She asked me to give her back my house keys."

"Did you give them back?"

"I did and walked out," Neil said.

"Let me get you a glass of wine."

"Thanks, honey."

It was ten o'clock, and the bedroom had gotten considerably darker since Neil had fallen asleep shortly after nine-thirty. The room had never been this dark before. The curtains were sheer and the moon was bright tonight. Then he felt a hand on his shoulder shaking him; he opened his eyes but couldn't see who it was because of the darkness, so he got up and went to the living room without hesitation.

Neil felt a chill and saw a shadow near the living room patio door. Uncertain if his eyes were deceiving him or his imagination was playing tricks, Neil walked towards the patio.

"Hello, son," a voice echoed throughout the living room.

"Dad? It's not possible. You're dead."

"You killed me, son. You knew my heart wasn't strong, and you went against my wishes. Your mother was right when she told me you were a selfish boy. I hope you're happy now," the voice said.

Neil began shaking as he got closer to the door. Then the shadow stepped out, illuminated by the moon, and Neil saw his father's face. *This isn't real.* Neil turned around and quickly walked to the bedroom to wake Trevor. The bedroom door handle was icy; Neil pulled his hand off the handle in a flash and stepped back. He then started yelling out Trevor's name.

"Help me," Neil said.

His father stood beside him and said, "You will kill your mother the same way if you don't get back on God's path. I will not let you do this, son." Then the shadow wrapped his hands around Neil's neck and began squeezing tighter and tighter. Neil's arms were reaching for the shadow's hands, and he started kicking the shadow, and suddenly he felt his whole body shaking.

Then Neil opened his eyes and saw Trevor's face hovering over him. He sat up in bed, drenched in sweat.

"Are you alright?" Trevor asked.

Breathless, Neil said, "I was dreaming that my father was blaming me for his death, and he was trying to choke me."

"You were mumbling something I couldn't make out, and then you started kicking. That's when I woke you up. I can stay up and wait until you fall asleep."

"No, I'll be okay. Thanks, honey. I hope I didn't scare you."

"You did." Trevor leaned over and kissed him.

Suzanne, Amanda's mother, called Neil a few days later to find out how he was. During the conversation, Suzanne let slip that his mother had been diagnosed with cancer a year ago, and they kept it a secret from him.

"Neil, your mother is not feeling well. I went to get her to bring her up to my place, and when I got there, she had changed her mind. I asked her if she saw her doctor. She has an appointment tomorrow, I offered to go with her. Neil, she told me what she told you. Your father's heart attack is not your fault. She's still grieving, and she probably didn't mean what she said. I'll call you tomorrow to let you know what the doctor says."

"Thank you, Suzanne." Neil hung up and turned to Trevor, his eyes watered up, and he told Trevor what Suzanne said about his mother's health. "I don't understand why they didn't tell me."

Suzanne and Beatrice sat in the doctor's office waiting room.

"Mrs. Fallon," the nurse called.

"I'm Mrs. Fallon," Beatrice said.

"Please follow me. I need to take some blood." After the extraction, the nurse said, "I'll take you to the doctor's office."

A few minutes later, the doctor came in. "Good morning, Beatrice. Sorry to hear about your husband. How are you coping?" the doctor asked, looking at Beatrice's file.

"I'm doing as best as I can. My friend Suzanne here takes care of me," Beatrice said.

"What about your son, Neil? Isn't he around?"

"I don't have a son anymore," Beatrice said. "My husband died because of him."

"What do you mean? Your husband had a heart attack," the doctor said.

"Yeah, I know. His homosexuality caused my husband's attack," she said.

"Beatrice, that's nonsense. Your husband had heart issues, you were with him when we told him. Being gay is not a choice. Neil was born this way, whether you like it or not," he said.

"I didn't come here to get lectured," she said.

"I know, I'm sorry. I have the results of your last tests. How have you been feeling?"

"I'm tired all the time. I have no appetite, and for the last two days, I've felt sick."

"Humm. The results of your blood test of two weeks ago are not good news, I'm afraid to say. Given what you've just said, I'm afraid this confirms your cancer is spreading. I'll send you for a scan to determine the extent of the spread."

"How long do I have?" Beatrice asked.

"It's hard to say," the doctor said, "it depends how far cancer has spread—maybe four to six months. With chemotherapy perhaps a year, a year and a half. If I were you, I'd talk with Neil and tell him about your health, and try to reconcile with him. He's a good guy, and he's your only child."

Despite her prognosis, Beatrice told Suzanne she would not have chemotherapy and would not to tell Neil about it.

"Didn't you hear what the doctor said about talking to Neil?" Suzanne said.

"Well, that's none of the doctor's business. He's a scientist, and scientists don't believe in the scriptures. I don't need a sinner in the family," Beatrice said.

"From where I stand, you don't have a family, Beatrice. You disowned the only family you had, your son," Suzanne said. "You have to come back to your senses, Beatrice. You're just as stubborn as you were ten years ago. Yes, I agree, you didn't plan to have a gay son. Neil didn't plan to be gay either, he was born this way. As your friend, I'm asking you to reach out to Neil and make amends before it's too late."

"The only way he can enter my life again is if he gets therapy for this sickness," Beatrice said.

"God, you make me mad, Bea. Continue to be this obstinate, and you'll die alone. I'm through arguing with you. I don't understand why you keep saying that homosexuality is a sickness," Suzanne said.

"Because it is. The bible says so."

"The bible *doesn't* say that. Those religious freaks-turned-therapists do, and it's been proven that the people who come out of those places are more fucked up than before they went in," Suzanne said.

"Homosexuality is not normal," Beatrice said. "The bible says men should not lay with men as they do with women," Beatrice said.

"The bible also says that rejecting his or her own child is unchristian," Suzanne said.

When she got home, Beatrice got out of the car and never said thank you or goodbye to Suzanne. She slammed the car door and disappeared inside the house.

Chapter Thirty-two: Evil Tongue

John walked into the house. "Where is he?"

"Where is who?" Teresa asked.

"Greg."

"He's in his room studying."

"I bet he is. Greg," John yelled.

"What?" Greg shouted from his room.

"Come out here."

"What now? I have to study," Greg said impatiently to his father.

"John, keep it down," Teresa said, teary-eyed. She had a feeling what her husband wanted to talk to Greg about.

"Someone told me you are still seeing this Tyler boy. Are you?"

"No. Who told you this?" Greg said.

"Not important. Don't lie to me."

"I'm not."

"What did you do after school?" John asked. Teresa shot another look at him.

"Nothing, I came directly home. Why?" Greg asked.

"You didn't meet up with him?" his father said.

"No. You're the one who told me to come home after school, remember? This is what I did," Greg said.

"Enough," his mother said. "When is your next practice, Greg?"

"Tomorrow night," Greg said.

"So what's on for tonight?" his father asked.

"What I was doing before you called me. Studying. Why?"

Greg said.

"You're not going out?" his father asked.

"No. What's up with all these questions? I told you, Tyler and I don't see each other outside of school."

"So you lied. You do see each other."

"No, we don't. We go to the same school. Of course, I see him during the day. I'm not going to hide whenever he walks by. You're acting weird," Greg said. "I'm going to my room." He left.

"You couldn't help yourself, could you, John? What if they see each other at school? What do you think will happen?" Teresa said.

John went to look for Layton Bradshaw's phone number. While Teresa was cleaning up, John walked by and said, "Honey, I'm going to the car, I forgot something."

Outside, he dialled Layton Bradshaw's number.

"Hi, Layton, this is John Miller. We've met when we picked up our boys at camp."

"Oh, yeah, I remember you. What can I do for you?" Layton said.

"A young girl came to my store today and insinuated that our boys still see each other. She told me they meet in a trailer in Lee Creek campground. I don't have a trailer there, do you?" John asked.

"What do you mean, still see each other? What's this about a trailer?" Layton said.

"This is what this girl told me."

"Who is this girl? Do you know her?"

"She goes to the same school as our boys. Anyway. I thought I'd call you to let you know what I've been told. I told Greg when we got back from camp that he was not allowed to see your son."

"We said the same to Tyler."

"Just so you are aware, I intend to follow Greg one night to see where he goes. I'm not certain if what she told me was true, but I don't trust my son, and I intend to find out the truth. If you want, I can send you a text to let you know when I'll be trailing Greg. If Tyler goes out around the same time, you can bet they are meeting."

"Thanks, John, but I'm confident my son has not been seeing your son. It could be that this girl may be jealous that one of our sons didn't want to go out with her," Layton said.

John slipped his phone in his front pocket and leaned against his car. *Layton might have a point. She's probably trying to spread rumours out of revenge. But for my own peace of mind, I will follow him.*

"What took you so long?" Teresa asked as John closed the door behind him.

"I was looking for my store sales receipts. I thought I had brought them with me. I looked all over the car, but I guess I left them at work," John said.

Adabelle asked Layton who was on the phone.

"It was John Miller, Greg's father."

"Everything okay?"

"Yeah. He called to ask if Tyler and his son were still seeing each other."

"Why didn't he ask his son?"

"Good question. I told him Tyler wasn't seeing his son."

Tyler sitting at his desk, grabbed his cell and texted Greg, *What are you up to? Do you feel like meeting tonight?*

I can't meet you tonight, sorry. I'm studying. I have finals coming up. What are you up to? Greg texted.

Not much. I have to study as well, but I don't feel like it. Have you heard from the University of Alberta yet? Tyler asked.

No, nothing yet. How are your parents these days? Mine are weird, man, Greg wrote back.

What do you mean, weird? My parents are okay, Tyler texted.

I don't know, tonight my father kept asking me if we see each other outside of school and what I do after school and when my next practice was. Usually, all he asks is how school was and about the store.

Just a sec, my dad just walked in, Tyler wrote.

"Who are you talking to?" Layton asked.

"A friend from school. Why?" Tyler said.

"Can I see your cell?" his father asked.

"It's private. Since when do you need to see my cell?" Tyler said.

"Who were you talking to then?" he asked again.

"I told you, a friend from school. What's going on?" Tyler asked.

"Are you and Greg seeing each other and texting each other?" his father asked.

"I see him at school. I can't help that we go to the same school. Why?" Tyler asked.

"No texting either?"

"What's wrong with texting? You asked me not to see him. You said nothing about texting," Tyler said.

"Tyler, I asked you not to contact him, and texting is contacting. He is a bad influence on you. Look what happened at camp," his father said.

"What makes you think he influenced me? Greg didn't force into anything. Dad, I'm sorry, but I am gay. I know it's not something you want to hear, but I can't keep lying and hiding and pretending to be who you want me to be," Tyler said.

"Listen, son, we will always love you, but we disapprove of this behaviour. There are many opinions out there, and many people believe that gay people can change."

"I will *not* see a therapist," Tyler said.

"Can I ask you to think about it, at least?" his father said as he left Tyler's room.

Tyler laid down in his bed. *There is no way I'm letting some-one fuck with my head. I'm not sick. Oh, shit, I left Greg hanging.*

Greg, sorry, Tyler wrote, *see you at school tomorrow.*

CHAPTER THIRTY-THREE: FOOTBALL PRACTICE

Greg, leaning back on the headboard, saw the moon set and the sun rise. His eyes were puffy and red from being up studying half of the night and spending the other half worrying if his father suspected something about him and Tyler. *How could he? It's not possible. He's pretending to know to trap me, that's what it is.*

"Good morning, Mom," Greg said, walking out of his bedroom in his pyjamas. "Is Dad gone already?"

"You just missed him. Did you want to talk to him?"

"No. What was the matter with him last night? It was as if he suspected that Tyler and I were still seeing each other."

"Are you? You can tell me."

"No. We're not."

Teresa picked up her coffee and suppressed a smile. She knew Greg was seeing Tyler; a mother knows when her child is fibbing. "Do you want any breakfast?"

"No. I'll just grab a coffee, I have to get to school." He reached for a cup in the cupboard, poured himself a coffee, and went back to his room to get ready. Rummaging through his pile of clothes on the floor, he pulled out a pair of jeans and a sweater.

Walking to school, he took out his cell and saw that Tyler had replied to his message. *Oh, yeah. His father walked in while we were chatting. Hopefully he didn't get caught.* Greg stopped and stared at his cell as if waiting for an answer. Then he shook his head, and shoved his cell in his back pocket and continued to school.

Before entering the school, Greg took out his cell and wrote, *Meet me behind the school at recess.*

Tyler felt the vibration of his phone in his jean pocket, saw the text from Greg and replied back, *Okay.*

The recess bell rang. Tyler hurried out of class and started running towards the exit when a teacher shouted, "No running in the hallway." Tyler slowed down until the teacher was out of sight, then sprinted towards the exit and grabbed the handlebar on the exit door, pushed it down and swung it open and sped to the back of the school.

When he got there, Tyler's inside started to flutter as he saw his guy standing there waiting for him. He looked around; there were only the two of them. Then he moved in closer, Greg grabbed his hand and drew him inches from his body, then swiftly backed him up against the brick wall and kissed him.

"You know, I keep falling in love with you whenever I see you and each time apart from you is harder than the last," Tyler said.

"I couldn't face the day without seeing you, this is why I asked you to meet here. The more I fall in love with you, the more butterflies I have inside of me . . . crazy, huh," Greg said.

"No," Tyler replied with a smile.

"Hey sorry about not texting you back last night. When my dad left my room, I lay there thinking about what just happened and then I realized I left you in limbo."

"Don't worry about it, I went back to studying. I bet he asked who you were chatting with."

"Yeah. I told him a friend from school, but he didn't believe me." *No. Please don't say you told him.* "Then he asked to see my cell, which I refused, of course. He kept insisting, and I told him that I was chatting with you." *Oh, shit.*

"How was his reaction when you told him about me?"

"He didn't get angry, but he brought up therapy again. I told him I wasn't going to therapy, and then I came out."

"Did he flip?" Greg asked, afraid that Tyler's father would turn around and call his father.

"No. I thought he was going to, but he remained calm and said I should think about therapy."

"Will he send you, you think?" Greg had done some research on the so-called therapy, and he would do anything to spare his boyfriend from this torture.

"I don't know. I'm definitely not going. I wonder what will happen if I refuse to go to therapy? I don't think they would throw me out . . ." Tyler said.

"I wish I could come out to my parents, but I know they'll flip. More so my father. I'd probably get a beating out of it . . . I can't wait to leave this place." Greg said loudly, raising his arms.

"I hear you. It sucks . . . Well, we might as well get back to class. Do you want to meet tonight?" Tyler asked.

Greg nodded yes and kissed Tyler before heading to meet James and Carl.

Around seven forty-five that evening, Greg, with his backpack, stopped by the living room on his way out to let his parents know he was going to football practice. Standing on the front step, Greg debated whether to take the pathway through the park or go through the village.

"Honey," John said. "I'm going to the store, I forgot something."

"Alright. Oh, can you stop and get some bread for tomorrow while you're out?" Teresa said.

"Yeah. See you in a minute," John said.

John checked his cell to see if he'd got any messages or texts. He backed out of the driveway and headed downtown. Parked in front of his shoe store, John checked his watch and went in the store to get an envelope he forgot on his desk. He got the bread for his wife and debated whether to go and watch his son's practice or return home. He'd missed seeing Greg play in Calgary, so decided to go on down.

I remember when my dad came to see me at football practice. I felt so proud. I feel bad for not having taken the time to go to his big game last month. Hopefully, this will make up for it.

Turning into Lion's Park, the tall post lights surrounded the field and illuminated the whole area. From the parking lot, John couldn't see any of the players on the football field. *Maybe the game is over, or they're sitting with the coach.* He looked at his watch, it was barely twenty after eight. *The game can't be over, can it?*

After waiting a few minutes, John decided to go back home. Driving by the campground, John elected to check it out, hoping the girl from the store was wrong. Pulling up to the campground, John saw a log building with a sign that read *Closed for the season. How can Greg be here? I don't see any trailers around. I knew she was lying.*

Backing out, John saw some light far back near the tree lines. *Is that a trailer?* Curious, John decided to check it out. He locked the car, walked down the dirt road leading to the back of the lot, and there was the light shining inside a compact, teardrop-shaped white-and-grey trailer. John propped his ear on the door to see if there was anyone inside. He didn't hear anything, so he wondered if the door was locked. *How could someone forget to turn off the light before leaving?*

Confirming no one was near the surroundings, John slowly turned the door handle and pulled back on the screen door; the hinges creaked. John froze, caught his breath then proceeded to open the main door. Stepping inside quietly, he looked around, but just as he began to close the door carefully, it slipped out of his hand and slammed shut. "Shit," John whispered.

"What was that?" a voice said from the bedroom at the far end of the trailer.

Greg, shirtless and jeans unbuttoned, came face to face with his father.

"What's going on here?" his father asked, white-knuckled and red-faced.

"What are you doing here?" Greg asked, putting on his sweater and buttoning his jeans.

"Who's in the bedroom with you?" His father was trying to look over Greg's shoulder.

"No one," Greg said, fidgeting and swaying from foot to foot.

"Don't lie to me," his father said. "I know you're with Tyler. Tyler," John yelled, "you can come out now."

"Dad, Tyler isn't here. Why don't you go, and I'll see you at home?" Greg pleaded.

"I know Tyler is with you. I know about this place."

"How do you know about this place?"

"Someone told me this is where you and Tyler meet, and God knows what else. Whose place is this?"

"Who told you about this place?"

"It's not important."

"Yes, it is. I want to know."

"You and I will have a serious talk. Now get your ass back home." As John opened the door to leave, he stopped and shouted, "Tyler, your father knows about what you've been up to." He slammed the door on his way out.

Tyler walked out of the bedroom, shaking like a leaf.

"Are you alright?" Greg asked. "Sorry about this. I don't know how he found out."

"I'm more worried about you. Your father sounded furious. I'm afraid of what he might do," Tyler said.

"I'm about to find out. Whatever it is, I'll handle it. First, I need to find out who told him about this place. Listen, whatever happens, I'll be fine. I'm going to head home now." Greg grabbed Tyler's hands and looked into his eyes, whispering into his ear, "I love you, Tyler Bradshaw." He kissed him passionately.

Walking back through the park, Greg stopped along the way, crashed to the ground and cried. "Give me a break," he muttered as he looked up to the sky. Then he took a deep breath wiped his eyes, got up, and continued his way home.

Standing in front of the house, hesitant to go in, Greg sensed his father's anger radiating from inside.

CHAPTER THIRTY-FOUR: MEDDLING FA-THER

Tyler remained in the camper a little longer after Greg left. He made the bed and threw a pillow against the wall, then sat on the bed and wept. *What will happen to us now? I don't want to lose him.* He cradled his head in his hands.

Tyler's thoughts of Greg were interrupted by a knock on the door. *Not Greg's father again. Why doesn't he leave us alone?*

He swung the door open. "Dad? Not you too? Who told you about this place?" Tyler went and sat down.

"Can I come in?" his father asked calmly. Tyler indicated that he could. "Greg's father told me all about it. He didn't seem too happy when he called to let me know that you guys were still seeing each other. Was Greg with you?"

"Yes, he was," Tyler answered, lowering his eyes.

"How long have you and Greg been coming here?" Layton asked, looking at his son.

"We've been meeting here for some time now," Tyler replied, looking everywhere but at his father.

"Whose trailer is this?"

"The trailer belongs to a friend of Greg's, and he lent it to us. Dad, I'm sorry. I know I lied, but I care for Greg a lot. I know it must be hard for you to accept that I'm not what you wanted me to be. I'm sorry if I'm a disappointment to you both," Tyler said, fighting back the tears. "I can't help it, Dad. I tried, but it's who I am. If you want me to leave I will."

"Why would you think your mom and me would want you

to leave? We love you, son. Come here," his father said, taking Tyler into his arms and holding him close to his heart. "Come, let's go home, your mother is waiting."

Greg walked up towards the entrance and noticed his parents sitting in the living room through the bay window. His heart racing and his hands clammy, he took a deep breath and entered to face the firing squad.

"Greg," his mother said, "come sit with us, please." Greg set his backpack on the floor, and put a brave face on.

"I thought I had been clear with you when I said I didn't want you to see this boy again," his father said. "How long have you two been seeing each other?"

"Since we came back from camp," Greg awkwardly said.

"What didn't you understand about what I said?"

Greg stood there, hands in his pockets, eyes lowered.

"Why do you continue to behave like this?" his father said sharply. "How many times do you have to be told homosexuality is a sin, and it will not be tolerated in this house?"

"Do you know how many times I've tried not to act on those feelings? Since I've been sixteen. Do you know how hard it is? No, I guess you don't. I can't control it. Every time I tried, I failed," Greg said, pleading for their understanding.

"I don't believe you," his father said in exasperation. "You can control feelings, you just don't want to. Homosexuality is an evil disease, and the devil is making you that way."

"Being gay is not a disease. Where did you hear that?" Greg said.

"I will never accept a faggot for a son!" his father vehemently said.

"John, you don't mean that," Teresa said, "watch what you're saying. He's your son."

"What do you want me to do?" Greg said sharply.

"Cloister myself, go out with a girl just because the church and your bible said so? How about if I kill myself, so I don't humiliate you anymore? Would that suit you?" he said, practically shouting.

"Don't say things like that, Greg," his mother fearfully said. "It's not what we want, honey."

"How dare you speak to us like that?"

Teresa shot a look at her husband. She tried to sit him down as he got up, but he yanked himself away from her and approached Greg and slapped him across the face. There was a look of horror in Teresa's face. She'd never seen that side of her husband.

Greg stared at his father, his eyes filling up with tears, then turned around and ran to his room. His father went after him but got the door slammed in his face.

Teresa went after her husband.

"Greg, open the door . . . I said, open this damn door," he screamed. Then he started banging on the door with his fist, screaming and yelling at Greg.

Greg, having had enough, yelled, "Leave me the fuck alone."

"John!" his wife said, trying to stop him from breaking down the door. "Leave him alone." John gave a last swing at the door and walked away.

"It's your fault he's that way," John said. "You've mothered him too much."

"How dare you say this to me? Our son will never be able to please you, no matter how hard he tries. Stop comparing our life and his with every bible passage," Teresa said, storming back the living room, wiping her tears with her fist.

Greg curled up in bed, brimming with resentment, grabbed his pillow and swung it against the wall. *I'm so sick and tired of this bullshit. If I find out who the bastard is that told on us . . .*

Greg woke up groggy and chilled. He had fallen asleep fully dressed, exhausted from all the emotions He stayed in his room until his father had left for the store because he didn't want to see or talk to him. Greg left his room carrying his backpack, and walked by the kitchen where his mother was sitting reading the newspaper. Greg kept on walking and didn't say a word to her, shutting the door behind him.

Teresa stared at the newspaper, her insides twisted in a knot and her heart torn apart.

Greg was walking up the school sidewalk when Tyler motioned to Greg to meet him behind the school. Greg stopped and waited for Tyler; he no longer cared who saw them together.

"Are you sure you're okay with us meeting out in the open?" Tyler asked, surprised by Greg's change of heart.

"Yes, I am. I'm done hiding. Are you okay with this?" Greg looked into Tyler's eyes.

"I am. How did it go when you got home?" Tyler said.

"Well, my father and I had it out last night. He slapped me across the face, and basically told me he would never accept me as a son if I was gay. I locked myself in my room and he tried to break in. My mother stopped him," Greg said. "How about you?"

"I had a surprise visit after you left the camper. My dad came to the trailer," Tyler said with a smirk.

"What?" Greg said, coming to a full stop and turning towards Tyler.

"Your father called him to let him know where I was, and

with whom."

"That fucking asshole," Greg blurted out, burning with rage. "I'm sorry, Tyler. Why can't he mind his own business?"

"It's okay. My dad and I had a discussion at the trailer, and then we went home, and we talked some more as a family. Therapy was brought up again, and I told them I don't need therapy; I am who I am." Tyler and Greg sat on the bench behind the school, face to face.

"I don't know what's going to happen to me. My father is pretty upset, and I'm sure he will make my life a living hell. Hopefully, he won't ruin my chance at getting this scholarship," Greg said anxiously. Tyler placed his hands on Greg's shoulder and looked at him.

"Life at home won't be easy for you then," Tyler said, brushing his hand on the side of Greg's face.

"No. I need to find the strength to hang in there until I leave for my football camp," Greg said in despair.

"Hey, I'm here if you need to vent." Tyler reached for Greg's hands. "You're not alone. We'll get through this together. As much as I want to spend the day here with you, we get need to get to class."

The school bell rang, that awful sound telling Greg it was time to go home. Any other day, he would be jumping and racing to leave, but not today. If he could take the longest route home, he would, but there was no such thing in his town. On his way home, Greg stopped at the coffee shop, grabbed a coffee and walked to the park. *God, I don't know if I can go through another night around him. I'd rather be dead than to listen to him tell me I'm evil.*

When Greg got home, his father was already there. Greg looked at the time. *It's just after four, why is he home that early?* Greg headed to his room when his father stopped him.

"I have homework to do," Greg said.

"Your homework can wait. Now sit," his father said. "I

made us an appointment next week at Hope and Faith Wellness Centre."

"Hope and what?" Greg asked. "What is this?"

"It's a reparative therapy centre."

"You're sending me to a mental institution?" Greg yelled.

"No," his mother said. "This place can cure you of this disease."

"I'm not sick, I don't need to get fixed," Greg said, exasperated.

"You have no choice in the matter," his father said.

"Of course I do. It's my life and my body, and I'm eighteen. No one will fuck with my mind."

"Listen to me, buddy. This is how it's going to play out. I had a chat with your coach today. I told him not to recommend you for the Golden Bears summer camp and the university scholarship unless you go to therapy."

"You did what? How dare you? You had no right," Greg screamed. "This is my life you are fucking with. Yours is already fucked, so keep your bible away from me."

Greg's mother tried to hold him back. "Don't touch me," Greg said, pulling away from her. "You disgust me, both of you."

"Greg," Teresa pleaded, "it's for your own good."

Greg ran to his room and slammed the door. Enraged, he threw himself on the bed and screamed into his pillow.

Teresa slumped down on her chair and wept.

"Oh, stop crying," John said. "He brought it upon himself."

Chapter Thirty-five: Unexpected

"Good morning, Neil Fallon speaking. How can I help you? Suzanne . . . I don't like it when you call, it's never good news."

"Hi, Neil. It's about your mother. She's not doing well. She was admitted to the hospital three days ago," Suzanne said on the other end of the line.

"What? Why didn't anyone call me?" Neil asked.

"She's dying. When I drove her to see her doctor the last time we talked, he didn't have good news. He told her she had two to three months to live, maybe four. It looks like she has less than that," Suzanne said. "Your mother had everyone promise not to tell you anything."

"Why? Why did she do this?"

"You know your mother. She doesn't want anybody to fuss over her. So today, I'm breaking that promise because it's not fair. I told her to make amends with you, but your mother is a stubborn old bat. She told me to mind my business."

"Which hospital is she at?" Neil asked.

"Canmore General," Suzanne said.

"Thanks for letting me know, Suzanne. You're a good friend to her," Neil said.

Neil threw his pen across his desk and grabbed his head with both hands. *Why didn't she tell me that her cancer was terminal?* He called Trevor to let him know he was leaving for the hospital to see his mother.

On his way to the hospital, Neil remembered how strict his mother could be; it had always been her way or the highway.

Neil's father once told him his mother grew up in a single-parent family, and her mother went from partner to partner. One of those partners abused her when she was fifteen. When her life spiralled out of control, she turned to religion.

For over fifty years of her life, Beatrice had considered religion to be the ultimate answer to all questions. She believed it should govern every part of someone's life. Every week she would spend at least three hours at the church, and she believed that the bible had the whole and only truth, that it was the literal word of God with all its implications. This ideology became her life.

Entering the hospital, Neil rushed in and asked for her room number at the front desk.

"I'm so sorry. I'm afraid you're too late. She passed away ten minutes ago," the nurse said, reaching out to him. "I'm sorry."

"Can I see her? I'm her son."

"Of course. We asked your mother if she had anybody we could call; she said there wasn't anyone."

"She would say that. She never wanted to disturb anyone," Neil said.

Dressed in a blue hospital gown, Beatrice lay there with her eyes closed and mouth slightly open. Her hair was greyer than the last time he saw her. His chest tightened. "Why didn't you want me to know, Mom?" Neil said, kissing her forehead, his voice quivering. "I wish you had called me."

"I love you, Mom. I wish you would have given me the chance to say goodbye," Neil said, sobbing. "Give Dad a hug for me."

Neil left her room, tears flowing down his face. As he sat in his car, drying his eyes, he called Suzanne to let her know that her friend had passed.

"She loved you with all her heart, Neil. It wasn't her that disowned you, it was her religion."

"I know," Neil said. "I'll let you know when the funeral is."

"Will you be alright?" Suzanne asked.

"I'll be fine."

An hour later, Neil arrived at home. Trevor was in the kitchen, making coffee when he came in. "How is your mother?" Trevor asked.

"She didn't make it. She passed away ten minutes before I got there," Neil said. "She had terminal cancer. I only found out today when Suzanne called me. She'd been rushed to the hospital three days ago."

"I'm so sorry, Neil," Trevor said. "How are you?"

"I'm okay. I wish I could have been with her in her last moments. Even though she tried to get me out of her life, she's still my mother, and I know I'll miss her," Neil said, blinking back his tears.

Trevor opened his arms, and Neil walked right into them and sobbed on Trevor's shoulder. "Are you hungry?" Trevor said.

"No, babe," Neil said, sniffling. "I'll have to find out if she had a will. I've never arranged a funeral before, I don't even know where to begin."

"We'll figure it out," Trevor said. "First, go take a shower, I'll make you some coffee."

Neil and Trevor spent the evening cuddling on the couch. Neil was going through an emotional rollercoaster with his father and mother passing away in such a short period of time. *I wish things could have been different between us. My mother shut me out of her life at a time I could have been there for her.*

A few days later, Neil drove to Bow River Funeral Home to arrange his mother's funeral.

"Mr. Fallon, please accept my condolences for the loss of your mother. How are you holding up?" the funeral director asked.

"It's hard. I have great support at home, though. I have to

tell you, I've never planned anything like this before," Neil said

"That's what I'm here for. Do you know what kind of funeral you would like for your mother?"

"A simple one. That's what she would have wanted," Neil said.

"What about her internment? Did you want a casket, or did you want her cremated?"

"My mother wanted to be cremated."

"When were you planning to have the funeral?"

"I don't want to delay it for too long. When could we have it?

"Is next Saturday suitable?" Neil nodded. "Perfect. We'll see you next week, and leave the arrangements to me. Again, I'm so sorry for your loss."

On the day of the funeral, Neil woke up early, unable to sleep. He started to make coffee, then went and looked outside, returned to the kitchen and sat on the stool waiting for the coffee to be ready. Trevor walked in and saw Neil tapping his finger on the counter, rubbing his neck and sighing.

"Are you okay, honey?" Trevor asked.

"Yeah. I was thinking about what I was going to say today," Neil said.

Trevor, handing Neil his coffee, said, "You'll be fine. I'll be there by your side."

"I'm not sure who will be there apart from friends. I don't have many relatives, and those I have are too old to travel. My father has a brother, but he's ten years older than he was and lives in a retirement home in the States. My mother had no siblings, and her parents passed a few years ago."

Neil and Trevor arrived at Bow River Funeral Home at one in the afternoon. Everything was ready; his mother's urn was placed at the front of the little chapel surrounded by her favourite flowers. Suzanne, Robert, and Amanda arrived first, followed by his mother's church friends. Neil had asked Father Williamson to perform the ceremony, something his mother would have wanted.

Suzanne walked over to Neil and asked, "How are you holding up?"

"I'm okay. I'll be happy when it's all over."

After the prayer, Father Williamson invited Neil to say a few words. Neil got up; his hands were cold and clammy as he walked to the front. He paused before speaking.

"Thank you for being here today to celebrate my mother's life. I'm Neil Fallon, Beatrice Fallon's son, for those of you who don't know me. Three weeks ago, my mother and I buried my father and today . . . we are here to say goodbye to her.

"My mother lived to please God. Father Williamson can attest to this. She found God at a moment in her life when she felt lost. Despite the hardship, she always believed that one day she would meet her Prince Charming. In the form of my father, she did.

"I am so honoured to have been her son. She taught us all what's really important in life: love, support and caring for friends and family. It was a great privilege to be part of her life. I will miss her. Yes, she was stubborn and did not mince her words when she spoke, but that was my mother. One thing you could count on her for is her help. She was always ready to lend a hand and sometimes to the chagrin of my father, who would say, *Slow down, Bea, you can't help everyone.* Mom, now is the time to rest. You deserve it. I love you."

CHAPTER THIRTY-SIX: FORCED

"Greg, get up, we have to leave soon," John yelled.

"What?" Greg said, jolted out of his sleep. He looked at the time. *For crying out loud, it's seven in the morning.*

"We have a long journey ahead of us, so get your ass out of bed and get dressed," John said.

"Where are we going?" *Oh shit. Today is the day he's bringing me to visit that concentration camp.*

Greg walked out of his room half-asleep, and saw his father with his coffee. "Dad, I thought about it, and I know I've wronged you and have been lying to myself, so I made the decision not to see Tyler ever again."

"I'm glad to hear you say this, Greg. Your stint over at Hope and Faith shouldn't be too long then. I'm glad you're embracing the process," his father said.

"No, Dad. What I'm saying is that I don't need to go. I know what's right now."

"Get dressed because we leave in thirty minutes."

"But, Dad . . ."

"You will go through this therapy, and that's final," his father said. "Now get dressed."

Fuck. Greg looked at his father and then at his mother, who shrugged. *Thanks, Mom, for standing up for me.* "Fine," he said. *I hate you.* Greg slammed his door, then after a series of rattles and thumps as he rummaged through his drawers and closet, he got dressed.

He texted Tyler before leaving his room to let him know his father was taking him to meet a conversion therapist against his will. He told Tyler that he would text him when he returned tonight.

During the tense car ride, Greg's mother tried to make conversation to break the silence, but Greg kept his nose in his cellphone playing games. Finally, she told him they were meeting a religious counsellor. *Is that what they call themselves? Are they stupid enough to think this religious counsellor is going to fix me? Make everything better, so they're not ashamed of their son?*

"They are professionals," his father said. "You'll see, you'll be fixed in no time, and then you'll be a normal man."

"I don't need fixing. I am cool with my so-called abnormality," Greg said. *I think you need fixing.*

On arrival at the Hope and Faith Wellness Centre, Grant Manley greeted them at the door. "Welcome," he said, extending his hand. "I'm Grant Manley. I hope you had a pleasant drive here. Would you please follow me?" He brought them to his office. "Please have a seat. You must be Greg. I'm sure you'll love this place. Tell me, Greg, were you ever sexually assaulted?"

"What? No," Greg said, looking at him with a disgusted look on his face.

"Have you had sex with a guy?" Grant asked.

"What business is it of yours? What's with these questions?" Greg said.

"Greg," his father said. "Answer the questions."

"Are you happy with your body?" Grant asked.

"Yeah."

"Do you want to be straight?" Grant asked.

Greg looked puzzled by the question and didn't immediately answer. His father kicked his foot, and Greg reluctantly said, "It depends how much suffering I have to go through." He offered Grant a fake smile.

His father slapped him behind the head. "Don't be such a smart ass. Yes, he wants to be straight," he told Grant.

"Thank you, Mr. Fallon. Greg, why do you think you'll be

suffering here?" Grant asked.

"Whenever you tamper with someone's intellect when there's nothing wrong with it, irreparable damage is done, and the person suffers," Greg said sarcastically.

"I see we have a clever young man here," Grant said facetiously, looking at Greg's father. "He'll do just fine here. When would you like to start, Greg?"

Who is this man? What is he going to do to me? And how is this charlatan going to help me become someone I am not?

"Start what?" Greg asked.

Greg's father jumped in. "Mr. Manley," John said.

"Call me Grant."

"We would like Greg to start next week, if possible."

"I can't. I have school, remember."

"Greg, now is a good time to begin," Grant said.

"No. What do you know about my life?" Greg said to Grant.

"I know that you need help returning to the righteous path."

"Says who? Listen, I can't do this right now, and I won't do this right now. I'm going to university next year, and I have to graduate." Greg turned to his parents. "You can't force me into this, I'm eighteen."

Greg sprung up of his chair, sending it backward and stormed out of the office, slamming the door behind him.

Greg's father excused himself and went after his son. "Greg Miller, you stop right there. You get back in there."

"No, I'm not dropping out of school mid-year and I'm not going through this. This is my life and my future."

"You won't have a life or a future if you don't go through with this. You can kiss your scholarship goodbye," his father said.

"I'm not dropping out of school, and that's final," Greg loudly said.

"Let's go and get your mother," his father said, grabbing

his son by an arm. Greg reluctantly followed his father back in Grant's office. "Sorry about this."

"No, that's alright," Grant said. "Tell me, Greg, will two weeks away from school affect your school year?"

"I don't know," Greg replied with a catatonic face.

"It should be alright, Greg," his mother said reassuring him. "You excel in all your classes."

"What if I tell you we could have you here for only two weeks at first to establish how many sessions you should have later on? Perhaps when school is over?"

Greg, uninterested, only wanted to get out of this awful place. His father then said, "Grant, that's perfect. I will bring him back next week. It's decided."

Grant walked them out to their car and said, "Greg, I'll see you next week. Drive safely. It was nice to meet you."

"Likewise," John said, starting the car.

"I hope you're satisfied with yourselves. You got your wish, getting your son fixed because he's defective in your eyes. If anything happens to me, it will be your fault," Greg said.

"Don't believe everything you read," his father said.

"Says someone who swears by every quote and phrase he reads in his bible," Greg said.

CHAPTER THIRTY-SEVEN: ONE LAST BLOW

W*hat a day.* Neil rolled his neck side to side. He and Trevor managed to drag themselves to their car after the funeral. "Thank you for being there with me today, sweetie. I don't know if I would have made it through the day if you hadn't been there."

"You did great. Your dedication to your mother was beautiful. I'm sure she liked it," Trevor said.

"Now the running around starts. Tomorrow I have to go to the house and find their will. Then I need to make an appointment with their bank and lawyer," Neil said.

"Anything I can do to help?" Trevor asked.

"Yes. When we get home, a glass of wine and cuddling with you is what I'm looking forward to. Thank you for being in my life."

"Thank you for being in mine," Trevor said. "Do you want me to drive?"

"No, I'm fine," Neil said.

An hour later, Neil and Trevor were finally home. After a relaxing shower, Trevor and Neil cuddled on the sofa with their glass of wine. Neil sank into Trevor's lap, and Trevor leaned over, and they shared a passionate kiss.

Trevor asked, "Are you worried that your mother took you out of the will?"

"Whether she did or not, it doesn't matter," Neil said. "I suspect that she might have because she was bitter to the very end."

"It's sad that she spent her last days being angry at you," Trevor said.

"Her and Dad were convinced that I would agree to get help without question. So they used the inheritance as their weapon to manipulate me into going to therapy."

"That's when your parents began shutting you out of their life."

"It was mostly my mother. I'm sure my father would have welcomed you with open arms. He was a religious man but not like my mother."

Greg sipped the last drops of his wine and stretched himself to set his glass on the coffee table. "Would you like more wine?" Trevor asked.

"No, thank you. What do you say if we go to bed? It's been a long day."

"Good idea. You need your rest," Trevor said.

They snuggled naked under the covers and inevitably ended up making love before falling sound asleep.

The next day, driving up to his parents' house, Neil wasn't sure if he could handle going in by himself. *I should have brought Trevor with me. My last memories of this place still haunt me.* Neil got out of the car, ran his fingers along the top of the back door frame, and found the door key. His mother always hid a house key there in case she lost hers, or if Neil happened to come home while they were out or asleep.

Entering through the back door, Neil walked into the kitchen. His mother's cup of coffee and newspaper was still sitting at the very place she was, the morning she was rushed to the hospital. It was hard to be in the house, every corner was filled with his parents' presence.

Down the dimmed corridor was his parents' bedroom. *Maybe the will is in there.* Looking through the wardrobe, Neil came across several photo albums. Flipping through the pages, he went on a trip down memory lane.

Further back behind his mother's hat collection on the top shelf, Neil found a shoebox. Neil opened the box, and inside was their will. He sat on his parents' bed and scanned through the document to see who the lawyer was. *Henry Watson. He's here in Canmore.*

Neil looked him up on his cell and called him. "Mr. Watson, I'm Neil Fallon, the son of Mr. and Mrs. Roger Fallon. My mother passed away a week ago, so I wondered if we could meet to discuss how to proceed with executing her will . . . I am the executor according to the copy I have, unless it has been modified recently . . . Next Thursday is perfect. Thank you."

"Hi, sweetie. You're home early. Any luck with the will?" Trevor asked.

"Yes, they had it stored in a shoebox," Neil said, chuckling. "Next week, I'll need your help to go through everything they have and determine what we'll keep, throw or donate."

"Sure," Trevor said. "How did you feel when you went in?"

"Even though my mother and I had fallen out, standing in the kitchen, seeing where she had breakfast last was heartbreaking. You know, it was the first time I've gone into their bedroom. Growing up, their door was always closed, and no one was allowed in. When I entered, I felt like I was breaking the rules. I sat on their bed for a minute and looked around. I could feel their presence around me. When I rummaged through their closet, I came across a dusty old box on the floor at the back of their wardrobe. Inside was, among other personal letters, my mother's diary. "

"Did you read any of it?" Trevor asked.

"I considered it, and then thought if it was private before her death, then it should continue to be private after."

"I think you did the right thing. What did you do with it?" Trevor asked.

"It's still at the house. When we go back next week, we'll burn it in the fireplace, along with the letters," Neil said.

"Do you feel like going out for dinner?" Trevor asked.

"That's a wonderful idea," Neil said. "We deserve a night out."

Neil, dressed in a navy and white fitted shirt and jeans and holding Trevor's hand, walked down to their favourite restaurant. Trevor opted to wear his black wool sweater that showed the definition of his muscled torso. On their way there, some people stared at them because of their hand-holding, and others looked jealous because they wished they had the guts to do the same.

After dinner, the couple decided to walk through the park and just be with one another. Neil stopped in front of a magnificent maple tree overlooking the river. With the sound of the water flowing downstream, Neil pressed Trevor's back against the tree and leaned in for a passionate kiss.

The soft indigo-blue comforter back at the apartment felt good against Neil's and Trevor's naked bodies as they rolled over it, caressing each other. Trevor moved on top of Neil, both with hard-ons. Neil brought his mouth to Trevor's rock-hard cock, and his tongue started waltzing around the shaft, arousing them both even more. Trevor rolled Neil on his stomach and lifted Neil's hips until Neil was on his knees. Lubing up his finger, Trevor ran it around Neil's hole, brushing the tip at the entrance and pushing it in teasingly. Neil moaned whenever Trevor's finger penetrated him.

Trevor reached for a condom, rolled it down on his penis, placed more lube in his right hand and stroked it on his shielded shaft. Trevor brought Neil's hips near his erection, and gently he worked his throbbing penis inside Neil's ass.

The feeling of being inside his lover and enjoying this incredible closeness with him was more than he could handle.

The moment Trevor began moving back and forth inside Neil, he felt his whole body starting to shake. "Ahhh!" he groaned as he filled the condom. Trevor pulled out, and immediately started tonguing Neil's shaft while he fingered his ass.

Sweaty, breathing heavily, they rolled on their backs and enjoyed the post-orgasmic rush. Following a shower, they got in bed and cuddled and fell asleep.

A week went by, and it was time to meet with the lawyer. Neil and Trevor arrived at Mr. Watson's office.

"Mr. Fallon, please come into my office," he said. "First, let me extend my condolences. It's not easy losing both parents in such a short time."

"Thank you, Mr. Watson," Neil said. Have you had the chance to review my parents' will?"

"Yes, you are still the executor. However your mother modified the will just a few weeks ago. Here is a copy of the new will." Bernard handed a copy to Neil.

Neil looked over the new will's pages, and Trevor registered his disappointed look. "Are you okay?"

"I am," Neil said. "Mr. Watson, you understand that my mother removed me from the will because I'm gay." Trevor reached for Neil's hand and held it. "But I'm not going to contest it. I just wanted you to know why she did what she did. I see she's leaving the money to the church, the proceeds of the sale of the house to charity and the amount of five thousand dollars in her bank account to me. One thing she forgot to change, though, is the executor."

"No, your mother was very clear on this. She wanted you to remain executor."

"This may have been her last wishes, but I decline to be the executor of this will," Neil said.

"Mr. Fallon, you realize that the court will appoint an administrator for your mother's will. Therefore, I recommend you think about your decision seriously."

"Mr. Watson, please tell me why I should remain the executor of my mother's will? I don't mind being cut out of it — as a matter of fact, I suspected that she would do exactly this. But to keep me as executor, don't you think that's rather below the belt? As I said, I want no part of it, not even the five thousand dollars."

Neil and Trevor got up and were at the door

"Wait, Neil," Mr. Watson said. "If I were you, I would contest the will. If you let me, I can help you with this."

"I'll let you know," Neil said as he left the office.

Neil thought about it for a few days. "Contesting the will," Neil said to Trevor, "would be an option, and if I won, I would have the last laugh. But I'm not sure that's what I want."

"Honey," Trevor said, "it's not. You're not a vengeful person."

"You're right. Besides, I don't want anything from her. It's best to let the church have it all."

"I think it's best," Trevor said.

That evening, Neil phoned Mr. Watson to let him know that he didn't want any part of his parents' inheritance.

Chapter Thirty-eight: Two Weeks in Hell

On his way to get fixed, as per his father's wish, Greg sent a text to Tyler to let him know where he was going and it would be a while before they see each other.

One of the first things to strike Greg when he arrived at Hope and Faith Wellness Centre was how much it seemed to perpetuate stereotypes of gay guys. Greg noticed most of the young guys attending wore designer jeans and tight-fitting T-shirts. They had pierced ears and modern haircuts. *This is the gayest thing I've been to so far.*

"Greg," Grant said, "welcome to the centre. Are you ready to embrace your new life as a new man?"

I don't need to be a new man, I like the way I am. While Greg was waiting for Grant to take him around, the guys going to their therapy session kept checking Greg out. "Let me show you your room. It's located down the hall on the right. You will be in room four hundred and one."

The panoramic windows along the hallway to the rooms showed beautiful flowers and shrubs on one side, and a majestic mountain on the other. Grant opened the door to Greg's room, which was sparsely furnished with a bed, a desk, and a small dresser.

Greg looked at Grant and said, "What's this, a broom closet? Is this how you make your guests comfortable? Where's the television, and why are there no windows?"

"This is not a hotel, Greg. It's a rehabilitation centre," Grant said. "Also, the rooms are used as isolation chambers when required."

"What do you mean by isolation chambers? Why would you want to put people in isolation? You're making this sound more like a concentration camp," Greg said with a blank face.

Grant cracked a faint smile and said, "Get settled and meet me in my office in fifteen minutes. I'll take you to your first session." Grant closed the door as he left.

I knew this was a bad idea coming here. Greg unpacked his suitcase, and then noticed that his door had no lock. "What the fuck?" he said "What about privacy? I guess trust is not in their vocabulary." With that, he left for Grant's office.

Grant accompanied Greg to a conference room a few doors from his office. Grant knocked before entering, then opened the door. Inside were a dozen young men sitting in two rows on wooden chairs, listening to the therapist.

"Here is Greg Fallon, the young man I was telling you about. He just arrived."

"Thank you, Grant. Greg, pleased to meet you. There's an empty chair between Jerold and Andrew." Both Jerold and Andrew waved at Greg to let him know where they were. "I'm John Merkle.

"Now as I was saying, your same-sex attraction can absolutely be changed. We need to rewire your brain, and it is completely doable. No one is born this way, and so if that's the case, it must be possible to change. Alcoholics change, thieves change, all sorts of people change. Homosexuals are broken. Broken in that something has caused you to be gay, like trauma, sexual abuse, bad parenting, or the need for acceptance.

"You need to recognize that you may believe you are gay for a variety of reasons that have nothing to do with your core sexual identity. Your sexual feelings may be rooted in a need for acceptance, approval. It may reflect your loneliness, boredom, or simple curiosity. Why do you struggle with same-sex attraction? You struggle with same-sex attraction because you are weak, you hate yourself, and you don't know how to be a man," John said.

What the fuck is he talking about? What am I doing here? I don't hate myself.

On the right side of the conference room stood six full-length mirrors. John ordered them to take off their shirts and look in the mirror. "Please describe what you see. Tell me what parts of your body make you insecure."

Greg was an athlete with a nicely developed upper body, so he told John there was nothing that was a source of insecurity. John encouraged Greg to look again. "What don't you like about your body?"

"Well, if you put it that way," Greg said, "what I don't like is not up here but down there." He pointed to his penis. "It's not as big as I want it to be." Laughter and whistles roared from the others in the room, and John's face turned bright red.

"Mr. Fallon, do you think this is funny?" John said.

"No, you asked me a question, and I answered it. There's nothing wrong with my upper body, as is the case for everybody else here. Jerold, Andrew, are you insecure about your body?" Greg asked.

"No. I work out, I like my body," Jerold said.

"I love my body," Andrew said.

"Body insecurities negatively impact your feelings of masculinity, and low levels of masculinity are the reason why you have same-sex attraction," John said. "Everyone, shirt back on and get back to your seats."

Greg, seconds after he sat down, put up his hand.

"Yes, Mr. Fallon?"

"Every human being has insecurities about some part of their bodies, so what you're saying is every human being has same-sex attraction issues?" Greg said.

"Enough, Mr. Fallon. I don't want to hear another word from you. Do you understand me? This session is over. Go back to your rooms," John said

The following day, Greg had a one-on-one session with a psychologist. He sat on the couch and looked around the room, his hands joined and leaning on his thighs. *I wonder what this session is all about.* The shrink came in and took out his pen and paper and looked at Greg, "Do you know why you're like this?"

Greg looked at him. "I'm sure you're going to tell me."

"It's because you had an over-involved relationship with your mother. It's okay to blame her for this, she made you this way without realizing it. I want you to kneel and pray so, God can forgive her and forgive your sin. I can't hear you, pray louder, and repent for your sins as a homosexual. Ask for the Lord's mercy.

"This is bullshit," Greg said, leaving the session. "Where does he get off accusing my mother of over-caring for me . . ."

Greg walked in for his other session, this time with behaviorist. There were twenty of them in a place that looked like an old gym, and this mid-fifty man broke them into groups. In their breakout groups, this man would teach them how to become more *manly*. They were told that if one walked, talked and sat different from other men, this was evidence of dysfunction that could be altered to instill heterosexual desires.

"Real men talk with a deep voice, and most of you speak with a soft feminine voice. You need to deepen your tone. Men don't sit with legs crossed at the knee or at the feet. Real men sit legs open and feet firmly planted on the ground." Greg and his pals spent the session practicing speaking and sitting. If it wasn't to the satisfaction of the teacher, they would be shouted at.

In the middle of their exercise, Grant Manley walked in with John Merkle. "Take a seat, everyone," Grant said. Then he motioned John to come front.

John grabbed Joshua from his seat and dragged him to the front, then pushed him in front of Grant and everyone. Joshua was a seventeen-year-old that started at the same time as Greg. He, like Greg and the others was forced into conversion. Joshua was shy and an introvert. Hating to displease anyone, he would do everything he is told to do.

"This," Grant said, "is a sinner, an advocate of the devil. Look at me, Joshua. Why do you think you are here?"

"I don't know, why?" Joshua answered, shaking.

"What were you doing in your room earlier this morning?" Grant asked.

"Nothing? What is there to do in that cell?"

"John, can you bring me what you found in Joshua's room?" John gave Grant a magazine all rolled up.

"Joshua, tell your friends here what this is." He waved the rolled-up magazine in front of the crowd.

Joshua, visibly uncomfortable, said, "I don't know what that is."

Grant unrolling it, shoved it in Joshua's face, "How dare you bring a porn magazine into this place." Joshua lowered his head. "Look at me when I'm talking to you. We saw you masturbating, flipping through the pages of this piece of trash, looking at erect naked men."

Joshua seemed shocked and angered,. "How could you see this? I was in my room with no windows," Joshua said. "Fucking shit, you're spying on us, aren't you? Where did you plant the cameras?"

"How dare you swear at me," Grant said, inches from his face. "John, give me the cable." John handed him the cable he had in his back pocket, and Grant started beating Joshua with it.

"Stop," Joshua cried out, trying to grab the cables. John then grabbed Joshua and held him while Grant lashed out at him. Josh was yelling in pain, his face wet from his crying. Then John released him and Joshua fell to the floor in pain, while Grant kept beating him. Everyone was terrorized, tears of fear and of compassion for Joshua flowing out of one and all.

"This is what happens when you don't follow the rules." Grant kept lashing at Joshua in front of everyone, panting from the physical effort but with a sense of enjoyment in his eyes, until Greg got up.

"Stop!" Greg shouted. Everyone turned towards Greg. "What do you think you're doing? You're killing him. Who are you people? Who gave you the right to treat this guy like a piece of trash?" Greg's face was the colour of beets from the anger he was channeling. "You call this place a Wellness Centre, and this is how you intend to treat us all?"

"Ah! Why am I not surprised by your interjection, Mr. Fallon. You seem to be the spokesperson and the shit disturber in every session." Grant handed over the cables to John and grabbed a chair to sit on it.

"Homosexuality is second only to murder in the eyes of God, Mr. Fallon. If we can't get through someone using our usual education, sometimes it is necessary to shame someone in public."

"This is not shaming, inflicting pain is not shaming. We're not in the Middle East," Greg yelled.

John moved to go and grab Greg by the collar, but Grant motioned him to stay still.

"Perhaps, Mr. Fallon, you would like to take Joshua's place? You're no better than him. We've seen your attitude in class and your rebellion against our help. I'm sure your father wouldn't be pleased to hear all about it. Now sit down. John, take Joshua to his room and lock the door. I hope, Joshua, you have learned something today. Everyone go back to your room."

John picked up Joshua off the floor, Joshua was limping from the beating; you could see cable marks on his arms in places where he used them to protect himself.

The next day, everyone was assigned a psychoanalyst for their session. Sitting in a rehabilitation lab, Greg was waiting for his so-called therapist when Grant Manley walked in and asked, "Greg, why are you here?"

"I'm waiting for my therapist. You should know. You design the sessions," Greg said snarkily.

"Don't get smart. Why did you come to this centre?"

"Because my father forced me," Greg replied.

"Do you think that your father sent you here for nothing?" Grant said, looking straight at Greg. "Your father brought you here because you're a troubled young man, and you have a serious identity problem."

"I would agree with you, but we would both be wrong," Greg said. "I don't have an identity problem. None of the guys here have an identity problem. You and my father have the problem."

"Now you listen to me," Grant said conceitedly, "I told your father that we would convert you, and we will. Your therapist is here." Grant walked out and slammed the door behind him.

Burt was an older guy; he didn't look like a therapist, more like angry old man. When Grant slammed the door, he turned to look back, shrugged and then turned to Greg and the first words out of his mouth were, "Your faith and your community reject your sexuality. Your parents dismiss your sexuality, and you are the abomination we had heard about in Sunday school." Greg was about to say something when the therapist interrupted him. "You don't speak. You don't say anything. You listen and do what you're told."

It didn't stop with his bullying and hurtful talk. Burt pulled out a mercury-filled tube and asked Greg to drop his pants. "What the hell for?" Greg asked.

Burt didn't like to play around and grabbed Greg's belt and began undoing it. Greg stopped him and undid his pants and dropped them. "Those too," Burt said, pointing to Greg's underwear.

"Fuck," Greg said has he got out of his underwear. Hiding his groin with his hands, Burt took the mercury-filled tube removed Greg's hands and placed the tube around the base of Greg's penis to measure the level of stimulation he should experience when viewing nude images of men and women.

"Sit on this table," Burt told Greg. Greg obliged and then Burt opened the door and somebody else came in and grabbed Greg, preventing him from moving while Burt bound his hand and feet so he couldn't move, then place electrode-wired suction cups on his back and quadriceps.

The thug left and Burt pulled down a projector screen and slides. A photo of a man naked popped up and Greg received an electric shock if his penis started to get erect. Then Burt showed a picture of a naked woman. He carefully monitored that mercury tube, and because Greg wasn't turned on by that photo, there was no consequence at all. Greg was given electroconvulsive shocks in three ten-second intervals in conjunction with slides of male and female nudity. This went on for hours.

At the end of his session, Greg was brought back to his room and locked in for the remainder of the day without food. Greg laid in his bed curled up in a ball, crying and in pain.

The following morning Greg, still weak from the shocks, banged his room door, yelling to let him out.

"Are you ready to conform, Mr. Fallon?" John asked. Greg bowed his head affirmatively. "Perfect," John answered. You can join the others for breakfast before your next session."

Session after session, Greg and the others were confronted with their own deviancy. As the days went by, repetition and duration of the cleansing ritual, forced nudity, and recitation of religious verse increased with intensity and importance.

Their goal was to get the residents to hate themselves for being gay. They removed everything that made them unique and tried to turn them into walking, talking robots for Jesus. To escape conversion therapy before more damage was done to him, Greg feigned complete rehabilitation.

On Friday morning, Grant asked Greg to meet him in his office. "Greg, I'm proud of you. You seemed to have responded to your therapist's treatment well, I am told. After your session with him, your therapist told me that you were starting to look down on same-sex attraction. How do you feel?"

"Ashamed. Dirty and disgusted. I hate myself for having lived a life of sin and bringing shame to my parents," Greg said with a straight face.

"I'm happy to hear this. I have taken the liberty to call your father; he is waiting for you outside. I told him because of your progress, I was allowing your therapy to continue from home. Your sessions will be done by phone with your therapist starting tomorrow. I'm proud of you. Keep up the good work. I'll be checking in once in a while," Grant said.

"Thank you."

"Go get your bags," Grant said.

Chapter Thirty-nine: Scarred

Greg was silent on the way home from the rehabilitation centre, his eyes glued to his cell, which was taken away from him two weeks ago. Greg's face winced whenever the car hit a bump or a hole; the jolt shook Greg's body, still sore from the treatments he received earlier in the week.

"I heard you responded well," his father said, looking at Greg in his rear-view mirror. "How are you feeling?" Greg looked at his father and went back to his cellphone. "Are you okay?" his father asked.

"Yeah," Greg replied in a dead voice.

"How was the centre?"

"How do you think it was?"

"You're not very talkative."

"What do you want me to say? That I had the time of my life? That having electricity shoved on my body was the highlight of my weeks? They electrocuted me, dad," Greg shouted, his voice cracking. "Every guy in that centre received electroshock and other means of torture. That is what they use to cure you." Greg swallowed his tears.

"Yes, Grant told me that they used electroshock therapy along with other methods as part of the cure."

"You were aware of this, and you sent me there anyway?" Greg said, his voice rising to a scream. "You put your image ahead of the wellbeing of your son? Wow, thanks, Dad." Greg turned to look out the window, wiping his tears occasionally. The he took out his cell and saw thousands of messages and texts. He plugged in his ear buds, turned on his music, leaned back in his seat, and didn't say another word the rest of the trip.

As soon as the car was parked, Greg got out, went directly to his room, and locked the door. He sat at the edge of his bed and wept. He could still feel the sting of the treatment they subjected him to. He stood up, lifted his sweater and looked in the mirror, and saw the red welts where his therapist stung him.

"Greg," his mother said, knocking at his door. "Are you alright? Can I come in?" Greg just closed his eyes, covered his head with his pillow to block his mother's voice. He just kept on crying.

"Don't waste your time," John said. "He was the same on the ride home. He probably needs some rest. Grant told me Greg's treatment went well, and we should notice a difference in him."

"What did they do to him?" Teresa asked.

"Oh, your normal therapy sessions, you know, talking to a therapist about how you feel and why do you think you're this way and how we can help. That sort of thing."

Early the next day, Greg stepped out of his room and noticed his mother standing at the kitchen island having her coffee, reading the newspaper. He poured himself a cup and sat at the table with his cellphone.

"How did it go?" his mother asked. Greg kept scrolling through all the emails he received while incarcerated at that centre. "How did it go?" she repeated.

"Hum, what did you say, Mom?" Greg lifted his head.

"I asked you how it went."

"Don't you know?" Greg said, his eyes back on his

cellphone. "I thought that Grant would have given you and Dad a detailed report."

Teresa snatched the cellphone from his hands and said, "Look at me when I ask you a question and don't be such a smart-ass. Yes, they called with your progress, but I want to hear how it went from you."

"What do you want me to say? That it went well and that I'm cured? That I finally saw the light? No. I didn't see the light, and no, I am not cured. I pretended to be so I could get the hell out of there. Don't worry, I'll make sure all the money Dad dumped into that place to satisfy his ego and his religion won't go to waste. My *conversion sessions* will continue by phone, but I'm sure you know about it. Now, if you'll excuse me, I'm going to my room." Greg threw his cup in the sink.

"Just wait until your father gets home," his mother yelled.

"What, so he can beat me and hope that will cure me?" Greg shouted from his room. "They tried that over there, and it didn't work. Oh, by the way," he said, coming back out shirtless, "this is what their therapy really looks like."

"Oh my God," she shrieked, "what happened to you?"

"Electroshock treatment, that's what happened to your son." Greg returned to his room and slammed the door.

Teresa's eyes watered at the sight of the swellings on Greg's body. She knocked at his door, "Greg, let me tend to your sores. Who did this to you?"

"Leave me alone. I'm fine."

Teresa went to the living room and phoned John at the store.

"John," Teresa said frantically, "something went on at the centre. Our son's upper body is covered in red burn marks. He said they gave him electroshock treatment. I want you to call Grant and ask him what happened."

Later that day, John called Teresa to let her know that Greg's red spots were caused by an allergic reaction to a medication they give to all their patients during treatment.

"Are you sure?" she asked. "They look like burn marks, not an allergic reaction."

"That's what Grant told me. What can I tell you," John said.

Greg knew his life at home wouldn't be the same. The centre had given his father a list of what Greg could and could not watch on television. Anything remotely alluding to homosexuality was forbidden. Grant specifically told John to carefully search through Greg's contacts on his cell for potential gay friends. His messages and emails were monitored, and his computer was moved to the living room to be used for homework only. Greg's father blamed technology for making him gay.

Everything about his life that had once been comforting was stripped away. He was being forced back into the closet. His love for who he was disappearing.

Despite some setbacks, Greg pretended to make progress. He informed his therapist that he was going through a grey area regarding his sexual orientation. It was all nonsense, of course. Greg was still just as gay as ever. He told his therapist his grey area consisted of a lack of sexual attraction to either sex. "This is a normal progression," his therapist informed him. "This represents the lessening of your same-sex attraction."

Little did he know that most of Greg's responses could be credited to Google. That was the power of the internet. Greg researched and became an expert on conversion therapy, and as such, was able to trick his therapist into believing that he was changing.

As his therapy continued, Greg progressed quickly and

turned into a proud heterosexual, just as his parents wanted him to be. But, in reality, nothing had changed except his self-confidence was gone. His parents and therapist analyzed everything he did. He felt trapped and could no longer be his authentic self.

As the days went by, Greg no longer had to deal with his therapist or the centre, as his parents now believed he was fixed. Greg was far from being cured; he was now suffering from anxiety, low self-esteem and depression.

After a month of intense therapy, Greg was given the okay to return to school. Now that his cellphone was no longer a threat for the success of his therapy, Greg texted Tyler to meet him at the trailer Monday morning at seven.

The weekend couldn't go by fast enough for neither of them. Greg got up early Monday, had breakfast and fifteen minutes before seven he grabbed his backpack to leave for school.

"Where are you going at this hour?" his father asked

"To school, why?" Greg looked at his father as if there was something wrong.

"It's not even seven, yet. School doesn't start until eight," his father said suspiciously.

"So. Some of my friends arrive at seven and hang out until class starts. There's nothing wrong with that. If you want me to wait until eight before leaving for school, just say so," Greg said, putting his backpack down.

"No, no. It's fine," his father said, going back to his newspaper. "You just never left this early for school before."

"I hadn't been removed from society in therapy before either. I haven't seen my friends in a month, we have some catching up to do," Greg said as he picked up his bag and walked out the door. *Fuck, is he going to watch me like this from now on?*

Tyler was already in the trailer when Greg walked in. Greg dropped his backpack and took Tyler in his arms, looked in his beautiful eyes, while his were tearing up and kissed him. Locked into each other's arms, they were afraid of letting go, they didn't want to be separated again.

"I missed the hell out of you," Tyler said. "I've sent you hundreds of emails and texts."

"Hi, Tyler. I'm sorry about not answering you back. At the centre, they confiscated our cellphones, and when they sent me back home, my parents had me erase all my messages and took away my cell when they went to bed."

"Are you okay?" Tyler asked.

"Yes, I am. Better now that I am here with you," Greg said, holding Tyler's hands.

"How long did you stay?" Tyler pulled Greg towards the couch and sat down.

"I was at the centre two weeks, then they sent me home for the rest of the treatment. At the centre, they tried everything to change me — isolation, electroshock, and hours of therapy." Greg lifted his sweater to show him the shadow mark left by the electric shock.

"Oh my God, babe. What did they do to you? It must have been so painful," Tyler said, running his hand over the wounds.

"I played their games and told them I was changing just to stop the torture. Greg pulling his sweater back down. They even beat guys in front of us to scare us. They couldn't change me and I didn't want to be changed. I'm still me, the Greg you know . . ." Greg smiled.

"I can't believe they do this to people, and in the name of the religion too."

"It's people like my father who keeps those places fueled. Right now, I have to pretend to be heterosexual for my parents until I can get the hell out of here. It won't be easy, I know."

"How are you going to do this?" Tyler asked, cuddling

against Greg.

"I have a plan, but I'll need your support and trust. I love you, you know I do, but for a little while, you and I need to keep some distance. I'll try and figure some other arrangement for you and I to meet secretly, because I'll go crazy, if I don't see you."

"I am here for you and I'm prepared to do anything so you don't have to face the wrath of your father," Tyler said, grabbing his hand.

"If it weren't for you, I wouldn't have been able to have gone through what I went through. I promise we'll be together soon." Greg leaned in and kissed him.

Chapter Forty: No Scruples

Patty was having a party this coming Friday night, and everyone from grade eleven and twelve was going to be there — except Elaine. Upset because she couldn't go, Elaine wrote on social media on her way to Saskatoon with her parents, *I wouldn't have gone to this party even if they'd paid me. Bunch of losers.*

The following week, Elaine made a pit stop at her favourite coffee shop and overheard two schoolmates talking about her comments on social media.

"What a bitch, talking about Patty like that," one said.

"Girls like that always think they're better than anyone else. Anyway, had she been there, I would have left. I can't stand her," the other said.

"I don't think many at school can."

Elaine decided to write derogatory remarks about them and posted them on her spam account. *Have heard the latest about Anna and Shirley,* she wrote. *If you see them walking home late some nights, it's because they are returning from turning tricks. Check out these photos of the sluts. Girls, watch your backs,* Elaine wrote under her pseudonym. Under the post, she posted a photoshopped picture of them lounging on a beach naked.

When Anna and Shirley saw this the following day, they were devastated. Elaine happened to walk by and asked, "Everything alright, girls? You guys look worried."

"Someone is cyberbullying us," one of them said.

"How awful. Why on earth would someone do this?"

Elaine said.

"Because they're crazy. They have nothing better to do but to harass people. When I find out who did it, I will report them to the school director," the other girl said.

"Good luck finding out," Elaine said as she entered the school. *You're not smart enough to figure out who it is.*

Walking down the hallway, Greg saw Elaine coming towards him. *Not her.*

"Hey, handsome, I haven't seen you in a while. Where have you been?" Elaine said.

"I was at a football camp for a few weeks," Greg said.

"Wow, that must have been interesting," Elaine said.

"Listen, I'm sorry for turning you down the other day," Greg said facetiously. "I had a lot on my mind, plus the coach wanted to see me. Hope I can make it up to you someday."

"I thought you and Tyler were an item?" Elaine said. "I saw the photo on social media."

"Oh, that. No. Actually, we knew someone was spying on us, so we decided to kiss. We didn't bank on that loser snapping a photo to post on social media," Greg said sarcastically.

"So you're not gay?" Elaine asked. "You guys were just pretending?"

"What you thought, Tyler and I . . . Oh my God, really?" Greg started to laugh.

"Everyone did when they saw the pic. Why didn't you or Tyler write a rebuttal?" Elaine asked.

"What for? All our friends knew that we weren't, and besides, we wanted the joke to be on the loser who posted it," Greg said.

"What about your parents?" Elaine asked.

"What about them?" Greg asked.

"What did they say when they saw the photo of you guys

kissing?" Elaine asked.

"Our parents are not on social media," Greg said.

"But someone told me that your father caught you guys having sex in a trailer at Lee Creek Campground," Elaine said.

"Really? Who told you that?" Greg asked with a stern look.

"I . . . I think it was Carl," Elaine said.

"How could he? I haven't seen or spoken to Carl for weeks," Greg said.

"Maybe it was somebody else, then," Elaine said aloofly. "So you really were at a football camp and not at conversion therapy?"

"Conversion therapy? Why would you think I was there?" Greg asked.

"I heard that as well," Elaine said.

"Wow, you do hear lots of things about me. And I guess you don't remember who told you that either," Greg said with a smirk.

Elaine shook her head. "No."

"It doesn't matter. I guess I should be getting to class and you too," Greg said, smiling. "Oh, by the way, have a nice day."

"Yeah," Elaine said.

What the fuck. I'm sure they weren't pretending to kiss. How dare he call me stupid and a loser? I need to get to the bottom of this. I don't believe he's straight.

CHAPTER FORTY-ONE: BARING MY HEART

Neil had been wrestling with grief. He blamed the universe's cruelty for taking away his parents in the space of three short weeks. It didn't matter if their relationship had turned sour before they passed; it didn't make Neil's loss hurt less.

"Sweetie," Neil said to Trevor, "I'm going to drive down to Canmore Cemetery. I want to visit my parents' resting place."

"Do you want me to go with you?" Trevor asked.

"No thanks, babe. I'd like to be alone with them," Neil said, taking Trevor in his arms and kissing him.

"Of course," Trevor said, caressing Neil's face.

Will I find the right words to say to her? This anger inside me is eating me up alive.

Walking to the columbarium that housed his parents' urns, Neil walked past an abandoned pioneer cemetery. *How old is this place? It must be at least a hundred years old just by the look of the wooden fence around each tombstone, discoloured with time.* Neil continued up the hill to the newer part of the cemetery, where his parents' final resting place was.

Neil sat on the wrought iron bench in front of the columbarium, staring at his parents' urns. A tear sprang free from his eye, and he lowered his head into his hands as he fought back his sorrow. Then, wiping his tear-stained face, Neil looked up to heaven and said, "Hi, Mom. There's something I need to tell you, but you're not going to like it. I didn't have time to have this discussion with you because I was scared, and you went to join Dad too fast.

"Yes, I was scared. I was afraid of your violent temper, the one you flashed when things weren't as you wanted them to be. You were perceived to be a loving person, caring for everything and everyone. You portrayed yourself as a model citizen and caretaker who people should adore. But in fact, in private, you were the opposite," Neil said sarcastically.

"You took care of my physical needs. You put food on the table, bought me clothes, and you and Dad built a roof over my head. But what about my feelings, Mom?" Neil said, raising his voice, trying not to cry. "Every time I tried to talk about how I felt growing up, you dismissed it. As an adult, I didn't have the right to be who I was; it didn't fit in with your worldview." Tears were rolling down Neil's face. "It was all about you and what people would say.

"Everything you gave came at a price; obedience and control was the price I had to pay," Neil said dryly, slapping his chest. "Your *love* was suffocating and dangerous. I came to understand why, Mom, your love was so dry. You probably received the same from your mother, conditional and unaffectionate, before she sent you to a convent.

"I still feel the profound pain of your rejection and criticism when you disowned me. Your hate-stricken face at the restaurant haunts me still.

"Why couldn't you just love me for who I was?" Neil said, crying. "Why did hurting me, who loved you so much, come so easy to you? I was your only son, and because I was different, you were ready to send me to conversion therapy."

Then with hatred he said, "I hated you for it and still do . . ." Neil got up, walked around the bench where he was sitting, trying to calm down, then he stopped and sneered. "Somehow you still managed to inflict more pain even after your death by disinheriting me but still keeping me as executor. Well, I'm sorry to tell you, Mom, I won't be treated this way. Now a total stranger will go through all your and Dad's personal things and discover what kind of person you really were."

Neil placing his hand on the Columbarium where his parents were resting. "I wish you to find peace and happiness someday if there's another life for us somewhere. But I don't want to meet you again. Not even in the afterlife . . . Before I go, Mom," Neil wiping his tears, "please know I forgive you, but I won't come back here."

Chapter Forty-two: Faking Who I'm Not

It was ten o'clock Sunday night. Greg, sitting on his bed, suddenly stopped moving and listened for noise. *Complete silence, this means they're in bed.* He quietly opened his bedroom door, tiptoed into the kitchen, reached in the cupboard over the refrigerator, and grabbed his cellphone that his parents took away from him every night as part of his therapy.

Back into his room, Greg texted Tyler, *Hi my love, I'm going to post something on social media about us; please don't believe a word I write. I'm asking you to play along. I love you.*

Greg logged on to his social media account and posted, *The rumours about Tyler and me, unfortunately, are true. I have shamed my parents and my church with my sexual orientation, and I needed to make things right for them and for me. I sought therapy, and I'm happy to say that I have become who I am supposed to be after my four weeks with the best therapist. Tyler and I are just friends, like I am friends with all of you.*

On Monday morning, the school was buzzing with *Did you read what Greg posted on his social media?* Tyler pretended to be crushed and upset when he saw Greg. Greg just looked away when Tyler looked at him and waved at Elaine and her entourage while walking towards her. Greg leaned in and kissed Elaine on both cheeks, and the stunned look on Elaine's face had her friends giggling with envy.

James, his teammate, didn't know what to make of Greg's social media confession. *I was certain Greg was comfortable with his sexuality. To come out as straight a month later doesn't quite jive with me.*

"Hey, Greg," James said, approaching him in the hallway. "How's it going, man? I saw your revelation this morning; wow, what a turnaround for you, hey?"

"James, bud. Good to see you," Greg said. "It's nice to be free from something that was eating me up inside." *I wish I could tell him the truth, but I need to keep this to myself.* "How was football while I was away?"

"We missed you. Practice wasn't the same without you. I saw you kissing Elaine just a while ago. Are you . . ."

"It was just a friendly kiss. Nothing is going on. But Cindy is pretty hot, don't you think?" Greg said.

"That she is. She's Elaine's gofer, though. Elaine may not like having her tied up dating someone," James said.

"I'll take my chance," Greg said, grinning.

Back home after school, Greg let himself fall back on his bed and thought how exhausting it was living like this.

The interrogations at dinner time had stopped since Greg's therapy. His parents were convinced that their boy had been fixed, as they put it.

"How was school?" his mother asked.

"School was okay, Mom. It's good to be back with my friends."

"Were you asked where you were this past month?"

"My friend James asked. I told him I was at a football camp. Oh, there's this girl . . . her name is Cindy, she's kind of cute. I've never noticed her before. I might ask her out," Greg said, taking a bite.

"I'm happy to hear this, son," his father said, smiling and looking at his wife. "You should bring her around sometime."

"Wait until I ask her out, Dad," Greg said, laughing. "I'm not sure she'll go out with me."

"She'd be a fool not to, sweetie," his mother said.

"Thanks for dinner, Mom. It was delicious," Greg said. "I'm going to do my homework and study."

"Greg," his father said, "your mother and I had a discussion earlier, and we decided to let you keep your phone from now on."

"Thank you."

"Therapy did him right. He's never thanked me for a meal before," Teresa said with a chuckle.

Alright, don't lay it on too thick. They're going to get suspicious. He closed the door to his room. Greg grabbed his cell from his jeans front pocket and texted Tyler. *Hey, babe, sorry for ignoring you today. I hope you can hang in there through this. I know it must be difficult for you to see me acting like this, it's difficult for me too. I love you, and soon we'll be together again, I promise.*

After texting Tyler, Greg sent a message to Cindy. *Hi Cindy, how are you? I was wondering if you would like to go out with me sometime. Maybe we could go for coffee or a walk after school one day.*

On the way to school the following morning, Cindy walked up behind Greg and surprised him.

"Hey, Cindy. I didn't hear you coming," Greg said.

"It would be hard with your earbuds in your ear," Cindy said. Greg laughed. "To answer your question, yes, I would like to go out with you if you still want to."

"Wow, that's wonderful. Of course I still want to. Did you want to grab a coffee after school?" Greg asked.

"Yes, and perhaps we can take a walk after," Cindy said.

"Cool," Greg said. "Walk with me to school. I'm sure we'll get the whole school talking."

Cindy met Greg at the only coffee shop in Cardston shortly

after four. Greg had already bought coffee for Cindy and was waiting for her outside.

"Do you want to take a walk down to Redford Park? We could chat and get to know each other," Greg said.

"Sounds good," Cindy said. "So I hear you went to a religious camp?" Cindy seemed surprised; she didn't think Greg was the type to go to that sort of thing.

"I did. My parents are Catholic, and they thought it would be good for me." Greg looked at Cindy, and tried to pretend this is where he went behind a fake smile. "Is your family in Cardston?" he asked.

"Yes. We grew up here. My family are Mormons." Cindy was expecting that sort of sneer she usually got when she told this to a guy, which she didn't get from Greg. "I was told that we come from a long line of Mormon ancestors here," Cindy continued.

"Is that so? I'm impressed. Most people I know either moved here or live close by. How is being a Mormon?" Greg asked, eager to learn the difference in beliefs.

"Normal. I mean, it's all I've known, really. I was born in the church, like many generations of my ancestors, it's kind of what it is. The religion forbids having sexual relations before marriage, no drugs, no drinking, and no studying on Sundays. Kissing is allowed, though," Cindy said, almost squinting and waiting for the lame excuse she always got after saying that from guys who saw their chances of having sex vanish.

"Do you find it strict?" Greg asked, unshaken by what she just said.

"No. I was raised this way. Guys find it hard, though," Cindy said, chuckling. "My older brother is away at university, I'm sure those rules went out the window."

"Here we are," Greg said. "Let's sit by the baseball field. As Catholics, we have similar restrictions, but a lot of people our age doesn't abide by them. Even though I like sex, I always respect the person I'm with. I was surprised but pleased when you said yes to going out with me because I thought you probably had a boyfriend." Greg was relieved that he wouldn't have to find clever ways or excuses not to go to bed with her.

"To tell you the truth, you're the first guy that hasn't run away from me so far. They usually disappear after I say that I'm forbidden to have sex before marriage. I guess for most guys, that's all they're looking for in a relationship," Cindy said.

"Well, I'm not most guys and like I said, I always respect the person I'm with. I think we should get back. I have studying to do, I'm sure you do as well. I'll see you at school tomorrow." Greg gave her a peck on the cheek before they went their separate ways.

CHAPTER FORTY-THREE: HONESTY

The news of Cindy and Greg exploded like a skyrocket. One pair of lips, that were doing more than just talking about it, belonged to Elaine. She grabbed Cindy by the arm and dragged her outside to the back of the school.

"What the fuck do you think you're doing?" Elaine said, looking directly at Cindy, her eyes as dark as a lump of coal. "Who told you you could date him?"

"And who do you think you are telling me who I can and can't date? I don't need your permission, or anyone else's," Cindy said as she attempted to leave.

"Get back here." Elaine pulled her back against the wall. "No, you can't date just anyone you like." Then Elaine's tone softened. "Come to think of it, maybe it's not a bad idea after all. Yes, go out with him. I want you to have sex with him, I'm sure you remember how."

"Fuck you, Elaine Thompson," Cindy said, insulted.

Elaine pulled her cell out and shook it at Cindy. "Remember what I have," Elaine said.

Cindy's face hardened. "I'm a Mormon, you know I'm not allowed to."

"This didn't seem to stop you with Mark," Elaine said pompously.

"I was lied to, you know that. I don't understand why you want me to sleep with Greg."

"Did you read the rumours on social media?" Elaine asked.

"I don't have a social media account," Cindy said.

"What? Are you for real? Who isn't on social media? Old

folks, maybe." Elaine said mockingly.

"My parents don't want us to be on social media. No one in my family is."

"What are you guys, Neanderthals? We're in the twenty-first century, get a life. Greg is gay," Elaine told her with a grin on her face.

"No, he isn't. He just came back from a religious camp. Didn't you get the news? Isn't everything on social media?" Cindy replied sarcastically.

"No, *you* didn't get the news. Greg spent four weeks in conversion therapy because he's gay. He and Tyler are lovers," Elaine said, chuckling. "Your new boyfriend prefers having a cock in his mouth than your pussy."

"*Shut up.* You're lying," Cindy said, tearing up. "Greg's not like that, he would have told me. He's nice to me, not like the other guys."

"Then find out for yourself. That's why I want you to sleep with him," Elaine said defiantly.

"I will do no such thing. Now leave me alone," Cindy said, running away from Elaine.

That bitch. She will if I blackmail her with the photos.

Cindy came running down the hall and bumped into Greg. "Hey, hey, hey, slow down," Greg said, stopping her. "What's wrong?"

"Nothing," Cindy said, taking a deep breath.

"It doesn't look like nothing to me," Greg said. "Talk to me, maybe I can help."

"Meet me after class, same place as yesterday," Cindy said and left, still upset.

During the afternoon break, Greg got a text from Tyler telling Greg not to worry about him but hurry up, because being away from him was getting harder every day. The final bell rang to signal the end of the day. His backpack ready to go, Greg ran out of school and cut through main street downtown, this was the fastest way to get to the park, and ten minutes later he was at Redford Park. He saw Cindy sitting in the same spot as the day before.

"Hi, Cindy," Greg said catching his breath. "Have you been waiting long?" Cindy looked sad.

"No," Cindy said as she got up and turned to face Greg.

"What happened today? You look upset."

"Can I ask you a question?"

"Of course," Greg said, not sure what to make out of her sudden stern look.

"Your religious camp. Why did you go there, exactly?" Cindy asked, staring at Greg.

"I needed to be alone for a while. Why do you ask?" Greg was unsure what she was getting at.

"Elaine told me that you went there to become heterosexual," Cindy said, her arms crossed.

Greg's face started to get flushed. "She's not wrong," he said. "My parents sent me there to get fixed, as they say."

"Did you get fixed?" Cindy said, laughing.

"Honestly, no." Cindy's jaw dropped. "Before you say anything, let me explain. I don't know what Elaine told you, but I have the best intentions . . . you have to believe me," Greg said, imploring.

"Elaine told me you were gay, and you're only going out with me because you pity me," Cindy said, feeling hurt.

"No. I don't pity you. On the contrary, I like you and admire you," Greg said proudly. "After I went home last night, I was going to text you to tell you that we shouldn't go out together. Not because of what you told me yesterday, but because I didn't want to lead you on and hurt you. I need to pretend that I'm not gay anymore to please my parents and get my father off my back. Also, I want to find out who sold me and Tyler out, and I have a suspicion that it might be Elaine."

"What do I have to do in all this?" Cindy asked curiously.

"When I saw you the other day standing beside Elaine, I saw someone who would understand how it is to be different," Greg said shyly. "I know Elaine uses you for her homework and assignments. Why you do it, I don't understand."

"I went to an ex-boyfriend's house for dinner, and Elaine took pictures of us having sex."

Greg's face dropped. He wasn't sure he understood correctly. He was about to ask something, when Cindy continued, "Elaine threatened to post them on social media and tell my parents unless I helped her get better marks. Her father threatened to cut her off financially, and you know how money-obsessed she is."

"I'm sorry this happened," Greg said sympathetically. "If your religion prevents you from pre-marital sex, why did you do it?"

"My ex told me he loved me, and if I loved him, I would have sex with him. I did, and the next day he dumped me," Cindy said shamefully.

"Wow," Greg said, not believing someone had no indignity from doing this. "I could never do that to someone."

"You still haven't told me why you wanted to go out with me, or what you want from me?" Cindy said, returning to sit beside Greg.

"No, you're right, but I can't ask this of you. It wouldn't be fair." Greg said, abashed.

"Ask anyway." Cindy grabbed his arm.

"As I said earlier, I need someone to be my girlfriend . . . fake girlfriend. They should be close enough to Elaine to find out if she was the one who told my father . . ."

"Tell your father what?" Cindy asked, perplexed.

"Someone told my father, that Tyler and I were at the

trailer having sex. This is why he sent me to conversion therapy," Greg said

"I wouldn't put it past her, if she's the one behind this," Cindy said, trying to contain her anger.

"Knowing Elaine, she can't keep her mouth shut for very long without bragging about her prowess. I'm hoping she might let it slip one day. But it wouldn't be fair of me to ask that of you. You deserve a real boyfriend," Greg said, squeezing her hand.

"I'll be your fake girlfriend," Cindy said. "If I have to do one more assignment for that bitch . . ."

"Are you sure?" Greg asked. "I don't want to put you in an awkward situation."

"You won't. Elaine tried to order me to sleep with you, and I told her it would never happen. We'll see how she reacts tomorrow when I kiss you."

"Thank you, Cindy, for helping me out," Greg said, grinning with joy.

"No, you're liberating me from her grip. Let's give her some of her own medicine. Thanks for being honest with me. I'll see you tomorrow at school." As Cindy was leaving, she stopped and asked, "Are you still with Tyler?"

"I am. He's aware of what I'm doing. We don't see each other these days because I'm supposed to be straight."

"Tell him not to be offended by our kiss tomorrow," Cindy said as she left.

"I will. See you tomorrow."

What a terrific person. She deserves to find someone who will love her with all of their heart.

CHAPTER FORTY-FOUR: GOT YOU

Startled by the chiming of his cellphone, Greg kicked the blanket off his bed and sat up, breathing heavily. He looked at his cell, seeing it was six-thirty already. He had set the alarm the night before because he knew his parents would still be sleeping at that time. Half-asleep, he texted Tyler that he would be leaving for the trailer in ten minutes. Tyler wrote back that he was on his way.

Greg jumped into a pair of jeans, put on his T-shirt and his favourite blue hoodie, then tiptoed to the front door and grabbed his sneakers on his way out. Then, on the porch, he slipped into his runners and ran to the trailer.

At seven sharp, Greg gave two quick knocks on the trailer door, followed by another a few seconds later, to signal Tyler that it was him. Greg barely had a foot in the door before Tyler grabbed him and pulled him close, and they locked into a passionate kiss.

"It's so good to see you," Tyler said.

"I missed you," Greg said. "It's hard seeing you at school and not being able to take you in my arms. How's life at home?"

"Okay. Things are cool between my folks and me. They don't accept that I'm gay, but they also know that I won't do therapy. I spend most of my evenings in my room, either on the computer or studying. At least I'll get good marks," Tyler said, laughing. "How are you holding up?"

"I'm happy I no longer have to deal with the therapist. As for my parents, well, they believe I am 'fixed.' I feel as though they are in denial, though. Do you know Cindy Roberts at school? She is always with Elaine." Tyler nodded. "I asked her if she would be my fake girlfriend."

"You did what?" Tyler asked, his voice growing bubbly.

"I suspect the one who told on us might be Elaine. Cindy is aware of my therapy and what it was for, and she knows I'm still gay. She agreed to help me out because it appears that Elaine is blackmailing her with compromising pictures she took of her."

"What's your plan?"

"That, I need to figure out. For now, I'm hoping Elaine will brag about her exploits in getting us caught. Cindy told me that Elaine told her to sleep with me. This tells me that Elaine is up to something. Cindy's hoping that Elaine will get all riled up when she kisses me today."

"I'll try not to be around when she kisses you then. I might get jealous," Tyler said, smiling.

"What time is it?" Greg asked. He looked at his watch — twenty after seven.

"We have time for a quickie," Tyler said.

The rushed to the bedroom and almost tore their clothes off, then they fell in bed and embraced, their lips locked in a passionate kiss, their bodies grinding against each other and the feeling of being one entity with their hearts beating in unison and moving as one. Then as their love heated up, their breath became faster, their moans announcing the inevitable and, with a cry of joy, sending their bodies into ecstasy.

And as they were putting their clothes back on, Greg said, "You know I love you, Cindy is just a pretend girlfriend. I can't wait for us to be together again."

Greg took Tyler's hands and pulled him gently towards him. Wrapping his arms around Tyler, he raised one hand and cupped Tyler's head, and he pressed his lips to Tyler's, and they kissed passionately. Tyler left first, followed by Greg ten minutes later.

Shortly after lunch, Greg was standing in front of his locker, sorting out his books for his next class, when Elaine dropped by.

"Greg, I thought about what you told me last time regarding you and I going on a date, and . . ."

As Elaine was about to say something, Cindy waltzed by and draped her arms around Greg's shoulders. She gave him an intense French kiss, causing Elaine to slam the door of Greg's locker and exclaim, "How . . . fucking . . . sick," before storming away.

Later that afternoon, Elaine went to Cindy's desk in class, leaned onto her desk and said, "You and I need to have a little chat. Meet me at the coffee shop after school, and don't be late."

Elaine couldn't wait for the day to be over. *I don't know what Greg sees in Cindy? I hope she did what I asked her to.*

"There she is, Miss Prim and Proper," Elaine said when Cindy came into the coffee shop.

"Hi, Elaine, nice to see you too," Cindy said with a smirk on her face. "What did you want to chat to me about?" Cindy sat, elbows on the table, and leaned towards Elaine.

"So I'm curious to find out if you did what I asked you," Elaine said, leaning forward as well and looking at Cindy inches from her face.

"What business is it of yours?"

"You're right, it's not my business, but you don't know him like I do. He's using you to prove something," Elaine said as she pulled out a mirror from her bag and checked herself in it.

"What are you talking about, Elaine? He's not using me," Cindy said, on the defense.

"Did you tell him as a Mormon you cannot have sex before marriage?" Elaine asked. *I hope that bitch told him.*

"It came up in one of our conversations. Greg told me that he would respect that," Cindy said with pride.

"Really. You believed him like you believed your last boyfriend. Ha! That's a joke," Elaine said, laughing.

"I do believe him. He's not like the other guys, or the guys you go out with anyway," Cindy replied sarcastically.

"Then let me tell you about your new boyfriend. He must be thrilled that you won't bug him to have sex. You know why? Because, like I already told you, he's gay," Elaine said.

"How do you know this?"

"I saw him and Tyler kissing behind the school a few months ago. So I followed Greg one evening and heard him and Tyler having sex at Lee Creek Campground," Elaine blurted out.

"I don't believe you. You're making that up just to get me to drop him," Cindy said, wanting to get her to tell her more.

"No, I'm not. You can ask Greg's father." There is it, Cindy thought. *Let's see if she has more to say.*

"Greg's father? What would he know about this?"

"I casually hinted where they met at night and how he must be proud of his gay son when I went to his store one day."

"You did what? That's insane. Why would you do such a thing?" Cindy said, looking shocked and surprised.

"Because he told my ex-boyfriend that I had been unfaithful. So he fucked up my sex life," Elaine said, frustrated. "Now listen to me—if you choose to continue to see Greg, your father will hear of your romp with Mark. Am I making myself clear this time?"

With that, Elaine got up and walked out.

Chapter Forty-five: Our Favourite Park

The sun was piercing through the bedroom curtains as Neil slowly woke up, stretching. He leaned over and kissed Trevor good morning and then got up and went to prepare coffee. The coffee was brewing when Trevor walked into the kitchen and looked at the clock.

"It's nine!" Trevor exclaimed. "I'm going to be late for work."

"It's Saturday, honey," Neil said.

"Oh, thank God. I can go back to bed then."

"No, you're not." Neil wrapped his arms around Trevor and kissed him. "Look at this beautiful day, why don't we go to the park later on?"

"Humm, can I wake up first?" Trevor said, smiling.

"I thought more after lunch, not now."

After breakfast, Neil picked up his book, got comfortable in the recliner chair, and started reading. After a few minutes into his book, he placed his book on his lap and peeked out the patio door watching the sun shine on the balcony steel ramp. Antsy to enjoy this radiant sun, he put the book back on the table, went to the kitchen, wrapped his arms around Trevor, who was washing the dishes, and said, "How about if we go to the park before lunch? We could stop at the canteen for lunch?" He leant in and placed a kiss on Trevor's neck. "What do you say?"

"Sure, why not. You've been eager to get outside since you

215

got up this morning."

"Thanks, babe. We sit in an office all week, it will do us good to get some fresh air."

Mallard Point Park was a twenty-minute walk from their place. The air was warm for March; the beams of sunlight were glowing on their skin, and their favourite pathway was up ahead. This pathway was nothing more than dirt littered with random rocks along the Bow River, with lavender along the path. It was the fragrance of the lavender that made this pathway a favourite of theirs.

There weren't too many walkers out that morning. Since they were alone, Neil took Trevor's hand and strode along to the sound of birds chirping and the river weaving its way downstream. A few minutes later, they crossed paths with a couple of guys jogging towards the main lodge. Behind the joggers were three guys in their mid-twenties, laughing and joking around until they saw Neil and Trevor.

Suddenly they stopped and asked Neil and Trevor where the lodge was. Trevor pointed in the direction they were heading and said, "It's about fifteen minutes from here."

Then one of the guys, the most muscular of the three, asked, "Are you guys queer?" as he looked back at his two friends and giggled.

"Why do you ask?" Neil said.

"You guys are holding hands, and it looks queer to me."

"Does that bother you?" Neil asked.

"As a matter of fact, it does," the guy said.

"I see," Trevor said. "Well, we'll be on our way. You guys have a nice day."

Neil and Trevor started walking away, and the same guy yelled, "Goddamn it, let go of your hands, it creeps me out."

"Then stop looking," Neil said, looking towards them. "Leave us alone."

Neil and Trevor continued their walk but sensed they were

being followed. Trevor looked back, and the three guys were walking behind them with stern looks on their faces, picking up their pace. Neil and Trevor sped up, fearing a confrontation, then Neil felt a sharp pain in the middle of his back.

"Ouch," he cried as he tried to catch his breath."

Trevor looked back and saw a stone fall to the ground. In a fit of anger, he looked at the guys and yelled, "Hey, you fucking assholes. You guys crazy or what? *Get the fuck out of here.*"

The three thugs wouldn't hear of it and ran towards Neil and Trevor. Trevor grabbed Neil by the arm and pulled him to get out of there, but the guys were too quick. One of them gripped Neil, and another pushed Trevor to the ground. With one swift kick in the legs, Neil tumbled down and the guy began kicking Neil in the gut. Neil curled into a ball, holding his stomach, crying out. Trevor saw him getting kicked and tried to come to his rescue, but someone punched Trevor across the face, and he fell flat on the ground.

Trevor tried to get up to fight back but got kicked back to the ground, then one of the guys started kicking him in the face and stomach. Neil, in agony, looked at his aggressor and, in a fit of rage, kicked him in the groin, sending him crouching in pain and giving Neil a chance to get up. "You fucking shit," Neil yelled and kicked his aggressor in the face; then one of the guys beating Trevor saw this and seized him by the arm and swung him to the ground, breaking his arm upon landing.

Neil, wailing in pain, tried to crawl towards Trevor but was dragged away by a thug. At that point, the two joggers that Neil and Trevor crossed earlier shouted at the three bullies, and one of them took out his cell and called 911 while the other ran to help Neil and Trevor.

One jogger removed his backpack and placed it under Trevor's head. Then he went to Neil and asked if he had anything broken. Neil gestured at his arm.

"The guys ran away," the jogger said.

"How is Trevor?" Neil asked, barely able to speak.

"He's pretty beaten up. Don't worry, the police are on their way with the paramedics."

The police arrived, followed by the ambulance. The officer got the story from the joggers.

"Can you describe them?"

"One of them had blond hair, the other two dark brown — the blond-haired one, his right arm was covered in tattoos. The beefy one had a black hoodie with a skull printed on its back, and the other one a red and black checkered shirt."

"Thank you." Then the officer walked over to Neil lying on the stretcher and asked, "Are you able to talk, sir?"

"A little," Neil said.

"Can you tell me what happened? Take your time."

The officer asked Neil if he could remember them if he saw them. Neil nodded yes, his eyes tearing up. They left for the hospital. As soon as they got into the emergency, they took Trevor to the examination room. His eye was bleeding, and he kept asking if he would be able to see again. The doctor said he couldn't tell because it was so swollen, but they bandaged his eye, cleaned his wounds, and told him his nose was broken.

Neil's arm was placed in a cast, and his wounds were cleaned and dressed. The doctor took Neil aside and told him that his biggest worry was the state of Trevor's internal organs. "Your friend has been pretty damaged from the fierce kicks that he got. We are trying to prevent any internal bleeding. I'm afraid he won't be going home for a little while."

"Will he be alright?" Neil asked.

"He should be."

Trevor was in the hospital for eighteen days, and then his breathing started changing. Neil prayed so much for Trevor to get better, but as the days went on, Trevor struggled more and more with his breathing from the trauma. Then a month later, Trevor took his last breath and died holding Neil's hand. Neil screamed, "Nooooooooooo." He bent over Trevor's body, holding on to him, crying hysterically. "Don't leave me. I need you."

Neil walked out of Trevor's room thirty minutes later, dragged himself to his car and just sat there. Then his tears turned to anger. His eyes darkened and he began screaming, "You fucking murderers, you killed the love of my life. I hope the cops catches you and you rot in hell."

Two months after Trevor's death, Neil was still devastated. He'd just finished burying his parents, and now he'd lost the love of his life. *I have to change something in my life, I can't go on this way.*

Neil grabbed a light jacket and his sunglasses to hide his puffy and red eyes, then he walked to the park nearby. Sitting, he thought about his life, his parents and the hurt he inflicted to them because he was different and wondered if he'd have a better life if he was straight. He remembered his parents telling him about this centre where he could get help. He went back to the apartment and picked up the phone and called his mother's best friend, Suzanne.

"Suzanne, it's Neil."

"Neil, how are you? Suzanne asked.

"I'm okay. Do you remember the centre, my mom wanted me to go to? Neil asked, his voice sounded like it was made of gravel.

"Why do you want to know this?" Suzanne asked, concerned about his state of mind as she heard him speak.

"Maybe if I talk to this guy, he can help me with what I'm going through," Neil said, his clear tone was undercut with a choking heaviness.

"But, Neil, I don't think they are in that type of business.

They treat homosexuality there. You probably need to see a psychologist or some sort of counsellor, to help you though your grief," Suzanne said.

"They are Christian aren't they?" Neil said sharply.

"Yes they are. The centre is called Hope and Faith Wellness and Grant Manley is the director. Listen before you make a harsh decision, why don't you call your cousin Carl. A friend of his, Greg Fallon, was sent there by his parents, he can probably tell you more about them," Suzanne said, hoping that Carl could convince him not to go.

Neil hung up. He went to his computer and googled the centre to find where it was located.

Neil had just returned from his doctor's appointment, when his phone rang. He hesitated to answer it, he didn't want to talk to anybody, then he thought it could be the center calling as he had left them a message yesterday.

"Hello," Neil answered.

"Neil! It's your cousin Carl."

"Carl? Is everything okay?" Neil said, waiting to hear something else had happened.

"Yeah, yeah. Just thought I'd find out how you're coping with everything that happened," Carl said reassuringly.

"Oh, that's thoughtful of you," Neil said softly.

"I hear through my mom's friend that you're looking at going to the Hope and Faith Wellness Centre," Carl said.

"You talked to Suzanne?" Neil asked. "She had no business telling you this."

"Listen, cousin, Suzanne is worried and rightly so. My friend Greg was sent there and he came back more traumatized than he went in. This is a bad place, man, Greg told us what they do to cure people and it's basically torture," Carl told him.

"Maybe your friend didn't follow the rules. Besides if I

choose to go, it's my business," Neil said, irritated.

"Neil, do you think you can change who you are? I know you blame yourself for what happened to your folks and to Trevor. It's not your fault, man. Whether you had been straight or gay, it wouldn't have changed nothing. You're going through a tough time now, give yourself time to heal and if you feel the same way in six months to a year from now, then go and get converted then. But for God's sake, man, pull yourself together. Come and spend some time with me in Cardston, we'll hang out. Think about it," Carl said, trying to get him to come to his senses.

"I'll think about it," Neil said. "Listen I have to go. Thanks for calling."

The following day, Neil drove to his work to drop off his leave of absence form that he got from his doctor two days ago. Before he left that morning, Neil had packed a small suitcase which was in the trunk. He returned to his car and drove off towards the Wellness Centre.

After parking his car in front of the main entrance, Neil entered the centre and asked to speak to Mr. Grant Manley. The receptionist informed Mr. Manley someone was here to see him. Soon after, he came out to meet Neil.

"Hello, I'm Grant Manley. How can I help you?"

"I'm here to enter your program. I've lost my father and mother because of my sin and I want to be cured," Neil said, his eyes watering up.

"Come in," Grant said, leading him to his office. "What's your name?"

"Neil Fallon."

Grant felt like he knew that name, so he looked it up in his computer, "Ha!" he said. "Are your parents Beatrice and Roger Fallon?"

"Yes they were."

"Where?"

"Both of them passed away recently," Neil said.

"I'm sorry to hear this. You said outside you wanted to join because you believe your sin killed your parents? Why do you think that?"

"My father had a heart attack when I moved in with my boyfriend, then my mother died of cancer shortly after. Then my boyfriend got beaten to death by thugs and died as well. If I was a heterosexual, none of this would have happened. All these maledictions are my fault and I want to be cured so no one else dies," Neil said, wiping his tears.

"I understand your grief. Let me tell you, your parents didn't die because of your homosexuality. They were concern about your life and living as a sinner, but God didn't take them away to punish you, he's not like that," Grant said. "He took them away so they wouldn't suffer. Your father had a bad heart and you mother had cancer, two horrible diseases. Unfortunately, for the man you were living with, if he had been living a life as God intended, he would probably be alive today. Were you with him when he was beaten?" he asked.

"We were walking in a park and three young adults attacked us. I tried to go to his rescue but I was held down and made to watch the whole thing. He didn't deserve to die, not like this. I'm the one who should have died," Neil said, raising his voice.

"Mr. Fallon, if you're serious about getting help, we can provide that help for you. Today, tomorrow or whenever you're ready. But seeing the state you're in, I recommend you start today."

"That's what I'm here for," Neil replied.

"Well, then." Grant reached in the top drawer of his desk and pulling out a sheet of paper. "If you could sign at the bottom,"

Neil signed. "Great, let me show you your room. I'll let you rest today and we'll start fresh tomorrow."

The next morning, Neil went to his first session. "The sins you may have committed" was Neil's first lecture. Sitting with twenty other guys in a classroom, chairs in a circle with the counsellor sitting in the centre, they were all presented with a check list of sins they may have committed and would need to repent of.

Homosexuality was on top of the list. Each of the participants had to stand up and voice that they were gay.

"You may all sit down. God didn't make you gay. This is what this modern world preaches because in today's society, sinning is the way of life. It is an abomination. Homosexuality is the work of demons and is likely the result of an early life experience. Put up your hand if any of you experimented with touching another guy's privates when you were young?" All of the hands went up. "There you have it. This is where your hormones got confused. The one thing that will correct this is prayers. Prayers will make you straight again, as God has made you."

The following day, Neil walked into a small auditorium with the conviction that he loved God, therefore he could be cured. Waiting for Neil and the others was a pastor who specialized in gay conversion. Standing in line on the stage, the pastor proceeded to the laying on of hands and intensive prayer, the casting out of demons, and each was being forced to describe their homosexual experiences and to repent publicly.

Then Neil was prayed for. Two adults stood in front of him, shouting and pushing down on his head, forcing him to his knees. The pastor had piercing eyes which would scare off the meanest person. The prayers went on and on, and would only stop until a change has been felt.

Two weeks later, Neil went into total denial about his

sexuality and embraced the idea he was cured. He returned to Calgary. Shortly thereafter his mental health bombed and he started to self-harm. Everywhere he looked in the apartment, he saw Trevor. Eating very little and just sitting around trying to find the will to go on, Neil went into a state of deep depression. He became sleep deprived. As time went by, Neil's heart still ached for Trevor. He still yearned to hold him, to make love to him, to kiss him. That's when he knew he wasn't cured, perhaps he didn't want to be.

The nightmares of that dreadful day in the park, came back. He would wake up drenched from dreaming of Trevor being savagely beaten up and not being able to help him.

Neil sank deeper in his depression, his guilt and loneliness darkening his world. In an effort to relieve that pain, he reached for the pills in the medicine cabinet, ingested the entire contents of the bottle, and went to bed.

A week later, Neil's work tried desperately to contact him to no avail. Neil's boss, worried, called the police. The building manager unlocked the door, and the police entered the apartment and found Neil dead in his bed, clutching a photo of Trevor.

Chapter Forty-six: Cougars against Beavers

The spring weather was perfect. It hadn't rained in a few days, which meant that the field would be dry. The buses to take the school's football team and their supporters to Magrath for the two schools' annual match was ready to depart.

Cindy and Matilda sat near the end of the bus owing to Cindy's motion sickness; being close to a washroom was a must.

Tyler boarded the second bus; he wanted to be there for Greg and his team but didn't want to draw attention to himself by going to the game because of their hidden relationship, so he tried to stay in the background. When they pulled up to Magrath Sports Field, Tyler walked out of the bus, and his eyes met Greg's. Tyler stood there for an instant, smiled at him, and went towards the bleachers to find a seat.

Cindy and Matilda decided to sit high enough to get a good view of the game without having to crane their necks. As the field was filling up, a young man hurried in front of Matilda and sat beside her. When he reached for his cell, he accidentally hit Matilda's arm. "Sorry," he said, turning towards Matilda. "Hey, I know you, how are you? I haven't seen you in a while."

"Scott, hi! We moved to Cardston last summer, that's why you haven't seen me."

"So you came to cheer for which team?" Scott asked, laughing.

"Whichever one wins," Matilda said, chuckling. "Any of the old gang still around?"

"Most, yeah. They're not football fans, as you know. Come to think of it, you weren't either in those days. Have you developed a liking for it?"

"No. I came with my friend Cindy here and to support the school team. How is Tim? Still the lady's man?"

"Well, Tim has calmed down a bit since he almost became a father," Scott said with a grin. "He got a girl pregnant in April last year, and that scared the shit out of him. Thank God she got an abortion last summer."

"Anyone I know?"

"I don't think so. Scott told me she was from out of town. She came down to visit a friend, and the four of them went out dancing, and apparently someone smuggled in a flask, so they spiked their sodas all night and got drunk. Her name was . . . Elaine, I think."

"Are you sure? There is an Elaine Thompson at our school, could that be her?"

"Oh, yeah, I remember the name. Maybe it's coincidence. I remember Tim describing her as a spoiled brat who liked to brag about her life."

"That sounds like the Elaine we know," Matilda said. "Wouldn't you agree, Cindy?"

"It does. I don't think the good Lord would have inflicted two of them on the world," Cindy said.

Cindy looked around; the seats around the field were filling up with both schools' students and parents. The teams entered the field at precisely two o'clock and took their position. After the toss, the referee blew the whistle, and the game started. The Cougars played very well from the beginning, and Greg was the star player as ever, leading his team to victory. The players went off the field chanting, "B-E-A-T beat 'em! B-U-S-T bust 'em! Beat 'em, bust 'em, that's our custom!

Gooooo Cougars!"

The school cafeteria was prepared to receive the crew upon their arrival home. Parents had prepared sandwiches while the school provided drinks and dessert, and the maintenance guys hung up the *Congratulations Cougars* banner at the entrance.

Midway through the celebrations, Cindy whispered something into Greg's ear, and both of them disappeared. Sitting on the stairs, Cindy said, "Did you know that our dear friend had an abortion last summer?"

"Where did you hear that?" Greg said

"A friend of Matilda told us at the game today. She spent a weekend with her friend in Magrath, and her friend introduced her to this guy. Apparently, after a night of dancing and drinking, our dear friend and this guy ended up together, and the rest is history."

"That sucks. I wonder what her parents thought when she told them she was pregnant."

"Knowing Elaine, she probably never told them."

"You can't hide a pregnancy, it would show at some point."

"Not if you got an abortion."

"No shit. Are you sure about this?"

"That's what Scott told us. What if we put her on the spot?"

"It would be cruel, though," Greg said.

"No crueller than telling your father about Tyler and you, or threatening to tell my dad about what I did," Cindy said sharply.

"Yeah, you're right. Let me think about it. Let's get back in, otherwise, they'll come looking for us."

Chapter Forty-Seven: Who's Life is It?

As she was walking home from the football gathering, Cindy thought about how she and Greg might enact their revenge on Elaine.

The house rules in the Roberts' home were clear. Anyone who needed a laptop for schoolwork would be given one; anyone who used their laptop for social media would be punished severely. Flipping her laptop cover up, Cindy couldn't resist creating a secret account to follow developments. Her hands sweaty, her breathing fast from both excitement and fear, she briefly flipped down the laptop screen. She got up and paced around her room, finally stopping in front of her laptop and giving in to temptation.

Cindy started to read some of the posts on there and was shocked. She then searched for Elaine, but couldn't find her. Then she found the post of Greg and Tyler kissing, clicked on it and saw DontFckWM had posted it. *Oh, this is Elaine for sure. This is her famous saying.*

Cindy looked for other posts she might have written and concluded Elaine was evil. *How could she write things like this? I don't think I could be this mean to people, no matter how badly they hurt me.* She closed her laptop and went to bed.

On Monday morning Elaine was standing by the school entrance, looking at her watch and waiting for Cindy and Matilda to show up. "Finally," Elaine said, seeing Cindy coming up the sidewalk. "Where were you all weekend? I've sent countless emails and texts to Matilda, since you don't have a social account."

"Good morning to you too, Elaine," Cindy said. "Matilda and I went to watch the football game in Magrath this weekend. What was so urgent? You're up to date with your assignments, and we had no homework to do."

"I needed a ride to my date yesterday. Because you guys weren't around, I had to ask my father to drive me. Do you know how embarrassing that was?" Elaine furiously said.

"Your emergency was you needed a ride? You expected us to drop everything to drive you to your date? Who do you think you are?"

"The one who knows your secret, and that can make your life a living hell. Besides, you are my bitches, aren't you?" Elaine said.

"I'm beginning to wonder who the biggest bitch out of us is. Have a nice day, Elaine," Cindy said, entering the school.

"Don't you walk away from me, Cindy Roberts," Elaine yelled. "Get back here."

Mid-afternoon, Cindy took Matilda aside and told her what Elaine said. Matilda became livid and wanted to strangle her, but Cindy said it would only fuel her vicious tongue.

"I created a profile on social media on the weekend," Cindy said. "Are you on it?"

"I am. I thought your parents didn't want you to be on there."

"They don't. I was curious to see what the big deal about social media was and what was going on there. So I created an account and logged on. Wow," Cindy exclaimed, "I thought Mormon women were gossipers, holy crap, they post everything on there. I was shocked. I started looking for Elaine but I couldn't find her. You think she might be using another name?" Cindy asked, unsure if that was possible.

"Oh, without a doubt. If someone doesn't want anyone to know who you are, you post under a pseudonym."

"Really. Listen, I'll talk to you later," Cindy said. "If you see Elaine, just smile and leave."

"Very funny," Matilda said. "Bye."

Cindy waited until her parents were in bed before logging on to social media. She looked for Matilda and found her profile. She sent her a friend request, accompanied by a message: *We need to find out which name Elaine uses for her nasty posts. I have an idea, but we need confirmation. Since she likes to gossip, when you see her next, tell her Greg and I are no longer together. You caught us leaving the cafeteria after the football get-together last Saturday, you followed us and heard us fight about Tyler. This should get her curiosity flowing. Keep me posted on here. Don't worry if I don't respond right away, I don't want my father catching me on here.*

Greg broke down and asked Tyler to meet him at the trailer at the usual time. Pretending to be someone else was starting to weigh heavy on Greg, and he needed to get Tyler's perspective on a thought he'd been turning over in his mind. As he arrived at the trailer, a message popped up on his cell. A message from Cindy. *I didn't think Cindy was on social media?* Greg opened the message, and read Cindy's plan for getting back at Elaine.

Greg walked into the trailer, and there was Tyler on his cell, waiting for him. "I was so glad when you asked me to meet you. I'm finding it hard being away from you," Tyler said, rushing to Greg's side.

"Me too." Greg wrapped his arms around Tyler and held him tight against him. "I've been thinking this past week," Greg said, coming out of their embrace. "I don't know how much longer I can go on pretending like this. Last weekend was a killer when I saw you in Magrath. My heart ached, not being able to go to you and kiss you, like this."

"It took all that I got to stay that far away from you. I didn't want to blow your cover," Tyler said.

"I don't want to pretend anymore," Greg said, looking at Tyler. "I want to be with you and see you whenever I want." Then with a shrug and shaking his head, he said, "It doesn't matter if my parents find out. It's my life, it's who I am, and I'm not ashamed of it."

"What will happen if they throw you out or send you back to therapy?" Tyler asked, anxiety eclipsing his thoughts.

"I'm not returning to that prison, and they can't force me to—I'm eighteen. They might throw me out, but if they do, I'll have to find somewhere to go until I leave for university next year."

"There are only a few months left until school is over. Then you'll be gone for a month at summer camp, and when you return from that, it will almost be time to leave for Calgary," Tyler said. "If your father does boot you out, can you ask James if you can live here for a while?"

"It crossed my mind. If his family agrees this place would be perfect," Greg said, looking around. "I would need to find a part-time job to pay for food and stuff, though. I won't do it if you don't think it's a good idea or would put you in an awkward position."

"I'm already out to my parents. Those close to me know, and the others, I don't care if they do or not. As long as you feel comfortable going forward with your idea, I am, and I will be by your side," Tyler replied, pulling Greg closer to him.

Tyler grabbed Greg's head with both hands, and kissed him. "I love you, and I'll always be here with you no matter what happens. Now let's get out of here before someone starts looking for us."

CHAPTER FORTY-EIGHT: STRIKE

What a difference one decision can make in a person's life. Two weeks ago, Greg was melancholic, playing along as a heterosexual man and missing the love of his life. Today, he was out and proud at school and to all of his friends, and at his happiest when Tyler was by his side. Still, Greg remained in the closet at home because he feared his father's reaction.

Matilda returned to school after a week away with a bad cold. Walking towards her locker, she saw Elaine walking down the hall. *I'm not in the mood for her this morning.*

Elaine, sporting a fake smile, stopped and said, "You look terrible. Where have you been?"

"Thanks, Elaine, for your concern."

"Sorry, you don't have to be so defensive. I was just asking because I care."

"That's real nice of you, Elaine. Since when do you care for anyone?" Matilda said sarcastically.

"Have you seen Cindy? I think she's trying to avoid me."

I don't blame her. "Why would she avoid you?"

"That's what it feels like. I think she is spending too much time with Greg if you ask me."

"And who would be asking you?" Matilda said tongue-in-cheek.

"Aren't you being the little bitch this morning?"

"Cindy and Greg have broken up," Matilda said.

"That didn't last long. What happened?" Elaine asked with a smirk.

"Greg told her he preferred boys and Cindy went into a depression. Now she's fed up with boys and is thinking of becoming a Sister Missionary."

Elaine looked at Matilda weirdly. "This is the same as nunhood."

"Where were you in the last couple of days?" Matilda asked with a frown. "Greg and Tyler have become an item again. Everyone at school have seen them together holding hands. I'm surprised you are not up on this, Miss Snoopy. Maybe if you stop looking at yourself in the mirror long enough, you'd find out that the world doesn't revolve around you."

"That's too bad. They made such a nice couple. Poor Cindy, hope she's okay," Elaine said snarkly.

"You're such a hypocrite, Elaine," Matilda replied, wanting to barf.

"Well, I hope you feel better soon, Matilda. I'd love to stick around and chat, but I don't want to catch what you have," Elaine said, twirling her finger at Matilda's nose.

Bitch. She went inside, grabbed her books and headed for her French class.

I warned her about him, and she didn't listen. Perhaps Cindy wanted to screw Greg after all and he refused and told her he was going back to Tyler. That sounds more like it. Elaine was exhilarated.

She ditched all her classes and went back home. Her mother was visiting her sister in Montreal and her father was at work, so she had the whole house to herself. Carl, who lived a few doors down from Elaine, saw her walking into her house and decided to pay a visit.

"You're not in school?" Elaine asked.

"And you?" Carl said.

"I didn't feel well, so I came home. Did you know that Greg and Cindy broke up?" Elaine asked as they were walking up to her room.

"That happened two weeks ago. You're a bit late in the news department, sweetie. Your girls aren't keeping you up to date,"

"Why did they break up?"

"Greg is in love with Tyler. Greg is gay. Come on Elaine don't play dumb. You've seen them around school," Carl said, tired of her games. "If you haven't then, you must have been elsewhere."

"Go home, Carl, and go fuck yourself." Elaine slammed the door behind him. *Fucking idiot.*

Elaine sat at her desk, staring at her social media page, getting ready to spread her venom.

The following morning Cindy opened her social media page and saw, *Hey, did you know that Cindy Roberts wants to be a nun? I'm not surprised, after being dumped again and by a fag on top. Looks like nobody wants you, Cindy. Hopefully they won't dump you as a nun either, LOL.* This was posted by DontfckWM.

Matilda and Cindy were talking at school when Elaine walked in on them and asked, "What are you guys talking about?"

"Didn't you read the post this morning?" Matilda said.

"I haven't turned on my cell yet. What's it about?" Elaine replied.

"Someone posted a comment about Cindy. It said she wanted to be a nun," Matilda said, shaking her head in disbelief.

"Oh, really. Is that true, Cindy?" Elaine asked

"No. I wonder where he or she got that information," Cindy said, looking at Elaine with a frown.

"I know," Matilda replied, pretending to be shocked.

"He or she must have heard about it from someone, I guess," Elaine replied swiftly.

"I don't who might that be. I'm the only one who knew," said Matilda, "and the only other person I told, was you Elaine."

"Are you insinuating that I'm responsible for that post, Matilda?" Elaine looked at her with fire in her eyes. "If you must know, Carl knew about it as well."

"How so? Nobody knew except me," Matilda said with a scowl face.

"Greg told him," Elaine said bluntly.

"Impossible," Cindy said, "why would I tell Greg this?"

"Well maybe somebody else told him," Elaine said, giving them a dirty look.

"Anyway, whoever posted this is a heartless bitch," Cindy said with a stern look.

"You know, I thought exactly the same," Matilda said, looking at Elaine. "Such a person must not have any feelings or heart, for that matter. Wouldn't you say, Elaine?" Maltilda asked with a smile on her face.

"Look at the time," Elaine said curtly. "I have to get to my class. Have a nice day."

"She looked a little bit upset, didn't she?" Cindy said.

"The heartless bitch was priceless," Matilda said.

Elaine slammed the door of her locker. *Heartless bitch, am I? I'll show her what a heartless bitch is.*

Chapter Forty-nine: Turn the Other Cheek

Elaine's post about Cindy did not have the results Elaine expected. Everyone in Cindy's senior class was sympathizing with her for the rude comment posted about her. Standing in front of her locker, Elaine heard, "Obviously, whoever wrote this awful post about you, Cindy, doesn't know you like we do. I hope this person sees what an asshole they've made of themselves."

Elaine quietly unlocked her locker; her face was flushed, and her eyes were practically bulging out of her head. Had she heard one more comment on her post, she would have lost it.

Cindy reached for her bag, locked her locker, and rushed home to her room to see if Elaine had posted anything else. With her laptop, Cindy sat on her bed, legs crossed, looking at her social media page before deciding to go ahead with the post she'd been dreaming up.

Guess which senior girl got knocked up last spring? Must have been quite the weekend away from home. I wonder if Mom and Dad know about this. At least she had the good sense to get an abortion.

"Cindy, dinner is ready," her mother called.

"Be right there." She logged off her laptop and went to dinner. Afterwards, Cindy went back to her room and logged into her social media.

Who the fuck is this? wrote an anonymous user under her

post.

Who wants to know? Cindy replied.

Minutes later, the same user replied, *Where did you get this information?*

It doesn't matter.

It's all lies.

Really. Which part, the pregnancy or abortion?

Both.

If they are lies, why are you worried?

If I ever find out who you are, I'll destroy you.

Not if I destroy you first, Cindy wrote.

When Matilda saw the post she had an idea who posted it. She sent a text to Cindy. *You posted this didn't you? It's a dangerous game you're playing.*

Hey Matilda, yeah, I did. I'd be curious to know how Elaine reacted. No name was mentioned, but I'm certain everybody in school will be curious to find out who it was. It should be fun tomorrow, Cindy wrote back. *Oh, by the way, I'm being careful.*

The following day Cindy was on her way to school when Greg yelled, "Hey, Cindy, wait up. Did you see what was posted on social media? Did you write this?"

"Why do you ask?"

"Because it's a piece of information that only you and Matilda knew about. I doubt that Matilda would post something like this."

"What makes you think I would?" Cindy said as she started walking.

"I'm just asking," Greg said. "Listen, if Elaine finds out you wrote this, she'll rip you apart, and what she holds against you will come out in the open. I wouldn't play this game with her, Cindy."

"All I meant to do was give her a taste of her own medicine," Cindy said. "I purposely didn't mention her name, so people won't know who it is."

"I agree she deserves every bit of it. But you know how she is. She will overturn every stone to find out who wrote it. Let me try to find out from a friend of hers if she took it personally," Greg said, smiling.

Elaine was taken aback when she saw Cindy and Greg walking up to school together. She turned to Carl and whispered, "What are they doing together? I thought they broke up."

Carl whispered back, "They did break up. Greg didn't tell us that they were back together. Maybe they're just friends."

Greg and Cindy walked past Elaine, and Carl smiled at both of them as they entered the school. "Cindy is becoming quite the little bitch," Elaine said to Carl.

"Why do you say this?" Carl asked surprised.

"She's mouthy, she's been ignoring me when I talk to her, and whenever I'm nearby, she and Matilda whispers to each other looking in my direction," Elaine said.

"Aren't you getting a little paranoid, Elaine," Carl said chuckling. "No one can be bitchier than you. That would be a first. Hey, I meant to ask. Did you see what someone posted on social media last night?"

"No. I was out last night. Who posted it?"

"I don't know, it was anonymous. Anyway, it was about a girl at school, a senior, who got pregnant and had an abortion," Carl said.

"What? Do we know who?" Elaine said, playing dumb.

"No. No name was mentioned. At first, I thought they were talking about you because of what you told me."

"You didn't tell anyone, did you?"

"Are you kidding? I know what you're capable of. Besides, what reason would I have to tell your secret?"

"If you get a hint of who wrote this, let me know immediately."

Chapter Fifty: Quick Trip

What I wouldn't give to spend a whole day with Tyler, Greg thought, lying in bed Saturday morning. *Somewhere nobody knows us.* Sliding off his bed, he walked towards his computer and started browsing the events happening around town this weekend. *Bingo.*

"Mom," Greg yelled from his room.

"What?" she yelled back.

He went through to the kitchen and poured himself a coffee. "Can I borrow your car this afternoon?"

"Why?" Teresa asked.

"I'd like to drive down to Magrath and take in the Beavers game."

"What time does the game end?" his mother asked.

"The game is over at four. I know a few guys on the team, and they asked me to stick around after. They want to grab a burger for dinner and then go for a few drinks later."

"Are you going by yourself? Or is Cindy going with you?"

"No, Cindy isn't coming. It's just us guys together."

"Alright. I don't want you to drink and drive, though. Call us if you think you're staying in Magrath overnight."

"Okay, Mom. Thank you."

Greg came back a few minutes later dressed in running pants and his red ball cap. "I'm going for a run," he said, walking out the door. He jogged to the school track, and saw Carl and James were already running when Greg got there. "Hey, guys, when did you get here?"

"This is our first lap. Hey, I meant to ask you—I thought

you and Cindy had broken up?" Carl said.

"We did. Why?" Greg said.

"Elaine and I were wondering when we saw you walking together to school yesterday," Carl said.

"No, dude, we are over. I saw her and decided to walk with her. Did you guys see that post on social media?"

"The one about the girl getting pregnant and having an abortion? Thank God she did. I wouldn't want to be stuck with a kid," James said, laughing.

"That's why condoms exist," Greg said. "Who's the girl, do we know? Poor her, going through an abortion at our age."

"No idea," James said. "How about you, Carl?"

"No. Could be anyone."

"I wonder who the guy was that knocked her up. Anyone at our school, you think?" James asked.

"No one from the team, I don't think. It's not you, is it, Carl?" Greg said jokingly. "You who swear by the pullout method, as you say."

"Hilarious. Maybe it's one of you?" Carl said, huffing.

"Don't think so," Greg said breathily. "I'm gay, remember?"

"And I'm still with the same girl since I broke up with Elaine," James said, breathing heavily.

"Well, that happened last spring. Not long after, you broke up with Elaine, James," Carl said

"What are you saying, Carl? That Elaine was pregnant with my child?" James asked.

"No, I'm not saying that," Carl said hastily.

"Then what are you saying?" Greg asked. "You just said the pregnancy happened sometime after James broke up with Elaine."

"Was I the guy that got her pregnant?" James asked.

"No," Carl said.

"Then who did?" Greg asked.

"Just a minute. This girl on social media is Elaine, isn't it Carl?" James asked.

"No," Carl said.

"I don't believe you," James said. "I know you, we've been friends for a long time, and I know when you're hiding something. Who was the guy that got Elaine pregnant?"

"I don't know. All I know it wasn't you. Can we talk about something else? Are we done running? Then I'm going home. I'll see you guys later," Carl said, walking away.

"Hey, Carl," Greg yelled. "Is the guy that got Elaine pregnant at our school?"

Carl gave James and Greg the finger and ran off.

"I don't blame him for not talking. Elaine would cut his balls off for sure if she found out," James said.

"What do you know," Greg said, "Elaine is the girl in question."

"I'm curious to find out who the guy was, though," James said. "Anyway, pal, I'm off. I'll see you later."

Greg took out his phone and messaged Tyler. *How would you like to go to Magrath with me this afternoon if you can get away? I feel like spending time with you away from Cardston. I told my mother I would be back by eight tonight. Let me know.*

Tyler replied, "I'd love to. What time do we leave? I can meet you near the campground."

"I'll pick you up at two-thirty. I can't wait to see you."

On their way to Magrath, Tyler asked, "How did you manage to get away without raising suspicion?"

"I told my mother I was going to the Beavers game this afternoon and would be going out with the guys after."

"Clever. Are we going?"

Greg shook his head. "No. We are spending this day together, just us and no one else. I was thinking about going to a bar and having a few drinks for starters, then grabbing something to eat and driving back to the trailer and spending the night together."

"I thought you had to be back by eight?"

"My mother doesn't want me to drink and drive and told me to call her if I was spending the night in Magrath."

"Nice."

Nestled to the right off the main road, Burt's Bar was about fifteen minutes from Magrath. It had a large patio at the back for drinks and food in the summer; in colder weather, the patio was open for smokers to indulge in their habit after a few beers.

This was the first time the boys had been to a gay bar. After they parked the car, they looked at each other, took a deep breath, and gathered the courage to walk to the entrance. They looked around for a place to sit, but luckily the place was hardly busy at three-thirty in the afternoon, so there were a few tables available.

"Let's sit towards the back," Greg said. "I don't feel comfortable sitting too close to the front door."

It was a quaint little bar, modestly decorated; the patrons, as the owner would say, were there to have a drink, a good time, and be with other LGBTQ people.

Greg and Tyler were deep in conversation when a blond, blue-eyed, handsome guy came over.

"What can I get you guys?" he said.

"We'll have two beers, please," Greg said.

"You look kind of young to be in here," he said.

"We're both eighteen. Would you like to see our ID?" Greg asked.

"No, that's cool. I believe you. Where are you from?"

"Cardston," Tyler said.

"Are you guys . . ." He pointed and moved his finger from Greg to Tyler.

"Yes, we are," Greg said.

"Cool. You guys make a cute couple. I'll get your drinks."

"This is a cool place," Tyler said as the waiter walked away. "How did you find it?"

"I googled *gay bar* near our town, and this place came up."

"You can't tell from the road this place exists. Nice to be out and not worry about running into someone you know," Tyler said.

"There you are, guys," said the waiter, placing the beers on the table. "Enjoy."

'Thanks," Greg said. "Oh, what's your name?"

"Brad."

"Nice to meet you, Brad. I'm Greg, and this is Tyler."

"First time here?" Brad asked.

"First time at a gay bar," Tyler said.

"You've come to the right place. This place is quiet, low-key, and the people in here are always friendly. If you want anything, just call me over," Brad said.

Sipping his beer, Tyler said, "I'd like to come out dancing here some weekend."

Greg waved at Brad to come over. "Two more already?" Brad asked.

"Actually, we were wondering if there was much going on here on a Friday night?" Greg asked.

"Friday night, the place is packed. The dance floor is where the action is, and you guys would have a ball. The crowd is around your age, and people gather from all over," Brad replied.

"Thanks, Brad," Greg said.

"Are you sure you don't want more beers?"

"No. We have to get back soon, but we'll be back for sure."

Greg and Tyler drove back to Magrath, stopping for a bite to eat before returning to Cardston. They arrived around six o'clock, parked the car behind the trailer so that no one would see it, and snuck into the trailer and locked the door. They knew that if they turned the light on, it would be seen by anyone nearby; instead, they used the torches on their cell-phones as candles.

Lying in bed, Greg asked, "How did you like your day—well, our half-day?"

"It couldn't have been any better, and it's not over yet," Tyler said, cuddling up to Greg. "I don't know how I will cope next year when you're at university. I have one more year before I can join you."

"We'll figure something out."

Tyler turned on his side and gazed into Greg's eyes, "I know I'm only eighteen, and I've only ever been with you, but I know in my heart you're the one I want to spend the rest of my life with."

Greg climbed on Tyler, looked at him, and said, "I just want to be with you too."

Tyler raised his head, pressed his lips against Greg's before scooping him up and pulling his sweater over his head. Kissing his upper body and covering it with kisses as he slid down towards Greg's waist, he reached Greg's pants and took them off. Then Tyler grabbed the waistband of Greg's boxers with his fingers and slid them off slowly, revealing every inch of his hardness. Tyler worked his way up, twirled a finger near his pubic hair and planted a kiss on his penis. Greg's hips rose off the bed, and he bit his lower lip as he closed his eyes. Tyler stood up on the bed and slowly began to lower his jeans and boxers inch by inch to prolong the excitement, finally revealing hard cock and firm ass. His cock had the perfect length and girth, capped by a beautiful head, eagerly waiting for Greg's mouth.

Greg pulled Tyler down, kissed him and flipped him on his back. He grabbed Tyler's cock gently between his fingers, lifted it and opened his mouth to wrap his wet lips around it and proceed to suck. A loud moan escaped Tyler's mouth.

"Haaa! It feels so good."

"You like that, don't you?"

"Like it? Man, if you keep this up, I'll shoot."

"That's the plan," Greg said, taking Tyler's dick back in his mouth. As he sucked him, Greg reached down and grabbed his hard-on and started jerking it. Greg wanted to cum at the same time as Tyler. Tyler's moans got louder and louder, his cock thrusting back and forth and hitting the back of Greg's throat, almost making him gag.

Tyler groaned, "Oh! Fuck, Greg, I'm going to cum, ahhhhhh, fuck!"

Greg kept his mouth on Tyler's cock as his hot sperm spurted out with each pulse of his cock. The sensation was enough to take Greg over the edge. He straddled Tyler and shot his load all over Tyler's stomach and chin.

Greg lay down beside Tyler, both breathing fast and smiling. He leaned over and kissed him. They lay side by side for several minutes, returning from their high, then got cleaned up before heading home.

Greg's mother, surprised to see him, asked how the game was and if he had a good time. Greg smiled and said it was the best day of his life. He said goodnight and went to his room.

He fell asleep thinking about Tyler.

CHAPTER FIFTY-ONE: GUILT-RIDDEN

Carl felt queasy when he got up. His head was spinning when he went to bed the night before; he had visions of Elaine ripping him apart on social media. Upon arriving at school, he walked up to James and Greg, looking pale.

"Guys," he said, "you have to swear you won't say anything about what I told you about Elaine. James, the dude that got her pregnant was from Magrath."

Both James and Greg swore they wouldn't say anything and went to class.

At mid-afternoon break, Elaine asked Carl if he found out if Greg and Cindy were back together or not. Carl reassured Elaine that they weren't. "Greg is still gay and was going out with Cindy to pretend he was cured, because his father would kill him if he ever found out his son was still gay despite the treatment."

"I knew it," Elaine cheerfully said. "I bet he is still seeing Tyler."

"And what does it matter to you if he is?" Carl said.

"Patrick broke up with me because of Greg," Elaine said.

"How so?"

"Well, I sort of invited Greg to meet me after class for some fun. Of course, he turned me down. He asked Patrick if he and I had an open relationship, which is what I'd told Greg. Patrick called me afterwards and trashed me over the phone before breaking up. Since that day, I swore revenge on Greg."

"Don't you think you had it coming? You were going out

with someone and wanted to fuck somebody else behind his back. No wonder you got pregnant, gallivanting from one guy to the next. Didn't you learn your lesson?" Carl said.

"I told you not to bring this up in public, Carl Birmingham."

"There's no one around," Carl said. But just as Carl said it, Joni sprung out of the corner and smiled at Elaine before running off.

"You fucking asshole," Elaine said. "The forked tongue of Cardston heard you."

"I wasn't that loud. How could she have heard me? You're getting paranoid," Carl said.

"If I see something on social media or if word gets around town, the whole world will find out about you, I swear to God," Elaine said as she stormed down the school walkway.

Oh shit. Carl, you idiot. I better make sure Joni doesn't say or write anything, or I'm dead.

Joni McMurray used gossip to get back at people. She wasn't always that mean—but when she started school, she met bullies instead of meeting new friends, and the die was cast.

Carl went back into the school and noticed Joni talking to Cindy and Matilda. "Joni," Carl said, coming her way. "Can I speak to you for a minute?"

"Sorry, girls, I'll be right back. What do you want?" Joni said.

"I'm not sure if you heard Elaine and me talking but, if you did, can I ask you to keep whatever you heard to yourself, please. This conversation was private," Carl said.

"Which part don't you want me to talk about? Greg being gay or Elaine's pregnancy?" Joni asked.

Oh, fuck. She heard every word we said.

"Eavesdropping isn't very cool."

"I just happened to be around when you guys were talking, I don't consider it eavesdropping."

"You were hiding listening to our conversation, that's eavesdropping. If you value your life, you better not repeat this to anyone, otherwise you will have Elaine to contend with. Something I wouldn't wish on my worst enemy."

"Thank you for your wisdom, Carl. Now, if you'll excuse me, I have friends waiting for me," Joni said as she left.

I have to warn Elaine, Joni heard us talking. She will kill me for sure.

Elaine ran into Greg when she stormed down the sidewalk leading to the parking lot. "Woah, woah," he said. "In a hurry, aren't we?"

"Oh, it's you. Sorry," Elaine said.

"What's wrong?"

"Nothing, I have an appointment, and I'm running late," Elaine said.

"Alright. Try to drive slowly."

Sitting in her car, Elaine banged the steering wheel with both her hands before starting her car and driving home. She ran to her room. *I have to do something before Joni does.*

Elaine logged into her social media and started writing a message from her spam account: *Hey, about that post yesterday. Like many of you, I've been asking myself who it could be. As I was leaving school, I overheard a conversation where Joni asked someone to keep her pregnancy and abortion secret. I bet all of you thought it was Elaine, didn't you? Nope.*

Then she hit enter on her keyboard and closed her social media.

Everybody turned to Joni the following morning, wanting to know who the guy that got her pregnant is. Joni kept telling them it wasn't her, it was Elaine, but nobody believed her.

Elaine walked in and Joni ran towards her, yelling, "You fucking bitch, you know it's a lie, you're the one who was pregnant."

"I don't know what you're talking about," Elaine said.

"Oh, yes, you do." Joni turned towards the onlookers and said, "You can ask Carl. I heard them talking about it yesterday."

Greg and Tyler came in and saw the fighting going on. Greg asked Joni, "What's going on?"

"Someone wrote on social media that I was the one who got pregnant, which is untrue. Now everyone thinks it's me. I overheard Carl yesterday talking to Elaine about it, and she told him to shut up."

Carl waltzed in and wondered why everyone was staring at him. Then he saw Elaine staring at him coldheartedly. He turned his attention to Greg, asking in a shaky voice, "What's up?"

"Beats me. I came in, and someone apparently posted on social media yesterday that Joni was the pregnant girl," Greg said.

"Really?" Carl said, with Elaine's eyes darting at him.

"You've been singled out as knowing who it really is," Greg said.

"Me? Why would I know who it is?"

"Because I overheard you and Elaine talking about it yesterday," Joni said.

"What are you talking about? I didn't see you or talk to you yesterday," Carl said.

Joni made a mad dash towards Carl; Greg grabbed her as she sprinted towards him, screaming, "You fucking asshole, I'll rip your eyes out, you pussy."

"Alright," Greg yelled. "Enough. I know for a fact it's not Joni. Right, Elaine?"

"You fucking bastard," Elaine said as she pushed her way out of the crowd and stood in front of Carl, slapping him across the face. Looking at the crowd that gathered around during the fight, she ran outside, screaming and yelling.

"Sorry, Carl," Greg said. "I couldn't let her ruin somebody else's life with despicable lies. I hope you understand."

"But she'll ruin both of our lives instead. Is that any better?" Carl said sharply.

"If she has something on us, we should come clean. She has nothing on me. What about you?"

CHAPTER FIFTY-TWO: TROUBLE AT HOME

After the confrontation, Elaine purposely isolated herself from her friends, classmates, and especially Carl. Despite Elaine's wrongdoing, Cindy and Matilda tried to talk to Elaine, console her, and tell her what happened was unfair, but Elaine pushed them away.

Carl, fearing what Elaine might do since she knew his secret, paid her a visit Friday night.

"Elaine is in her room. Come on in," her mother said. As Carl was heading for the stairs, she asked, "Do you know what the matter with her is? She's been quiet, moody, and hasn't come out of her room most of the week."

"I noticed," Carl said. "I don't know. She hasn't said anything to me."

Carl hurried up the stairs, stood at Elaine's bedroom door, took a deep breath and knocked. "Elaine, it's Carl. Can I talk to you, please?"

"No. Leave me alone. All this is your fault," she said, shouting.

"How is this my fault? You're the one that didn't deny it. I didn't say anything."

"Oh, no. Then tell me, how did Greg know it was me?"

"Are we going to talk about this through the door? Let me in," Carl said.

"Not until you tell me how Greg knew."

Carl slid down the door frame and sat on the floor. "Last

Saturday James, Greg, and I were training at the track. While running, the conversation turned towards what had been posted the night before about the pregnant girl. They insinuated that I might be the father, but I told them it was more likely one of them. James feared it could be him because he had broken up with you around that time, and me and my big mouth told him you discovered you were pregnant shortly after you guys broke up. James panicked, and I told James he wasn't the father. At that moment, they knew it was you. I had them swear not to tell."

"Had you kept your mouth shut at school, nobody would have known."

"Had you not written on your social media it was Joni to cover your ass, nobody would have known. You went too far this time, to protect your image."

"Fuck off, Carl. Go home."

Elaine's mother, Maureen, was standing at the foot of the staircase and heard everything. Devastated by what she heard, she rushed into her husband's office and said, her eyes tearing up, "Phillip, I just learned that our daughter is pregnant."

"When did you hear that?" Phillip asked, getting up from his desk.

"Just now. Carl and Elaine were discussing how someone knew at school."

Phillip sped up the stairs to Elaine's room. Carl's face turned white as a ghost when he saw Elaine's father in front of him, so he got out of the way rapidly.

"Elaine, open the door!" Phillip yelled, banging on the door.

"What?" she yelled back.

"Open this door immediately, or I'll break it down." Phillip heard a click, and the door opened. Elaine's parents stormed in. Carl tried to leave but was immediately pulled in by Maureen.

"What were you guys talking about?" Elaine's mother asked Carl. Carl looked at Elaine, and Elaine's mother said, "Look at me, Carl. I'm asking the question."

"We were talking about school and my running with James and Greg," Carl carefully said.

"And what else?"

"Mom, why are you doing this?" Elaine said.

"Elaine, stay out of this."

"I don't understand what you want me to say. It was just school talk, Mrs. Thompson," Carl said.

"Let me rephrase my question then. Did you get my daughter pregnant?"

"What. No. Why are you asking this?"

"I heard you and Elaine talking about it just a minute ago. So did you or not?"

"No, it wasn't me."

"Mom, it wasn't Carl. It was someone else. A guy from Magrath," Elaine said.

"When did you go to Magrath?"

"Excuse me," Carl said. "Sorry to interrupt, but I'm going to go now." He raced down the stairs and out the door, slamming the door shut behind him.

"Late last spring, remember. I went to visit Christina for a few days. We had a bit too much to drink, so I slept with this guy, Christina's friend, and his condom broke." Elaine's mother closed her eyes and shook her head. "A month later, I found out I was pregnant. I didn't want to upset you, so I got an abortion not long after."

"Oh, no, no, no," Elaine's mother said.

"No one knew except Carl," Elaine continued. "But last week, a message was posted on social media about someone having had an abortion. I tried to save my reputation by saying it was Joni who got pregnant, and Joni and I got into a big fight and someone said it was me. Now the whole school knows."

"Wonderful," her father said. "Now the whole town will know about my daughter, my irresponsible daughter who had an abortion. Have you thought about how this will affect my reputation? What went through your mind? Aren't you on the pill?"

"I wasn't."

"What do you mean you weren't?" her mother said.

"I stopped taking it a few months after I started because I was gaining weight," Elaine said.

"Of course your figure is more important to you than not getting pregnant," her father said. "If you're not going to take birth control, then keep your pants on, young lady."

"I don't care if the pill makes you gain weight, as long as you live in this house and as long as we support you financially," her mother said, "you will take the pill. Is this clear?"

"I am back on it," Elaine said furiously.

"You better be," her mother said. "Tomorrow you will go and apologize to Joni for what you did."

"I didn't do anything."

"You call trying to tarnish someone's reputation in front of their classmates nothing? If she hadn't had a friend defend her, I'm sure with all the gossip that goes on in a schoolyard, word would have gotten to her parents. And then what would have happened to her and her family?"

Elaine shrugged as if she didn't care.

"You know, Elaine," her mother said, "the world doesn't revolve around you. You are a spoiled little girl, and that's our fault. We gave you everything because you are our only child. But you wanted more, so you whined and cried until your father gave in; you knew that would work, and you took advantage of it. I heard how you behave at school. You're manipulative, you think you're better than everybody else, and you get someone else to do your dirty work and classwork. This stops now. You are grounded for three months."

"What? You can't do this to me. Daaad?" Elaine said, latching on to her father's arm, imploring.

"Oh, stop whining," Elaine's father said, pulling his arm away from her. "We should have done this a long time ago. Give me your cell. You'll get it back in three months."

"No, not my cell. It's my life. I won't give it to you," Elaine said defiantly.

"Elaine, your cell please," her father said.

"No!" Elaine said, clutching her cell against her chest. "I'm eighteen, and you can't force me to do anything I don't want to."

"Fine. Here are your choices," her father said sternly. "You hand over your phone, or I'm cutting you off financially, and you can find another place to live."

"You can't throw me out," Elaine said, holding her cellphone and staring at her father.

"Sure I can. You just said you're eighteen," her father, replied as he turns to leave.

"You can't do this," Elaine yelled. "I'm still in school."

"So? You can find a job to pay for your studies. What's it going to be?" he said loudly and bluntly.

Elaine handed her cell to her father. "I hate you," she said. She slammed the door behind her parents and threw herself on her bed, kicking and screaming.

"I fucking hate all of you!"

CHAPTER FIFTY-THREE: YOU'RE OUT

Eight o'clock Sunday morning, Maureen knocked on Elaine's bedroom door and told her to get up and be downstairs in fifteen minutes.

"What for?" Elaine asked. "It's Sunday."

Elaine marched downstairs fifteen minutes later, and her mother was waiting for her at the entrance, holding Elaine's jacket.

"What's this? Why are you holding my jacket?

"We're driving to Joni's to apologize for your behaviour."

"Yeah, right. No, I'm not. I'll do it at school tomorrow. Did you wake me up for this?" Elaine turned around and went back to her room. "What's the matter with you people? Joni is a bitch anyway. Her reputation is as bad as mine."

"Elaine, get back down here." A slammed door was the next thing Maureen heard. She went to Elaine's room and knocked again.

"I told you I'm not going, period," Elaine said. "Leave me alone and stop bothering me."

"I'm not going to fight with you, Elaine. I'll call the school tomorrow to advise them that you'll apologize to Joni in front of the class."

Elaine opened the door and said, "No, you won't. If you do, I won't do it anyway."

"Suit yourself, Elaine."

Smiling, Elaine logged on to her social media to brag about how she stood up to her parents. But the comments she received were not what she expected. One of her friends said, *I*

used to like you, but you're turning out to be a real bitch. I'm delet-
ing you from my friend list. Another one commented, *What you
did to Joni was inexcusable. I'd never thought you would stoop that
low. I don't ever want to talk to you again.*

Rage quickened Elaine's pulse, and she posted, *Fuck you all.*
She flipped the screen of her laptop shut. *Arrgh, this is all Carl's
fault. He can't keep his damn trap shut.* Elaine flipped her screen
back up, logged back into her social media, and lashed out at
Carl.

*Friday at school, I was fed to the wolves when my secret was re-
vealed. Only one person knew about it, and that person couldn't
keep his trap shut. Have you ever wondered why you haven't seen
Carl with a girl? Well, he tasted pussy and decided he preferred cock
instead. Yes, folks, our self-proclaimed Casanova is a homo. Well,
Carl, at least you're not alone – right, Greg?*

With a smirk on her face, Elaine put her laptop aside and
went downstairs. She grabbed her jacket, opened the door but
as she was stepping out, her father pulled her back in. "You're
grounded, remember, now get back to your room."

"But, Daddy," Elaine pouted, "I was going to Joni's to apologize, like Mom wanted me to. Please, Daddy."

"Alright. I want you back here right after. You have an
hour," her father said.

"Thank you, Daddy," Elaine said sweetly.

Carl, his fists clenched, came up the driveway as Elaine
was getting in her car. "Elaine, what the fuck?" he yelled.
"How dare you do this to me?"

Elaine's parents came out to see what was going on and
heard Carl screaming and shouting at their daughter. "What
the hell is going on?" Phillip said, walking towards Carl.

"Why don't you ask your daughter?"

"Elaine?" his father asked.

"I don't know what he's talking about," Elaine said in a
honeyed tone.

"No?" Carl took out his phone to show to her father, and

Elaine snatched the phone out of his hand and threw it on the pavement.

"Oops," she said.

"You bitch, look what you've done!" Carl yelled.

"Watch your language, young man," Phillip said. "Elaine, why did you do that?"

"Sorry, the phone fell out of my hand," Elaine said. "I wanted to give it to you, Daddy, so you could look at what Carl wanted to show you." Elaine looked at Carl and winked.

"Liar," Carl said, getting angrier. He turned to her father and said, "Your daughter is evil. She posted on social media that I'm gay. She has just made my life a living hell." With that, Carl turned around and ran home.

"Is this true?" her father asked Elaine.

"Why would I do such a thing? Anyway, you guys have my cell, how could I possibly have done this?" Elaine said, looking at her parents as if her feelings were hurt.

"She has a point," her mother said. "Carl must have made a mistake."

"What about your computer," her father asked.

"What about it?" Elaine said playing dumb.

"Did you post something about Carl on social media from your computer?" Phillip asked.

"I already told you, I would never do such a thing," Elaine said as she threw her hands in the air.

Her father looked at her wondering if he should believe what she's saying or check for himself. "I better not find out you did this," he said, pointing his finger at her.

Carl felt a fury twisting inside of him on his way home. When he saw Elaine leave in her father's Audi, he decided to follow her and settle this once and for all. Carl ran and jumped in his car and sped off, hoping she hadn't got far.

Carl followed her to the Southern Country Inn Motel, parked, and waited. Ten minutes later, a dark blue BMW parked up beside Elaine's car, and both she and the man got out of their vehicles. Carl was parked at the restaurant next to the motel, close enough to see both of them chatting. He took out his cell and used his camera to zoom in closer to see who this guy was.

No, no, no, it can't be. It's the fucking mayor's son. Isn't he married? Holy shit, man.

Elaine waited for him when he went into the motel, and when he returned, they entered a room. *That fucking slut, she's having sex with a married man. I bet her father would have a coronary if he knew.*

Carl drove back home, found out this guy's name, and called his wife to let her know her husband's whereabouts.

CHAPTER FIFTY-FOUR: FRIENDS

"Holy shit," James said upon opening his social media. "What is this?"

He texted Carl, asking where he was. No response. James then texted Greg to meet him at the track and field. James left home and ran towards the school, where he saw Carl on the track.

James went towards him, tried to get him to stop running, but Carl wouldn't. Greg arrived and asked James what was going on.

"Someone outed Carl on social media. When he's upset, he runs, and he will run until he drops if we don't stop him."

Greg and James finally got Carl to stop running, and Carl fell to his knees and started crying. James sat beside him and pulled him close. "Sorry about this," James said. "Whoever did this will have to deal with us?"

"I have a pretty good idea who's behind this," Greg said.

"Me too," James said. "I want you to know, I don't care if you are gay, straight, or bisexual. We are friends, and nothing will change that. I'll always be there for you."

"Was it Elaine that did this?" Greg asked. Carl nodded yes. "I bet it's because of what happened Friday. That bitch."

"Someone needs to put her in her place, for good," James said.

"How will I be able to face everyone at school?" Carl said.

"The same way you did last week and the week before," Greg said. "Nobody cares who you love in this day and age. The only person who thinks it's a big deal is Elaine, and maybe my parents."

"And my parents," Carl said.

"Yes, parents find it difficult to accept, but they usually come around. If they don't, you have to think about your happiness. It's your life, not theirs. Promise me one thing, though. Don't let them send you to conversion therapy as mine did. I pretended to be cured so I could get out of there and stop the pain," Greg said.

"Why did you go? Did you want to change?" Carl asked.

"I went because I was forced to, not because I wanted to. I went to get my father off my back and because he threatened to fuck my football scholarship," Greg said.

"I didn't know that," James said. "It's fucked up for a father to do that to his son."

"He'll never accept it, neither will my mother. They're being driven by religion. I've been pretending to be straight ever since I got back. I told Cindy, and she agreed to play along. I broke up with her because what I was doing wasn't fair to her and Tyler. What I'm saying, Carl, is that you can pretend to be someone you're not, but eventually it catches up with you. Be yourself. James and I will always be there for you, regardless."

"Thanks, guys. I was afraid that I'd lose you as friends. I've hurt so many people with my arrogance and selfishness, that I have some major apologizing to do," Carl said.

"What do you say we get out of here and head over to my place for video games?" James asked.

"I'm hungry," Carl said. "Do you guys want to get a burger? We can go to that place in front of Southern Country Inn."

"Sounds good," James said.

They barely started eating when suddenly, everyone in the restaurant was staring out the window. James stood and tried to see what was going on, but too many people blocked the view. So the three of them went out with their burgers, and the spectacle at the motel in front became immediately clear.

"What the hell?" Carl said. "Looks like someone got caught with their pants down."

A woman was standing outside of one of the motel rooms and yelling, "You bastard, how could you? And you, you little tramp." The woman walked into the room, dragged the girl out wearing a towel and pulled the towel off her, leaving the girl naked for everyone to see. Her husband ran out in his underwear, tried to restrain his wife from attacking the girl, and she turned and slapped him across the face.

Greg took out his cell and zoomed in; he turned towards Carl and James, his eyes squinting, and looked again. "Holy fuck!" Greg exclaimed. "Guys, that's Elaine out there." Greg took a picture.

"You're shitting us," James said. "Let's see."

"Let's get back inside. I'll show you. Fucking unbelievable," Greg said, laughing.

Greg and the guys returned inside, and Greg pulled up the picture he took.

"I don't believe it," James said.

"What if this appeared on social media, what a payback that would be," Greg said with a grin.

"I can't wait to see her wiggle out of this," Carl said, with a wry face.

"Elaine will get all the attention she deserves," James said.

CHAPTER FIFTY-FIVE: LAST STRAW

M onday morning, with dark circles under her eyes from having spent a sleepless night, Elaine stuffed her alarm clock in her night table when she heard its dreadful sound. Dragging herself out of bed, she looked in the mirror, seeing her red and puffy eyes.

After stepping out of the shower, she looked at herself again. *I can't go to school looking like this.* Elaine left her room and went to the kitchen to pour herself a coffee.

Her mother was already sitting at the counter, sipping her coffee and reading the newspaper. "Good morning."

"Morning, Mom."

"Are you wearing makeup to school?" she asked.

"My skin broke out last night. It must have been something I ate at Joni's yesterday," Elaine said

"How did it go?" her mother asked, setting down the newspaper.

"It was hard, but she accepted my apology," Elaine said with a half-smile.

"What did you do after you left? Your father asked you to come home right after."

"Joni asked me to spend the afternoon with her. Was I supposed to tell her that you guys grounded me? The whole school will find out if I had told her that. Besides, I would have called, but you guys have my cell."

"Even if you had a phone, you were grounded." Her mother's face hardened. "When we tell you something, I want you to do as you're told. I didn't hear you come in, how late was it?"

"I'm too old to be grounded. This is ridiculous," Elaine said, flinging her arms in the air. "If you must know, I came home, it was dark and went to my room. Enough with the questions."

"It doesn't matter how old you are, you are still grounded," her mother said with authority. "You need to change your attitude young lady. In this house your father and I make the rules, not you. Understood?" Elaine nodded her head.

"Any good stuff in the newspaper?" Elaine asked softly and nervously, hoping what happened yesterday didn't make the news.

"Nothing newsworthy ever happens in this town," her mother said, calmer.

"I'm off to school," Elaine said blankly. "Have a nice day."

Entering the school, the buzzing was so loud that Elaine wondered what the fuss was all about at this time of the morning. When she turned the corner, the whole corridor went silent when they saw her. *Okay, is there someone behind me?* Elaine looked behind her and saw no one. Walking towards her locker, she glanced at everyone standing around, and approaching her locker, she stopped dead in her tracks.

When she saw the photo of her in all her glory outside the motel, her heart started pounding in her chest, and she began to hyperventilate. She grabbed the picture and tore it up, and threw the pieces on the floor. "Who is the asshole that did this?" she yelled, fighting her tears. Everyone dispersed, laughing on the way to class.

She saw Cindy and Matilda standing there. "Did one of you see who did this?"

"No. The picture was already there when most of us came in. There's more," Matilda said. She showed her what had been posted on social media.

"Oh, no, no, no. Fuuuck. Someone posted a video of the whole scene. You guys have to help me and say I was with you all day yesterday. This girl could be anyone, you can't tell who it is in the video."

"But you can from the picture," Matilda said. "The photo is also on social media. So you're on your own, don't count on us to bail you out."

"If you don't help me, I swear I'll tell the world your secret," Elaine threatened.

Cindy walked up to Elaine and, standing an inch from her face, "You go ahead. Who is going to believe a slut like you? Come, Matilda, let's go." Then Cindy stopped and turned to face Elaine. "By the way, you can do your own assignments and homework from now on. We're through being your puppets."

Elaine slammed the door of her locker shut, stormed out, and went to her car. *Fuck, fuck, fuck. Thank God it didn't make the newspaper.*

Elaine drove around town; she didn't want her parents to find out she skipped school. After a few hours, Elaine went to Waterton Park and sat by the lake, trying to figure out how she would get out of this one if ever it made the news. She went home around three o'clock, grabbed an apple and went to her room. She logged on to her social media and tried to find clues about who posted the video. Elaine spent the night plotting her next move.

The following day, Elaine's father bulldozed his way into her room. She was startled out of bed and screamed. Her father threw the newspaper at her. On the front page was his daughter naked, underneath the headline, "Cardston mayor's son caught with his pants down by his wife."

"Daddy, I can explain . . ."

"Shut up," he yelled. "I want you out of here this morning."

"Where will I go?"

"I don't care. You have made a fool of this family for the last time."

"Daddy, I'm sorry. It will never happen again," Elaine cried. "Please, Daddy, don't do this. Mom, please."

"You have two hours to pack your bags," her father yelled.

"Mom, please."

"Here is a cheque for five thousand dollars," he said, throwing it at her. "This is the last penny you'll ever get from me."

Elaine, enraged, kicked her door shut and screamed at the top of her lungs, "You'll never see me again, you hear? Hope you fucking die."

Her bags packed, Elaine stomped down the stairs, pulled the front door open and smashed the entrance mirror when the door flew into it. Next, she dragged her suitcase to her car and threw it on the back seat. Then, squealing her wheels, she drove off and gave her parents the finger as she left.

Elaine stopped to grab a coffee, took a newspaper, and browsed the apartment listings. She found one in Magrath: a one-bedroom apartment, fully furnished.

Elaine walked into her new home and dropped her suitcase at the door. This was far from the luxury she was used to living in. The furniture was old and not in the best shape, but at least it was clean. The bedroom was three times smaller than her old room, furnished with a small dresser and a double bed.

Sitting in the living room, she looked at the cheque for five thousand dollars, and knew it wouldn't get her far. *How am I supposed to live and go to school on five fucking thousand dollars?* Elaine suddenly realized after unpacking her suitcase that she needed to buy bed linens and dishes. *Shit.* She hopped back in her car and drove to downtown Magrath. Strolling by the few stores in search of a general store, Elaine noticed a cellphone shop. *I need a cell.*

Elaine was handed the shock of her life when she saw the cost of cellphones. Her father had always paid for them, so she had no idea what they cost. Elaine couldn't do without one, so she got herself a new cellphone. Elaine then made a sprint into the Walmart to buy bed linens and a bedspread, then she bought dishes and utensils and stopped by a grocery store to get food. *There goes a grand. Fuck, I won't have a choice but to find a fucking job.*

CHAPTER FIFTY-SIX: TRUTH HURTS

Elaine thought one of the perks of being on her own was that she didn't have to ask permission for anything. The downside, though, was she had to do everything herself, such as doing laundry in a laundromat. Another downside was she didn't have access to Daddy's bank account anymore, and her cash flow was drying up. *Time to get a job.* Checking the ads in the local newspaper, Elaine spotted a store clerk job at the gas station on the corner of West Third. She grabbed her car keys and shoulder bag and headed to the gas station.

Elaine arrived at the gas station and glanced at her reflection in the glass door before walking in. Approaching the counter, she looked at the cashier. "Hi, I'd like to see the manager, please."

"Just a moment. Jack," the cashier yelled, "someone is here to see you." Then, turning towards Elaine, he asked, "Are you here for the job?"

"Yes."

"Jack needs someone for the evening shift and some weekends."

"Hello," Jack said. "How can I help you?"

"Jack, I'm Elaine Thompson. I would like to apply for the store clerk job I saw in the newspaper."

"Have you ever worked at a gas station before?"

"No."

"Do you have any experience working in a store?"

"No, but I learn fast. I was just told you are looking for someone who can work evenings. Evenings are perfect for me, I have school during the day."

"Alright, when can you start?" Jack asked, fortunate to have found someone willing to work evenings.

"I'm available anytime," Elaine replied cheerfully, while she cringed inside at the thought of having to work.

"Perfect. Charles here . . ."

Charles looked at Elaine and smiled.

"Will be with you from four to eight for the first two weeks to show you everything you need to know."

Great Mr. Nerdy himself will be my tutor.

"Can you start next week?" Jack asked.

"Yes, I can," Elaine replied.

"You'll be working from four to midnight. Are you okay with this?"

"I am, thank you." Elaine replied. *Do I have a choice?*

"The clients will buzz you to let them in because gas must be paid before the pump is authorized. The door locks automatically on exit. Welcome to the team, Elaine, I hope you'll enjoy it here."

Cindy asked Matilda after school if she had seen Elaine lately. Cindy replied she hadn't seen her in a week and wondered if something had happened to her. "I did hear, though, that her father booted her out of the house," Matilda said.

Wow, that must be rough for someone who had everything.

Then, Greg happened to walk by. "Hey, Greg," Cindy said. "Did you know Elaine left home?"

"Carl told me last week. I heard she lives in Magrath. Must be rough for a spoiled brat like her," Greg said.

"I guess her father wasn't impressed by what she did," Cindy said.

"I don't think any parent would be. I guess her behaviour and her attitude became too much for them. I must go, sorry.

I'm on my way to meet Tyler. Catch you guys later," Greg said, leaving.

Elaine, savouring her latte and browsing her new cellphone, saw Greg heading towards the campground. I bet I know where he's going, she thought as she watched Greg strolling down the street. Elaine gulped down her latte and followed him to the campground. When she saw Tyler walking into the camper, her blood began boiling, and she ran back to her car.

Wandering downtown, Elaine purposely walked into the Miller's shoe store.

"Hi, can I help you?" John asked. "I remember you. Weren't you in a few months ago?"

"I was. You have a good memory. I go to school with your son Greg," Elaine replied, smiling.

"That's right. Are you here to buy shoes? The last time you came in was to spread rumours about Greg," John said, bluntly.

"I'm sorry," Elaine said, lowering her head. "I thought you knew about Greg." She added with a half shrug, "I hear though, he's been through therapy?"

"Yes, he has. He's much happier now that he saw the light. He has a girlfriend, Cindy Roberts, you must know her," John said, probing. "She goes to the same school as you."

"Yes, Cindy. She's a nice little Mormon girl, I'm told, and religious too. A bit nerdy though," Elaine said, snooping around. "I see you got new stuff in . . ."

"What's wrong with being religious?" John replied, offended.

"Nothing." Elaine said, turning towards John and flashing a half smile.

"My wife and I are very religious," John said proudly, "and this is why Greg decided to get therapy because he knew what he was doing was sinful."

"I guess it didn't work," Elaine chuckled, opening the door to leave. She turned and looked at John her eyes fixed on his. "That's why he's with Tyler at the trailer as we speak, probably sucking him off." Then she laughed, closing the door behind her.

Running towards the door and pulling it open, John yelled, "Come back here you little witch. How dare you spread lies about my son?"

Elaine stopped and turned. "If you think I'm lying, then go check for yourself." Elaine gave him the finger and walked away with a big smile on her face.

John rushed back inside, went to his office and called his wife. "Is Greg at home?" he asked. Teresa told him that he hadn't returned from school yet and that he was probably with Cindy. "Thanks, honey," John said as he hung up. John flipped the sign on his door and drove quickly to the campground, praying it was all lies.

Reaching the trailer, John grabbed the door handle and tried to open it, but it was locked. Then he heard some laughter inside the camper, so he propped his ear closer to the door and heard the laughter again, this time coming from the front end of the trailer. John took a few steps towards the bedroom, moved closer to the window to look inside, but the curtains were drawn, so he stood silently listening before hearing the sounds of boys moaning and groaning. John, disheartened, took a step backwards, and a branch snapped under his foot, which startled the two boys.

"Shhh," Tyler said. "Did you hear that?"

John ran out of sight. He took a deep breath, his body trembling with rage as he rushed back to the store.

Later that evening, he slammed the front door and said,

"Where is that son of a bitch?"

Teresa, her voice thick with fear, asked what was going on. She pulled on John's arm to have him look at her, but he wouldn't budge and kept pounding at Greg's bedroom door. "Open that door, or I'll break it open," John yelled.

Greg opened the door and said, "What the fuck?" With that, John rammed his fist in Greg's face. Greg fell backwards on impact; Teresa held John back, screaming, unsure what was happening. John pushed her away, and as Greg was getting up, his father kicked him in the stomach. Greg crumbled to the floor, holding his stomach, writhing in pain.

"John, have you gone mad?" Teresa screamed. "Leave him alone. Get out of here."

John grabbed his son by the front of his sweater, lifted him up from the floor and slugged him across the face a few times before throwing him back on the bed, bruised and bleeding. John ran out the front door into his car and drove off, the wheels squealing.

Teresa ran into the bathroom, grabbed the first aid kit, and cleaned and bandaged Greg's wounds. *What the hell has gotten into him? I've never seen such rage in him before.* She said, "I don't know what came over him, sweetie. I'm so sorry. I remember he called around three-thirty to see if you were home yet, and I told him that you weren't."

Greg had a feeling that the noise he and Tyler heard outside the trailer might have been him. *How could he have known that I was there? We didn't tell anyone.* Greg got up from his bed and went into his closet to grab a duffle bag.

"What are you doing?" his mother asked.

"I'm leaving. I'm not staying one more minute in this house

with him around." Greg shoved clothes in his bag. "I'm going to stay with friends until he calms down."

"No, don't. I'm going to talk to him, you can stay in your room. I'll forbid him to come near here until he apologizes to you and me. Stay, don't go," his mother tearing up.

"Sorry, Mom, I can't," Greg said, walking out of his room.

"Wait," his mother said, going into the kitchen. "Here, take this." She handed Greg three hundred dollars that she'd been saving up. "Where can I reach you?"

"I'll call you when Dad is at work to let you know how I am and when I'll come back," Greg said. "I love you, Mom."

An hour later, John returned home. Teresa was waiting for him in the living room, still shaking. When he walked in, she stood up, her fists clenched, and looked at him with daggers in her eyes. "What the *hell* came over you beating your son to a pulp like that? *Answer me,* you bastard," she yelled.

John looked at her on his way to the liquor cabinet and poured himself a drink, his hands still trembling from shock. "Where is he?" he asked calmly.

"He left," she screamed.

"What do you mean he left? Where did he go?" John asked.

"I don't know, he went to a friend's place. He doesn't want to see or talk to you." Teresa began hitting John in the chest with her fists, crying out, "How could you do this to him, to us? I don't care what you think he might have done or has done; you had no right to lay a hand on him like you did. Get out, get out of this house *Now.*" She ran to her bedroom and locked the door.

"Teresa, open this door," John said. "Do you hear me? Open the fucking door. I need to get some clothes, and I'll be out of here."

Teresa opened the door, threw a selection of his clothes at

his face, and slammed the door shut again. John picked the bundle of clothes from the floor, kicked the bedroom door, threw his clothes in the back seat of his car, and drove off.

Greg, his hoodie partially covering his face, took the trail to the trailer. He sent a text to James telling him what happened and asked if it would be okay with his family if he stayed at the trailer for a while. Thirty minutes later, James walked into the trailer and saw Greg's face.

"Holy shit, man. Your father do this to you?" Greg nodded. "Why? What the fuck? This is insane."

"I don't know. I really don't know. I've never seen him in this state before. He kept banging on my bedroom door, and when I opened it, he pounced on me like a madman."

"Man, I don't know what to say. I'm so sorry."

At that moment, Tyler stormed into the trailer, took a look a Greg, and teared up. "Oh my God, oh my God. Who did this to you?"

"My father," Greg said.

Tyler was filled with rage. "I'll fucking kill him," he said, bursting into tears.

Greg pulled him over and put his arm around him, and said, "Don't worry, I'm fine. James said that I could stay here for a while."

"Thank you, James. What happened? Why did he beat you up? I don't understand," Tyler said, his voice quivering.

"He started beating me without telling me why. Then he threw me on the bed and ran out to his car and drove off." Greg's eyes became watery. "I never want to see him again."

"Are you going to be okay staying here?" James asked. "You can come stay at my place anytime."

"I'll be fine. I need to be on my own for a while," Greg said.

"I will ask my dad to get the campground to turn the

electricity back on for you. The nights are still cool, and at least you could watch some television and not be in the dark," James said. "What about school tomorrow?"

"If someone at school asks where I am, tell them I'm sick or something. I'll go back next week."

"Okay, bud. I'll head back home. I'll text you when the power is back on. Take care and stay safe." James walked out and went home.

"Do you think your father found out about us? That would explain his rage, but that wouldn't excuse the beating," Tyler said.

"How would he? No one knew."

They sat there holding hands, trying to figure out what could have provoked Greg's father to do such a thing to his son. Finally, Tyler looked at Greg and noticed he'd fallen asleep in his arms.

Chapter Fifty-seven: Working Part-Time

Elaine thought working part-time would be enough to live independently and finish school, but the reality kicked in soon enough.

"I need another job, this four to midnight shit doesn't pay enough," she said as she watched her bank account emptying with each month that went by. Elaine didn't see any other solution but to work more hours and she couldn't get more at the gas station, so she looked for another job.

Elaine saw an opening in a retail store. With her fashion sense, Elaine got the job at a lingerie boutique in the shopping plaza in Magrath. She worked from four until nine every evening except for Friday, which she got off, and needed to work every weekends. This schedule would provide enough revenue for Elaine to pay for rent, groceries, utilities, and her cell use. One thing Elaine didn't thoroughly think about was leaving enough time for homework and exam preparation.

Elaine managed to get through her first few weeks of work and school without much difficulty. But with barely two months left before the end of the school year, assignments that counted towards her final grades started to flow her way.

One Sunday, having worked all weekend, an exhausted Elaine collapsed on her couch. *Ouch.* She reached in her back pocket to pull her cell out. She set her phone beside her on the sofa, and a reminder pinged. *Shit, I forgot all about this fucking paper.* Her paper on *Civil society protest from the 1950s to 1970s* was due next Friday, and Elaine had not written one word yet. *When am I supposed to find time to write it?*

The following morning, walking up the stairs to the school, Cindy and Matilda were chatting. "Hi, girls," Elaine said with a smile. "You guys are looking beautiful today. Matilda, did you lose weight? You look terrific."

"What do you want, Elaine?" Cindy said.

"Nothing. I wanted to say hi, that's all. Have you guys started your research on our assignment?" Elaine asked.

"Which assignment? We have two," Matilda said.

"What do you mean two? I only know about the one on civil society protest," Elaine said.

"There's that one and the one on social study," Cindy said.

"Fuck. When that's due?"

"The same deadline. Have you started them?" Cindy asked.

"Obviously not," Elaine said, irritated. "Can I borrow your notes?" she asked.

"No," both of them said in unison.

"Remember, I can post both of your secrets on social media. If I were you, to avoid any embarrassment, I would just hand over the notes," Elaine defiantly said.

"Elaine, we told you a few weeks ago, we didn't care what you say about us. So stop your blackmailing and go fuck yourself." Matilda and Cindy entered the school, leaving Elaine dumbfounded at the door.

"You know what you guys are? Fucking bitches." *Now, what am I supposed to do? I've never done an assignment, and I have to work until nine every night. I'm screwed.* She then saw Tyler coming up the steps. "Hi, Tyler, do you know where Greg is? I haven't seen him all last week," Elaine said, trying to make believe she cared.

"No," Tyler said without stopping.

"Of course you do, you were with him at the trailer last week," Elaine said, realizing what she just said. Fuck, she thought after the words came out.

With the door halfway opened, Tyler released the handle and turned to Elaine, who had a grin on her face. "What did you just say?"

"N . . . othing," Elaine said in her honeyed voice.

"Why did you say Greg and I were at a trailer?" Tyler probed.

"I took a wild guess," Elaine said, her mouth drying up.

"Why would you think we see each other at a trailer?" Tyler asked, tilting his head and staring at her.

"That's what I heard," Elaine replied defensively.

"Oh! From who?"

"James," Elaine shyly said.

"Sorry, Elaine, James doesn't like you, let alone trust you. I have a hard time believing this. Where did you hear about a trailer? Come on, speak up." Tyler was getting angry.

"Oh, look at the time, I must get to class." She tried to get past Tyler. Tyler grabbed her by the arm and stopped her from going anywhere.

Pulling her back close to him, he said, "You're not going anywhere until you tell me what you know."

"Ouch, you're hurting me," Elaine said, trying to pull away from Tyler's grasp.

"I'll ask you one more time. Where did you hear Greg and I were together last week? Answer me, or I'll go to the director and tell him you were blackmailing Cindy and Matilda to do your assignments."

"Go ahead, you have no proof," Elaine said.

"That's where you're mistaken. I have signed confessions from both of them."

"You're lying," Elaine said nervously.

"Try me." Tyler pulled out his cell and showed Elaine a photo of the letter from Cindy.

"That fucking bitch," Elaine said, throwing her hands up

in the air. "Alright. I saw Greg walking towards the campground and followed him and hid behind a trailer. Minutes later, I saw you entering the camper. Happy now?"

"Who did you tell?" Tyler asked, clenching his teeth.

"No one." Fear could be seen in Elaine's eyes.

"I don't believe you, Elaine."

"I swear, I didn't tell anyone. Why do you think I told someone?"

"Because you like to gossip. Oh, by the way, everyone campus is aware of you bullying others into getting your homework done," Tyler blurted out.

"What about Cindy? Did she really give you a letter?"

"Not Cindy Roberts," Tyler replied smugly. "The letter I showed you was from another Cindy and not about you." Tyler opened the door and walked in.

Elaine struck the brick wall with her hands, then screamed in pain after scraping her hands. She opened the door to get into the school when she saw Greg.

"Greg, I haven't seen you in ages," Elaine said as he was walking up the steps, his head bowed. "Where have you . . ." Elaine's eyes widened. "What happened to your face?"

"My face met my father's fist," Greg said.

"What? Why?" she said, pretending not to know.

"For something I did, I guess. You can ask him because he didn't tell me."

"He must have been pissed," Elaine said.

"That he was," Greg said. "I have to get to class."

Elaine wondered if what happened to Greg was a result of her visit to the store. *Shit.*

Tyler texted Greg, telling him that he would stop by the trailer after school. *I have a feeling that Elaine has something to do with your father beating you. I'll tell you all about it after school.*

When Greg read the message, his hands tightened into a

fist and his eyes darkened. He looked at the time—he had an hour before his next class, so he went to the locker room and changed into his running gear. He went at the school track and field and ran to burn his anger out of his system.

Sitting in his last class of the day, Greg kept looking at the time, anxious to see Tyler and also to find out what he discovered. Soon after the last bell rang, Greg walked to the trailer and waited for Tyler.

Greg heard the door opening and his serious face, lightened up. "Hey, how was your day?" Tyler said walking in.

"It was okay." Greg walked up to Tyler and kissed him.

"How did people react when they saw you today?" Tyler asked, brushing Greg's face.

"Shocked. Especially Elaine," Greg said.

"Speaking of Elaine, you know when we thought someone was outside the trailer when we were making love . . . I think it might have been Elaine," Tyler said as he and Greg sat down.

"What makes you think that?" Greg asked, eager to find out what she did or said.

"She asked me if I had seen you lately and told her no, then she said that I should know because I was with you at the trailer," Tyler told Greg, who frowned.

"How could she know you were there with me, unless she was spying on us," Greg said, his eyes widening.

"Exactly. So, to get her to spill the beans, and curious to see how she knew. I had a letter from a friend of mine on my cell and told her I have a signed affidavit from Cindy that you were bullying her into doing her assignments and I would give it to the director if she didn't talk," Tyler proudly said.

"What did she say?" Greg asked with a laugh.

"She said, she was having a coffee downtown when she saw you heading this way, so she followed you here," he told Greg.

"You think Elaine went to the store to tell my father?" Greg asked, frowning.

"Why not? Wasn't it your father who said a girl from school went to see him and told him about us before he sent you to therapy? The only girl at school who seemed to be bothered by us being together is Elaine. She was humiliated in front of everyone after the social media post," Tyler said, stating facts. "She was further embarrassed with the photo of her naked out front of the motel. Don't you think she would seek revenge?"

Chapter Fifty-eight: Karma

It was Saturday night, and the Red Barn was where all the young adults gathered to dance the night away. The Red Barn was a country and western bar six days a week, but the bar switched their line-dancing music to pop music on Saturday night.

Christina hadn't seen Elaine in months, so she texted and invited her to the Red Barn after her shift. The last time Elaine went dancing was the weekend Elaine had too much fun and wound up pregnant, and it was also when she last saw Christina. The boys they were with that weekend had a hard time keeping them on the dance floor. One was always missing. Throughout the night, Christina and Elaine ran back and forth to their table to have a sip of their drink. The boys suggested they get their drinks and bring them to the dance floor, but both refused to do that out of fear of ending up wearing their drink. Christina remembered this from last time, and managed to get a table near the dance floor.

Elaine got in her car and rushed home after work, freshened up, then hopped back in her car to meet Christina. She drove into the parking lot and after going around a few times, she found an empty spot. Elaine spotted Christina as soon as she entered the bar. She waved at her and walked to her table.

"How have you been?" Christina asked, giving her a hug. "I haven't seen you in forever. How's the apartment?"

"The apartment is okay. It's not the best, but it's all I can afford right now." She sighed. "What's new with you?"

"Working too much. My life is boring right now," Christina

replied with a scrunched-up face. "You?"

"I've been busy with work, working every night and week-end and studying on top of that. I'm running on adrenaline," she said, flagging the waiter.

"Wow, that's a lot. Have you spoken to your folks since?"

"No. I'm still pissed at them for throwing me out." She gave a dismissing wave of her hand. "They haven't even both-ered to call me to see how I'm doing." The waiter came by and she ordered two beers.

"Do they have your new cell number?" Christine asked. "Maybe they've tried to reach you?"

"I doubt it. Have you seen the dipshit who got me preg-nant?" Elaine snarkily said.

"Scott? No, he moved to Calgary shortly after your abor-tion. His father got a job there. He got the scare of his life when he found out you were pregnant. His father almost kicked him out too."

Elaine laughed sarcastically and shook her head. "What about you? Still with . . ." Elaine asked.

"Brad? No. When Scott moved, he became withdrawn and quiet. They were best buds, and he took it very hard when Scott left."

"Bummer . . . Still in school?" Elaine asked

"No," Christina shaking her head, "I never liked it. I went to please my parents and because I didn't have a choice. I didn't return this year. I got a job in retail, and I like it."

"I didn't have much of a choice either. My folks were going to cut me off financially if I didn't go to university, which they did anyway. Now I work to support myself, how fucked up is that?" Elaine said with a smirk on her face. "Hey, you want another beer?"

"Hey, why not, the night is young."

Elaine went to the bar and returned with two beers.

"I meant to tell you, did you know your friend Carl is gay?"

Christina asked.

"Yeah, I know," Elaine replied, snickering. "I outed him on social media a couple of weeks ago."

"You did what?" Christina said, laughing. "That is nasty."

"I know, but he humiliated me at school."

"Well, his boyfriend lives here. Carl comes around often to see him."

"What do you know? Maybe I'll run into Carl," Elaine said.

"I shouldn't tell you this but, I overheard Jeremy, Carl's boyfriend, at the fast-food joint a couple of weeks ago, telling his buddy the whole story about you and the mayor's son getting caught by his wife that Carl tipped. I thought you'd like to know."

"What a prick," Elaine said with malice.

"Maybe he did it out of revenge for outing him," Christina said.

"I don't care what his motive was. He fucked up my life, and he'll pay for it," she said bluntly.

"Didn't you fuck up his?"

"I don't care about his life. I'm financially wrecked because of him."

"Let's not allow this to spoil our fun. Hey! I love this song," Christina said. "Come dance!"

On the dance floor, two guys began flirting with them; Christina turned towards one of the guys and wrapped her arms around his neck, and began swaying right to left, sliding up and down the young guy's body to the beat of the music. His friend thought of getting the same treatment from Elaine, but she was not in the mood—she threw her glass of beer in his face and left.

"Elaine," Christina yelled. "Where are you going?"

"Home. Have fun."

Monday morning, Elaine was eagerly waiting for Carl at the school entrance. She looked at the time; it was nearly eight o'clock, and there was no sign of Carl. Then she heard someone running up the cement stairs, stretching her neck to see who it was.

"Greg," Elaine said. "Do you know where Carl is?"

"No. Why do you ask?" Greg replied as he walked past her.

"I need to talk to him," Elaine yelled.

"Too bad, he doesn't want to talk to you after what you've done," Greg said as he turned around and walked towards her.

"Who are you to say he doesn't want to talk to me?" she said defiantly.

"A friend, one that wouldn't meddle in his life because it's none of my business. One that would support him no matter what, and one who wouldn't throw his friend under the bus out of revenge," Greg told her, staring down her face.

"Fuck right off, Greg. That asshole tipped off the wife of the guy I was with at the motel," Elaine said bluntly, giving Greg the finger.

"That's what happens when you don't mind your own fucking business. Stop using social media to spread your vile comments. Now, if you don't mind, get lost and leave us alone." Greg walked into the school.

Elaine lost it. She grabbed her backpack in a fit of rage, swung it at the door, and shattered the window. The glass breaking resounded throughout the hallway, and one of the maintenance crew ran to the front door, saw glass shards all over the floor, and asked, "What happened here?"

Elaine shrugged, turned around and walked back to her car, and sped away. *Carl and Greg will pay for this, no one treats me this way.* She drove to Cardston shopping mall and returned a half-hour later with a bag. Elaine drove to Lee Creek campground, roamed around Greg's trailer for twenty minutes and then returned to Magrath.

Tyler stopped at a grocery store after school and entered the trailer carrying a paper bag.

"Hi, sweetie, what's in the bag?" Greg grabbed the bag from Tyler.

"Dinner," Tyler said. "I stopped and bought us a salad, a roast chicken, and French fries so you can have a decent dinner . . . and because your cooking sucks, babe," Tyler said, laughing.

"Oh my God, it smells so good. You're so sweet. My cooking really sucks, doesn't it?" Greg moved closer and began poking Tyler on the side.

"It does, but I'm not good at it either," Tyler replied, giggling. "I'm glad James's father came through and got the electricity back in the trailer."

"Me too. His father won't take a penny from me, though. It makes me uncomfortable, and I mentioned it to James." Greg emptied the shopping bag.

"What did James say?" Tyler asked, getting plates and utensils.

"You know James, he said don't worry about it," Greg said, shrugging. "I owe them big time."

"Have you seen your mother?" Tyler asked, wrapping his arms around Greg.

"No, not yet. I miss her a lot, and I want to see her, but I don't want to go to the house."

"Ask her to meet you somewhere. The coffee shop or, better yet, ask her to meet you for burgers or something," Tyler said, giving Greg a kiss.

"Yeah, that's a good idea." Greg kissed him back. "I could ask her to meet me on Thursday or Friday night when Dad is working."

"Do you want to eat now or later?" Tyler teasingly said. "We can always re-heat the chicken in the microwave." He flashed a wink at Greg.

Greg locked the door then, with smouldering eyes, took Tyler's face between his hands and guided Tyler's lips to his. As their mouths came together, their lips parted and their tongues interlaced and danced together, breaking into a fervent kiss as they made their way to the bedroom.

Greg took the bottom edge of Tyler's sweater, slowly sliding it over Tyler's erect nipples from Greg's touch on his skin. Gentle with his teeth, Greg nibbled Tyler's nipple, which elicited a sensual moan from Tyler. Greg began to feel a tightness in his jeans. Tyler raised his arms, and his sweater fell to the floor. Unbuckling Greg's jeans, Tyler knelt in front of Greg's bulge, caressing it with his other hand as he pulled the zipper down. Greg's penis pushed against the fabric of his boxers and forced open the unzipped fly of his pants.

Tyler grabbed the waistband of Greg's jeans and boxers and pulled them down; Greg's manhood sprang out, pointing straight at Tyler's mouth. Greg sensed warmth around his shaft as Tyler engulfed the length of it. Greg murmured as he took a deep breath and closed his eyes, savouring every moment. He lightly pushed Tyler on the bed, slid a condom over Tyler's erection, and lubed it up before guiding it to his waiting hole. He slowly lowered himself over Tyler's cock to the moaning and groaning of his lover.

Taken by their surmounting arousal, they climaxed at the same time. Greg collapsed beside Tyler, breathing heavily, their bodies glistening from sweat.

"I love you," Greg said to Tyler. "I don't know what I would do without you."

"I love you too. Ready for some food? I'm starving," Tyler said.

Chapter Fifty-nine: No More Lies

How quickly a month went by; it had been that long since Greg had seen his mother. Tonight was going to change this, they were going to dinner together. Greg, antsy, felt the need to move around; if his limbs were moving, the anxiety would go, or at least he could ignore it a while. The store was opened late tonight, so his father was there until nine o'clock, which meant he and his mother would have some quality time together. What Greg was looking forward to above all was to feel her arm around him, and see her smile.

When she walked into the restaurant, Greg's eyes watered up and a smile grew of its own accord. When Teresa saw her son, she swallowed her tears and rushed to his side. The month without Greg had been one of the most difficult times in her life. She still hadn't forgiven her husband for what he did.

"Mom," Greg said when he saw her. He opened his arms, she walked into them and wrapped hers around him, and they held onto each other, tears running down their cheeks. Then Greg said, "I missed you so much." He squeezed her again and gave her a kiss on the cheek.

"I missed you too. It's so good to see you," Teresa said as they sat down.

"How's life at home?" Greg asked, his eyes tenderly looking into hers.

"It's okay. It's not the same without you," Teresa said, grabbing Greg's hands and holding them.

"I'm sorry I don't visit." Greg bowed his head. "I'm afraid

I'll run into Dad, and I haven't gotten over what he did to me."

"I know," Teresa said, squeezing Greg's hands. "Your father spends his evening praying. He hasn't said much to me since I told him to leave the night you left."

"You kicked him out?" Greg, his wide eyes, put his hand over his mouth.

"I didn't want to see him for a few days, I was so angry with him," Teresa said, letting go of Greg's hands and folding her arms.

"How long was he gone?"

"Two days," Teresa answered with a bit of a blush.

"Has he asked about me?" Greg was curious to find out how caring his father was.

"He asked where you went the night you left, but otherwise, no." Teresa felt bad telling her son this. He saw the sadness in her eyes. "How have you been?"

"I've been okay. I missed a few days of school after that night as my face was all swollen. But I went back the following week." Greg smiled.

"How is school?" Teresa asked, hoping the incident didn't affect his grade.

"Good, thanks. I'm studying hard and looking forward to university next year." Greg said, reassuring her.

"Which friend are you staying with?"

"No one you know. Don't worry about me, I'm okay." Greg leaned forward and touched her hand that was resting on the table.

"I can't help but worry about you; you're my son, and I care," she said, her eyes full of love and gratitude.

"Thanks, Mom. I care about you too. I'm worried sometimes that Dad would hurt you," Greg said, leaning back.

"Your father hasn't laid a hand on me, Greg, and he wouldn't. I don't know what came over him that day. He's not a violent man," Teresa said, trying to reassure her son. "Are you eating enough? Do you need any money?"

"I'm fine. I'm working part-time at a fast-food restaurant, which helps me pay for what I need." Teresa put a hand in front of her mouth, and her face became covered in sadness when Greg told her he had to work to survive. "Speaking of eating, let's order — I'm starving."

"Tell me, are you still seeing that guy?" Teresa asked.

"His name is Tyler. Yes, I am."

"Are you . . ." Teresa was hesitant, but wanted to know.

"Yes, I am gay, Mom. I pretended to be cured to get away from that place. I came home more traumatized than when I went in. I have great friends, and if it weren't for them, I wouldn't be here." Teresa teared up and clutched her aching heart. "I've accepted who I am because that's how God created me."

"I'm so sorry we put you through this," Teresa said, drying her tears.

"Mom, it's not your fault." Greg reached out to her and grabbed her hand.

"I agreed to send you there with your father; therefore, I'm just as guilty. Had I known about the treatments, I would have never agreed to it."

"Mom, stop blaming yourself. You didn't do anything wrong, you didn't know," Greg told her.

"After you left, I wanted to understand what makes one person gay and another not. I went to the doctor to find out why you were that way. He basically told me it is programmed into the brain before birth, based on a mix of genetics and prenatal conditions, none of which are a choice." Teresa looked down and then up. "What I'm trying to say, Greg, is that it's your life, and I want you to be happy. If Tyler makes you happy, then I'm happy, and I'd like to meet him someday," she said, and sighed.

"He makes me very happy, and I love him, Mom." Greg's eyes lit up and his face gleamed of joy when he thought of Tyler.

"I'm glad. You deserve to be loved. Do you think you'll come back home?" Teresa asked as she called the waiter over.

"I don't know. I don't know if I could be in the same room as Dad. We'll see."

"I understand. Your father doesn't know how to control his temper. It's always been a problem with him. The store would be busier if he would just learn to shut up. We've lost so many customers because of his short fuse."

Greg looked outside and saw Elaine going towards downtown. *I wonder where she's going.* He shook his head and turned to his mother. "What do you want to eat?" he asked.

"I'll have the chicken burger, no fries," Teresa said to the waiter.

"I'll have the cheeseburger and fries."

"Are you okay? You got distracted," Teresa said to Greg.

"Humm. Yeah. I saw Elaine Thompson going downtown."

"The daughter of the realtor?" she asked.

"Yeah." Greg reached for his phone. "Here's a picture of her." He turned his phone towards his mother.

"She looks like a nice girl," she said, smiling.

"She isn't," Greg replied, shaking his head.

Elaine drove to Carl's place, hoping he would be home, but his car wasn't in the driveway, and neither was his parents'. She swung by her parents' house, stopped in front for a minute looking at the house, then she saw her mother pulling up the driveway on her way back from her volunteer work at the hospital.

When her mother came out of the garage, she noticed a car parked in front of her driveway. She slowly walked down the driveway towards Elaine; however, Elaine still resented her mother's silence when her father threw her out, so she sped away, looking straight ahead.

Pulling into the parking lot of her apartment building, Elaine noticed Carl's car parked across the street. *What is he doing there? Oh, maybe it's where Jeremy, his boyfriend, lives.*

She was tempted to go over and confront Carl, but decided to wait until she saw him at school. Unzipping her backpack, she took her cellphone out, viewed the video that she captured from a hidden camera, and transferred the footage to her computer and onto a DVD. This should get someone's blood flowing, she thought as she placed the DVD in an envelope and stuffed it in her handbag.

Standing in front of the living room window, she saw Carl and Jeremy get into Carl's car and leave. *Where are they going?* She grabbed her bag and keys, got in her car, and followed them. Fifteen minutes out of the city, Carl made a right turn on a side road; Elaine slowed down and trailed them. She kept on driving but at a distance, then Carl and Jeremy turned and parked at Burt's Bar.

Elaine looked at herself in her rear-view mirror, grabbed the ball cap on the seat beside hers and put it on, tucking her hair inside. She opened her bag and applied makeup, making sure her eyes were heavily done so Carl didn't recognize her.

Satisfied with her look, she went into the bar and spotted Carl and Jeremy sitting towards the back of the room. Elaine glanced over the place and spotted a table far enough from Carl and Jeremy but close enough to hear their conversation. She called the waiter over and ordered a beer. Pretending to be busy on her cell, Elaine listened attentively to what they were talking about.

"I enjoyed meeting your parents tonight," Carl said

"They've enjoyed meeting you. Now they will have a face in their mind whenever I talk about you," Jeremy said.

Elaine snuck a look at Jeremy. *Whoa! Look at this guy's body. Lean and muscular with blond hair to boot. A five o'clock shadow. There's nothing that turns me on more than a five o'clock shadow. Why are all the good-looking guys gay?*

"I wish my parents would be as accepting as yours. I'm not sure they would."

"I thought the same about my parents. When I was outed on social media, it came to my parents' attention from friends of theirs. I thought I would be kicked out, but instead, they told me it didn't matter who I fell in love with, as long as I was being loved back. Give them a chance, you never know."

Elaine almost choked on her beer. *Oh, give me a break. They certainly never said this — what a crock of shit.*

"How was it at school after?" Carl asked.

"To my surprise, no one cared, and no one mentioned it. My close friends knew about me before I was outed and kept the secret until then."

"A friend of mine wasn't so lucky. Remember that evil, self-centered bitch I told you about, Elaine? Well, she told my friend's father that his son was having sex with another guy. So when his father came home after work, he beat him up. Man, you should have seen the poor guy's face. Of course, we all hope she gets what's coming to her."

"Maybe she did when you called the guy's wife to let her know where her husband was. Man, I would have given anything to have seen her when she was taken out naked out of the motel room," Jeremy said, laughing.

Elaine toppled her chair when she abruptly got up, stared at the guys, and gave them the finger as she hastily left. Pacing in front of her car, Elaine screamed as she kicked her tires. She rifled through her handbag and pulled out her lipstick. *I'll show those fuckers who they're fucking with.* Elaine walked over to Carl's car, and wrote on his windshield *FAGGOT* in red lipstick, before getting in her car and driving away.

"Who was that?" Jeremy asked.

"I'm not sure," Carl said somewhat puzzled. "She had a resemblance to the girl I was just telling you about, Elaine.

"Really?" Jeremy said.

"Yeah. And the fact that she became angry after listening to our conversation . . . If it was her, then that's what happen when you eavesdrop," Carl said.

"Well, whoever that was, maybe she needs to get laid or something. Speaking of sex, I wish there could be somewhere we could make love instead of the backseat of your car," Jeremy said with a smile.

"Let me see if I can come up with something for tomorrow night. How does that sound?"

"Sounds naughty. I can't wait."

"Great. Oh my God, it's my favourite song. Come on, let's dance."

Elaine, still miffed, went to Cardston with the intention of outing Carl to his parents. *What a payback this will be. This asshole thinks he can fuck with me, well we'll see who has the last laugh.*

She walked up to Carl's house and rang the doorbell. She rocked back and forth as she waited, but no one answered, so she rang the doorbell again. She waited a few more moments, then frustration kicked in, and she started pounding the doorbell over and over again, then kicked the door and left.

"Last call," the waiter announced.

Carl looked at the time. *Wow! Two o'clock already.* "Do you want another drink, or are you ready to go?" Carl asked Jeremy.

"Let's go if you don't mind," Jeremy answered.

Walking towards their car, Jeremy exclaimed, "What the

f . . ."

"Oh my god," Carl cried out. "Who did this?" Carl ran his finger over the writing and noticed it was lipstick. Carl removed his shirt and wiped the graffiti from the windshield. Then ran his wipers to wipe off the grime as much as he could before driving away.

Chapter Sixty: Out of Control

On Saturday morning, John stopped by the coffee shop to grab his morning coffee. Then, he went by the corner store to buy a pack of cigarettes before opening the shoe store. John occasionally smoked to kill time on days and evenings when clients were few and far between.

Approaching the store, John noticed a large envelope sitting on his doorstep. *I don't remember ordering anything.* Intrigued, he picked up the envelope and noticed there was no return address. Juggling his coffee, newspaper and the envelope, John managed to grab his keys to open the door.

Thirty minutes before the store opened, John returned to his office to check the invoices for the shipment he received yesterday. But first, he wanted to see what was in the brown envelope. So he took the envelope, tore it open, and pulled out what looked like a DVD. *What's this? There is no label on it. Maybe it's photographs of a new shoe collection.*

Greg worked late at the restaurant last night, serving burgers to all the teenyboppers of Cardston who decided to drop by for a snack. The community centre was hosting a dance for teens Friday night and they were usually famished after.

While Greg was sleeping soundly, and a loud knock jolted him out of his dream state. Half awake, Greg looked at the time; it was nine-fifteen. *It's Saturday, who could this be . . .* He crawled out of bed, looked for his sweatpants, which were on the floor, jumped into them, and zombied his way to the door.

"Hey, James," Greg said when he opened the door, "come on in. You caught me sleeping."

"I think you still are," James said, smiling. "Sorry for waking you up."

"No, no, that's okay. I've been lazy lately," Greg said, running his hand through his hair. "Do you want a coffee?" Greg asked, filling the kettle.

"Sure, why not. How are you getting on?"

"Great, thanks," Greg said, reaching for two cups. "Hey, please thank your dad for me. Having electricity is great."

"Hey, no problem. What are friends for?" James said.

"Sorry, I only have instant coffee," Greg said, setting the table with the bottle of milk and sugar he poured in a small bowl. "So what's up?"

"I was wondering if you could do Carl and me a favour," James said, resting his hands on the table.

"Sure, what do you guys need?" Greg replied, intrigued.

"Carl called me late last night asking if he could borrow the trailer tonight. He and Jeremy wanted to spend some time together, and they have nowhere to go besides renting a motel. Would you mind spending the night at my place so that they could have their alone time? Just for tonight," James said, leaning back in his chair.

"Of course I don't mind, if it's okay with your folks that I spend the night there," Greg replied as he got up to make coffee.

"Perfect, I'll let Carl know," James said, giving Greg the thumbs up.

"How long have they been together?" Greg asked, bringing the coffee.

"Not long. I think they met when we played in Calgary. Jeremy was there with a friend, Jeremy's friend is a big fan of the Golden Bears, and Carl saw him when we went out partying the night before. I remember the two of them spending a lot of time together, but I didn't think anything of it." James shrugged.

"I'm glad for him. What time do you want me to come over?"

"Come over for dinner, then we can play video games after and watch movies," James said, coffee in hand. "Tyler is welcome to join us after dinner if he wants to as well."

"I can ask him," Greg said. "What on the program for today?"

"I have to help my dad around the house, then I'll probably go for a run," James said, setting his cup on the table.

"Cool."

I'll see you tonight, then," James said, getting up. "Thanks for doing this."

"Don't mention it." Greg got up, put the cups in the sink and went to shower.

John looked at the disc and pondered what was on it. He inserted the DVD into the player and pressed play. A few minutes into the video, John stood staring at the screen, his eyes bulging out of his head — he rose and sent his chair flying across the room. He stumbled back with his eyes still riveted on the image in front of him, then he grabbed his head with both hands and screamed, "That son of a bitch."

John pulled the DVD out and shoved it in a drawer in his desk. Huffing and puffing, he picked up the phone.

"Did you fucking know your stupid son is still a faggot?" John yelled at his wife.

"John," Teresa said. "Calm down. You're scaring me. What's the matter?"

"I just saw a video of your son having sex with another guy."

"First, he's your son too and what he does in private is

none of your business, nor is it mine. The guy's name is Tyler, and yes, our son is gay. It's his life, his happiness, not yours. We'll talk about it later." Teresa hung up.

Did she just hang up on me? John left the store and returned thirty minutes later, carrying a brown paper bag and a coffee. He walked back to his office, opened the back door, lit a cigarette, and sat in the doorway inhaling nicotine to calm his nerves. Then he reopened the store and went about his day, haunted by the images on the video. *I am your servant God, and I will execute your wrath on those who have sinned.*

Teresa was in the kitchen preparing dinner when she heard the door slam. "John, is that you?" she asked.

"Yes, it's me. I'm going in the shower," John said.

"Alright. Dinner will be ready in half an hour."

John went to the bedroom, got undressed, and his eyes landed on the bed in front of him. He stared at it, and he kept seeing the image of Greg and Tyler making love. He took a deep breath and went to take his shower. Water spraying over his head, his hands firmly pressed against the ceramic wall of the shower stall, rage churned inside of him. *I will never accept this sinful behaviour.*

After showering and getting dressed, John walked into the kitchen and grabbed a beer out of the refrigerator. Teresa asked, "Do you want to talk about it?"

"No. I thought about what you said, and you're right. It is his life, and if that makes him happy, then who am I to stand between him and that boy?" John said in a honeyed tone.

"His name is Tyler, John. Whether we like it or not, Greg was born like this. It's not a choice like the conversion therapist told us. Tell me, I have a feeling the Wellness center was not honest with us." Teresa said, looking at John.

"Why do you say this," John replied.

"Did you know torture was a method they used there?"

"Who fed you that crap? Your son? It's a Wellness center, why would they torture people there," John said, being defensive.

"What did they tell you when you went down?" Teresa asked, looking at John straight into his eyes.

"Why do you want to know? I don't remember. They said they use prayers and positive reinforcement to help them see the light." John said, avoiding eye contact.

"Greg told me that he complained to you in the car coming back home about their use of electroshock as one of their treatment."

"I don't recall," John said

"Where did you think he got the welts from?" Teresa said. "His body was covered. Don't tell me they didn't do anything to him." Teresa's voice got louder.

"I told you, the center said it was an allergic reaction to a medication they use there. Some sort of a tranquilizer to calm people down because of the stress they feel when they realize how hurtful, selfish and disrespectful they have been towards their parents, religion, and their bodies," John replied.

"Oh! Really. If I remember correctly, you only said that it was an allergic reaction to a medication. You never told me the specifics. For your information, I called our family doctor and asked if an allergic reaction to some medication can cause red puffy spots on someone's back, not blotches but welts in specific areas. And you know what he told me?" Teresa said as her face took on a look of horror. "It's not possible."

John sat there silent. He grabbed his beer and went to the living room.

"You allowed those people to inflict electrical burns on our son's body . . . how dare you. What evil person have you become? And then you beat Greg up . . ." Tearing up, Teresa said, "He told me he wanted to commit suicide when he came back from that place. But, thanks to his friends, he didn't. I would have never forgiven myself. He needs our love, our support."

"Your love and your support. As long as he continues this disgusting behaviour, he won't get mine," John said, turning on the television.

Teresa got up and ran to her room. "What about dinner?" John yelled.

Teresa opened her door and yelled, "Fix it yourself." Then she slammed the door.

Excited about spending the night ahead with Jeremy, Carl hopped in his car and drove to Magrath to collect his lover. Greg had left the trailer's door unlocked for them, and when they arrived, Jeremy jumped out and said, "Wow, look at this place, how did you find this?"

"It belongs to a friend of mine's father. He said we could have it for the night. I told my folks I was spending the night at a friend's place," Carl said.

"I did too. So we can stay here all night then?"

"Yep. I even got us some beer and munchies. We don't have to go anywhere. We can make love all night."

"I like the sound of that." Jeremy grabbed Carl's waist, pulled him closer, and kissed him. "See what you do to me," he said, placing Carl's hand on his crotch to make him feel his hard-on.

"The bedroom is back there. Follow me," Carl said.

Around nine o'clock, John got up from the sofa, looked in his coat pocket, and then went to the bedroom, then to the kitchen. Teresa asked what he was looking for, and he said his cellphone. "I must have forgotten it on my desk at the store. I'm going to drive down to get it. I shouldn't be gone long," John said.

"Fine," Teresa said, still upset at her husband.

John drove to the store, tossed a small package in the backseat, put his cell in his pocket and drove off. He took Highway Two to Seventh Avenue, went down to the end, and parked. He opened the car door, remained seated, and lit up a cigarette. John quietly sat there smoking, deep in thoughts.

He threw half of his cigarette outside, reached over to the back seat, grabbed what was in the package, and got out. After shutting his door, he looked around the parking area, then he started walking. Strolling down the grass patched laneway, he stopped for a minute to spot the trailer he was looking for, since he came in from another direction. He stood outside the camper where Greg was staying and quietly pressed the door handle and pulled on the door and stepped inside.

The place was quiet. John looked around and saw several empty beer bottles on the table and discarded bags of chips. Carefully watching where he was stepping, he walked slowly towards the bedroom peeked inside, and saw the guys sleeping soundly, probably from too much drinking. John then pulled a gun out of his coat pocket, aimed it at the one sleeping to his right, who he thought was Tyler, and pulled the trigger.

The noise jolted Carl awake.

John, realizing it wasn't Tyler, removed the blanket from the bed and panicked. Carl, alert by now, saw this man in front with a gun pointed at Jeremy and then he turned towards Jeremy to wake him and saw the blood. Terror took over his face, he grabbed Jeremy by the arm and turned him and saw the blood seeping out of his forehead. He threw himself on him.

"Nooooooo!" Carl screamed. He repeated Jeremy's name hysterically. "You fucking prick," Carl screamed as he lunged towards John. John's reflex kicked in and he pulled the trigger, sending Carl backwards in the bed with a bullet through the heart.

John ran out to his car in a frenzy. In the dark stillness, he couldn't see much, but the dim glow of the moon on the ground lit his path to the car. John fumbled with his gun, trying to shove it in his coat pocket while running erratically. He stumbled, scraped his elbow and tore part of his sleeve, then got up, looked behind to make sure he wasn't being followed, got in his car, and sped away.

Breathing laboriously from fear, John drove to a park along the way and threw the gun into the lake. He crouched by the lake to recover. *What did I do? What did I do? Calm down, John. No one saw you. Breathe, breathe.* John got up and paced along the shore, grabbing his head with both hands, his whole body shaking uncontrollably.

Teresa knows I went to the store to pick up my cellphone. How long has it been? John checked his watch. *Shit, I've been gone forty-five minutes.*

John ran to his car and drove home.

Chapter Sixty-One: Dazed and Con-fused

In the ten hours John had been in bed, he must have woken up six times. Each time it was the same disturbance—the sound of a gun going off. This time the gunshot sounded real and close, and he could still hear the ringing in his ears. In his dream state, John got up and walked towards the window, searching for where the shot came from. The moonlight shone through the window, and its ray of light highlighted the red blotches on his bare chest.

Seeing this reflection in the windowpane, John lowered his head, and saw that his body was covered in red spots and streaks. He looked at his hands, and they were blood-covered as well. Panicked, he turned towards the bed, and lying in it was a body covered in blood and a gun resting next to it. Terrified, holding his head, John tried to scream for help, but the words wouldn't come out of his mouth.

The loud ring of his alarm clock jolted him out of his dream.

Paralyzed and haunted by his nightmare, John lay there a minute before getting up, breathing deeply and drenched in sweat. Then, he slowly turned towards Teresa, sleeping next to him, hoping it was only a dream. Reassured, John finally got up, turned on the shower and, reflected in the mirror, saw a man distraught and haunted by what he did. Once dressed, John went to make himself a coffee before leaving for work, but thought the caffeine would put him over the edge, so he left without it.

John got to the store, dropped off his briefcase, then went to the corner store to pick his newspaper. He decided that he needed a coffee after all, so he walked across the street to get the strongest coffee he could buy. Back in the store, John went to his office and leafed through the newspaper a few times, looking for anything related to what he did; fortunately, there was no mention of it. Breathing a sigh of relief, John lit a cigarette and sat out back with his coffee.

But John knew it was just a matter of time before someone discovered the bodies.

Greg stopped by the supermarket to buy tomatoes, lettuce, and radishes to make a salad with the leftover chicken on his way to the trailer. Walking along, Greg wondered if Carl and Jeremy were still there. *I hope they had a wonderful evening together.*

Entering the trailer, Greg noticed a strange smell as if someone urinated, then spotted the mess in the kitchen.

"What the hell?" he said when he saw the empty beer bottles all over the table and chips crumbs on the seats. *I cleaned this place before I left; they could at least have cleaned up after themselves.* Greg put down his bags on the small kitchen counter, then picked up the empties and cleaned the table. Next, he stored the vegetables in the fridge and tidied up the living area. *I thought Carl would have been tidier. But maybe I'm too quick to judge, they probably planned to clean up when they got back. Still, what's that smell?*

Greg grabbed his backpack and went to the bedroom to unpack. Greg let out a blood curdling scream, then ran outside, threw up and collapsed to the ground, quivering. Gathering his nerve, he stood up and slowly went back in, praying it wasn't what he saw. Standing at the bedroom entrance, Greg hesitated to step in. Then, inhaling deeply, he walked in and froze when he caught a glimpse of what looked like Carl and Jeremy. He began convulsing uncontrollably when he realized the blood-soaked bodies in the bed were those of his friend Carl and his boyfriend. Greg fell to his knees, crying and howling, his heart had been ripped out of his chest. Greg shaky reached for his cell in his back pocket and dialled 911.

Crying hysterically, he said, "Hello . . . Someone killed my friend and his friend."

"Sir, calm down. What is your name?" the operator asked.

"Greg Miller," Greg replied, trying to contain his crying long enough to answer.

"Where did this happen?" the operator asked.

Greg, swallowed then took a deep breath, "Lee Creek Campground. The third camper on the last row, near the tree line," he said, his voice cracking.

"Okay, stay with me. Help is on the way. How did they die?" the operator calmly asked.

"I guess they were shot; there is blood all over the bed," Greg managed to say, his voice quivering.

"What is your friend's name?" the operator said before asking Greg to take a deep breath, to calm him down.

Sniffling, Greg replied, "Carl and the other guy is his boyfriend, Jeremy, I think. Please hurry."

Before too long, the paramedics and police arrived and went straight into the trailer. While they were in the trailer, the police brought Greg to a bench nearby to ask him some questions.

"Hi, I'm Constable Mercer. Can I have your name?"

"Greg Miller," Greg said, breathing noisily and drying his eyes.

"Where do you live?" Constable Mercer asked, standing in front of Greg pad in hand.

"I live here." Greg said, pointing to the trailer.

"You live in this trailer?" Greg nodded yes. "When did you

discover the bodies?" he asked, writing.

"About fifteen minutes ago," Greg replied, wiping his wet hands on the front of his jeans.

"Is this your trailer?"

"No. It belongs to a friend of mine's father. I've been staying in it for a little over a month with his permission." Greg took his backpack and laid it on the ground and sat on it.

"What's your friend's full name?" Constable Mercer asked, pen in hand looking at Greg.

"James Sutton."

"They live in Cardston?"

"Yeah," Greg said, shaking his head, his eyes looking at the ground, his chin resting on his knees.

"Do you know the people inside?" Constable Mercer asked.

"The guy with the blond hair is Jeremy, I think, and the other is my friend Carl," Greg replied, tearing up again.

"Why do you say *think*?" he asked with a frown.

Greg looked up at Constable Mercer and with a cracking in his voice, "Carl and Jeremy borrowed the trailer last night for the night, and I went to stay with James for the night. I've never met Jeremy before."

"Did Carl have any enemies?"

"Not that I'm aware of."

"Has he ever been intimidated by someone?" Constable Mercer asked.

"I know he was outed on social media by a girl at school. Her name is Elaine Thompson. But she bullies everyone on social media." Greg started fidgeting; his rear end was getting numb sitting on his backpack.

"Do you think Elaine would be involved in this?" he asked bluntly.

"I don't know."

"Do you know where she lives?"

"In Magrath," Greg said.

"That's all I need for now. Do you have a place to go?" Constable Mercer asked. Greg nodded his head yes.

"When will I be able to return to the trailer?"

"In a few days," Constable Mercer said.

"Can I get some clothes and my school stuff?" Greg asked, unsure if he wanted to go back in the room.

"Yes. Just tell the officer," he said as he was writing in his pad.

Greg watched as Carl and Jeremy's bodies were carried to the ambulance. He turned away for a moment, as they passed in front of him, his heart aching so much. Greg went in and saw the bed stripped from all the linen, stained with blood. He stood there a moment. *It could have been me and Tyler.* He quickly grabbed what he needed and ran out.

When he arrived at James's house, the police were already there. Greg knocked, and James opened the door and saw Greg. "Are you okay, man? What the fuck happened? Who could have done this? The police are in the living room questioning my parents."

Greg asked if he could spend a couple of days there. James said, "Of course you can. I don't understand who could do such a thing." Greg wrapped his arms around James and held him tight as they both cried, grieving for their murdered friend.

Greg and James joined James's parents and the officer in the living room. James's mother got up, took both boys in her arms, and said, "I'm so sorry for your friend's death. It's horrible. I hope they catch the monster who did this."

"Greg's going to spend a few days here until he can go back to the trailer," James said.

"Greg, you can stay as long as you want," James's mother said.

"Do you have an idea who might have done this?" James's

father asked.

"No. We're searching the area for clues that might have been left behind," the officer said, getting ready to leave.

"Listen, boys, what is going through your minds must be overwhelming. If ever you need to talk, I'm here. I'm really sorry for your loss," James's father said.

James and Greg went down to the basement, sat on the couch in silence while their eyes overflowed with tears. Their world had been turned upside down.

Greg asked, "Do you think this happened because of Elaine's post on social media?"

"If it was viewed only by the guys at our school, I don't think so. But, if she shared it wider, maybe," James said, drying his eyes.

"I guess they will announce it tomorrow at school. Do you think we should get the team together tomorrow night?" Greg asked.

"It might be a good idea. We can check with the guys tomorrow."

Monday morning, the school director asked all the students to gather in the cafeteria for an announcement. Greg and James sat with Tyler and some of the guys from the football team. Shawn from the team asked where Carl was. James and Greg didn't say anything. The director's voice came on the intercom.

"Good morning, everyone. I'm sorry to say I don't have good news today. Unfortunately, we lost one of our students on the weekend. Carl Springfield died yesterday." Gasps of shock reverberated around the room. "We have no word to express our sadness. In his memory, please join me in a minute of silence to think about our friend . . . Class is suspended for the rest of the day. Our staff will be on hand for anyone who would like to talk. Thank you, and God bless everyone."

Elaine came over and asked what happened. James got up and said, "Someone shot him dead, and it better not be because of what you posted." With that, Tyler, James, and Greg walked away.

Elaine looked like she'd seen a ghost. Feeling faint, she sat down.

Chapter Sixty-two: Investigation

Detective Jack Gordon arrived at the scene around seven o'clock Monday morning. Already there were Sergeant Paul Ramsay and Sergeant Carlos Banderos, examining every inch of the path from the trailer to the parking lot, painstakingly searching for evidence.

"Paul, have you found anything yet?" Detective Gordon asked.

"No."

"Let's go in."

Jack pulled the tape off the door and entered the trailer. Jack and Paul began their examination with a walkthrough. "There is no sign of forced entry," Jack said, "which means that the door wasn't locked." Paul turned on his flashlight and fanned the floor back and forth to detect any traces of shoeprints while Jack examined the kitchen and living area.

"I wonder how come they didn't hear anything," Jack said. Then he saw the empty beer bottles Greg had been in the middle of clearing up. "Ah, that's probably why. They were sound asleep."

Jack took out his camera and began snapping photos of the area. At the same time, Paul went to the bedroom to start his investigation.

"Jack, you need to see this," Paul said from the bedroom.

Jack hurried into the bedroom. Paul opened one of the overhead cabinets and pointed to a camera hidden there. "The camera is pointed towards the mirror which right in front of the bed. Was this intentional? Were the guys being spied on, or were they filming themselves?" Paul said.

"Can we find out who this camera belongs to?" Jack said.

"Yes, sir," Paul said.

"Paul, dust it for fingerprints also. Can you asked Carlos to package those bloodstained bedsheets and send them to the lab?" Jack continued his investigation, noting everything they found and collected. "Paul, did we get fingerprints off the door handles inside and out?"

"Carlos and I dusted them first thing this morning."

Standing in the bedroom doorway, Jack looked at the picture that the guys took of the victims. Based on how the bodies were found, Jack deduced the shooter shot the first victim from here. *The first victim was sleeping when he was shot; it looks like the other tried to stop his assailant, and the shooter fired when he was coming at him.*

"Okay. I think we're done here. We can head back to the station," Jack said.

Sergeant Banderos stopped Sergeant Ramsay and Detective Gordon on their way to their car. "Looks like someone fell here," Carlos said.

"Collect a sample of the soil, and we'll send it to forensics," Detective Gordon said.

Sergeant Ramsay knocked on Jack's door at the police station. Jack waved at him to come in. "What do you have for me?"

"Detective," Paul said, "they got a hold of Mr. Sutton, and the camera is not his. He doesn't know who placed it there."

"Can you get in touch with Greg Miller, the guy that lives there, to see if it's his?" Jack asked.

Sergeant Ramsay, picked up the phone and called the school to speak to Greg.

"He's in class right now, the receptionist said. I can have him call you back."

"It the Cardston Police department, I really need to talk to him now. Can someone get him please? Sergeant Ramsay insisted.

The receptionist went and talk to the director about the request, unsure of what to do. The director told her to page him. "Greg Miller please come to the director's office please."

"Sergeant Ramsay," the receptionist said, "I have asked Mr. Miller to come to the office. He should be here in five minutes. Oh, Greg, Sergeant Ramsay would like to talk to you." She handed him the phone.

"Hi, this is Greg," he said nervously.

"Greg, this is Sergeant Paul Ramsay, I'm investigating what happened at your trailer. We found a camera hidden in the bedroom and we were wondering if it was yours."

"A camera? No. I never saw a camera in the bedroom, before. Have you asked Mr. Sutton or James?" Greg replied, shocked.

"We did, it's not theirs. Are you sure it's not yours? I don't know, kids now a days like to play jokes on each other and catch people by surprise . . ." Paul said, prying.

"I've already told you, it's not mine. Who would I play a joke on? Myself? Greg replied in annoyance.

"Very well," Paul said. "Thank you, Greg. We'll get in touch if we have more questions." Paul hung up.

Greg returned to class, scratching his head, wondering who would hide a camera in the bedroom and how long had it been there.

Paul returned to Detective Sutton's office. "Detective, the camera wasn't Greg Miller's either. He was surprised to know that a camera had been planted in his room."

"Thank you Sergeant," the detective said.

Later that afternoon, Paul received a call from forensics, they were able to get prints off the camera. Paul went and got the report from them, then read through it before he brought it to Detective Sutton.

"Sir, here the report for the prints they found on the camera. Unfortunately they didn't come up with anything. So I called the store here in Cardston to verify if they had sold this type of security camera to anyone lately, and it turned out they did. They sold one to Elaine Thompson from Magrath. She is a student at Cardston High and the daughter of Phillip Thompson of Thompson Realty."

"Bring her in for questioning." Jack said.

"Oh, before I forget . . . the camera has an application that can relay the video directly to a cellphone or tablet. I thought you should know. We should get results from forensic in a few days."

"Thanks, Sergeant."

Greg went to the park to unwind. He sat silently overlooking the river, thinking how he missed Carl. He would cry at one moment and then laugh the next, remembering some special time they shared. He also found himself getting angry that he had not been able to do anything to prevent it. He tried repeatedly to make some sense of something that did not make sense at all. Tears flowed down his cheeks when Tyler arrived. He took Greg into his arms and held him tight, feeling his immense loss and pain.

"What's going through your mind right now?" Tyler asked.

Greg blinked back his tears. "I can't stop thinking about Carl. Who could have done this and why? I don't understand. Only James and I knew they were there."

"Could it be that Carl told somebody else?"

"I don't see why he would have done. He and Jeremy wanted to be together, alone and away from onlookers."

"You're right. His parents must be devastated."

"Shit, this is awful. One other thing keeps haunting me. What if the shooter didn't know it was Carl and Jeremy staying at the trailer last Saturday? Who was he there to kill?"

"Woah," Tyler said, creeped out. "You're scaring me. What are you saying?"

"I'm saying was he there to shoot me? Why? All this shit is going through my mind."

"How will you feel going back there?"

"I have no choice. I can't go back home, not with my dad still the way he is. So I will probably sleep on the sofa bed for a while, then we'll see. One thing for sure—I'm going to make sure the door is always locked."

"Do you want to come over for dinner?"

"At your place? What about your parents?"

"I told them what happened, and I asked them if you could come to dinner. So it's going to be okay, and it will give them a chance to get to know you."

"Thanks, I'd like that."

Chapter Sixty-three: Connection

John had retreated inside of himself; his eyes were blank as he stared at the television. It was as if sound was not registering in his brain and came from far, far away. He seemed disconnected from reality.

"What happened to your shirt?" Teresa asked.

"Huh?" John said, snapping out of his trance. "What shirt?"

"The one you put in the wash. The one you had on went back to the store to get your cell. I pulled it out to wash it, and the right sleeve was torn at the elbow."

"Oh, I fell at the store that night and scraped my elbow." John lifted his right arm to show the scratch on his elbow.

Teresa nodded when John showed her his elbow. Something wasn't right though. John always went to Teresa to get tears and split seams fixed. He never just dropped the item in the laundry basket. Something else Teresa found peculiar about her husband was that he was unusually quiet since the weekend and had not argued once, which was rare for John.

"You've been distant all week. What's going on?" Teresa asked.

"I'm fine. I keep thinking about what happened at the campground," John replied with a blank expression.

"It's awful. I can't imagine what the family is going through. What a senseless crime. Two young men killed because of who they were. This is what discrimination does to people," Teresa said staring at John, who didn't react to what she said.

Seconds later, John bluntly said, "I think it's a sign that God is not happy about how his children are behaving."

Teresa looked at John, frowning. "What are you talking about, John?" she asked, staring at him and shaking her head in disbelief.

"Is this not God's way of warning us that sinners will be punished?"

"Sinners? Who says these teenagers were sinners? They were only eighteen," Teresa said, simmering with anger.

"They were involved in an immoral act," John replied, lashing out at Teresa.

"What immoral act? How do you know it was immoral?"

"It was in the newspaper. They were in bed together." His face contorted in disgust.

"So what?" she said. "Maybe they were friends, you don't know."

"They were homos."

"Are you listening to yourself? Are you saying your son should be shot because he's gay?" Teresa choked as she said it.

John didn't answer. He got up and said, "I'm going to bed. I have a busy day tomorrow." Then he left the room with a dull expression on his face.

"John. John, answer me! Look at me," she said tears rolling down her face. John went on his way, he didn't turn once to look at Teresa.

"You bastard," she yelled, "How dare you think this about your own son?" She ran to the front door, took a sweater and slammed the door behind her and sat on the porch crying furiously.

Around four in the morning, John lay awake, his mind replaying the events of that night. The absolute horror of his actions paralyzed him, and the thought of running away terrified him. Yet, he didn't remember being that scared in his life. John retraced every move he made that night and wondered if anyone saw him.

The guilt sat not on his chest but inside his brain. What he had done, he could not undo. One second passed, two seconds passed, three seconds passed, and the guilt continued eating away at him. He checked the time and carefully slipped out of bed, grabbed his clothes, and closed the bedroom door. Once dressed, he got in his car — it was still dark out when he drove to the store.

Sitting in his office, the fear looped around in John's mind until there was no room for anything else. *Will I be caught? Did anyone see me? Look what you've made me do, you fucking homo. My own son, a sinner.*

"You were supposed to die," John screamed out. "You were supposed to be in that bed, not him." John broke down and started to moan.

The sun was starting to rise when Elaine arrived at the trailer, still covered in crime scene tape. Before entering, she looked around to make sure no one was nearby, then she grabbed her cellphone to light her way to the bedroom. Elaine stopped in her tracks at the sight of the bloody mattress in front of her. She covered her mouth and nose because of the stench, then carefully walked around the bed until she reached the right overhead cabinet door. Elaine looked inside, but the camera wasn't there. *I thought I placed it on this side.* She walked to the other side and checked there, but to no avail. *Fuck! They found it. Shit.*

Elaine rushed back to her car, her mind in turmoil. *I must erase the video of Greg and Tyler, I don't want it to lead back to me.*

Elaine scrolled to the video capture on her cell and noticed two videos had been recorded. *What is the other one?* Elaine pressed play, then her brain stuttered for a moment, and her eyes took time to catch up to what she was watching. After a brief moment, her emotions changed gears, and shock took over her body. *I have to get rid of this video. If the police get a hold of it, Greg will find out who killed Carl and Jeremy.* Elaine swiftly deleted both files from her cell.

Elaine arrived at school just in time for her classes. Trying to stay awake during her English class, she heard her name being called through the intercom. "Will Elaine Thompson report to the principal's office?" the director announced.

She gathered her books and marched to the director's office. Approaching his door, Elaine noticed two police officers inside. *Why am I being summoned? What are those officers doing here?*

The director motioned for Elaine to come in. "Elaine, these gentlemen are here to see you," the director said.

"Ms. Thompson, we have some questions for you. Can you please come with us to the station?" Sergeant Paul Ramsay said.

"What questions?" Elaine asked.

"Regarding the crime that occurred at the campground. Please follow us." Sergeant Ramsay guided Elaine outside the office.

"Is she under arrest?" the director asked.

"No. We only want to ask her some questions."

Elaine's heart twisted and sunk with nerves as she sat in the detective's office. Her breaths came in sharp pants, and she tried to gain control, but nothing was working. She tried to breathe calmly, but the wait was making her anxiety worse.

"Sorry to drag you away from school, Ms. Thompson," Detective Gordon said. "We found this camera in the trailer, specifically in the bedroom of the trailer." Elaine broke out in a cold sweat when she saw her camera in the plastic evidence bag on the table. "We traced it back to you. Can you tell us what it was doing in the trailer's bedroom?"

"I placed it there when I stayed at the camper recently while I was looking for an apartment. Being a woman living alone, I was afraid of someone breaking in while I was asleep," Elaine said, straight-faced.

"How long ago was this?"

"A few weeks ago."

"How long did you stay in the camper?"

"Only a few nights."

"Any recordings from the camera while you were there?" Detective Gordon asked.

"No, I realized you needed to download an application to be able to view anything that was captured by it."

"Can we borrow your cell for a minute?"

"What for?" Elaine's hands became moist. She tried to keep her expression neutral but she felt her heart thumping inside her chest.

"We want to check if there were any video captures in the last seven days that might help us with this investigation."

"I'm telling you, there was nothing recorded." Beads of cold sweat formed on her forehead as she desperately trying to regulate her breathing.

"Just the same, we'd like to check, Ms. Thompson."

Elaine reached in her pocket and pulled out her cell, thankful that she deleted the videos. She extended her arm to give her phone to the detective, flashing a forced smile. "Here you go. Will I get it back?"

"It shouldn't be long."

Jack waved at Sergeant Ramsay to come in and handed him Elaine's cellphone and a note. "Did you know Carl Springfield?" Jack asked.

"He was a neighbour, and we went to the same school." Elaine replied, pretending to wipe a tear.

"You knew he was gay?" Jack asked sharply.

"A friend of mine told me," Elaine replied, nodding her head yes and forcing a sad face.

"Do you know of anyone that might have done this? Did Carl or his friend have enemies, someone who had an issue with them being gay?"

"No," Elaine replied.

Sergeant Ramsay returned with the cellphone and a note. Jack read the message and said, "When did you stay at the camper again?" Detective Sutton asked again, his hands on his desk and leaning forward, staring at Elaine's who began fidgeting.

"About one week or so ago? Why?" Elaine crossed her arms to hide her shaky hands.

"Because Mr. Sutton, the trailer's owner, said that the only person who he knew stayed at the trailer was Greg Miller."

Elaine heard those words being spoken, and she watched the anger flash across the detective's face. She crumpled inside, trying to remain composed as she tried to explain her lie. "Alright," Elaine said. "I installed the camera in the trailer because I wanted to capture the lies being spread about me."

"Why did you install it in the bedroom and not the living room?" the detective asked, getting up from behind his desk.

"Because I couldn't find a spot to put it where they couldn't find it?"

"Who are they?" Detective Sutton asked authoritatively, his eyes fixed on Elaine.

"I meant Greg," Elaine said, her voice cracking.

"Do you know, Ms. Thompson, that this is an invasion of privacy? You could be sued for it."

"No, I didn't know," Elaine replied, feeling uneasy.

"Thank you for your time, Ms. Thompson. Sergeant Banderos will drive you back to school. We may need to talk to you again. Have a good day."

Elaine put her hands in her jeans pocket as she walked out, keeping her arms close to her body to hide her quivering.

"Were you able to retrieve data from her cellphone?" Jack asked Sergeant Ramsay a little while later.

"Yes we were, though Ms. Thompson erased the videos this morning. However, they were still on the cloud. The videos have been transferred to the case file. You can view them from your computer."

"Thank you."

Chapter Sixty-four: Search

John usually called Teresa after lunch to let her know how things were at the store, but she hadn't heard from him today. Worried about his state of mind in light of his comments he made the night before, Teresa picked up the phone and dialled the store.

"J.T. Miller shoes, how can I help you?" John answered.

"Hi, John. How is it at the store today?"

"It's slow. I had a few clients this morning, but the afternoon looks quiet. Is there something wrong?"

"No. I thought perhaps you were busy and needed a hand because you usually call around lunchtime."

"No, everything is fine."

"Do you need help with something? I can come to the store."

"There isn't much to do, but if you want, I need help with entering the sales in the ledger."

"Sure, no problem. Did you want a coffee? I can get one across the street," Teresa said.

"Yeah, I could go for a coffee."

John was gathering the samples of his new line of shoes when he heard the door chime. "I'll be there in just a minute, Teresa. You can put the coffee on my desk."

John came out of the storage room with a few boxes of shoes in his arms and noticed two police officers standing in the middle of the store. "Gentlemen, how can I help you?" John asked, setting the shoe boxes on a chair.

Teresa walked in and saw the two police officers, and

looked at John to ask what they were doing here. "Hi, honey," John said. "All the sales slips are on the desk. I'll be right with you." Teresa walked past the officers, glanced at them sideways on her way to the office, flashing a half-smile.

"We're looking for Mr. John Miller," one of the officers said.

"I am John Miller. What is this all about?"

"You're under arrest for the murder of Carl Springfield and Jeremy Simmons."

"What?" John said in a complete state of panic. "You've made a mistake. I didn't kill anyone."

Teresa bolted out of the office as the officers were cuffing her husband. "What is going on? John, what's happening?"

"Your husband is accused of murdering the two guys at the campground," the officer said.

"This must be a mistake, my husband would never do such a thing."

"I have a warrant to search this place and your house. Take him away," the officer told his partner.

"Search for what?" Teresa asked.

Teresa slapped the store closed sign in the window and followed the officer into the office. The officer searched John's desk and found a brown envelope with a DVD inside, in the bottom drawer. He inserted the DVD into the player and pressed play.

A few minutes into the video, the police officer took a step back. *What is this video doing here? It's the same one that we got from this girl's cellphone.* He stopped the player, shoved the DVD back in the envelope and stuffed it in a plastic bag.

"Is everything okay?" Teresa asked when she noticed the officer's facial expression looking at the video.

The officer said nothing and continued his search. He

looked everywhere thoroughly, but didn't find what he was looking for. He turned to Teresa, who was sitting at John's desk "Ma'am, I need to search your house. Is there someone at home?"

"No," Teresa said.

"Can you come with me?" the officer asked with a stern look.

"What about the store? I can't just close." Teresa tried to delay the house search until she could look through it herself.

"Is there anybody else that can open the door of your house? Unfortunately, I am required to search your home today."

Teresa looked at the officer. "You're making a big mistake. My husband is innocent. I'll meet you at the house."

The officer entered John and Teresa's bedroom, opened the closet and began to search behind the hung clothes, then he looked on the closet floor and the top shelf. He carefully searched the dresser drawers and didn't find anything. He went into Greg's room, saw a picture on a dresser, and called Teresa.

"Who is this?" the officer asked, pointing at the photo on the dresser. The officer recognized the face.

"This is my son Greg," she said with a smile.

"How was the relationship between your son and your husband?"

"They had a falling out not too long ago," Teresa said nervously, "and Greg went and stayed with friends for a while. Unfortunately, my husband has a temper and sometimes loses it," she added.

"How long has he been away?"

"A little over a month."

"Is he in Cardston?" the officer asked.

"Yes, he goes to Cardston High. Why?" Teresa asked,

wondering why the officer was asking about her son.

"The fallout, was it because your son is gay?" he asked bluntly.

"Yes, it was. My husband is very religious, and homosexuality is a sin, according to him. He sent our son to conversion therapy and recently found out that Greg hadn't changed. So he lost his temper and hit Greg. That is why Greg left," Teresa said, shameful.

"Did Greg and his boyfriend ever go to the trailer at Lee Creek Campground?"

"Yes, a few months ago. My husband went over one night and confronted Greg. This was what prompted us to send him to therapy."

"How did he know that Greg would be there?" he asked, hoping to find out who told him.

"He told me that a girl that went to school with Greg dropped into the store and told my husband that he must be proud of his gay son. She then told him that she saw him and his boyfriend at a trailer at the campground," Teresa said, taking a deep breath.

"Do you know the girl's name?"

"I'm afraid I don't."

"Thank you."

"How long will my husband be detained?" she asked as the officer turned to leave.

"I couldn't say. Have a good day, Mrs. Miller." The officer smiled and left.

CHAPTER SIXTY-FIVE: ACCESSORY

Sergeant Ramsay walked into Detective Gordon's office. "Sir, I have some information you might be interested in. One of the two guys having sex in the video is John Miller's son, Greg Miller. According to his wife Teresa, John Miller is a religious nut, and having a gay son was not something he was going to stand. So when he found out that his son and this other guy were seeing each other and had been lying about it, he went over to the trailer, the same trailer where the crime took place, to surprise his son and his lover. Guess who tipped him off? A girl from his school. How did John Miller end up with this video?"

"Why don't we ask Ms. Thompson?" Detective Gordon said, sending Carlos off to pick her up at school.

Elaine entered Detective Gordon's office thirty minutes later, accompanied by Sergeant Banderos.

"Ms. Thompson, sorry to bring you back here again, but we have a few more questions. Mrs. Miller told my sergeant that Mr. Miller found out about his son Greg and his friend still saw each other from a schoolmate of theirs. Would you happen to know who this might be?"

"No. Why would I know that?" Elaine said icily.

"Do you know anyone that could have tipped Mr. Miller off?" Detective Gordon insisted.

"No."

"Are you sure it wasn't you who informed Mr. Miller about his son and his friend?" Detective Gordon asked.

"Why would I want to do that? I don't care if they are gay

or not," Elaine said.

"Didn't you out your neighbour Carl on social media?"

"What does Carl have to do with Greg Miller?"

"You just said that you didn't care if Greg Miller was gay or not, but you publicly denounced your neighbour. Aren't you contradicting yourself, Ms. Thompson?" Detective Gordon said matter-of-factly.

Elaine just looked at Detective Gordon. "Who do you think would have informed Mr. Miller then?" Jack asked her.

"I don't know."

"Did you know that Greg's father was religious, and that he considered homosexuality a sin?"

"I knew he was religious. Why else would he send his son to conversion therapy?"

"How did you know that Mr. Miller sent Greg to conversion therapy?" he asked, sitting on his desk in front of Elaine, his hands crossed on his lap.

"Greg told me," Elaine said, looking at him expressionless.

"Has Greg ever come to school looking like he had been beaten up?"

"Yes, about a month ago. His face was badly bruised."

"Were you aware that his father did this to him?" Detective Gordon asked.

"Yes, I was. Greg told me," Elaine said impatiently.

"Do you think his father beat him because he found out he was having sex with another guy?

"Maybe, I don't know."

"When we questioned Mr. Miller, we showed him a photo of you and asked him if this was the girl that went into his store. Do you want to know his answer?" Detective Gordon leaned back into his chair and looked at Elaine straight in the eyes.

Elaine's insides began churning, her heart started palpitating and the palm of her hands were sweating. With no other choice, she said, "Alright, I went to see him and told him about Greg seeing Tyler, and the place where they meet."

"Was it the only time you went to the store?" he asked bluntly.

"No. I went to tell Greg's father that he and Tyler were having sex at the trailer," Elaine replied sheepishly.

"It's probably why his father beat him up, wouldn't you agree, Ms. Thompson? Was there another time you went to the store?"

"No. Those were the only times."

"Then perhaps you might explain how Mr. Miller happened to have a video of his son and Tyler having sex?" he said, looking down at her.

"What video? I don't know anything about that," Elaine replied, her voice sounding panicky.

"We found a DVD at the store." Detective Gordon motioned his Sergeant to give him the video.

"I know nothing about a video."

"Are you sure? It's the same video we got from your cell the other day." Detective Gordon waved the video at her.

"What video? I have no video on my cell," Elaine said.

"We know you deleted the security videos from your cell. We were able to get them back. Now, did you drop him a copy of that video?"

"No. I don't know how he could have gotten this."

"Are you sure?"

"Yes, I'm sure." Elaine felt her chest tightening up with anxiety.

"What if I send one of my guys to get your home computer and have our forensic experts look at your hard drive? What do you think they might find? It's amazing what these guys can recover. Also, your fingerprints are all over the DVD. Let me ask you again, how did . . ."

"I left a copy on the doorstep at the store. I did it to get back at Greg for posting a picture of me standing half-naked out-side a motel," Elaine said, tearing up.

"You knew of Greg's father's violent nature, as Greg told you himself when you saw him. So you left him a video of his son having sex with another man, knowing his father would become aggressive towards his son—therefore, you would have your revenge," the detective said in an accusing manner.

"No," Elaine said loudly. "Are you saying that I'm respon-sible for what Greg's father did to him? That's bullshit."

"No, Ms. Thompson. What Mr. Miller did to Carl and Jer-emy? Suppose it's proven that your video provoked Mr. Mil-ler to commit a crime. You can be accused of being an acces-sory to a crime. Do you understand?" he said sharply.

"What crime? Greg is still alive, isn't he?" she said defi-antly.

"Fortunately for him. If he hadn't permitted Carl and Jer-emy to use the trailer that night, Greg and his boyfriend would be dead today. You see, Ms. Thompson, the video trig-gered John to commit these murders. Mr. Miller confessed that he thought Greg and Tyler were in that bed that night. It's as if you handed him the gun." Jack motioned for the of-ficer to come in.

"Ms. Thompson, you are under arrest as an accessory to murder. Take her away."

"No, you can't do this," Elaine yelled. "I didn't do any-thing. Let go of me! I want to speak to a lawyer."

Chapter Sixty-six: Superior Court of Cardston

Teresa drove to the campground to pick up her son. When she walked into the trailer, Greg was sitting at the table looking gloom and his hands were shaking. Teresa sat in front of him and took his hands and looked at him with mother's eyes and squeezed his hands to comfort him. Greg has been dreading this day.

"Are you okay?" Teresa asked.

"I'll be okay. I'm not sure how I'll react when I see him in that courtroom. I have a hard time conceiving that my own father took the lives of two human beings, and for what?" Greg said, tears filling his eyes. "Because their relationship went against his beliefs? One of them was my friend," Greg said as he burst out crying. "I hope they hang him."

Teresa went around the table and took Greg into his arm and held him tight as Greg sobbed. "You will be okay," Teresa softly said to him.

Greg lifting his head and sitting back, swallowed and said, "I know. I want to see his face when they sentence him. I want him to see me when they call me to testify. See his reaction when I tell the court what he did to me."

"Then we better get going," his mother said. "Otherwise we'll be late."

Greg grabbed a jacket and some Kleenex and got in the car with his mother.

Inside the courtroom, Tyler went and sat beside Greg and

his mother. He took Greg's hand, and squeezed it. In front of them sat Carl's parents and a few relatives. Seated near the back were Elaine's parents, and two rows in front of them were Jeremy's folks.

The officers brought John and Elaine, released them from their handcuffs and sat them at their lawyer's table. The judge walked in, and the court clerk said, "Order in the court. All rise! The Honourable Mister Justice Bernard presiding."

Everyone stood as the judge entered the room. The judge sat and looked around the courtroom and said, "You may be seated. Are all parties present?"

The crown attorney stood up and said, "Yes, Your Honour. I am Dennis Pratt, and this is my associate Carol Armstrong. We are acting on behalf of the Crown in this matter."

The Defence got up and looked at the judge and said, "Your Honour. I am Mark Gregory. I am acting on behalf of the accused, John Miller and Elaine Thompson."

"Thank you, the judge said. "John Miller and Elaine Thompson, please rise to hear the charges."

"John Miller," the court clerk said, "you are charged with murder in the second degree for causing the death of Carl Springfield and Jeremy Simmons. Elaine Thompson, you are charged as an accessory to murder. How do you plead?"

John replied, "Not guilty."

Greg's face flushed with anger and his hands began to clench so tight, his knuckles were turning white. Tyler saw his reaction and whispered, "Honey, calm down. We all know he's guilty so will the jury." Greg took a deep breath and began to relax a little.

Elaine, expressionless, replied, "Not guilty."

"I'm not surprised that bitch would say that," Greg quietly said to Tyler.

"Thank you, you may sit," the judge said, looking at both of them.

"Good afternoon, ladies and gentlemen of the jury," the judge began, turning and looking at the jury. "I shall begin with some general comments on your roles during this trial. Throughout these proceedings, you shall act as judges of the facts and I, the judge of the law. Although I may comment on the evidence, you are the exclusive judges of the evidence. By the same token, when I tell you what the law is, my view of the law must prevail.

"Two basic principles are fundamental to your role as jurors. They are the requirement for proof beyond a reasonable doubt and the presumption of innocence. The requirement for proof beyond a reasonable doubt means that no person accused of an offence can be found guilty unless the Crown proves each and every part or element of that offence beyond a reasonable doubt. Similarly, our system of law requires that an accused person be presumed innocent until proven guilty.

"Before calling the Crown counsel to give their opening statement, I will tell you something of the offence with which John Miller and Elaine Thompson have been charged. The Crown has charged John Miller with one count of second-degree murder, and Elaine Thompson as an accessory to that murder. Before you can legally return a guilty verdict on the homicide, the Crown must prove all the elements beyond a reasonable doubt. I now call upon the Crown to proceed with their case," he finished, then motioned to the crown's lawyer.

Dennis got up and said, "Your Honour, ladies and gentlemen of the jury. We intend to prove that John Miller killed Carl Springfield and Jeremy Simmons and that he did so willfully, therefore committing second-degree murder. We also intend to prove that Elaine Thompson pushed John Miller to commit this crime by providing him images and information that caused him mental anguish. To prove our case, we intend to call the following witnesses: Grant Manley; Tyler Bradshaw; Greg Miller; Detective Jack Gordon; and Sergeant Paul

Ramsay. We now wish to call our first witness, Greg Miller."

Greg got up, and Tyler gave him a smile and let go of his hand. Greg turned and look at his mother, who winked and smiled. Holding his head up high, he walked down the aisle, glanced at his father and Elaine on his way to the bench, his face was expressionless.

"Do you swear that the evidence you shall give shall be the truth, the whole truth and nothing but the truth, so help you, God?" the court clerk asked.

"Yes," Greg replied, looking at the clerk.

"State your name and address for the court, please."

Greg cleared his throat and said, "I am Greg Miller, and I live in Cardston, AB."

"Greg," the Crown attorney said, "please tell the court what happened on the afternoon of March twentieth."

"At around two in the afternoon. I went back to Lee Creek campground to the trailer I live in," Greg said.

"Why did you spend the night with a friend?" the Crown attorney asked.

Greg, looking at the attorney said, "James asked me if I could lend the trailer to Carl and Jeremy for the night."

"What happened once you got there?"

Greg swallowed. "I went in and saw the guys had left a mess in the kitchen, so I cleaned it up."

"What happened after you had finished cleaning up?" the Crown attorney asked.

"I entered the bedroom to put away my clothes," Greg replied.

"And what did you see?"

Greg choked up; he was having a hard time containing his grief. "Take your time," Dennis said.

"I saw Carl and Jeremy lying in bed, covered in blood." Greg burst out in tears. Tyler couldn't help but tearing up as well. "I . . . I suddenly felt ill and ran outside."

"What did you do next?"

"I grabbed my cellphone and called 911."

"Do you know the accused?" the Crown attorney asked.

Greg looked at him and said, "I do. John Miller is my father, and Elaine Thompson attends the same school as me."

"How would you describe your father?" The Crown attorney asked.

Greg looked at the attorney, confused. "I don't understand the question."

"Is he a compassionate man, a violent man?"

Greg, hesitant, looked at his mother who blinked, to let him know it's okay. "Generally, he is a good father, but I've seen the violent side of him."

"Under what circumstances is he violent?" the attorney asked.

"When he sees my behaviour as a sin," Greg replied.

"Can you be more specific?" the Crown attorney said, prying. "Swearing is a sin, hating someone is a sin."

Greg, this time looked at his father with a stern look and said, "He became violent when he found out conversion therapy didn't cure me of my homosexuality."

"When was this, and what happened?"

Greg's face hardened. "One month ago. After spending time with my boyfriend at the trailer, I came home, and he barged into my room and started kicking me in the stomach and punching me in the face. My mother tried to stop him but she couldn't. It was like he was possessed. So once he left, I told my mother I couldn't stay there anymore and went and lived in the trailer."

"Thank you, Greg. I have no further questions, Your Honour."

The judge asked, "Does the Defense wish to cross-examine the witness?"

"No, Your Honour," replied the defense attorney.

Greg got up, stopped and looked at his father for a moment. With his lowered his head and eyes, Greg's face was blank as if the man he was looking at was a complete stranger. He was devoid of emotions for the man that gave him life, who had tried to take it away. He remembered the easygoing man from when he was growing up and the hours they spent playing together. But that was then, and this man sitting in the accused bench is not him. He was a heartless, selfish imposter who used religion to justify the monster that he became. His father's face turned red when Greg looked at him. Greg smirked and continued to his seat.

"We call Detective Jack Gordon to the stand," the Crown attorney said.

"Do you swear that the evidence you shall give shall be the truth, the whole truth and nothing but the truth, so help you, God?" the court clerk said.

"Yes," Detective Gordon said.

"State your name and position, please," said the clerk.

"I am Detective Jack Gordon, I am the investigating officer."

"Detective, what happened on the afternoon of March 20th?" the Crown attorney asked.

"A call came into the police station about two young people found dead at Lee Creek campground," he replied.

"Who was there when you arrived?"

"Mr. Greg Miller, Sergeant Paul Ramsay and Sergeant Carlos Banderos," Detective Gordon replied, looking at the attorney.

"Did you determine the time of death?" the Crown attorney asked.

"It was determined that the victims had been dead for twelve hours at least," Jack answered.

"Did you find anything that confirmed the crime was committed by the accused during your search?" the Crown attorney asked, approaching the bench.

"Yes," Jack answered. "We found a security camera hidden in the bedroom's overhead cabinet with footage of Mr. Miller shooting both victims."

"What is John Miller's association with Elaine Thompson, who is also accused today?" the Crown attorney asked, pointing to Elaine.

"The security camera belongs to Elaine Thompson. She placed it in the bedroom to spy on Greg Miller and his boyfriend," Jack said.

"Why would Ms. Thompson do this?"

"Ms. Thompson told us she wanted to find out if Greg had been spreading lies about her," Jack answered promptly.

"If the purpose was to capture information," the Crown attorney said with emphasis, "why use a security camera? And why the bedroom?"

"Ms. Thompson told us the store didn't have anything else, and she was told she didn't have to turn on the video capability," Jack said. "We checked with the store clerk, and the clerk said that Ms. Thompson specifically asked for a security camera. There was never a discussion about capturing audio only. As for why the bedroom, Ms. Thompson told us she couldn't find a place to put the camera anywhere else."

"What did you find on the security camera?"

"There was nothing captured on the security camera. The video feed was sent directly to Ms. Thompson's cellphone. When we checked her cell, we noticed the video had been erased. My team was able to find out the video was still available remotely, so we were able to download it," Jack said.

"What did the recording show?"

"Greg Miller and Tyler Bradshaw having sex," he replied.

"How did Mr. Miller end up with the video at his store?" the Crown attorney asked.

"Before erasing the video from her cell, Ms. Thompson

transferred the contents onto a DVD. She confessed to dropping the DVD on the doorstep of Mr. Miller's store."

"What motivated the accused to do this?"

"She knew when Mr. Miller would see his son engaged in what he classifies as a sin, he would react violently," Jack said.

"Objection, Your Honour. This is speculation," the Defence attorney said, standing up.

"Mr. Pratt, have your witness rephrase," the judge said.

"Detective Gordon, why do you believe Ms. Thomson knew Mr. Miller would have reacted to the video?"

"When Ms. Thompson went to Mr. Miller's shoe store to tell him his son was with his boyfriend at the campground, she saw Greg Miller a few days later bruised and battered. Ms. Thompson asked what happened, and Greg Miller told her his father beat him up. Mrs. Miller told Sergeant Ramsay that her husband came home and brutalized his son after learning Greg and his friend were still seeing each other, from a girl at his school that stopped by his store," Jack replied.

"Would it be safe to say that the video triggered Mr. Miller's action?" the Crown attorney asked.

"Yes," Jack answered. "That afternoon, Mr. Miller purchased a firearm at a hunting and fishing store, in Cardston."

The Crown attorney handed a piece of paper to the court clerk, a scanned register slip. "Your Honour, here is a copy of the purchase from the store and the gun registration with Mr. Miller's name on it." The court clerk showed the evidence to the judge. "Detective, what was Mr. Miller's motivation?"

"Given his intolerance to homosexuality, he became consumed by rage and went to the trailer, intending to kill his son and his friend. He fired his gun at the first person on the right, thinking it was his son because the blanket partially covered the victim's head. The sound of the gunshot woke up Carl Springfield, who was sleeping next to the victim and at that moment, Mr. Miller pulled the blanket off the person he had shot and realized it wasn't his son. Mr. Springfield jumped at the shooter in order to defend himself, at which time Mr. Miller shot him. The security camera captured everything that night," Jack said while the Crown attorney gave the court clerk a DVD copy of the shooting, captured by the camera.

"Thank you, Detective. No more questions, Your Honour," Dennis said.

"Does the Defence wish to cross-examine the witness?" the judge asked.

"In light of the video showing Mr. Miller committing the crime, the Defence will not cross-examine," Mark Gregory said.

Detective Gordon got up from the stand and went to sit down behind the accused.

"Your Honour, we would like to call Ms. Cindy Roberts to the stand," the Crown attorney said. "We would like to show the court how manipulative and conniving Ms. Elaine Thompson can be. How Ms. Thompson uses people through blackmail and whatever she does is for revenge." The judge nodded his approval.

"The Crown calls Cindy Roberts to the stand," the attorney said.

Greg looked at Tyler, wondering why Cindy was here today. He quietly asked Tyler if he had heard anything about her being asked to testify. Tyler was as clueless as he was. When she came through the doors, she noticed Greg sitting to the right, she smiled at him as she walked by.

"Do you swear that the evidence you shall give shall be the truth, the whole truth and nothing but the truth, so help you, God?" the court clerk asked.

"I do," Cindy said.

"Please state your name for the record," the clerk said.

"Cindy Roberts," she replied.

"How do you know the accused, Elaine Thompson?" the

Crown attorney asked.

Cindy looked at Elaine, who had rage written all over her face when she saw Cindy. Then Cindy turned towards the attorney. "She goes to the same school as me."

"What is Ms. Thompson's interaction with the other students?" he asked.

"Elaine bullies her way through school," Cindy answered without hesitation.

"What do you mean bullies her way through school?

"She blackmails students into doing her homework and assignments," Cindy said.

"She blackmails them with what?" the Crown attorney asked.

"With whatever dirt she can find out on the student."

"Did she ever blackmail you?" he asked, looking at Elaine.

"Yes," Cindy replied.

"With what?"

Cindy, took a deep breath, then looked at Greg, and said embarrassed, "She had photos of her next door neighbour and me having sex."

"How did she get those?" he asked.

"She took them herself," Cindy said.

"Speculation," the defence said.

"Ms. Roberts, how do you know she took them herself?" the Crown attorney asked.

"She showed them to me from her photo album on her cellphone," Cindy said.

"Is there anybody else being blackmailed by Ms. Thompson?"

"There are several students who she blackmails," Cindy answered a matter-of-factly.

"Did she ever blackmail Greg Miller?" he asked.

"No. But she got him in trouble.

"How?" the Crown attorney asked.

"She told me she had gone to his father's store to tell him where Greg and Tyler meet," Cindy replied.

"Why do you think she did this?" the Crown attorney asked with a frown.

"Elaine always seeks revenge on anybody that crosses her. Greg came to the defence of another student whom she accused of lying to cover something that happened to her, and vowed revenge on Greg and Carl. This was when she outed Carl on social media."

"Ms. Roberts, did Ms. Thompson know that informing Mr. Miller of his son's homosexuality would bring rage out in him?" he asked.

"She did. She saw the consequences of her action when she told Mr. Miller that Greg and Tyler still saw each other, which sent Greg to conversion therapy. Then when she told him they were having sex that is when Greg came to school with his face beaten to a pulp," Cindy said.

"Did Ms. Thompson ever mention the video that she had of the two boys having sex?" he asked.

"No." Cindy answered.

"Given what you know of her, do you think she was hoping something would happen to Greg and Tyler by dropping the video at the store?" the Crown attorney probed.

"Whatever Elaine does, it is for a reason, and Elaine's reason is always revenge.

"Thank you, Ms. Roberts. No more questions, Your Honour."

"Does the Defence wish to cross-examine the witness?" the judge asked.

"Yes, Your Honour. Ms. Roberts," Mark said, getting up from his seat, "did you actually see Ms. Thompson drop the video at Mr. Miller's store?

"No," Cindy answered.

"Then how do you know she did?" Mark asked.

"I don't know. I didn't say she did," Cindy replied with assurance.

"Why did you say her motive is always revenge? Isn't it the motive of all teens when posting things on social media?" Mark asked.

"No," Cindy said with a frown.

"What makes you think Elaine sought revenge on Greg and Tyler? Did you hear her say this?" the attorney asked

"Yes. She said so when Greg posted a photo of her on her locker when she got caught with someone else's husband at a motel."

"Thank you, Ms. Roberts. No more questions, Your Honour." Mark sat down.

Cindy got up and left the room, emotionally exhausted.

"Members of the jury, you have heard all the evidence," the judge said. "You are asked to review all that was presented to you and come up with a verdict. We will reconvene tomorrow morning. Court is adjourned."

People began leaving the courtroom, Greg sat for a moment and watched his father being taken away, handcuffed. His mother nudged him, Greg turned towards her, she smiled, and she knew how difficult this is for Greg. She motion Greg and Tyler it was time to leave. Once outside, Greg's mother asked them over to her house.

"Come in," Theresa said, entering the house. "Do you guys want anything to drink?"

Greg shrugged, looking at Tyler, who was a little bit shy, as it was the first he'd been to Greg's house. Teresa came back with beers, the only alcohol she had in the house, and said, "We deserve one after the day we had.

"How are you feeling Greg?" Teresa asked. She knew it had been an emotional day for him; it was for her.

"It was hard, testifying against a member of the family. I looked at him and I saw his lifeless eyes and thought, what's going through his mind right now?" Then Greg started tearing up. Tyler grabbed his hand. "I feel heartless, Mom," Greg said looking at her. "All the tears I'm shedding none of them are for him, I feel dry inside." Greg sobbed.

Tyler took him in his arms. "Oh! Honey," his mother said. "You're the least heartless person I know. Your father has put you through a lot in the last year. Not crying when you think of him in that cell or see him in handcuffs is perfectly normal. You've been hurt deeply . . ." She looked at Tyler. "I am grateful for your strength and your love for my son. You've been by side through all of this, you helped him, supported him and made him happy."

"I love your son. There is nothing I wouldn't do for him," Tyler said.

Teresa saw for the first time, the glow in her son's eyes when he's around Tyler. The love that exhumes when they look at each other.

"Are you guys hungry?" Teresa asked." I can make you something."

"No, mom. If you don't mind, Tyler and I will go back to the trailer and rest."

"We're all pretty tired. Do you want me to drive you?" Teresa asked.

"No," Greg said, getting up. "We'll walk. It's not far from here." Greg went and took his mother in his arms, I love you . . ." The he gave her a kiss on the cheek.

Teresa took Tyler in her arms and held him close to her as tears ran down her face. "Thank you," she said.

Greg and Tyler took the path near his house towards the campsite. They walked hand in hand, anxious to get home and cuddle in bed.

Greg got up at six, went into the kitchen, sat at the table after having made himself a coffee, and thought about the day that was about to unfold. Greg wasn't looking forward to being at the courthouse and watching his father being sentenced and sent to prison. Never in his life had he even fathomed living something like this. Around seven, Tyler walked out of the bedroom, eyes still glued together with sleep, and fumbled his way to the table.

Greg smiled and got him a coffee and gave him a kiss. "You know, you don't have to assist to the sentencing today," Greg said. "I'll be alright, my mom will be there."

"I want to be there with you and for you," Tyler replied, reaching for his hands. "I know it's going to be horrible seeing someone you once cared for, go to jail. And I know you won't be alright because you'll pretend to be strong for your mother and swallow your emotions. I'll be there if you want a shoulder to cry on, or even someone to scream at to release all that pent-up crap you have been avoiding dealing with. Thank you for thinking of me, but I am going with you."

Later that morning Teresa, Greg, and Tyler entered the courtroom and sat at the same place as the day before. From where they were, Greg could see his father very well.

"Order in the court. All rise! The Honourable Mister Justice Bernard presiding," the court clerk said.

"Please sit," the judge said.

The jury entered the courtroom and sat down. The clerk approached the jury, and the foreperson handed the clerk their verdict. The clerk provided the judgement to Judge Bernard.

"Mister Foreperson, have you reached a verdict?" the judge asked.

"Yes, we have Your Honour. We, the jury, find the accused, John Miller guilty of second-degree murder, and Elaine

Thompson of accessory to murder."

Greg lowered his head, and Tyler placed a hand on his thigh. Teresa teared up, seeing the man she'd married eighteen years ago was a criminal today. She turned to Greg, placed a hand on his shoulder, and gave him a gentle squeeze.

"Members of the jury, we have heard your verdict of guilty, so say you all. Please stand to confirm your verdict. Ladies and gentlemen of the jury, thank you for acting as jurors in this matter," the judge said.

"John Miller and Elaine Thompson, you have been found guilty of the offences you are accused of and will now be sentenced. Crown, do you have a submission on the appropriate sentence?" the judge asked.

"Yes, Your Honour, I do," Dennis Pratt said. "I suggest that the appropriate sentence is twenty years of imprisonment for Mr. Miller and ten years for Ms. Thompson."

"Defence, do you have anything to say?" the judge asked.

"No, Your Honour."

"John Miller and Elaine Thompson, please stand. You have been found guilty of a serious criminal offence and must not take these proceedings lightly.

"Ms. Thompson, your role in this senseless crime cannot be ignored. Your actions in your quest for revenge fueled what happened, and as such, it was as if you handed the gun to Mr. Miller yourself. Due to your role in this crime, I hereby sentence you to ten years imprisonment with a possibility of probation in five years. I hope you will take this opportunity to think about your actions and seek help.

"Mr. Miller, I am concerned about your violent nature when it relates, in this case, to homosexuality. We live in a society that should be tolerant and accepting. This court feels a psychiatric evaluation and treatment is recommended, followed by fifteen years in a correctional facility for the murder of Carl Springfield and Jeremy Simmons."

"This court stands adjourned," the judge said.
"Order in the court. All rise," said the clerk.

Chapter Sixty-seven: Unlucky

Teresa got in her car after the verdict, sat there and collapsed into tears. Images of the two innocent lives her husband had taken away kept haunting her. *How could he do this? He went there intending to kill our son, his own flesh and blood. What kind of a man did I marry?* She swallowed her tears. *He can rot in hell and burn with his stupid beliefs.*

Early that afternoon, Teresa called the Correctional Facility of Cardston to find out if John Miller was still being held there or if he had been transferred to the psychiatric hospital in Calgary. She was told that he wasn't scheduled to leave until next week.

Teresa arrived at the correctional facility around ten o'clock the following morning. As she entered the facility, her hands began shaking, her heartbeat increased rapidly, and she had to loosen the scarf around her neck because she couldn't catch her breath. When it came time to sign the registry, she had to steady her hand. Holding back her tears, she followed the officer down the hall to the visitation room.

Entering the room, John was sitting on a folding chair across a round wooden table and got up to hug Teresa, but she swiftly sat down before he could put his arms around her.

John looked at Teresa. "I'm sorry . . ." John started to say.

"Don't even finish that sentence," she said. "I don't want to hear it." Drying the tears rolling down her face, Teresa then asked, "Why? I don't understand what drove you to do such a thing?"

John, his hands clenched together on the table, said, "When

I saw the video of our . . . your son engaged in this immoral and unnatural act, rage took over my body. Your son provoked me into doing this."

"You bastard. How dare you blame this on Greg?"

"He's a sinner, Teresa. Open your eyes, your son is evil."

"You're the evil one, John Miller. I don't know who you are anymore," Teresa said, sobbing. "Our son, he is *our* son, is far from being a sinner. He's a loving and caring human being. He is a normal eighteen-year-old no matter what you and your bible think. You killed two innocent men because of your own insecurities. Who are you to pass judgement and decide what is shameful or not? Read your bible and look at who's the sinner here."

"My beliefs are the words of God. If everyone believed and lived by his words, we wouldn't have these sexual deviants in this world."

"You are mad. The only abnormal person around here is you. May God have pity on you." Teresa walked out and went back home. She had heard enough.

Teresa didn't want to spend one more minute in that house. She called a real estate agent the moment she got home and put the house up for sale. *I would have never imagined the man I married would one day commit such a heinous crime.*

Fortunately for Teresa, the house sold within a month. She rented an apartment for her and Greg, and she took over the business, hoping that sales would see a resurgence under new management. It took some time. Teresa had to work hard to dissociate her name from that of her ex-husband.

She noticed most of the shoe sales were made by women. The store carried men's shoes as well, but sold very few of them as most men in town wore work boots and the young men's sneakers. She visited the shoe store in the small plaza in Cardston and the larger one in Magrath to view their selections. She surveyed the women and teens in her town to find out what style of shoes they would like to see in her store that were nowhere else nearby, and made changes. The business bounced back from near bankruptcy with the careful planning and marketing she did.

Teresa needed to find a way to express her feelings about what her husband did to the Springfield and Simmons families. She wanted to make amends to ease the pain she felt in her heart as a mother.

She decided to invite them over to her apartment on Saturday for coffee, letting them know she wanted to talk about something important. At first, Mr. and Mrs. Simmons declined. They were still overwhelmed with grief and resentment, but Teresa managed to convince them to meet her.

That Saturday, Teresa didn't open the store, leaving a note in the window apologizing to customers about the store being closed for the day.

"Thank you for having accepted my invitation. I know it must be hard for you to be here with a murderer's wife. First of all, I want you to know how sorry I feel about what my husband has done to you and your family.

"His behaviour was deplorable and inexcusable. When I think about what he did, it tears my heart open," Teresa said, her eyes tearing up and her voice cracking. "All the hurtful and horribleness he has done to you, you did not deserve this. No family deserves this. He minimized, justified, denied, and even blamed his own son for his actions. I know this won't bring back your sons. But I wanted you to know that I am deeply remorseful for what he did, and I hope you can someday find it in your heart to forgive me."

"Mrs. Miller," Carl's mother said. "We don't blame you for what your husband did, and you don't need to ask for our forgiveness. We imagine it is as hard on you, as a mother, as it is on us. You are a good person, and Greg is lucky to have you."

A year later, Teresa decided to sell her existing shoe inventory to the shoe store in the plaza and reopened her business as a women's sportswear emporium, something Cardston lacked.

EPILOGUE

Crystal Mountain Correctional Centre was a place where no cameras existed, and lockdowns were a near-daily occurrence. For the first four weeks, Elaine sat in the exact same spot day-in, day-out, staring at the reflection through a cell-door window to make sure nobody would sneak up behind her.

Nobody talked to her except to measure her up and see if they could try and punk her.

"Who the fuck are you," one inmate said to Elaine.

"Who's asking?"

"Me."

"And who the fuck are you?" Elaine said, inches from her face.

"This bitch has a mouth on her," the inmate said to the onlookers.

"Fuck you," Elaine said.

That's all it took. Suddenly this girl started to swing at Elaine. Elaine began hitting her; then the inmate ducked and kicked Elaine in the gut, sending her flying backwards to land on her back. Next, the inmate jumped on Elaine and began punching her. Elaine tried desperately to push her off, but her assailant was more muscular and had pinned Elaine with her knees. Blood flew through the air, the other inmates kept cheering, and finally the alarm sounded. The guards pried the inmate off Elaine's unconscious body. The inmate was sweating with rage when the guards cuffed her and led her away. The correctional officers picked Elaine off the floor, sat her in a wheelchair, and took her to the infirmary.

After serving his sentence, Greg's father left Cardston and went to work for Grant Manley at the Hope and Faith Wellness Centre. When the government passed a bill banning conversion therapy, John and Grant opened a Christian youth centre with the intention of continuing their rehabilitation work anonymously. Unfortunately, word spread soon enough on what was going on at this centre, and it was shut down, and both John and Grant were fined. John had nowhere to go and nothing to live for, so in a desperate act to free himself from this sordid world, he committed suicide.

Greg underwent psychotherapy to deal with his nightmares and the damage caused by conversion therapy. Then, he and Tyler returned to where it all happened, hoping to face his ghosts head-on. Standing inside their old retreat at the campground, they remembered the wonderful moments they spent there and created a new and happy one together. Now, when Greg's mind took him back there, he was able to feel the happy and loving memory of that place.

Two years after both having graduated from university, Greg and Tyler married. They bought a house and made it a shelter for LGBTQ youth whose families had rejected or abused them. Greg and Tyler knew the community would continue to face discrimination, so through financial support from the wider community and their friends, Greg and Tyler were able to help these young people find a safe and secure haven and life.

Greg's parting message to his guests was, "Don't let anyone tell you you're not normal. You are. Don't let anyone tell you need to get fixed. You're not broken, you are perfect the way you are, a beautiful human being. Do not be afraid of who you are. This is how the universe wanted you to be, and remember: Love is love, no matter who you love."

ABOUT THE AUTHOR

Kristian Daniels is a published author. His first novel Stolen Heart was published a little more than one year ago. An Information Technologist by profession, he retired a few years ago to dedicate his time to his story telling. Kristian is passionate about writing. Fiction and coming–of-age stories are what he likes to write about. Kristian lives and works out of his home in Canada and spends his summers traveling and enjoying a drink a good book and the sun by his pool with his husband and their two dogs.

www.ingramcontent.com/pod-product-compliance
Lightning Source LLC
Chambersburg PA
CBHW062009170626
46813CB00001B/91